William Faulkner

MOSQUITOES

William Faulkner was born in 1897 and raised in Oxford, Mississippi, where he spent most of his life. One of the towering figures of American literature, he is the author of *The Sound and the Fury*, *As I Lay Dying*, and *Absalom, Absalom!*, among many other remarkable books. Faulkner was awarded the Nobel Prize in Literature for 1949 and France's Legion of Honor in 1951. He died in 1962.

INTERNATIONAL

BOOKS BY WILLIAM FAULKNER

The Marble Faun
Soldiers' Pay
Mosquitoes
Sartoris (Flags in the Dust)
The Sound and the Fury
As I Lay Dying
Sanctuary
These 13
Light in August
A Green Bough
Doctor Martino and Other Stories
Pylon
Absalom, Absalom!
The Unvanquished
The Wild Palms (If I Forget Thee, Jerusalem)
The Hamlet
Go Down, Moses
Intruder in the Dust
Knight's Gambit
Collected Stories of William Faulkner
Notes on a Horsethief
Requiem for a Nun
A Fable
Big Woods
The Town
The Mansion
The Reivers
Uncollected Stories of William Faulkner

William Faulkner

MOSQUITOES

VINTAGE INTERNATIONAL
Vintage Books
A Division of Penguin Random House LLC
New York

A Note on the Text: This book was published in 1927 and reflects the attitudes of its time. The publisher's decision to present it as it was originally published is not intended as endorsement of cultural representations or language contained herein.

FIRST VINTAGE INTERNATIONAL EDITION 2023

The Library of Congress has cataloged the Boni & Liveright edition as follows:
Name: Faulkner, William, 1897–1962
Title: Mosquitoes, by William Faulkner
Description: First edition. | New York : Boni and Liveright, 1927.
Identifiers: LCCN 27010732
Classification: LCC PZ3.F272 Mo PS3511.A86
LC record available at https://lccn.loc.gov/27010732

Vintage International Trade Paperback ISBN: 978-0-593-47098-5
eBook ISBN: 978-0-593-47099-2

Book design by Steve Walker

vintagebooks.com

Printed in the United States of America
1st Printing

To Helen

Contents

Prologue   5

The First Day   53

The Second Day   104

The Third Day   173

The Fourth Day   253

Epilogue   317

MOSQUITOES

In spring, the sweet young spring, decked out with little green, necklaced, braceleted with the song of idiotic birds, spurious and sweet and tawdry as a shopgirl in her cheap finery, like an idiot with money and no taste; they were little and young and trusting, you could kill them sometimes. But now, as August like a languorous replete bird winged slowly through the pale summer toward the moon of decay and death, they were bigger, vicious; ubiquitous as undertakers, cunning as pawnbrokers, confident and unavoidable as politicians. They came cityward lustful as country boys, as passionately integral as a college football squad: pervading and monstrous but without majesty: a biblical plague seen through the wrong end of a binocular: the majesty of Fate become contemptuous through ubiquity and sheer repetition.

Prologue

1

"The sex instinct," repeated Mr. Talliaferro in his careful cockney, with that smug complacence with which you plead guilty to a characteristic which you privately consider a virtue, "is quite strong in me. Frankness, without which there can be no friendship, without which two people cannot really ever 'get' each other, as you artists say; frankness, as I was saying, I believe—"

"Yes," his host agreed. "Would you mind moving a little?"

He complied with obsequious courtesy, remarking the thin fretful flashing of the chisel beneath the rhythmic maul. Wood scented gratefully slid from its mute flashing, and slapping vainly about himself with his handkerchief he moved in a Bluebeard's closet of blonde hair in severed clots, examining with concern a faint even powdering of dust upon his neat small patent leather shoes. Yes, one must pay a price for Art. . . . Watching the rhythmic power of the other's back and arm he speculated briefly upon which was more to be desired—muscularity in an undershirt, or his own symmetrical sleeve, and reassured he continued:

". . . frankness compels me to admit that the sex instinct is perhaps my most dominating compulsion." Mr. Talliaferro believed that Conversation—not talk: Conversation—

with an intellectual equal consisted of admitting as many so-called unpublishable facts as possible about oneself. Mr. Talliaferro often mused with regret on the degree of intimacy he might have established with his artistic acquaintances had he but acquired the habit of masturbation in his youth. But he had not even done this.

"Yes," his host agreed again, thrusting a hard hip into him. "Not at all," murmured Mr. Talliaferro quickly. A harsh wall restored his equilibrium roughly and hearing a friction of cloth and plaster he rebounded with repressed alacrity.

"Pardon me," he chattered. His entire sleeve indicated his arm in gritty white and regarding his coat with consternation he moved out of range and sat upon an upturned wooden block. Brushing did no good, and the ungracious surface on which he sat recalling his trousers to his attention, he rose and spread his handkerchief upon it. Whenever he came here he invariably soiled his clothes, but under that spell put on us by those we admire doing things we ourselves cannot do, he always returned.

The chisel bit steadily beneath the slow arc of the maul. His host ignored him. Mr. Talliaferro slapped viciously and vainly at the back of his hand, sitting in lukewarm shadow while light came across roofs and chimneypots, passing through the dingy skylight, becoming weary. His host labored on in the tired light while the guest sat on his hard block regretting his sleeve, watching the other's hard body in stained trousers and undershirt, watching the curling vigor of his hair.

Outside the window New Orleans, the vieux carré, brooded in a faintly tarnished languor like an aging yet still beautiful courtesan in a smokefilled room, avid yet weary too

of ardent ways. Above the city summer was hushed warmly
into the bowled weary passion of the sky. Spring and the
cruellest months were gone, the cruel months, the wantons
that break the fat hybernatant dullness and comfort of Time;
August was on the wing, and September—a month of languorous days regretful as woodsmoke. But Mr. Talliaferro's
youth, or lack of it, troubled him no longer. Thank God.

No youth to trouble the individual in this room at all.
What this room troubled was something eternal in the race,
something immortal. And youth is not deathless. Thank
God. This unevenly boarded floor, these rough stained
walls broken by high small practically useless windows beau-
tifully set, these crouching lintels cutting the immaculate
ruined pitch of walls which had housed slaves long ago,
slaves long dead and dust with the age that had produced
them and which they had served with a kind and gracious
dignity—shades of servants and masters now in a more gracious region, lending dignity to eternity. After all, only a few
chosen can accept service with dignity: it is man's impulse to
do for himself. It rests with the servant to lend dignity to an
unnatural proceeding. And outside, above rooftops becoming slowly violet, summer lay supine, unchaste with decay.

As you entered the room the thing drew your eyes: you
turned sharply as to a sound, expecting movement. But it
was marble, it could not move. And when you tore your eyes
away and turned your back on it at last, you got again untar-
nished and high and clean that sense of swiftness, of space
encompassed; but on looking again it was as before: motionless and passionately eternal—the virginal breastless torso
of a girl, headless, armless, legless, in marble temporarily
caught and hushed yet passionate still for escape, passionate

and simple and eternal in the equivocal derisive darkness of the world. Nothing to trouble your youth or lack of it: rather something to trouble the very fibrous integrity of your being. Mr. Talliaferro slapped his neck savagely.

The manipulator of the chisel and maul ceased his labor and straightened up, flexing his arm and shoulder muscles. And as though it had graciously waited for him to get done, the light faded quietly and abruptly: the room was like a bathtub after the drain has been opened. Mr. Talliaferro rose also and his host turned upon him a face like that of a heavy hawk, breaking his dream. Mr. Talliaferro regretted his sleeve again and said briskly:

"Then I may tell Mrs. Maurier that you will come?"

"What?" the other asked sharply, staring at him. "Oh, Hell, I have work to do. Sorry. Tell her I am sorry."

Mr. Talliaferro's disappointment was tinged faintly with exasperation as he watched the other cross the darkening room to a rough wood bench and raise a cheap enamelware water pitcher, gulping from it.

"But, I say," said Mr. Talliaferro fretfully.

"No, no," the other repeated brusquely, wiping his beard on his upper arm. "Some other time, perhaps. I am too busy to bother with her now. Sorry." He swung back the open door and from a hook screwed into it he took down a thin coat and a battered tweed cap. Mr. Talliaferro watched his muscles bulge the thin cloth with envious distaste, recalling anew the unmuscled emphasis of his own pressed flannel. The other was palpably on the verge of abrupt departure and Mr. Talliaferro, to whom solitude, particularly dingy solitude, was unbearable, took his stiff straw hat from the

bench where it flaunted its wanton gay band above the slim
yellow gleam of his straight malacca stick.

"Wait," he said, "and I'll join you."

The other paused, looking back. "I'm going out," he
stated belligerently.

Mr. Talliaferro, at a momentary loss, said fatuously:
"Why—ah, I thought—I should—" The hawk's face brooded
above him in the dusk remotely and he added quickly: "I
could return, however."

"Sure it's no trouble?"

"Not at all, my dear fellow, not at all! Only call on me. I
will be only too glad to return."

"Well, if you're sure it's no trouble, suppose you fetch
me a bottle of milk from the grocer on the corner. You know
the place, don't you? Here's the empty one."

With one of his characteristic plunging movements the
other passed through the door and Mr. Talliaferro stood in
a dapper fretted surprise, clutching a coin in one hand and
an unwashed milk bottle in the other. On the stairs, watching the other's shape descending into the welled darkness,
he stopped again and standing on one leg like a crane he
clasped the bottle under his arm and slapped at his ankle,
viciously and vainly.

2

Descending a final stair and turning into a darkling corridor he passed two people indistinguishably kissing, and
he hastened on toward the street door. He paused here in

active indecision, opening his coat. The bottle had become
clammy in his hand. He contemplated it through his sense
of touch with acute repugnance. Unseen, it seemed to have
become unbearably dirty. He desired something, vaguely—a
newspaper, perhaps, but before striking a match he looked
quickly over his shoulder. They were gone, hushing their
chimed footsteps up the dark curve of the stair: their chimed
tread was like a physical embrace. His match flared a puny
fledged gold that followed his clasped gleaming stick as if
it were a train of gun powder. But the passage was empty,
swept with chill stone, imminent with weary moisture . . .
the match burned down to the even polished temper of
his fingernails and plunged him back into darkness more
intense.

He opened the street door. Twilight ran in like a quiet
violet dog and nursing his bottle he peered out across an
undimensional feathered square, across stencilled palms
and Andrew Jackson in childish effigy bestriding the terrific
arrested plunge of his curly balanced horse, toward the long
unemphasis of the Pontalba building and three spires of the
cathedral graduated by perspective, pure and slumbrous
beneath the decadent languor of August and evening. Mr.
Talliaferro thrust his head modestly forth, looking both ways
along the street. Then he withdrew his head and closed the
door again.

He employed his immaculate linen handkerchief reluctantly before thrusting the bottle beneath his coat. It bulged
distressingly under his exploring hand, and he removed the
bottle in mounting desperation. He struck another match,
setting the bottle down at his feet to do so, but there was
nothing in which he might wrap the thing. His impulse was

to grasp it and hurl it against the wall: already he pleasured in its anticipated glassy crash. But Mr. Talliaferro was quite honorable: he had passed his word. Or he might return to his friend's room and get a bit of paper. He stood in hot indecision until feet on the stairs descending decided for him. He bent and fumbled for the bottle, struck it and heard its disconsolate empty flight, captured it at last and opening the street door anew he rushed hurriedly forth.

The violet dusk held in soft suspension lights slow as bell-strokes, Jackson square was now a green and quiet lake in which abode lights round as jellyfish, feathering with silver mimosa and pomegranate and hibiscus beneath which lantana and cannas bled and bled. Pontalba and cathedral were cut from black paper and pasted flat on a green sky; above them taller palms were fixed in black and soundless explosions. The street was empty, but from Royal street there came the hum of a trolley that rose to a staggering clatter, passed on and away leaving an interval filled with the gracious sound of inflated rubber on asphalt, like a tearing of endless silk. Clasping his accursed bottle, feeling like a criminal, Mr. Talliaferro hurried on.

He walked swiftly beside a dark wall, passing small indiscriminate shops dimly lighted with gas and smelling of food of all kinds, fulsome, slightly overripe. The proprietors and their families sat before the doors in tilted chairs, women nursing babies into slumber spoke in soft south European syllables one to another. Children scurried before him and about him, ignoring him or becoming aware of him and crouching in shadow like animals, defensive, passive and motionless.

He turned the corner. Royal street sprang in two directions and he darted into a grocery store on the corner, passing the proprietor sitting in the door with his legs spread for comfort, nursing the Italian balloon of his belly on his lap. The proprietor removed his short terrific pipe and belched, rising to follow the customer. Mr. Talliaferro set the bottle down hastily.

The grocer belched again, frankly. "Good afternoon," he said in a broad West End accent much nearer the real thing than Mr. Talliaferro's. "Meelk, hay?"

Mr. Talliaferro extended the coin, murmuring, watching the man's thick reluctant thighs as he picked up the bottle without repugnance and slid it into a pigeonholed box and opening a refrigerator beside it, took therefrom a fresh one. Mr. Talliaferro recoiled.

"Haven't you a bit of paper to wrap it in?" he asked diffidently.

"Why, sure," the other agreed affably. "Make her in a parcel, hay?" He complied with exasperating deliberation, and breathing freer but still oppressed, Mr. Talliaferro took his purchase and glancing hurriedly about, stepped into the street. And paused, stricken.

She was under full sail and accompanied by a slimmer one when she saw him, but she tacked at once and came about in a hushed swishing of silk and an expensive clashing of impediments—handbag and chains and beads. Her hand bloomed fatly through bracelets, ringed and manicured, and her hothouse face wore an expression of infantile trusting astonishment.

"Mister Talliaferro! What a surprise," she exclaimed, accenting the first word of each phrase, as was her manner. And she really was surprised. Mrs. Maurier went through the world continually amazed at chance, whether or not she had instigated it. Mr. Talliaferro shifted his parcel quickly behind him, to its imminent destruction, being forced to accept her hand without removing his hat. He rectified this as soon as possible. "I would never have expected to see you in this part of town at this hour," she continued. "But you have been calling on some of your artist friends, I suppose?"

The slim one had stopped also, and stood examining Mr. Talliaferro with cool uninterest. The older woman turned to her. "Mr. Talliaferro knows all the interesting people in the Quarter, darling. All the people who are—who are creating—creating things. Beautiful things. Beauty, you know." Mrs. Maurier waved her glittering hand vaguely toward the sky in which stars had begun to flower like pale and tarnished gardenias. "Oh, do excuse me, Mr. Talliaferro— This is my niece, Miss Robyn, of whom you have heard me speak. She and her brother have come to comfort a lonely old woman—" her glance held a decayed coquetry, and taking his cue Mr. Talliaferro said:

"Nonsense, dear lady. It is we, your unhappy admirers, who need comforting. Perhaps Miss Robyn will take pity on us, also?" He bowed toward the niece with calculated formality. The niece was not enthusiastic.

"Now, darling," Mrs. Maurier turned to her niece with rapture. "Here is an example of the chivalry of our southern men. Can you imagine a man in Chicago saying that?"

"Not hardly," the niece agreed. Her aunt rushed on:

"That is why I have been so anxious for Patricia to visit me, so she can meet men who are—who are— My niece is named for me, you see, Mr. Talliaferro. Isn't that nice?" She pressed Mr. Talliaferro with recurrent happy astonishment.

Mr. Talliaferro bowed again, came within an ace of dropping the bottle, darted the hand which held his hat and stick behind him to steady it. "Charming, charming," he agreed, perspiring under his hair.

"But, really, I am surprised to find you here at this hour. And I suppose you are as surprised to find us here, aren't you? But I have just found the most won-derful thing! Do look at it, Mr. Talliaferro: I do so want your opinion." She extended to him a dull lead plaque from which in dim bas-relief of faded red and blue simpered a Madonna with an expression of infantile astonishment identical with that of Mrs. Maurier, and a Child somehow smug and complacent looking as an old man. Mr. Talliaferro, feeling the poised precariousness of the bottle, dared not release his hand. He bent over the extended object. "Do take it, so you can examine it under the light," its owner insisted. Mr. Talliaferro perspired again mildly. The niece spoke suddenly:

"I'll hold your package."

She moved with young swiftness and before he could demur she had taken the bottle from his hand. "Ow," she exclaimed, almost dropping it herself, and her aunt gushed:

"Oh, you have discovered something also, haven't you? Now I've gone and shown you my treasure, and all the while you were concealing something much, much nicer." She waggled her hands to indicate dejection. "You will consider mine trash, I know you will," she went on with heavy assumed displeasure. "Oh, to be a man, so I could poke around in shops all day and really discover things! Do show us what you have, Mr. Talliaferro."

"It's a bottle of milk," remarked the niece, examining Mr. Talliaferro with interest.

Her aunt shrieked. Her breast heaved with repression, glinting her pins and beads. "A bottle of milk? Have you turned artist, too?"

For the first and last time in his life Mr. Talliaferro wished a lady dead. But he was a gentleman: he only seethed inwardly. He laughed with abortive heartiness.

"An artist? You flatter me, dear lady. I'm afraid my soul does not aspire so high. I am content to be merely a—"

"Milkman," suggested the young female devil.

"—Mæcenas alone. If I might so style myself."

Mrs. Maurier sighed with disappointment and surprise. "Ah, Mr. Talliaferro, I am dreadfully disappointed. I had hoped for a moment that some of your artist friends had at last prevailed on you to give something to the world of Art. No, no; don't say you cannot: I am sure you are capable of it, what with your—your delicacy of soul, your—" she waved her hand again vaguely toward the sky above Rampart street. "Ah, to be a man, with no ties save those of the soul! To create, to create." She returned easily to Royal street. "But, really, a bottle of milk, Mr. Talliaferro?"

"Merely for my friend Gordon. I looked in on him this afternoon and found him quite busy. So I ran out to fetch him milk for his supper. These artists!" Mr. Talliaferro shrugged. "You know how they live."

"Yes, indeed. Genius. A hard taskmaster, isn't it? Perhaps you are wise in not giving your life to it. It is a long lonely road. But how is Mr. Gordon? I am so continually occupied with things—unavoidable duties, which my conscience will not permit me to evade (I am very conscientious, you know)—that I simply haven't the time to see as much of the Quarter as I should like. I had promised Mr. Gordon faithfully to call, and to have him to dinner soon. I am sure he thinks I have forgotten him. Please make my peace with him, won't you? Assure him that I have not forgotten him."

"I am sure he realizes how many calls you have on your time," Mr. Talliaferro assured her gallantly. "Don't let that distress you at all."

"Yes, I really don't know how I get anything done: I am always surprised when I find I have a spare moment for my own pleasure." She turned her expression of happy astonishment on him again. The niece spun slowly and slimly on one high heel: the sweet young curve of her shanks straight and brittle as the legs of a bird and ending in the twin inky splashes of her slippers, entranced him. Her hat was a small brilliant bell about her face, and she wore her clothing with a casual rakishness, as though she had opened her wardrobe and said, Let's go downtown. Her aunt was saying:

"But what about our yachting party? You gave Mr. Gordon my invitation?"

Mr. Talliaferro was troubled. "We-ll— You see, he is quite busy now. He— He has a commission that will admit of no delay," he concluded with inspiration.

"Ah, Mr. Talliaferro! You haven't told him he is invited. Shame on you! Then I must tell him myself, since you have failed me."

"No, really—"

She interrupted him. "Forgive me, dear Mr. Talliaferro. I didn't mean to be unjust. I am glad you didn't invite him. It will be better for me to do it, so I can overcome any scruples he might have. He is quite shy, you know. Oh, quite, I assure you. Artistic temperament, you understand: so spiritual. . . ."

"Yes," agreed Mr. Talliaferro, covertly watching the niece who had ceased her spinning and got her seemingly boneless body into an undimensional angular flatness pure as an Egyptian carving.

"So I shall attend to it myself. I shall call him to-night: we sail at noon to-morrow, you know. That will allow him sufficient time, don't you think? He's one of these artists who never have much, lucky people." Mrs. Maurier looked at her watch. "Heavens above! seven thirty. We must fly. Come, darling. Can't we drop you somewhere, Mr. Talliaferro?"

"Thank you, no. I must take Gordon's milk to him, and then I am engaged for the evening."

"Ah, Mr. Talliaferro! It's a woman, I know." She rolled her eyes roguishly. "What a terrible man you are." She lowered her voice and tapped him on the sleeve. "Do be careful what you say before this child. My instincts are all bohemian, but she . . . unsophisticated . . ." Her voice bathed him warmly and Mr. Talliaferro bridled: had he had a mustache he would have stroked it. Mrs. Maurier jangled and glittered again: her expression became one of pure delight. "But, of course! We will drive you to Mr. Gordon's and then I can run in and invite him for the party. The very thing! How fortunate to have thought of it. Come, darling."

Without stooping the niece angled her leg upward and outward from the knee, scratching her ankle. Mr. Talliaferro recalled the milk bottle and assented gratefully, falling in on the curbside with meticulous thoughtfulness. A short distance up the street Mrs. Maurier's car squatted expensively. The negro driver descended and opened the door and Mr. Talliaferro sank into gracious upholstery, nursing his milk bottle, smelling flowers cut and delicately vased, promising himself a car next year.

3

They rolled smoothly, passing between spaced lights and around narrow corners, while Mrs. Maurier talked steadily of hers and Mr. Talliaferro's and Gordon's souls. The niece sat quietly. Mr. Talliaferro was conscious of the clean young odor of her, like that of young trees; and when they passed beneath lights he could see her slim shape and the impersonal revelation of her legs and her bare sexless knees. Mr. Talliaferro luxuriated, clutching his bottle of milk, wishing the ride need not end. But the car drew up to the curb again, and he must get out, no matter with what reluctance.

"I'll run up and bring him down to you," he suggested with premonitory tact.

"No, no: let's all go up," Mrs. Maurier objected. "I want Patricia to see how genius looks at home."

"Gee, Aunty. I've seen these dives before," the niece said. "They're everywhere. I'll wait for you." She jackknifed her body effortlessly, scratching her ankles with her brown hands.

"It's so interesting to see how they live, darling. You'll simply love it." Mr. Talliaferro demurred again, but Mrs. Maurier overrode him with sheer words. So against his better judgment he struck matches for them, leading the way up the dark tortuous stairs while their three shadows aped them, rising and falling monstrously upon the ancient wall. Long before they reached the final stage Mrs. Maurier was puffing and panting, and Mr. Talliaferro found a puerile vengeful glee in hearing her labored breath. But he was a gentleman; he put this from him, rebuking himself. He knocked on a door, was bidden, opened it:

"Back, are you?" Gordon sat in his single chair, munching a thick sandwich, clutching a book. The unshaded light glared savagely upon his undershirt.

"You have callers," Mr. Talliaferro offered his belated warning, but the other looking up had already seen beyond his shoulder Mrs. Maurier's interested face. He rose and cursed Mr. Talliaferro, who had begun immediately his unhappy explanation.

"Mrs. Maurier insisted on dropping in—"

Mrs. Maurier vanquished him anew. "Mister Gordon!" She sailed into the room, bearing her expression of happy astonishment like a round platter stood on edge. "How *do* you do? Can you ever, ever forgive us for intruding like this?" she went on in her gushing italics. "We just met Mr. Talliaferro on the street with your milk, and we decided to brave the lion in his den. How do you do?" She forced her effusive hand upon him, staring about in happy curiosity. "So this is where genius labors. How charming: so—so original. And that—" she indicated a corner screened off by a draggled length of green rep "—is your bedroom, isn't it? How delightful! Ah, Mr. Gordon, how I envy you this freedom. And a view—you have a view also, haven't you?" She held his hand and stared entranced at a high useless window framing two tired looking stars of the fourth magnitude.

"I would have if I were eight feet tall," he corrected. She looked at him quickly, happily. Mr. Talliaferro laughed nervously.

"That would be delightful," she agreed readily. "I was so anxious to have my niece see a real studio, Mr. Gordon, where a real artist works. Darling—" she glanced over her shoulder fatly, still holding his hand "—darling, let me present you to a real sculptor, one from whom we expect great things. . . . Darling," she repeated in a louder tone.

The niece, untroubled by the stairs, had drifted in after them and she now stood before the single marble. "Come and speak to Mr. Gordon, darling." Beneath her aunt's saccharine modulation was a faint trace of something not so sweet after all. The niece turned her head and nodded slightly without looking at him. Gordon released his hand.

"Mr. Talliaferro tells me you have a commission." Mrs. Maurier's voice was again a happy astonished honey. "May we see it? I know artists don't like to exhibit an incomplete work, but just among friends, you see. . . . You both know how sensitive to beauty I am, though I have been denied the creative impulse myself."

"Yes," agreed Gordon, watching the niece.

"I have long intended visiting your studio, as I promised, you remember. So I shall take this opportunity of looking about— Do you mind?"

"Help yourself. Talliaferro can show you things. Pardon me." He lurched characteristically between them and Mrs. Maurier chanted:

"Yes, indeed. Mr. Talliaferro, like myself, is sensitive to the beautiful in Art. Ah, Mr. Talliaferro, why were you and I given a love for the beautiful, yet denied the ability to create it from stone and wood and clay. . . ."

Her body in its brief simple dress was motionless when he came over to her. After a time he said:

"Like it?"

Her jaw in profile was heavy: there was something masculine about it. But in full face it was not heavy, only quiet. Her mouth was full and colorless, unpainted, and her eyes were opaque as smoke. She met his gaze, remarking the icy blueness of his eyes (like a surgeon's she thought) and looked at the marble again.

"I don't know," she answered slowly. Then: "It's like me."

"How like you?" he asked gravely.

She didn't answer. Then she said: "Can I touch it?"

"If you like," he replied, examining the line of her jaw, her firm brief nose. She made no move and he added: "Aren't you going to touch it?"

"I've changed my mind," she told him calmly. Gordon glanced over his shoulder to where Mrs. Maurier pored volubly over something. Mr. Talliaferro yea'd her with restrained passion.

"Why is it like you?" he repeated.

She said irrelevantly: "Why hasn't she anything here?" Her brown hand flashed slimly across the high unemphasis of the marble's breast, and withdrew.

"You haven't much there yourself." She met his steady gaze steadily. "Why should it have anything there?" he asked.

"You're right," she agreed with the judicial complaisance of an equal. "I see now. Of course she shouldn't. I didn't quite—quite get it for a moment."

Gordon examined with growing interest her flat breast and belly, her boy's body which the poise of it and the thinness of her arms belied. Sexless, yet somehow vaguely troubling. Perhaps just young, like a calf or a colt. "How old are you?" he asked abruptly.

"Eighteen, if it's any of your business," she replied without rancor, staring at the marble. Suddenly she looked up at him again. "I wish I could have it," she said with sudden sincerity and longing, quite like a four-year-old.

"Thanks," he said. "That was quite sincere, too, wasn't it? Of course you can't have it, though. You see that, don't you?"

She was silent. He knew she could see no reason why she shouldn't have it.

"I guess so," she agreed at last. "I just thought I'd see, though."

"Not to overlook any bets?"

"Oh, well, by to-morrow I probably won't want it, anyway. . . . And if I still do, I can get something just as good."

"You mean," he amended, "that if you still want it to-morrow, you can get it. Don't you?"

Her hand, as if it were a separate organism, reached out slowly, stroking the marble. "Why are you so black?" she asked.

"Black?"

"Not your hair and beard. I like your red hair and beard. But you. You are black. I mean . . ." her voice fell and he suggested Soul? "I don't know what that is," she stated quietly.

"Neither do I. You might ask your aunt, though. She seems familiar with souls."

She glanced over her shoulder, showing him her other unequal profile. "Ask her yourself. Here she comes."

Mrs. Maurier surged her scented upholstered bulk between them. "Wonderful, wonderful," she was exclaiming in sincere astonishment. "And this . . ." her voice died away and she gazed at the marble, dazed. Mr. Talliaferro echoed her immaculately, taking to himself the showman's credit.

"Do you see what he has caught?" he bugled melodiously. "Do you see? The spirit of youth, of something fine and hard and clean in the world; something we all desire until our mouths are stopped with dust." Desire with Mr. Talliaferro had long since become an unfulfilled habit requiring no longer any particular object at all.

"Yes," agreed Mrs. Maurier. "How beautiful. What—what does it signify, Mr. Gordon?"

"Nothing, Aunt Pat," the niece snapped. "It doesn't have to."

"But, really—"

"What do you want it to signify? Suppose it signified a—a dog, or an ice cream soda, what difference would it make? Isn't it all right like it is?"

"Yes, indeed, Mrs. Maurier," Mr. Talliaferro agreed with soothing haste, "it is not necessary that it have objective significance. We must accept it for what it is: pure form untrammeled by any relation to a familiar or utilitarian object."

"Oh, yes: untrammeled." Here was a word Mrs. Maurier knew. "The untrammeled spirit, freedom like the eagle's."

"Shut up, Aunty," the niece told her. "Don't be a fool."

"But it has what Talliaferro calls objective significance," Gordon interrupted brutally. "This is my feminine ideal: a virgin with no legs to leave me, no arms to hold me, no head to talk to me."

"Mister Gordon!" Mrs. Maurier stared at him over her compressed breast. Then she thought of something that did possess objective significance. "I had almost forgotten our reason for calling so late. Not," she added quickly, "that we needed any other reason to—to—Mr. Talliaferro, how was it those old people used to put it, about pausing on Life's busy highroad to kneel for a moment at the Master's feet? . . ." Mrs. Maurier's voice faded and her face assumed an expression of mild concern. "Or is it the Bible of which I am thinking? Well, no matter: we dropped in to invite you for a yachting party, a few days on the lake—"

"Yes. Talliaferro told me about it. Sorry, but I shall be unable to come."

Mrs. Maurier's eyes became quite round. She turned to Mr. Talliaferro. "Mister Talliaferro! You told me you hadn't mentioned it to him!"

Mr. Talliaferro writhed acutely. "Do forgive me, if I left you under that impression. It was quite unintentional. I only desired that you speak to him yourself and make him reconsider. The party will not be complete without him, will it?"

"Not at all. Really, Mr. Gordon, won't you reconsider? Surely you won't disappoint us." She stooped creaking, and slapped at her ankle. "Pardon me."

"No. Sorry. I have work to do."

Mrs. Maurier transferred her expression of astonishment and dejection to Mr. Talliaferro. "It can't be that he doesn't want to come. There must be some other reason. Do say something to him, Mr. Talliaferro. We simply must have him. Mr. Fairchild is going, and Eva and Dorothy: we simply must have a sculptor. Do convince him, Mr. Talliaferro."

"I'm sure his decision is not final: I am sure he will not deprive us of his company. A few days on the water will do him no end of good; freshen him up like a tonic. Eh, Gordon?"

Gordon's hawk's face brooded above them, remote and

insufferable with arrogance. The niece had turned away, drifting slowly about the room, grave and quiet and curious, straight as a poplar. Mrs. Maurier implored him with her eyes doglike, temporarily silent. Suddenly she had an inspiration.

"Come, people, let's all go to my house for dinner. Then we can discuss it at our ease."

Mr. Talliaferro demurred. "I am engaged this evening, you know," he reminded her.

"Oh, Mr. Talliaferro." She put her hand on his sleeve. "Don't you fail me, too. I always depend on you when people fail me. Can't you defer your engagement?"

"Really, I am afraid not. Not in this case," Mr. Talliaferro replied smugly. "Though I am distressed . . ."

Mrs. Maurier sighed. "These women! Mr. Talliaferro is perfectly terrible with women," she informed Gordon. "But you will come, won't you?"

The niece had drifted up to them and stood rubbing the calf of one leg against the other shin. Gordon turned to her. "Will you be there?"

Damn their little souls, she whispered on a sucked breath. She yawned. "Oh, yes. I eat. But I'm going to bed darn soon." She yawned again, patting the broad pale oval of her mouth with brown fingers.

"Patricia!" her aunt exclaimed in shocked amazement. "Of course you will do nothing of the kind. The very idea! Come, Mr. Gordon."

"No, thanks. I am engaged myself," he answered stiffly. "Some other time, perhaps."

"I simply won't take No for an answer. Do help me, Mr. Talliaferro. He simply must come."

"Do you want him to come as he is?" the niece asked.

Her aunt glanced briefly at the undershirt, and shuddered. But she said bravely: "Of course, if he wishes. What are clothes, compared with this?" she described an arc with her hand; diamonds glittered on its orbit. "So you cannot evade it, Mr. Gordon. You must come."

Her hand poised above his arm, pouncing. He eluded it brusquely. "Excuse me." Mr. Talliaferro avoided his sudden movement just in time, and the niece said wickedly:

"There's a shirt behind the door, if that's what you are looking for. You won't need a tie, with that beard."

He picked her up by the elbows, as you would a high narrow table, and set her aside. Then his tall controlled body filled and emptied the door and disappeared in the darkness of the hallway. The niece gazed after him. Mrs. Maurier stared at the door, then to Mr. Talliaferro in quiet amazement. "What in the world—" Her hands clashed vainly among her various festooned belongings. "Where is he going?" she said at last.

The niece said suddenly: "I like him." She too gazed at the door through which, passing, he seemed to have emptied the room. "I bet he doesn't come back," she remarked.

Her aunt shrieked. "Doesn't come back?"

"Well, I wouldn't, if I were him." She returned to the marble, stroking it with slow desire. Mrs. Maurier gazed helplessly at Mr. Talliaferro.

"Where—" she began.

"I'll go see," he offered, breaking his own trance. The two women regarded his vanishing neat back.

"Never in my life—Patricia, what did you mean by being

so rude to him? Of course he is offended. Don't you know how sensitive artists are? After I have worked so hard to cultivate him, too!"

"Nonsense. It'll do him good. He thinks just a little too well of himself as it is."

"But to insult the man in his own house. I can't understand you young people at all. Why, if I'd said a thing like that to a gentleman, and a stranger . . . I can't imagine what your father can mean, letting you grow up like this. He certainly knows better than this—"

"I'm not to blame for the way he acted. You are the one, yourself. Suppose you'd been sitting in your room in your shimmy, and a couple of men you hardly knew had walked in on you and tried to persuade you to go somewhere you didn't want to go, what would you have done?"

"These people are different," her aunt told her coldly. "You don't understand them. Artists don't require privacy as we do: it means nothing whatever to them. But any one, artist or no, would object—"

"Oh, haul in your sheet," the niece interrupted coarsely. "You're jibbing."

Mr. Talliaferro reappeared panting with delicate repression. "Gordon was called hurriedly away. He asked me to make his excuses and to express his disappointment over having to leave so unceremoniously."

"Then he's not coming to dinner." Mrs. Maurier sighed, feeling her age, the imminence of dark and death. She seemed not only unable to get new men any more, but to hold to the old ones, even . . . Mr. Talliaferro, too . . . age, age. . . . She sighed again. "Come, darling," she said in a strangely chastened tone, quieter, pitiable in a way. The niece put both her firm tanned hands on the marble, hard, hard. O beautiful, she whispered in salutation and farewell, turning quickly away.

"Let's go," she said, "I'm starving."

Mr. Talliaferro had lost his box of matches: he was desolated. So they were forced to feel their way down the stairs, disturbing years and years of dust upon the rail. The stone corridor was cool and dank and filled with a suppressed minor humming. They hurried on.

Night was fully come and the car squatted at the curb in patient silhouette; the negro driver sat within with all the windows closed. Within its friendly familiarity Mrs. Maurier's spirits rose again. She gave Mr. Talliaferro her hand, sugaring her voice again with a decayed coquetry.

"You will call me, then? But don't promise: I know how completely your time is taken up"—she leaned forward, tapping him on the cheek—"Don Juan!"

He laughed deprecatingly, with pleasure. The niece from her corner said:

"Good evening, Mr. Tarver."

Mr. Talliaferro stood slightly inclined from the hips, frozen. He closed his eyes like a dog awaiting the fall of the stick, while time passed and passed . . . he opened his eyes again, after how long he knew not. But Mrs. Maurier's fingers were but leaving his cheek and the niece was invisible in her corner: a bodiless evil. Then he straightened up, feeling his cold entrails resume their proper place.

The car drew away and he watched it, thinking of the girl's youngness, her hard clean youngness, with fear and a troubling unhappy desire like an old sorrow. Were children really like dogs? Could they penetrate one's concealment, know one instinctively?

Mrs. Maurier settled back comfortably. "Mr. Talliaferro is perfectly terrible with women," she informed her niece.

"I bet he is," the niece agreed, "perfectly terrible."

4

Mr. Talliaferro had been married while quite young by a rather plainfaced girl whom he was trying to seduce. But now, at thirty-eight, he was a widower these eight years. He had been the final result of some rather casual biological research conducted by two people who, like the great majority, had no business producing children at all. The family originated in northern Alabama and drifted slowly westward ever after, thus proving that a certain racial impulse in the race, which one Horace Greeley summed up in a slogan so excruciatingly apt that he didn't have to observe it himself, has not yet died away. His brothers were various and they attained their several milieus principally by chance; milieus ranging from an untimely heaven via some one else's horse and a rope and a Texas cottonwood, through a classical chair in a small Kansas college, to a state legislature via some one else's votes. This one got as far as California. They never did know what became of Mr. Talliaferro's sister.

Mr. Talliaferro had got what is known as a careful raising: he had been forced while quite young and pliable to do all the things to which his natural impulses objected, and to forgo all the things he could possibly have had any fun doing. After a while nature gave up and this became a habit with him. Nature surrendered him without a qualm: even disease germs seemed to ignore him.

His marriage had driven him into work as drouth drives the fish down stream into the larger waters, and things had gone hard with them during the years during which he had shifted from position to position, correspondence course to correspondence course, until he had an incorrect and impractical smattering of information regarding every possible genteel method of gaining money, before finally and inevitably gravitating into the women's clothing section of a large department store.

Here he felt that he had at last come into his own (he always got along much better with women than with men) and his restored faith in himself enabled him to rise with comfortable ease to the coveted position of wholesale buyer. He knew women's clothes and, interested in women, it was his belief that knowledge of the frail intimate things they preferred gave him an insight which no other man had into the psychology of women. But he merely speculated on this, for he remained faithful to his wife, although she was bedridden: an invalid.

And then, when success was in his grasp and life had become smooth at last for them, his wife died. He had become habituated to marriage, sincerely attached to her, and readjustment came slowly. Yet in time he became accustomed to the novelty of mature liberty. He had been married so young that freedom was an unexplored field to him. He took pleasure in his snug bachelor quarters in the proper neighborhood, in his solitary routine of days: of walking home in the dusk for the sake of his figure, examining

the soft bodies of girls on the street, knowing that if he cared
to take one of them, that there was none save the girls themselves to say him nay; to his dinners alone or in company
with an available literary friend.

Mr. Talliaferro did Europe in forty-one days, gained
thereby a worldly air and a smattering of esthetics and a
precious accent, and returned to New Orleans feeling that
he was Complete. His only alarm was his thinning hair, his
only worry was the fact that some one would discover that he
had been born Tarver, not Talliaferro.

But long since celibacy had begun to oppress him.

5

Handling his stick smartly he turned into Broussard's. As he
had hoped, here was Dawson Fairchild, the novelist, resembling a benevolent walrus too recently out of bed to have
made a toilet, dining in company with three men. Mr. Talliaferro paused diffidently in the doorway and a rosy cheeked
waiter resembling a studious Harvard undergraduate in
an actor's dinner coat, assailed him courteously. At last he
caught Fairchild's eye and the other greeted him across the
small room, then said something to his three companions
that caused them to turn half about in their chairs to watch
his approach. Mr. Talliaferro, to whom entering a restaurant alone and securing a table was an excruciating process,
joined them with relief. The cherubic waiter spun a chair
from an adjoining table deftly against Mr. Talliaferro's knees
as he shook Fairchild's hand.

"You're just in time," Fairchild told him, propping his fist and a clutched fork on the table. "This is Mr. Hooper. You know these other folks, I think."

Mr. Talliaferro ducked his head to a man with iron gray hair and an orotund humorless face like that of a thwarted Sunday school superintendent, who insisted on shaking his hand, then his glance took in the other two members of the party—a tall, ghostly young man with a thin evaporation of fair hair and a pale prehensile mouth, and a bald Semitic man with a pasty loose jowled face and sad quizzical eyes.

"We were discussing—" began Fairchild when the stranger interrupted with a bland and utterly unselfconscious rudeness.

"What did you say the name was?" he asked, fixing Mr. Talliaferro with his eye. Mr. Talliaferro met the eye and knew immediately a faint unease. He answered the question, but the other brushed the reply aside. "I mean your given name. I didn't catch it to-day."

"Why, Ernest," Mr. Talliaferro told him with alarm.

"Ah, yes: Ernest. You must pardon me, but traveling, meeting new faces each Tuesday, as I do—" he interrupted himself with the same bland unconsciousness. "What are your impressions of the get-together to-day?" Ere Mr. Talliaferro could have replied, he interrupted himself again. "You have a splendid organization here," he informed them generally, compelling them with his glance, "and a city that is worthy of it. Except for this southern laziness of yours. You folks need more northern blood, to bring out all your possibilities. Still, I won't criticize: you boys have treated me pretty well." He put some food into his mouth and chewed it down hurriedly, forestalling any one who might have hoped to speak.

"I was glad that my itinerary brought me here, to see the city and be with the boys to-day, and that one of your reporters gave me the chance to see something of your bohemian life by directing me to Mr. Fairchild here, who, I understand, is an author." He met Mr. Talliaferro's expression of courteous amazement again. "I am glad to see how you boys are carrying on the good work; I might say, the Master's work, for it is only by taking the Lord into our daily lives—" He stared at Mr. Talliaferro once more. "What did you say the name was?"

"Ernest," suggested Fairchild mildly.

"—Ernest. People, the man in the street, the breadwinner, he on whom the heavy burden of life rests, does he know what we stand for, what we can give him in spite of himself—forgetfulness of the trials of day by day? He knows nothing of our ideals of service, of the benefits to ourselves, to each other, to you"—he met Fairchild's burly quizzical gaze—"to himself. And, by the way," he added coming to earth again, "there are a few points on this subject I am going to take up with your secretary to-morrow." He transfixed Mr. Talliaferro again. "What were your impressions of my remarks to-day?"

"I beg pardon?"

"What did you think of my idea for getting a hundred percent church attendance by keeping them afraid they'd miss something good by staying away?"

Mr. Talliaferro turned his stricken face to the others, one by one. After a while his interrogator said in a tone of cold displeasure: "You don't mean to say you do not recall me?"

Mr. Talliaferro cringed. "Really, sir—I am distressed—" The other interrupted heavily.

"You were not at lunch to-day?"

"No," Mr. Talliaferro replied with effusive gratitude, "I take only a glass of buttermilk at noon. I breakfast late, you see." The other man stared at him with chill displeasure, and Mr. Talliaferro added with inspiration: "You have mistaken me for some one else, I fear."

The stranger regarded Mr. Talliaferro for a cold moment. The waiter placed a dish before Mr. Talliaferro and he fell upon it in a flurry of acute discomfort.

"Do you mean—" began the stranger. Then he put his fork down and turned his disapproval coldly upon Fairchild. "Didn't I understand you to say that this—gentleman was a member of Rotary?"

Mr. Talliaferro suspended his fork and he too looked at Fairchild in shocked unbelief. "I a member of Rotary?" he repeated.

"Why, I kind of got the impression he was," Fairchild admitted. "Hadn't you heard that Talliaferro was a Rotarian?" he appealed to the others. They were noncommittal and he continued: "I seem to recall somebody telling me you were a Rotarian. But then, you know how rumors get around. Maybe it is because of your prominence in the business life of our city. Talliaferro is a member of one of our largest ladies' clothing houses," he explained. "He is just the man to help you figure out some way to get God into the mercantile business. Teach Him the meaning of service, hey, Talliaferro?"

"No: really, I—" Mr. Talliaferro objected with alarm. The stranger interrupted again.

"Well, there's nothing better on God's green earth than Rotary. Mr. Fairchild had given me to understand that you

were a member," he accused with a recurrence of cold suspicion. Mr. Talliaferro squirmed with unhappy negation.
The other stared him down, then he took out his watch.
"Well, well. I must run along. I run my day to schedule.
You'd be astonished to learn how much time can be saved by
cutting off a minute here and a minute there," he informed
them. "And—"

"I beg your pardon?"

"What do you do with them?" Fairchild asked.

"When you've cut off enough minutes here and there to
make up a sizable mess, what do you do with them?"

"—Setting a time limit to everything you do makes a
man get more punch into it; makes him take the hills on
high, you might say." A drop of nicotine on the end of the
tongue will kill a dog, Fairchild thought, chuckling to himself. He said aloud:

"Our forefathers reduced the process of gaining money
to proverbs. But we have beaten them; we have reduced the
whole of existence to fetiches."

"To words of one syllable that look well in large red
type," the Semitic man corrected.

The stranger ignored them. He half turned in his chair.
He gestured at the waiter's back, then he snapped his fingers
until he had attracted the waiter's attention. "Trouble with
these small second-rate places," he told them. "No pep, no
efficiency, in handling trade. Check, please," he directed
briskly. The cherubic waiter bent over them.

"You found the dinner nice?" he suggested.

"Sure, sure, all right. Bring the bill, will you, George?"
The waiter looked at the others, hesitating.

"Never mind, Mr. Broussard," Fairchild said quickly.

"We won't go right now. Mr. Hooper here has got to catch a train. You are my guest," he explained to the stranger. The other protested conventionally: he offered to match coins for it, but Fairchild repeated: "You are my guest to-night. Too bad you must hurry away."

"I haven't got the leisure you New Orleans fellows have," the other explained. "Got to keep on the jump, myself." He arose and shook hands all around. "Glad to've met you boys," he said to each in turn. He clasped Mr. Talliaferro's elbow with his left hand while their rights were engaged. The waiter fetched his hat and he gave the man a half dollar with a flourish. "If you're ever in the little city"—he paused to reassure Fairchild.

"Sure, sure," Fairchild agreed heartily, and they sat down again. The late guest paused at the street door a moment, then he darted forth shouting, "Taxi! Taxi!" The cab took him to the Monteleone hotel, three blocks away, where he purchased two to-morrow's papers and sat in the lobby for an hour, dozing over them. Then he went to his room and lay in bed staring at them until he had harried his mind into unconsciousness by the sheer idiocy of print.

6

"Now," said Fairchild, "let that be a lesson to you young men. That's what you'll come to by joining things, by getting the habit of it. As soon as a man begins to join clubs and lodges, his spiritual fiber begins to disintegrate. When you are young, you join things because they profess high ideals. You believe in ideals at that age, you know. Which is all right, as long as you just believe in them as ideals and not as criterions of conduct. But after a while you join more things, you are getting older and more sedate and sensible; and believing in ideals is too much trouble so you begin to live up to them with your outward life, in your contacts with other people. And when you've made a form of behavior out of an ideal, it's not an ideal any longer, and you become a public nuisance."

"It's a man's own fault if the fetich men annoy him," the Semitic man said. "Nowadays there are enough things for every one to belong to something."

"That's a rather stiff price to pay for immunity, though," Fairchild objected.

"That need not bother you," the other told him. "You have already paid it."

Mr. Talliaferro laid aside his fork. "I do hope he's not offended," he murmured. Fairchild chuckled.

"At what?" the Semitic man asked. He and Fairchild regarded Mr. Talliaferro kindly.

"At Fairchild's little joke," Mr. Talliaferro explained.

Fairchild laughed. "I'm afraid we disappointed him. He probably not only does not believe that we are bohemians, but doubts that we are even artistic. Probably the least he expected was to be taken to dinner at the studio of two people who are not married to each other, and to be offered hashish instead of food."

"And to be seduced by a girl in an orange smock and no stockings," the ghostly young man added in a sepulchral tone.

"Yes," Fairchild said. "But he wouldn't have succumbed, though."

"No," the Semitic man agreed. "But, like any Christian, he would have liked the opportunity to refuse."

"Yes, that's right," Fairchild admitted. He said: "I guess he thinks that if you don't stay up all night and get drunk and ravish somebody, there's no use in being an artist."

"Which is worse?" murmured the Semitic man.

"God knows," Fairchild answered. "I've never been ravished . . ." He sucked at his coffee. "But he's not the first man that ever hoped to be ravished and was disappointed. I've spent a lot of time in different places laying myself open, and always come off undefiled. Hey, Talliaferro?"

Mr. Talliaferro squirmed again, diffidently. Fairchild lit a cigarette. "Well, both of them are vices, and we've all seen tonight what an uncontrolled vice will lead a man into— defining a vice as any natural impulse which rides you, like the gregarious instinct in Hooper." He ceased a while. Then he chuckled again. "God must look about our American scene with a good deal of consternation, watching the antics of these volunteers who are trying to help Him."

"Or entertainment," the Semitic man amended. "But why American scene?"

"Because our doings are so much more comical. Other nations seem to be able to entertain the possibility that God may not be a Rotarian or an Elk or a Boy Scout after all. We don't. And convictions are always alarming, unless you are looking at them from behind."

The waiter approached with a box of cigars. The Semitic man took one. Mr. Talliaferro finished his dinner with decorous expedition. The Semitic man said:

"My people produced Jesus, your people Christianized him. And ever since you have been trying to get him out of your church. And now that you have practically succeeded, look at what is filling the vacuum of his departure. Do you think that your new ideal of willynilly Service without request or recourse is better than your old ideal humility? No, no"—as the other would have spoken—"I don't mean as far as result go. The only ones who ever gain by the spiritual machination of mankind are the small minority who gain emotional or mental or physical exercise from the activity itself, never the passive majority for whom the crusade is set afoot."

"Katharsis by peristalsis," murmured the blond young man, who was nurturing a reputation for cleverness. Fairchild said:

"Are you opposed to religion, then—in its general sense, I mean?"

"Certainly not," the Semitic man answered. "The only sense in which religion is general is when it benefits the greatest number in the same way. And the universal benefit of religion is that it gets the children out of the house on Sunday morning."

"But education gets them out of the house five days a week," Fairchild pointed out.

"That's true, too. But I am not at home myself on those days: education has already got me out of the house six days a week." The waiter brought Mr. Talliaferro's coffee. Fairchild lit another cigarette.

"So you believe the sole accomplishment of education is that it keeps us away from home?"

"What other general result can you name? It doesn't make us all brave or healthy or happy or wise, it doesn't even keep us married. In fact, to take an education by the modern process is like marrying in haste and spending the rest of your life making the best of it. But, understand me: I have no quarrel with education. I don't think it hurts you much, except to make you unhappy and unfit for work, for which man was cursed by the gods before they had learned about education. And if it were not education, it would be something else just as bad, and perhaps worse. Man must fill his time some way, you know."

"But to go back to religion"—"the spirit protestant eternal," murmured the blond young man hoarsely—"do you mean any particular religion, or just the general teaching of Christ?"

"What has Christ to do with it?"

"Well, it's generally accepted that he instigated a certain branch of it, whatever his motives really were."

"It's generally accepted that first you must have an effect to discern a cause. And it is a human trait to foist the blunders of the age and the race upon some one or something too remote or heedless or weak to resist. But when you say religion, you have a particular sect in mind, haven't you?"

"Yes," Fairchild admitted. "I always think of the Protestant religion."

"The worst of all," the Semitic man said. "To raise children into, I mean. For some reason one can be a Catholic or a Jew and be religious at home. But a Protestant at home is only a Protestant. It seems to me that the Protestant faith was invented for the sole purpose of filling our jails and morgues and houses of detention. I speak now of its more rabid manifestations, particularly of its activities in smaller settlements. How do young Protestant boys in small towns spend Sunday afternoons, with baseball and all such natural muscular vents denied them? They kill, they slay and steal and burn. Have you ever noticed how many juvenile firearm accidents occur on Sunday afternoon?" He ceased and shook the ash from his cigar carefully into his coffee cup. Mr. Talliaferro seeing an opening, coughed and spoke.

"By the way, I saw Gordon to-day. Tried to persuade him for our yachting party to-morrow. He doesn't enthuse, so to speak. Though I assured him how much we'd all like to have him."

"Oh, he'll come, I guess," Fairchild said. "He'd be a fool not to let her feed him for a few days."

"He'd pay a fairly high price for his food," the Semitic man remarked drily. Fairchild looked at him and he added: "Gordon hasn't served his apprenticeship yet, you know. You've got through yours."

"Oh," Fairchild grinned. "Well, yes, I did kind of play out on her, I reckon." He turned to Mr. Talliaferro. "Has she been to him in person to sell him the trip, yet?"

Mr. Talliaferro hid his mild retrospective discomfort behind a lighted match. "Yes. She stopped in this afternoon. I was with him at that time."

"Good for her," the Semitic man applauded, and Fairchild said with interest:

"She did? What did Gordon say?"

"He left," Mr. Talliaferro admitted mildly.

"Walked out on her, did he?" Fairchild glanced briefly at the Semitic man. He laughed. "You are right," he agreed. He laughed again, and Mr. Talliaferro said:

"He really should come, you know. I thought perhaps"—

diffidently—"that you'd help me persuade him. The fact that you will be with us, and your—er—assured position in the creative world . . ."

"No, I guess not," Fairchild decided. "I'm not much of a hand for changing folks' opinions. I guess I won't meddle with it."

"But, really," Mr. Talliaferro persisted, "the trip would benefit the man's work. Besides," he added with inspiration, "he will round out our party. A novelist, a painter—"

"I am invited, too," the blond young man put in sepulchrally. Mr. Talliaferro accepted him with apologetic effusion.

"By all means, a poet. I was about to mention you, my dear fellow. Two poets, in fact, with Eva W——."

"I am the best poet in New Orleans," the other interrupted with sepulchral belligerence.

"Yes, yes," Mr. Talliaferro agreed quickly, "—and a sculptor. You see?" he appealed to the Semitic man. The Semitic man met Mr. Talliaferro's importunate gaze kindly, without reply. Fairchild turned to him.

"We—ll," he began. Then: "What do you think?"

The Semitic man glanced briefly at him. "I think we'll need Gordon by all means." Fairchild grinned again and agreed.

"Yes, I guess you're right."

7

The waiter brought Fairchild's change and stood courteously beside them as they rose. Mr. Talliaferro caught

Fairchild's eye and leaned nearer, diffidently, lowering his tone.

"Eh?" Fairchild said in his burly jovial voice, not lowering it.

"Would like a moment, if you've time. Your advice—"

"Not to-night?" Fairchild asked in alarm.

"Why, yes." Mr. Talliaferro was faintly apologetic. "Just a few moments, if you are alone—" he gestured meaningly with his head toward the other two.

"No, not to-night. Julius and I are spending the evening together." Mr. Talliaferro's face fell, and Fairchild added kindly: "Some other time, perhaps."

"Yes, of course," Mr. Talliaferro agreed faultlessly. "Some other time."

8

The car swept sibilantly up the drive and on around the house. There was a light on the veranda vaguely beyond vines. They descended and Mrs. Maurier crossed the veranda and passed clashing and jangling through a French window. The niece turned the corner and followed the veranda to where beyond a nook spaced with wicker and chintz, and magazines gaily on a table, her brother sat coatless on a divan beneath a wall lamp. There was a faint litter of shavings about his feet and clinging to his trousers, and at the moment he bent with a carpenter's saw over something in his lap. The saw scraped fretfully, monotonously, and she stopped beside him and stood scratching her knee. Presently he raised his head.

"Hello," he remarked without enthusiasm. "Go to the library and get me a cigarette."

"I've got one on me, somewhere." She searched the pockets of her linen dress, but without success. "Where—" she said. She mused a moment, spreading her pocket with her hand and staring into it. Then she said, oh, yes, and took off her hat. From the crown of it she produced one limp cigarette. "I ought to have another," she mused aloud, searching the hat again. "I guess that's all, though. You can have it: I don't want one, anyway." She extended the cigarette and skirled her hat onto the lounge beside.

"Look out," he said quickly, "don't put it there. I need all this space. Put it somewhere else, can't you?" He pushed the hat off the divan, onto the floor, and accepted the cigarette. The tobacco was partially shredded from it and it was limp, like a worm. "Whatcher been doing to it? How long've you had it, anyway?" She sat beside him and he raked a match across his thigh.

"How's it coming, Josh?" she asked, extending her hand toward the object on his lap. It was a cylinder of wood larger than a silver dollar and about three inches long. He fended her off with the hand that held the lighted match, thrusting the elbow beneath her chin.

"Let it alone, I tell you."

"Oh, all right. Keep your shirt on." She moved slightly away and he took up the saw again, putting the burning cigarette on the wicker lounge between them. A thin pencil of smoke rose from it into the windless air, and soon a faint smell of burning. She picked up the cigarette, drew once at it and replaced it so it would not scorch the wicker. The saw grated jerkily and thinly; outside, beyond the vines, insects

scraped monotonously one to another in the heavy, swooning darkness. A moth, having evaded the screen wire, gyrated
idiotically beneath and about the light. She raised her skirt
to stare at a small feverish spot on her brown knee. . . . The
saw grated jerkily, ceased, and he laid it aside again. The
cylinder was in two sections, fitted one to another, and she
drew one foot beneath the other knee, bending nearer to
watch him, breathing against his neck. He moved restively
and she said at last:

"Say, Gus, how long will it take you to get it finished?"

He raised his face, suspending his knife blade. They
were twins: just as there was something masculine about her
jaw, so was there something feminine about his.

"For God's sake," he exclaimed, "let me alone, can't
you? Go away and pull your clothes down. Don't you ever
get tired of waving your legs around?"

A yellow negro in a starched jacket stepped silently
around the corner. When they looked up he turned without speaking. "All right, Walter," she said. But he was gone.
They followed, leaving the cigarette to lift its unwavering
plume and a thin smell of burning wicker into the somnolent air.

9

fool fool you have work to do o cursed of god cursed and forgotten form shapes cunningly sweated cunning to simplicity
shapes out of chaos more satisfactory than bread to the belly
form by a madmans dream gat on the body of chaos le gar-
çon vierge of the soul horned by utility o cuckold of derision.

The warehouse, the dock, was a formal rectangle without perspective. Flat as cardboard, and projecting at a faint
motionless angle above it, against a lighter spaciousness and
sky not quite so imminent and weary, masts of a freighter
lying against the dock. Form and utility, Gordon repeated
to himself. Or form and chance. Or chance and utility.
Beneath it, within the somber gloom of the warehouse where
men had sweated and labored, across the empty floor lately
thunderous with trucks, amid the rich overripe odors of the
ends of the earth—coffee and resin and tow and fruit—he
walked, surrounded by ghosts, passing on.

The hull of the freighter bulked, forecastle and poop
soaring darkly sharp, solid, cutting off vision, soaring its
superstructure on the sky. The unseen river continued a
ceaseless sound against the hull, lulling it with a simulation
of the sea, and about the piles of the wharf. The shore and
the river curved away like the bodies of two dark sleepers
embracing, curved one to another in slumber; and far away
opposite the Point, banked lights flickered like a pile of yet
living ashes in a wind. Gordon paused, leaning over the
edge of the wharf, staring down into the water.

stars in my hair in my hair and beard i am crowned with
stars christ by his own hand an autogethsemane carved darkly
out of pure space but not rigid no no an unmuscled wallowing fecund and foul the placid tragic body of a woman who
conceives without pleasure bears without pain

what would i say to her fool fool you have work to do
you have nothing accursed intolerant and unclean too warm
your damn bones then whisky will do as well or a chisel
and maul any damn squirrel keeps warm in a cage go on
go on then israfel revolted surprised behind a haycock by

a male relation fortitude become a matchflame snuffed by a small white belly where was it i once saw a dogwood tree not white but tan tan as cream what will you say to her bitter and new as a sunburned flame bitter and new those two little silken snails somewhere under her dress horned pinkly yet reluctant o israfel ay wax your wings with the thin odorless moisture of her thighs strangle your heart with hair fool fool cursed and forgotten of god

He flung back his head and laughed a huge laugh in the loneliness. His voice surged like a dark billow against the wall behind him, then ebbing outward over the dim, formless river, it died slowly away . . . then from the other shore a mirthless echo mocked him, and it too died away. He went on treading the dark resin-scented wharf.

Presently he came to a break in the black depthless monotony of the wall, and the wall again assumed a pure and inevitable formal significance sharp against the glow of the city. He turned his back to the river and soon was among freight cars black and angular, looming; and down the tracks, much further away than it appeared, an engine glared and panted while filaments of steel radiating from it toward and about his feet were like incandescent veins in a dark leaf.

There was a moon, low in the sky and worn, thumbed partly away like an old coin, and he went on. Above banana and palm the cathedral spires soared without perspective on the hot sky. Looking through the tall pickets into Jackson square was like looking into an aquarium—a moist and motionless absinthe—cloudy green of all shades from ink black to a thin and rigid feathering of silver on pomegranate and mimosa—like coral in a tideless sea, amid which globular lights hung dull and unstraying as jellyfish, incandescent yet without seeming to emanate light; and in the center of it Andrew's baroque plunging stasis nimbused about with thin gleams as though he too were recently wetted.

He crossed the street into shadow, following the wall. Two figures stood indistinguishably at his door. "Pardon me," he said touching the nearer man peremptorily, and as he did so the other man turned.

"Why, here he is now," this one said. "Hello, Gordon, Julius and I were looking for you."

"Yes?" Gordon loomed above the two shorter men, staring down at them, remote and arrogant. Fairchild removed his hat, mopping his face. Then he flipped his handkerchief viciously about his head.

"I don't mind the heat," he explained fretfully. "I like it, in fact. Like an old racehorse, you know. He's willing enough, you know, but in the cool weather when his muscles are stiff and his bones ache, the young ones all show him up. But about Fourth of July, when the sun gets hot and his muscles loosen up and his old bones don't complain any more, then he's good as any of 'em."

"Yes?" repeated Gordon looking above them into shadow. The Semitic man removed his cigar.

"It will be better on the water to-morrow," he said.

Gordon brooded above them. Then he remembered himself. "Come up," he directed abruptly, elbowing the Semitic man aside and extending his latchkey.

"No, no," Fairchild demurred quickly, "We won't stop. Julius just reminded me: we came to see if you'd change your mind and come with us on Mrs. Maurier's boat to-morrow? We saw Tal—"

"I have," Gordon interrupted him. "I'm coming."

"That's good," Fairchild agreed heartily. "You probably won't regret it much. He may enjoy it, Julius," he added. "Besides, you'll be wise to go on and get it over with, then she'll let you alone. After all, you can't afford to ignore people that own food and automobiles, you know. Can he, Julius?"

The Semitic man agreed. "When he clutters himself up with people (which he can't avoid doing) by all means let it be with people who own food and whisky and motor cars. The less intelligent, the better." He struck a match to his cigar. "But he won't last very long with her, anyway. He'll last even a shorter time than you did," he told Fairchild.

"Yes, I guess you're right. But he ought to keep a line on her, anyhow. If you can neither ride nor drive the beast yourself, it's a good idea to keep it in a pasture nearby: you may some day be able to swap it for something, you know."

"A Ford, for instance, or a radio," the Semitic man suggested. "But you've got your simile backward."

"Backward?" repeated the other.

"You were speaking from the point of view of the rider," he explained.

"Oh," Fairchild remarked. He emitted a disparaging sound. "'Ford' is good," he said heavily.

"I think 'radio' is pretty good, myself," the other said complacently.

"Oh, dry up." Fairchild replaced his hat. "So you are coming with us, then," he said to Gordon.

"Yes. I'm coming. But won't you come up?"

"No, no: not to-night. I know your place, you see." Gordon made no reply, brooding his tall head in the shadow.

"Well, I'll phone her and have her send a car for you tomorrow," Fairchild added. "Come on, Julius, let's go. Glad you changed your mind," he added belatedly. "Good night. Come on, Julius."

They crossed the street and entered the square. Once within the gates they were assailed, waylaid from behind every blade and leaf with a silent, vicious delight.

"Good Lord," exclaimed Fairchild, flipping his handkerchief madly about, "let's go over to the docks. Maybe there ain't any nautical ones." He hurried on, the Semitic man ambling beside him, clamping his dead cigar.

"He's a funny chap," the Semitic man remarked. They waited for a trolley to pass, then crossed the street. The wharf, the warehouse, was a formal rectangle with two slender masts projecting above it at a faint angle. They went on between two dark buildings and halted again while a switch engine drew an interminable monotony of cars up the track.

"He ought to get out of himself more," Fairchild commented. "You can't be an artist all the time. You'll go crazy."

"You couldn't," the other corrected. "But then, you are not an artist. There is somewhere within you a bewildered stenographer with a gift for people, but outwardly you might be anything. You are an artist only when you are telling about people, while Gordon is not an artist only when he is cutting at a piece of wood or stone. And it's very difficult for a man like that to establish workable relations with people. Other artists are too busy playing with their own egos, workaday people will not or cannot bother with him, so his alternatives are misanthropy or an endless gabbling of esthetic foster sisters of both sexes. Particularly if his lot is cast outside New York city."

"There you go: disparaging our Latin Quarter again. Where's your civic pride? Where's your common courtesy, even? Even the dog won't bite the hand that holds the bread."

"Corn belt," the other said shortly, "Indiana talking. You people up there are born with the booster complex, aren't you? Or do you acquire it with sunburned necks?"

"Oh, well, we Nordics are at a disadvantage," Fairchild replied. His tone was unctuous, the other detected something falsely frank in it. "We've got to fix our idea on a terrestrial place. Though we know it's second rate, that's the best we can do. But your people have got all heaven for your old home town, you know."

"I could forgive everything except the unpardonable clumsiness of that," the other told him. "Your idea is not bad. Why don't you give it to Mark Frost—roughly, you know—and let him untangle it for you? You and he could both use it then—if you are quick enough, that is."

Fairchild laughed. "Now, you lay off our New Orleans bohemian life; stay away from us if you don't like it. I like it, myself: there is a kind of charming futility about it, like—"

"Like a country club where they play croquet instead of golf," the other supplied for him.

"Well, yes," Fairchild agreed. "Something like that." The warehouse loomed above them, and they passed into it and amid the ghosts of the ends of the earth. "A croquet player may not be much of a go-getter, but what do you think of a man that just sits around and criticizes croquet?"

"Well, I'm like the rest of you immortals: I've got to pass the time in some way in order to gain some idea of how to pass eternity," the Semitic man answered. They passed through the warehouse and onto the dock. It was cooler here, quieter. Two ferry boats passed and repassed like a pair of golden swans in a barren cycle of courtship. The shore and the river curved away in a dark embracing slumber to where a bank of tiny lights flickered and trembled, bodiless and far away. It was much cooler here and they removed their hats. The Semitic man unclamped his dead cigar and cast it outward. Silence, water, night, absorbed it without a sound.

The First Day

The *Nausikaa* lay in the basin—a nice thing, with her white, matronly hull and mahogany-and-brass superstructure and the yacht club flag at the peak. A firm, steady wind blew in from the lake and Mrs. Maurier, having already got a taste of the sea from it, had donned her yachting cap and she now clashed and jangled in a happy, pointless ecstasy. Her two cars had made several trips and would make several more, creeping and jouncing along the inferior macadam road upon and beside which the spoor of coca cola and the almond bar betrayed the lair of the hot dog and the less-than-one-percent. All the jollity of departure under a perfect day, heatridden city behind, and a breeze too steady for the darn things to light on you. Her guests each with his or her jar of almond cream and sunburn lotion came aboard in bright babbling surges, calling, "Ship ahoy, every one," and other suitable nautical cries, while various casuals, gathered along the quay, looked on with morose interest. Mrs. Maurier in her yachting cap clashed and jangled in a happy and senseless excitement.

On the upper deck where the steward broke out chairs for them, her guests in their colored clothing gathered, dressed for deep water in batik and flowing ties and open collars, informal and colorful with the exception of Mark Frost,

the ghostly young man, a poet who produced an occasional
cerebral and obscure poem in four or seven lines reminding
one somehow of the function of evacuation excruciatingly
and incompletely performed. He wore ironed serge and
a high starched collar and he borrowed a cigarette of the
steward and lay immediately at full length on something, as
was his way. Mrs. Wiseman and Miss Jameson, flanking Mr.
Talliaferro, sat with cigarettes also. Fairchild, accompanied
by Gordon, the Semitic man and a florid stranger in heavy
tweeds, and carrying among them several weighty looking
suitcases, had gone directly below.

"Are we all here? Are we all here?" Mrs. Maurier chanted
beneath her yachting cap, roving her eyes among her guests.
Her niece stood at the afterrail beside a soft blonde girl in
a slightly soiled green dress. They both gazed shoreward
where at the end of the gangplank a flashy youth lounged
in a sort of skulking belligerence, smoking cigarettes. The
niece said, without turning her head, "What's the matter
with him? Why doesn't he come aboard?" The youth's attention seemed to be anywhere else save on the boat, yet he was
so obviously there, in the eye, belligerent and skulking. The
niece said, "Hey!" Then she said:

"What's his name? You better tell him to come on,
hadn't you?"

The blonde girl hissed "Pete" in a repressed tone. The
youth moved his slanted stiff straw hat an inch and the
blonde girl beckoned to him. He slanted the hat to the back
of his head: his whole attitude gave the impression that he
was some distance away. "Ain't you coming with us?" the
blonde girl asked in that surreptitious tone.

"Whatcher say?" he replied loudly, so that everybody looked at him—even the reclining poet raised his head.

"Come on aboard, Pete," the niece called. "Be yourself."

The youth took another cigarette from his pack. He buttoned his narrow coat. "Well, I guess I will," he agreed in his carrying tone. Mrs. Maurier held her expression of infantile astonishment up to him as he crossed the gangplank. He evaded her politely, climbing the rail with that fluid agility of the young.

"Are you the new steward?" she asked doubtfully, blinking at him.

"Sure, lady," he agreed courteously, putting his cigarette in his mouth. The other guests stared at him from their deck chairs and slanting his hat forward he ran the gauntlet of their eyes, passing aft to join the two girls. Mrs. Maurier gazed after his high vented coat in astonishment. Then she remarked the blonde girl beside her niece. She blinked again.

"Why—" she began. Then she said: "Patricia, who—"

"Oh, yes," the niece said, "this is—" she turned to the blonde girl. "What's your name, Jenny? I forgot."

"Genevieve Steinbauer," the blonde girl submitted.

"—Miss Steinbauer. And this one is Pete Something. I met them downtown. They want to go, too."

Mrs. Maurier transferred her astonishment from Jenny's vague ripe prettiness to Pete's bold uncomfortable face. "Why, he's the new steward, isn't he?"

"I don't know." The niece looked at Jenny again. "Is he?" she asked. Jenny didn't know either. Pete himself was uncomfortably noncommittal.

"I dunno," he answered. "You told me to come," he accused the niece.

"She means," the niece explained, "did you come to work on the boat?"

"Not me," Pete answered quickly. "I ain't a sailor. If she expects me to run this ferry for her, me and Jenny are going back to town."

"You don't have to run it. She's got regular men for that. There's your steward, anyway, Aunt Pat," the niece said. "Pete just wanted to come with Jenny. That's all."

Mrs. Maurier looked. Yes, there was the steward, descending the companionway with a load of luggage. She looked again at Pete and Jenny, but at that moment voices came aft breaking her amazement. The captain wished to know if he should cast off: the message was relayed by all present.

"Are we all here?" Mrs. Maurier chanted anew, forgetting Jenny and Pete. "Mr. Fairchild— Where is he?" She roved her round frantic face, trying to count noses. "Where is Mr. Fairchild?" she repeated in panic. Her car was backing and filling to turn around and she ran to the rail and screamed to the driver. He stopped the car, completely blocking the road, and hung his head out with resignation. Mrs. Wiseman said:

"He's here: he came with Ernest. Didn't he?"

Mr. Talliaferro corroborated her and Mrs. Maurier roved her frantic gaze anew, trying to count them. A sailor sprang ashore and cast off head- and sternlines under the morose regard of the casuals. The helmsman thrust his head from the wheelhouse and he and the deckhand bawled at each other. The sailor sprang aboard and the *Nausikaa* moved

slightly in the water, like a soundless awakening sigh. The
steward drew in the gangplank and the engine room telegraph rang remotely. The *Nausikaa* waked further, quiver-
ing a little, and as a gap of water grew between quay and boat
without any sensation of motion whatever, Mrs. Maurier's
second car came jouncing into view, honking madly, and
the niece sitting flat on the deck and stripping off her stockings said:

"Here comes Josh."

Mrs. Maurier shrieked. The car stopped and her nephew
descended without haste. The steward, coiling the sternline
down, gathered it up and flung it outward across the growing gap of water. The telegraph rang again and the *Nausikaa*
sighed and went back to sleep, rocking sedately. "Shake it
up, Josh," his sister called. Mrs. Maurier shrieked again and
two of the loungers caught the line and dug their heels as
the nephew, coatless and hatless, approached without haste
and climbed aboard, carrying a new carpenter's saw.

"I had to go downtown and buy one," he explained casually. "Walter wouldn't let me bring yours."

ELEVEN O'CLOCK

At last Mrs. Maurier succeeded in cornering her niece. New
Orleans, the basin, the yacht club, were far behind. The
Nausikaa sped youthfully and gaily under a blue and drowsy
day, beneath her forefoot a small bow wave spread its sedate
fading fan. Mrs. Maurier's people could not escape her now.
They had settled themselves comfortably on deck: there was
nothing to look at save one another, nothing to do save wait

for lunch. All, that is, except Jenny and Pete. Pete, holding his hat on, stood yet at the afterrail, with Jenny beside him. Her air was that of a soft and futile cajolery, to which Pete was smoldering and impervious. Mrs. Maurier breathed a sigh of temporary relief and astonishment and ran her niece to earth in the after companionway.

"Patricia," she demanded, "what on earth did you invite those two—young people for?"

"God knows," the niece answered, looking past her aunt's yachting cap to Pete, belligerent and uncomfortable beside Jenny's bovine white placidity. "God knows. If you want to turn around and take 'em back, don't let me stand in your way."

"But why did you ask them?"

"Well, I couldn't tell that they were going to turn to be so wet, could I? And you said yourself there were not enough women coming. You said so yourself last night."

"Yes, but why ask those two? Who are they? Where did you ever meet such people?"

"I met Jenny downtown. She—"

"I know: but where did you come to know her? How long have you known her?"

"I met her downtown this morning, I tell you; in Holmes' while I was buying a bathing suit. She said she'd like to come, but the other one was waiting outside on the street for her and he put his foot down: he said she couldn't go without him. He's her heavy, I gather."

Mrs. Maurier's astonishment was sincere now. "Do you mean to tell me," she asked in shocked unbelief, "that you never saw these people before? That you invited two people you never saw before to come on a party on my boat?"

"I just asked Jenny," the niece explained patiently. "The other one had to come so she could come. I didn't want him specially. How could I know her when I never saw her before? If I had known her, you can bet I wouldn't have asked her to come. She's a complete washout, far as I'm concerned. But I couldn't see that this morning. I thought she was all right, then. Gabriel's pants, look at 'em." They both looked back at Jenny in her flimsy green dress, at Pete holding his hat on. "Well, I got 'em here: I guess I'll have to keep 'em from getting stepped on. I think I'll get Pete a piece of string to tie his hat down with, anyway." She swung herself easily up the stairs: Mrs. Maurier saw with horrified surprise that she wore neither shoes nor stockings.

"Patricia!" she shrieked. The niece paused, looking over her shoulder. Her aunt pointed mutely at her bare legs.

"Haul in your sheet, Aunt Pat," the niece replied brusquely, "you're jibbing."

ONE O'CLOCK

Lunch was spread on deck, on collapsible card tables set end to end. When she appeared her guests all regarded her brightly, a trifle curiously. Mrs. Maurier, oblivious, herded them toward it. "Sit anywhere, people," she repeated in singsong. "Girls will be at a premium this voyage. To the winner belongs the fair lady, remember." This sounded a little strange to her, so she repeated: "Sit anywhere, people; the gentlemen must make . . ." She looked about upon her guests and her voice died away. Her party consisted of Mrs. Wiseman, Miss Jameson, herself, Jenny and Pete clotting unhappily behind her niece, Mr. Talliaferro and her nephew, who had already seated himself. "Where are the gentlemen?" she asked at large.

"Jumped overboard," muttered Pete darkly, unheard, clutching his hat. The others stood, watching her brightly.

"Where are the gentlemen?" Mrs. Maurier repeated.

"If you'd stop talking a minute you wouldn't have to ask," her nephew told her. He had already seated himself and he now spooned into a grapefruit with preoccupied celerity.

"Theodore!" his aunt exclaimed.

From below there came an indistinguishable mixture of sound somehow vaguely convivial. "Whooping it up," the nephew added, looking up at his aunt at her expression of reproof. "In a hurry," he explained. "Got to get done. Can't wait on those birds." He remarked his sister's guests for the first time. "Who're your friends, Gus?" he asked without interest. Then he fell anew upon his grapefruit.

"Theodore!" his aunt exclaimed again. The indistinguishable convivial sound welled, becoming laughter. Mrs. Maurier roved her astonished eyes. "What can they be doing?"

Mr. Talliaferro moved deferentially, tactfully. "If you wish—?"

"Oh, Mr. Talliaferro, if you would be so kind," Mrs. Maurier accepted with emotion.

"Let the steward go, Aunt Pat. Let's eat," the niece said, thrusting Jenny forward. "Come on, Pete. Gimme your hat," she added, offering to take it. Pete refused to surrender it.

"Wait," the nephew interjected, "I'll get 'em up." He picked up the thick plate and flipping his grapefruit hull overboard he turned sideways in his chair and hammered a brisk staccato on the deck with the dish.

"Theodore!" his aunt exclaimed for the third time. "Mr. Talliaferro, will you—" Mr. Talliaferro sped toward the companionway, vanished.

"Aw, let the steward go, Aunt Pat," the niece repeated. "Come on, let's sit down. Let up, Josh, for God's sake."

"Yes, Mrs. Maurier, let's don't wait for them," Mrs. Wiseman abetted, seating herself also. The others followed suit. Mrs. Maurier roved her fretted eyes. "Well," she submitted at last. Then she remarked Pete, still clutching his hat. "I'll take your hat," she offered, extending her hand. Pete foiled her quickly.

"Look out," he said, "I've got it." He moved beyond Jenny and put his hat behind him in his chair. At this moment the gentlemen appeared from below, talking loudly.

"Ah, wretches," began the hostess with flaccid coquetry, shaking her finger at them. Fairchild was in the lead, burly and jovial, a shade unsteady as to gait. Mr. Talliaferro brought up the rear: he too had now a temporarily emancipated air.

"I guess you thought we'd jumped the ship," Fairchild suggested, happily apologetic. Mrs. Maurier sought Mr. Talliaferro's evasive eyes. "We were helping Major Ayers find his teeth," Fairchild added.

"Lost 'em in that little rabbit hutch where we were," explained the florid man. "Couldn't find 'em right off. No teeth, no tiffin, y'know. If you don't mind?" he murmured politely, seating himself next Mrs. Wiseman. "Ah, grapefruit." He raised his voice again. "How jolly: seen no grapefruit since we left New Orleans, eh, Julius?"

"Lost his teeth?" repeated Mrs. Maurier, dazed. The niece and her brother regarded the florid man with interest.

"They fell out of his mouth," Fairchild elaborated, taking the seat next Miss Jameson. "He was laughing at something Julius said, and they fell out of his mouth and somebody kicked 'em under the bunk, you see. What was it you said, Julius?"

Mr. Talliaferro essayed to seat himself beside the florid man. Mrs. Maurier again sought his eye, forced him and vanquished him with bright command. He rose and went to the chair next to her, and she leaned toward him, sniffing. "Ah, Mr. Talliaferro," she murmured with playful implacability, "naughty, naughty."

"Just a nip—they were rather insistent," Mr. Talliaferro apologized.

"You men, you naughty men. I'll forgive you, however, this once," she answered. "Do ring, please."

The Semitic man's flaccid face and dark compassionate eyes presided at the head of the table. Gordon stood for a time after the others were seated, then he came and took the seat between Mrs. Maurier and her niece, with abrupt arrogance. The niece looked up briefly. "Hello, Blackbeard." Mrs. Maurier smiled at him automatically. She said:

"Listen, people. Mr. Talliaferro is going to make an announcement. About promptness," she added to Mr. Talliaferro, putting her hand on his sleeve.

"Ah, yes. I say, you chaps almost missed lunch. We were not going to wait on you. The lunch hour is half after twelve, hereafter, and every one must be present promptly. Ship's discipline, you know. Eh, Commodore?"

The hostess corroborated. "You must be good children," she added with playful relief, looking about her table. Her worried expression returned. "Why, there's an empty place. Who isn't here?" She roved her eyes in growing alarm. "Some one isn't here," she repeated. She had a brief and dreadful vision of having to put back short one guest, of inquest and reporters and headlines, and of floating inert buttocks in some lonely reach of the lake, that would later wash ashore with that mute inopportune implacability of the drowned. The guests stared at one another, then at the vacant place, then at one another again. Mrs. Maurier tried to call a mental roll, staring at each in turn. Presently Miss Jameson said:

"Why, it's Mark, isn't it?"

It was Mark. They had forgotten him. Mrs. Maurier dispatched the steward, who found the ghostly poet still at full length on the upper deck. He appeared in his ironed serge, bathing them briefly in his pale gaze.

"You gave us rather a turn, my dear fellow," Mr. Talliaferro informed him with reproof, taking upon himself the duties of host.

"I wondered how long it would be before some one saw fit to notify me that lunch was ready," the poet replied with cold dignity, taking his seat.

Fairchild, watching him, said abruptly: "Say, Julius, Mark's the very man for Major Ayers, ain't he? Say, Major, here's a man to take your first bottle. Tell him about your scheme."

The florid man regarded the poet affably. "Ah, yes. It's a salts, you see. You spoon a bit of it into your—"

"A what?" asked the poet, poising his spoon and staring at the florid man. The others all poised their tools and stared at the florid man.

"A salts," he explained. "Like our salts at home, y'know—"

"A—?" repeated Mrs. Maurier. Mr. Talliaferro's eyes popped mildly.

"All Americans are constipated," the florid man continued blithely, "do with a bit of salts in a tumbler of water in the morning. Now, my scheme is—"

"Mr. Talliaferro!" Mrs. Maurier implored. Mr. Talliaferro girded himself anew.

"My dear sir," he began.

"—is to put the salts up in a tweaky phial, a phial that will look well on one's night table: a jolly design of some sort. All Americans will buy it. Now, the population of your country is several millions, I fancy; and when you take into consideration the fact that all Americans are con—"

"My dear sir," said Mr. Talliaferro, louder.

"Eh?" said the florid man, looking at him.

"What kind of a jar will you put 'em in?" asked the nephew, his mind taking fire.

"Some tweaky sort of thing that all Americans will buy—"

"The American flag and a couple of doves holding dollar marks in their bills, and a handle that when you pull it out, it's a corkscrew," suggested Fairchild. The florid man glared at him with interest and calculation.

"Or," the Semitic man suggested, "a small condensed table for calculating interest on one side and a good recipe for beer on the other." The florid man glared at him with interest.

"That's just for men," Mrs. Wiseman said. "How about the women's trade?"

"A bit of mirror would do for them, don't you think?" the florid man offered, "surrounded by a design in colors, eh?" Mrs. Wiseman gave him a murderous glance and the poet added:

"And a formula for preventing conception and a secret place for hairpins." The hostess moaned, Mr. Talliaferro! Mrs. Wiseman said savagely:

"I have a better idea than that, for both sexes: your photograph on one side and the golden rule on the other." The florid man glared at her with interest. The nephew broke in once more:

"I mean, have you invented a jar yet, invented a way to get the stuff out of the jar?"

"Oh, yes. I've done that. You spoon it out, you know."

"But tell 'em how you know all Americans are constipated," Fairchild suggested. Mrs. Maurier rang the service bell furiously and at length. The steward appeared and as he removed the plates and replaced them with others, the florid man leaned nearer Mrs. Wiseman.

"What's that chap?" he asked indicating Mr. Talliaferro.

"What is he?" Mrs. Wiseman repeated. "Why— I think he sells things downtown. Doesn't he, Julius?" She appealed to her brother.

"I mean, what—ah—race does he belong to?"

"Oh. You'd noticed his accent, then?"

"Yes. I noticed he doesn't talk like Americans. I thought perhaps he is one of your natives."

"One of our—?" She stared at him.

"Your red Indians, y'know," he explained.

Mrs. Maurier rang her little bell again, sort of chattering to herself.

TWO O'CLOCK

Mrs. Maurier put an end to that luncheon as soon as she decently could. If I can only break them up, get them into a bridge game, she thought in an agony. It had got to where every time one of the gentlemen made the precursory sound of speech, Mrs. Maurier flinched and cringed nearer Mr. Talliaferro. At least she could depend on him, provided . . . But she was going to do the providing in his case. They had discussed Major Ayers' salts throughout the meal. Eva Wiseman had turned renegade and abetted them, despite the atmosphere of reproof Mrs. Maurier had tried to foster and support. And, on top of all this, the strange young man had the queerest manner of using knife and fork. Mr. Fairchild's way was—well, uncouth; but after all, one must pay a price for Art. Jenny, on the other hand, had an undeniable style, feeding herself with her little finger at a rigid and elegant angle from her hand. And now Fairchild was saying:

"Now here's a clean case of poetic justice for you. A hundred odd years ago Major Ayers' grandpa wants to come to New Orleans, but our grandfathers stop him down yonder in those Chalmette swamps and lick hell out of him. And now Major Ayers comes into the city itself and conquers it with a laxative so mild that, as he says, you don't even notice it. Hey, Julius?"

"It also confounds all the old convictions regarding the

irreconcilability of science and art," the Semitic man suggested.

"Huh?" said Fairchild. "Oh, sure. That's right. Say, he certainly ought to make Al Jackson a present of a bottle, oughtn't he?"

The thin poet groaned sepulchrally. Major Ayers repeated: "Al Jackson?"

The steward removed the cloth. The table was formed of a number of card tables; by Mrs. Maurier's direction he did not removed these. She called him to her, whispered to him: he went below.

"Why, didn't you ever hear of Al Jackson?" asked Fairchild in unctuous surprise. "He's a funny man, a direct descendant of Old Hickory that licked you folks in 1812, he claims. He's quite a character in New Orleans." The other guests all listened to Fairchild with a sort of noncommittal attention. "You can always tell him because he wears congress boots all the time—"

"Congress boots?" murmured Major Ayers, staring at him. Fairchild explained, raising his foot above the level of the table to demonstrate.

"Sure. On the street, at formal gatherings, even in evening dress he wears 'em. He even wears 'em in bathing."

"In bathing? I say." Major Ayers stared at the narrator with his round china-blue eyes.

"Sure. Won't let any one see him barefoot. A family deformity, you see. Old Hickory himself had it: that's the reason he outfought the British in those swamps. He'd never have whipped 'em otherwise. When you get to town, go down to Jackson square and look at that statue of the old fellow. He's got on congress boots." He turned to the Semitic man, "By the way, Julius, you remember about Old Hickory's cavalry, don't you?" The Semitic man was noncommittal, and Fairchild continued:

"Well, the old general bought a place in Florida. A stock farm, they told him it was, and he gathered up a bunch of mountaineers from his Tennessee place and sent 'em down there with a herd of horses. Well, sir, when they got there they found the place was pretty near all swamp. But they were hardy folks, so they lit right in to make the best of it. In the meantime—"

"Doing what?" asked the nephew.

"Huh?" said Fairchild.

"What were they going to do in Florida? That's what we all want to know," Mrs. Wiseman said.

"Sell real estate to the Indians," the Semitic man suggested. Major Ayers stared at him with his little blue eyes.

"No, they were going to run a dude ranch for the big hotels at Palm Beach," Fairchild told them. "And in the meantime some of these horses strayed off into the swamps, and in some way the breed got crossed with alligators. And so, when Old Hickory found he was going to have to fight his battle down there in those Chalmette swamps, he sent over to his Florida place and had 'em round up as many of those half-horse half-alligators as they could, and he mounted some of his infantry on 'em and the British couldn't stop 'em at all. The British didn't know Florida—"

"That's true," the Semitic man put in. "There were no excursions then."

"—and they didn't even know what the things were, you see."

Major Ayers and Mrs. Maurier stared at Fairchild in quiet childlike astonishment. "Go on," said Major Ayers at last, "you're pulling my leg."

"No, no: ask Julius. But then, it is kind of hard for a foreigner to get us. We're a simple people, we Americans, kind of childlike and hearty. And you've got to be both to cross a horse on an alligator and then find some use for him, you know. That's part of our national temperament, Major. You'll understand it better when you've been among us longer. Won't he, Julius?"

"Yes, he'll be able to get us all right when he's been in America long enough to acquire our customs. It's the custom that makes the man, you know."

"Ah, yes," said Major Ayers, blinking at him. "But there's one of your customs I'll not be able to acquire: your habit of eating apple tarts. We don't have apple tarts at home, y'know. No Englishman nor Welshman nor Scot will eat an apple tart."

"You don't?" repeated Fairchild. "Why, I seem to remember—"

"But not apple tarts, old lad. We have other sorts, but no apple tarts. You see, years ago it was the custom at Eton for the young lads to pop out at all hours and buy apple tarts. And one day a chap, a cabinet member's son, died of a surfeit of apple tarts, whereupon his father had parliament put through a bill that no minor should be able to purchase an apple tart in the British dominions. So this generation grew up without them; the former generation died off, and now the present generation never heard of apple tarts." He turned to the Semitic man. "Custom, as you just remarked."

The ghostly poet, waiting his chance, murmured "Secretary of the Interior," but this was ignored. Mrs. Maurier stared at Major Ayers, and Fairchild and the others all stared at Major Ayers' florid bland face, and there was an interval of silence during which the hostess glanced about hopelessly among her guests. The steward reappeared and she hailed him with utter relief, ringing her little bell again commandingly. The others looked toward her and she passed her gaze from face to face.

"Now, people, at four o'clock we will be in good bathing water. Until then, what do you say to a nice game of bridge? Of course, those who really must have a siesta will be excused, but I'm sure no one will wish to remain below on such a day as this," she added brightly. "Let me see—Mr. Fairchild, Mrs. Wiseman, Patricia and Julius, will be table number one. Major Ayers, Miss Jameson, Mr.—Talliaferro—" her gaze came to rest on Jenny. "Do you play bridge, Miss—child?"

Fairchild had risen with some trepidation. "Say, Julius, Major Ayers had better lie down a while, don't you think? Being new to our hot climate, you know. And Gordon, too. Hey, Gordon, don't you reckon we better lie down a while?"

"Right you are," Major Ayers agreed with alacrity, rising also. "If the ladies will excuse us, that is. Might get a touch of sun, you know," he added, glancing briefly at the awning overhead.

"But really," said Mrs. Maurier helplessly. The gentlemen, clotting, moved toward the companionway.

"Coming, Gordon?" Fairchild called.

Mrs. Maurier turned to Gordon. "Surely, Mr. Gordon, you'll not desert us?"

Gordon looked at the niece. She met his harsh arrogant

stare calmly, and he turned away. "Yes. Don't play cards," he answered shortly.

"But really," repeated Mrs. Maurier. Mr. Talliaferro and Pete remained. The nephew had already taken himself off to his new carpenter's saw. Mrs. Maurier looked at Pete. Then she looked away. Not even necessary to ask Pete if he played bridge. "You won't play at all?" she called after the departing gentlemen, hopelessly.

"Sure, we'll come back later," Fairchild assured her, herding his watch below. They descended noisily.

Mrs. Maurier looked about on her depleted party with astonished despair. The niece gazed at the emptied companionway a moment, then she looked about at the remainder of the party grouped about the superfluous card tables. "And you said you didn't have enough women to go around," she remarked.

"But we can have one table, anyway," Mrs. Maurier brightened suddenly. "There's Eva, Dorothy, Mr. Talliaferro and m—Why, here's Mark," she exclaimed. They had forgotten him again. "Mark, of course. I'll cut out this hand."

Mr. Talliaferro demurred. "By no means. I'll cut out. You take the hand: I insist."

Mrs. Maurier refused. Mr. Talliaferro became insistent and she examined him with cold speculation. Mr. Talliaferro at last averted his eyes and Mrs. Maurier glanced briefly toward the companionway. She was firm.

* * *

"Poor Talliaferro," the Semitic man said. Fairchild led the way along the passage, pausing at his door while his gang trod his heels. "Did you see his face? She'll keep him under her thumb from now on."

"I don't feel sorry for him," Fairchild said. "I think he kind of likes it: he's always a little uncomfortable with men, you know. Being among a bunch of women seems to restore his confidence in himself, gives him a sense of superiority which his contacts with men seem to have pretty well hammered out of him. I guess the world does seem a kind of crude place to a man that spends eight hours a day surrounded by lace trimmed crêpe de chine," he added, fumbling at the door. "Besides, he can't come to me for advice about how to seduce somebody. He's a fairly intelligent man, more sensitive than most, and yet he too labors under the illusion that art is just a valid camouflage for rutting." He opened the door at last and they entered and sat variously while he knelt and dragged from beneath the bunk a heavy suitcase.

"She's quite wealthy, isn't she?" Major Ayers asked from the bunk. The Semitic man, as was his way, had already preempted the single chair. Gordon leaned his back against the wall, tall and shabby and arrogant.

"Rotten with it," Fairchild answered. He got a bottle from the suitcase and rose to his feet and held the bottle against the light, gloating. "She owns plantations or something, don't she, Julius? First family, or something like that?"

"Something like that," the Semitic man agreed. "She is a northerner, herself. Married it. I think that explains her, myself."

"Explains her?" Fairchild repeated, passing glasses among them.

"It's a long story. I'll tell it to you some day."

"It'll take a long story to explain her," Fairchild rejoined.

"Say, she'd be a better bet for Major Ayers than the laxative business, wouldn't she? I'd rather own plantations than a patent medicine plant, any day."

"He'd have to remove Talliaferro, somehow," the Semitic man remarked.

"Talliaferro's not thinking seriously of her, is he?"

"He'd better be," the other answered. "I wouldn't say he's got intentions on her, exactly," he corrected. "He's just there without knowing it: a natural hazard as regards any one else's prospects."

"Freedom and the laxative business, or plantations and Mrs. Maurier," Fairchild mused aloud. "Well, I don't know. . . . What do you think, Gordon?"

Gordon stood against the wall, aloof, not listening to them hardly, watching within the bitter and arrogant loneliness of his heart a shape strange and new as fire swirling, headless, armless, legless, but when his name was spoken he stirred. "Let's have a drink," he said.

Fairchild filled the glasses: the muscles at the bases of their noses tightened.

"That's a pretty good rejoinder to every emergency life may offer—like Squire Western's hollo," the Semitic man said.

"Yes, but freedom—" began Fairchild.

"Drink your whisky," the other told him. "Take what little freedom you'll ever get while you can. Freedom from the police is the greatest freedom man can demand or expect."

"Freedom," said Major Ayers, "the only freedom is in wartime. Every one too busy fighting or getting ribbons or a snug berth to annoy you. Samurai or headhunters—take your choice. Mud and glory, or a bit of ribbon on a clean tunic. Mud and abnegation and dear whisky and England full of your beastly expeditionary forces. You were better than Canadians, though," he admitted, "not so damned many of you. It was a priceless war, eh? . . . I like a bit of red, myself," he confided. "Staff tabs worth two on the breast: only see the breast from one side. Ribbon's good in peacetime, however."

"But even peace can't last forever, can it?" the Semitic man added.

"It'll last a while—this one. Can't have another war right off. Too many would stop away. Regulars jump in and get all the cushy jobs right off: learned in the last one, you know; and the others would all get their backs up and refuse to go again." He mused for a moment. "The last one made war so damned unpopular with the proletariat. They overdid it. Like the showman who fills his stage so full chaps can see through into the wings."

"You folks were pretty good at war bunk yourselves, weren't you?" Fairchild said. "War bunk?" repeated Major Ayers. Fairchild explained.

"We didn't pay money for it, though," Major Ayers answered. "We only gave ribbons. . . . Pretty good whisky, eh?"

*　*　*

"If you want me to," Jenny said, "I'll put it away in my room somewheres."

Pete crammed it down on his head, holding his head tilted rigidly a little to windward. The wind was eating his cigarette right out of his mouth: he held his hand as a shield, smoking behind his hand.

"It's all right," he answered. "Where'd you put it, anyway?"

". . . Somewheres. I'd just kind of put it away somewheres." The wind was in her dress, molding it, and clasping her hands about the rail she let herself swing backward to the full stretch of her arms while the wind molded her thighs. Pete's coat, buttoned, ballooned its vented flaring skirts.

"Yes," he said, "I can just kind of put it away myself, when I want. . . . Look out, kid." Jenny had drawn herself up to the rail again. The rail was breast high to her, but by hooking her legs over the lower one she could draw herself upward, and by creasing her young belly over the top one she leaned far out over the water. The water sheared away creaming: a white fading through milky jade to blue again, and a thin spray whipped from it, scuttering like small shot. "Come on, get back on the boat. We are not riding the blinds this trip."

"Gee," said Jenny, creasing her young belly, hanging out over the water, while wind molded and flipped her little skirt, revealing the pink backs of her knees above her stockings. The helmsman thrust his head out and yelled at her, and Jenny craned her neck to look back at him, swinging her blown drowsy hair.

"Keep your shirt on, brother," Pete shouted back at the helmsman, for form's sake. "What'd I tell you, dumbness?" he hissed at Jenny, pulling her down. "Come on, now, it's their boat. Try to act like somebody."

"I wasn't hurting it," Jenny answered placidly. "I guess I can do this, can't I?" She let her body swing back again at the stretch of her arms. ". . . Say, there he is with that saw again. I wonder what he's making."

"Whatever it is he probably don't need any help from us," Pete answered. . . . "Say, how long did she say this was going to last?"

"I don't know . . . maybe they'll dance or something after a while. This is kind of funny, ain't it? They are not going anywhere, and they don't do anything . . . kind of like a movie or something." Jenny brooded softly, gazing at the nephew where he sat with his saw in the lee of the wheelhouse, immersed and oblivious. "If I was rich, I'd stay where I could spend it. Not like this, where there's not even anything to look at."

"Yeh. If you were rich you'd buy a lot of clothes and jewelry and an automobile. And then what'd you do? Wear your clothes out sitting in the automobile, huh?"

"I guess so. . . . I wouldn't buy a boat, anyway. . . . I think he's kind of good looking. Not very snappy looking, though. I wonder what he's making?"

"Better go ask him," Pete answered shortly. "I don't know."

"I don't want to know, anyhow. I was just kind of wondering." She swung herself slowly at arms' length, against the wind, slowly until she swung herself over beside Pete, leaning her back against him.

"Go on and ask him," Pete insisted, his elbows hooked over the rail, ignoring Jenny's soft weight. "A pretty boy like him won't bite you."

"I don't mind being bit," Jenny replied placidly. . . . "Peter—. . . ?"

"Get away, kid: I'm respectable," Pete told her. "Try your pretty boy; see if you can compete with that saw."

"I like peppy looking men," Jenny remarked. She sighed. "Gee, I wish there was a movie to go to or something." (I wonder what he's making.)

* * *

"What horsepower does she develop?" the nephew asked, raising his voice above the deep vibration of the engine, staring at it entranced. It was clean as a watch, nickeled and redleaded—a latent and brooding power beneath a thin film of golden lubricating oil like the film of moisture on a splendid animal functioning, physical with perfection. The captain in a once white cap with a tarnished emblem on the visor, and a thin undershirt stained with grease, told him how much horsepower she developed.

He stood in a confined atmosphere oppressive with energy: an ecstatic tingling that penetrated to the core of his body, giving to his entrails a slightly unpleasant sensation of lightness, staring at the engine with rapture. It was as beautiful as a racehorse and in a way terrifying, since with all its implacable soulless power there was no motion to be seen save a trivial nervous flickering of rockerarms—a thin bright clicking that rode just above the remote contemplative thunder of it. The keelplates shook with it, the very bulkheads trembled with it, as though a moment were approaching when it would burst the steel as a cocoon is burst, and soar upward and outward on dreadful and splendid wings of energy and flame. . . .

But the engine was bolted down with huge bolts, clean and firm and neatly redleaded; bolts that nothing could break, as firmly fixed as the nethermost foundations of the world. Across the engine, above the flickering rockerarms, the captain's soiled cap appeared and vanished. The nephew moved carefully around the engine, following.

There was a port at the height of his eye and he saw beyond it sky bisected by a rigid curving sweep of water stiff with a fading energy like bronze. The captain was busy with a wisp of cotton waste, hovering about the engine, dabbing at its immaculate anatomy with needless maternal infatuation. The nephew watched with interest. The captain leaned nearer, wiped his waste through a small accumulation of grease at the base of a pushrod, and raised it to the light. The nephew approached, peering over the captain's shoulder. It was a tiny speck, quite dead.

"What is it, Josh?" his sister said, breathing against his neck. The nephew turned sharply.

"Gabriel's pants," he said. "What are you doing down here? Who told you to come down here?"

"I wanted to come, too," she answered, crowding against him. "What is it, Captain? What've you and Gus got?"

"Here," her brother thrust at her, "get on back on deck where you belong. You haven't got any business down here."

"What is it, Captain?" she repeated, ignoring him. The captain extended his rag. "Did the engine kill it?" she asked. "Gee, I wish we could get all of 'em down here and lock the door for a while, don't you?" She stared at the engine, at the flickering rockerarms. She squealed. "Look! Look how fast they're going. It's going awfully fast, isn't it, Captain?"

"Yes, ma'am," the captain replied. "Pretty fast."

"What's her bore and stroke?" the nephew asked. The

captain examined a dial. Then he turned a valve slightly. Then he examined the dial again. The nephew repeated his question and the captain told him her bore and stroke.

"She revs up pretty well, don't she?" the nephew suggested after a while.

"Yes, sir," the captain answered. He was busy doing something with two small wrenches, and the nephew offered to help. His sister followed, curious and intent.

"I expect you'd better let me do it alone," the captain said, courteous and firm. "I know her better than you, I expect. . . . Suppose you and the young lady stand over there just a little."

"You sure do keep her clean, Captain," the niece said. "Clean enough to eat off of, isn't she?"

The captain thawed. "She's worth keeping clean. Best marine engine made. German. She cost twelve thousand dollars."

"Gee," the niece remarked in a hushed tone. Her brother turned upon her, pushing her before him from the room.

"Look here," he said fiercely, his voice shaking, when they were again in the passage. "What are you doing, following me around? What did I tell you I was going to do if you followed me any more?"

"I wasn't following you. I—"

"Yes, you were," he interrupted, shaking her, "following me. You—"

"I just wanted to come, too. Besides, it's Aunt Pat's boat: it's not yours. I've got as much right down there as you have."

"Aw, get on up on deck. And if I catch you trailing around behind me again . . ." his voice merged into a dire and nameless threat. The niece turned toward the companionway.

"Oh, haul in your sheet: you're jibbing."

FOUR O'CLOCK

They sat at their bridge on deck, shuffling, dealing, speaking in sparse monosyllables. The *Nausikaa* surged sedately onward under the blue drowsing afternoon. Far away on the horizon, the lazy smudge of the Mandeville ferry.

Mrs. Maurier on the outskirt of the game, gazed at intervals abstractedly into space. From below there came an indistinguishable sound, welling at intervals, and falling, and Mr. Talliaferro grew restive. The sound died away at intervals, swelled again. The *Nausikaa* paced sedately on.

They played their hands, dealt and shuffled again. Mr. Talliaferro was becoming distrait. Every once in a while his attention strayed and returning found Mrs. Maurier's eyes upon him, coldly contemplative, and he bent anew over his cards. . . . The indistinguishable sound welled once more. Mr. Talliaferro trumped his partner's queen and the gentlemen in their bathing suits surged up the stairs.

They completely ignored the cardplayers, passing aft in a body and talking loudly; something about a wager. They paused at the rail upon which the steward leaned at the moment; here they clotted momentarily, then Major Ayers detached himself from the group and flung himself briskly and awkwardly overboard. "Hurray," roared Fairchild. "He wins!"

Mrs. Maurier had raised her face when they passed,

she had spoken to them and had watched them when they
halted, and she saw Major Ayers leap overboard with a
shocked and dreadful doubt of her own eyesight. Then she
screamed.

The steward stripped off his jacket, detached and flung
a lifebelt, then followed himself, diving outward and away
from the screw. "Two of 'em," Fairchild howled with joy.
"Pick you up when we come back," he megaphoned through
his hands.

Major Ayers came up in the wake of the yacht, swimming strongly. The *Nausikaa* circled, the telegraph rang.
Major Ayers and the steward reached the lifebelt together,
and before the yacht lost way completely the helmsman and
the deckhand had swung the tender overside, and soon they
hauled Major Ayers savagely into the small boat.

The *Nausikaa* was hove to. Mrs. Maurier was helped
below to her cabin, where her irate captain attended her
presently. Meanwhile the other gentlemen plunged in and
began to cajole the ladies, so the rest of the party went below
and donned their bathing suits.

Jenny didn't have one: her sole preparation for the voyage
had consisted of the purchase of a lipstick and a comb. The
niece loaned Jenny hers, and in this borrowed suit which fit
her a shade too well, Jenny clung to the gunwale of the tender, clutching Pete's hand and floating her pink-and-white
face like a toy balloon unwetted above the water, while Pete
sat in the boat fully dressed even to his hat, glowering.

Mr. Talliaferro's bathing suit was red, giving him a
bizarre desiccated look, like a recently extracted tooth. He
wore also a red rubber cap and he let himself gingerly into
the water feet first from the stern of the tender, and here he

clung beside the placid Jenny, trying to engage her in small talk beneath Pete's thunderous regard. The ghostly poet in his ironed serge—he didn't swim—lay again at full length on four chairs, craning his pale prehensile face above the bathers.

Fairchild looked more like a walrus than ever: a deceptively sedate walrus of middle age suddenly evincing a streak of demoniac puerility. He wallowed and splashed, heavily playful, and, seconded by Major Ayers, annoyed the ladies by pinching them under water and by splashing them, wetting Pete liberally where he sat smoldering with Jenny clinging to his hand and squealing, trying to protect her make-up. The Semitic man paddled around with that rather ludicrous intentness of a fat man swimming. Gordon sat on the rail, looking on. Fairchild and Major Ayers at last succeeded in driving the ladies back into the tender, about which they splashed and yapped with the tactless playfulness of dogs while Pete refraining "Look out goddam you look out christ watcher doing lookout" struck at their fingers with one of his discarded and sopping shoes.

Above this one-sided merriment the niece appeared poised upon the top of the wheelhouse, unseen by those in the water. They were aware first of a white arrow arcing down the sky. The water took it lazily and while they stared at the slow green vortex where it had entered there was a commotion behind Fairchild, and as he opened his mouth his gaping surprise vanished beneath the surface. In its place the niece balanced momentarily on something under the water, then she fell plunging in the direction of Major Ayers' yet passive astonishment.

The ladies screamed with delight. Major Ayers also vanished, and the niece plunged on. Fairchild appeared presently, coughing and gasping, and climbed briskly into the tender where Mr. Talliaferro with admirable presence of mind already was, having deserted Jenny without a qualm. "I've got enough," Fairchild said when he could speak.

Major Ayers, however, accepted the challenge. The niece trod water and awaited him. "Drown him, Pat!" the ladies shrieked. Just before he reached her, her dark wet head vanished and for a while Major Ayers plunged about in a kind of active resignation. Then he vanished again and the niece, clad in a suit of her brother's underwear—a knitted sleeveless jersey and short narrow trunks—surged out of the water and stood erect on his shoulders. Then she put her foot on the top of his head and thrust him deeper yet. Then she plunged on and trod water again.

Major Ayers reappeared at last, already headed for the boat. He had enough also, and the gentlemen dragged him aboard and they dripped across the deck and passed below, to the derision of the ladies.

The ladies got aboard themselves. Pete standing erect in the tender was trying to haul Jenny out of the water. She hung like an expensive doll-confection from his hands, raising at lax intervals a white lovely leg, while Mr. Talliaferro, kneeling, pawed at her shoulders. "Come on, come on," Pete hissed at her. The niece swam up and thrust at Jenny's sweet thighs until Jenny tumbled at last into the tender in a soft blonde abandon: a charming awkwardness. The niece held the tender steady while they boarded the yacht, then she slid skilfully out of the water, sleek and dripping as a seal; and as she swung her short coarse hair back from her face she saw hands, and Gordon's voice said:

"Give me your hands."

She clasped his hard wrists and felt herself flying. The setting sun came level into his beard and upon all his tall lean body, and dripping water on the deck she stood and looked at him with admiration. "Gee, you're hard," she said. She touched his forearms again, then she struck him with her fist on his hard high chest. "Do it again, will you?"

"Swing you again?" he asked. But she was already in the tender, extending her arms while sunset was a moist gold sheathing her. Again that sensation of flying, of space and motion and his hard hands coming into it; and for an instant she stopped in midflight, hand to hand and arm braced to arm, high above the deck while water dripping from her turned to gold as it fell. Sunset was in his eyes: a glory he could not see; and her taut simple body, almost breastless and with the fleeting hips of a boy, was an ecstasy in golden marble, and in her face the passionate ecstasy of a child.

At last her feet touched the deck again and she turned. She sped toward the companionway and as she flashed downward the last of the sun slid upon her and over her with joy. Then she was gone, and Gordon stood looking at the wet and simple prints of her naked feet on the deck.

SIX O'CLOCK

They had raised land just about the time Major Ayers won his wager, and while the last of day drained out of the world the *Nausikaa* at halfspeed forged slowly into a sluggish river mouth, broaching a timeless violet twilight between solemn bearded cypresses motionless as bronze. You might, by listening, have heard a slow requiem in this tall nave, might have heard here the chanted orisons of the dark heart of the world turning toward slumber. The world was becoming dimensionless, the tall bearded cypresses drew nearer one to another across the wallowing river with the soulless implacability of pagan gods, gazing down upon this mahogany-and-brass intruder with inscrutable unalarm. The water was like oil and the *Nausikaa* forged onward without any sensation of motion through a corridor without ceiling or floor.

Mr. Talliaferro stood at the sternrail beside Jenny and her morose hatted duenna. In the dusk Jenny's white troubling placidity bloomed like a heavy flower, pervading and rife like an odor lazier, heavier than that of lilies. Pete loomed beyond her: the last light in the world was concentrated in the implacable glaze of his hat, leaving the atmosphere about them darker still; and in the weary passion of August and nightfall Mr. Talliaferro's dry interminable voice fell lower and lower and finally ceased altogether; and abruptly becoming aware of an old mislaid sorrow he slapped suddenly at the back of his hand, with consternation, remarking at the same time that Pete was also restive and that Jenny was agitating herself as though she were rubbing her body against her clothing from within. Then, as if at a signal, they were all about them, unseen, with a dreadful bucolic intentness; unlike their urban cousins, making no sound.

Jenny and Pete and Mr. Talliaferro evacuated the deck. At the companionway the ghostly poet joined them hurriedly, flapping his handkerchief about his face and neck and the top of his unnurtured evaporating head. At that instant Mrs. Maurier's voice rose from somewhere in astonished adjuration, and presently the *Nausikaa* put about and felt her way back to open water and stood out to sea. And not at half-speed, either.

SEVEN O'CLOCK

Years ago Mrs. Maurier had learned that unadulterated fruit juice was salutary, nay, necessary to a nautical life. A piece of information strange, irrelevant at first draught, yet on second thought quite possible, not to mention pleasant in contemplation, so she had accepted it, taking it unto her and making of it an undeviating marine conviction. Hence there was grapefruit again for dinner: she was going to inoculate them first, then take chances.

Fairchild's gang was ultimately started from its lair in his quarters. The other guests were already seated and they regarded the newcomers with interest and trepidation and, on Mrs. Maurier's part, with actual alarm.

"Here comes the dogwatch," Mrs. Wiseman remarked brightly. "It's the gentlemen, isn't it? We haven't seen any gentlemen since we left New Orleans, hey, Dorothy?"

Her brother grinned at her sadly. "How about Mark and Talliaferro?"

"Oh, Mark's a poet. That lets him out. And Ernest isn't a poet, so that lets him out, too," she replied with airy feminine logic. "Isn't that right, Mark?"

"I'm the best poet in New Orleans," the ghostly young man said heavily, mooning his pale, prehensile face at her.

"We were kind of wondering where you were, Mark," Fairchild told the best poet in New Orleans. "We got the idea you were supposed to be on the boat with us. Too bad you couldn't come," he continued tediously.

"Maybe Mark couldn't find himself in time," the Semitic man suggested, taking his seat.

"He's found his appetite, though," Fairchild replied. "Maybe he'll find the rest of himself laying around somewhere nearby." He seated himself and stared at the plate before him. He murmured, Well, well, with abstraction. His companions found seats and Major Ayers stared at his plate. He murmured Well, well, also. Mrs. Maurier chewed her lip nervously, putting her hand on Mr. Talliaferro's sleeve. Major Ayers murmured:

"It does look familiar, doesn't it?" and Fairchild said:

"Why, it's grapefruit: I can tell every time." He looked at Major Ayers. "I'm not going to eat mine, now. I'm going to put it away and save it."

"Right you are," agreed Major Ayers readily. "Save 'em by all means." He set his grapefruit carefully to one side. "Advise you people to do the same," he added at large.

"Save them?" Mrs. Maurier repeated in astonishment. "Why, there are more of them. We have several crates."

Fairchild wagged his head at her. "I can't risk it. They might be lost overboard or something, and us miles from land. I'm going to save mine."

Major Ayers offered a suggestion. "Save the rinds, anyway. Might need 'em. Never can tell what might happen at sea, y'know," he said owlishly.

"Sure," Fairchild agreed. "Might need 'em in a pinch to prevent constipation." Mrs. Maurier clasped Mr. Talliaferro's arm again.

"Mr. Talliaferro!" she whispered imploringly. Mr. Talliaferro sprang to the breach.

"Now that we are all together at last," he began, clearing his throat, "the Commodore wishes us to choose our first port of call. In other words, people, where shall we go to-morrow?" He looked from face to face about the table.

"Why, nowhere," answered Fairchild with surprise. "We just came from somewhere yesterday, didn't we?"

"You mean to-day," Mrs. Wiseman told him. "We left New Orleans this morning."

"Oh, did we? Well, well, it takes a long time to spend the afternoon, don't it? But we don't want to go anywhere, do we?"

"Oh, yes," Mr. Talliaferro contradicted him smoothly. "To-morrow we are going up the Tchufuncta river and spend the day fishing. Our plan was to go up the river and spend the night, but this was found impossible. So we shall go up to-morrow. Is this unanimous? or shall we call for a ballot?"

"Gabriel's pants," the niece said to Jenny, "I itch just to think about that, don't you?"

Fairchild brightened. "Up the Tchufuncta?" he repeated. "Why, that's where the Jackson place is. Maybe Al's at home. Major Ayers must meet Al Jackson, Julius."

"Al Jackson?" Major Ayers repeated. The best poet in New Orleans groaned and Mrs. Wiseman said:

"Good Lord, Dawson."

"Sure. The one I was telling you about at lunch, you know."

"Ah, yes: the alligator chap, eh?" Mrs. Maurier exclaimed. "Mr. Talliaferro" again.

"Very well," Mr. Talliaferro said loudly, "that's settled,

then. Fishing has it. And in the meantime, the Commodore invites you all to a dancing party on deck immediately after dinner. So finish your dinner, people. Fairchild, you are to lead the grand march."

"Sure," Fairchild agreed again. "Yes, that's the one. His father has a fish ranch up here. That's where Al got his start and now he's the biggest fisherd in the world—"

"Did you see the sunset this evening, Major Ayers?" Mrs. Wiseman asked loudly. "Deliciously messy, wasn't it?"

"Nature getting even with Turner," the poet suggested.

"That will take years and years," Mrs. Wiseman answered. Mrs. Maurier sailed in, gushing.

"Our southern sunsets, Major Ayers—" But Major Ayers was staring at Fairchild.

—"Fisherd?" he murmured.

"Sure. Like the old cattle ranches out west, you know. But instead of a cattle ranch, Al Jackson has got a fish ranch out in the wide open spaces of the Gulf of Mexico—"

"Where men are sharks," put in Mrs. Wiseman. "Don't leave that out." Major Ayers stared at her.

"Sure. Where men are men. That's where this beautiful blonde girl comes in. Like Jenny yonder. Maybe Jenny's the one. Are you the girl, Jenny?" Major Ayers now stared at Jenny.

Jenny was gazing at the narrator, her blue ineffable eyes quite round, holding a piece of bread in her hand. "Sir?" she said at last.

"Are you the girl that lives on that Jackson fish ranch out in the Gulf of Mexico?"

"I live on Esplanade," Jenny said after a while, tentatively.

"Mr. Fairchild!" Mrs. Maurier exclaimed. Mr. Talliaferro said:

"My dear sir!"

"No, I reckon you are not the one, or you'd know it.
I don't imagine that even Claude Jackson could live on a
fish ranch in the Gulf of Mexico and not know it. This girl
is from Brooklyn, anyway—a society girl. She went down
there to find her brother. Her brother had just graduated
from reform school and so his old man sent him down there
for the Jacksons to make a fisherd out of him. He hadn't
shown any aptitude for anything else, you see, and his old
man knew it didn't take much intelligence to herd a fish.
His sister—"

"But, I say," Major Ayers interrupted, "why do they herd
their fish?"

"They round 'em up and brand 'em, you see. Al Jackson
brands—"

"Brand 'em?"

"Sure: marks 'em so he can tell his fish from ordinary
wild fish—mavericks, they call 'em. And now he owns
nearly all the fish in the world; a fish millionaire, even if he
is fish-poor right now. Wherever you see a marked fish, it's
one of Al Jackson's."

"Marks his fish, eh?"

"Sure: notches their tails."

"Mr. Fairchild," Mrs. Maurier said.

"But our fish at home have notched tails." Major Ayers
objected.

"Well, they are Jackson fish that have strayed off the
range, then."

"Why doesn't he establish a European agent?" the ghostly poet asked viciously.

Major Ayers stared about from face to face. "I say," he began. He stuck there. The hostess rose decisively.

"Come, people, let's go on deck."

"No, no," the niece said quickly, "go on: tell us some more." Mrs. Wiseman rose also.

"Dawson," she said firmly, "shut up. We simply cannot stand any more. This afternoon has been too trying. Come on, let's go up," she said, herding the ladies firmly out of the room, taking Mr. Talliaferro along also.

NINE O'CLOCK

He needed a bit of wire. He had reached that impasse familiar to all creators, where he could not decide which of a number of things to do next. His object had attained that stage of completion in which the simplicity of the initial impulse dissolves into a number of trivial necessary details; and lying on his bunk in the cabin he and Mr. Talliaferro shared, his saw at hand and a thin litter of sawdust and shavings well impermeating the bed clothing, he held his wooden cylinder to the small inadequate light and decided that he could do with a bit of stiff wire or something of that nature.

He swung his legs out of the berth and flowed to the floor in a single beautiful motion, and crossing the room on his bare feet he searched Mr. Talliaferro's effects without success, so he passed from the cabin.

Still on his bare feet he went along the passage, and

opening another door he let subdued light from the passage into a room filled with snoring, discerning vaguely the sleeper and, on a peg in the wall, a stained white cap. Captain's room, he decided, leaving the door open and traversing the room silently to another door.

There was a dim small light in this room, gleaming dully on the viscid anatomy of the now motionless engine. But he ignored the engine now, going about his search with businesslike expedition. There was a wooden cabinet against the wall: some of the drawers were locked. He rummaged through the others, pausing at times to raise certain objects to the light for a closer inspection, discarding them again. He closed the last drawer and stood with his hand on the cabinet, examining the room.

A piece of wire would do, a short piece of stiff wire . . . there were wires on one wall, passing among and between switches. But these were electric wires and probably indispensable. Electric wires . . . battery room. It must be there, beyond that small door.

It was there—a shadow filled cubbyhole smelling of acids, of decomposition; a verdigris of decay. Plenty of wires here, but no loose ones. . . . He stared around, and presently he saw something upright and gleaming dully. It was a piece of mechanism, steel, smooth and odorless and rather comforting in this tomb of smells, and he examined it curiously, striking matches. And there, attached to it, was exactly what he needed—a small straight steel rod.

I wonder what it does, he thought. It looked . . . a winch of some kind, maybe. But what would they want with a winch down here? Something they don't use much, evidently, he assured himself. Too clean. Cleaner than the engine. Not greased all over like the engine. They mustn't hardly ever use it. . . . Or a pump. A pump, that's what it is. They won't need a pump once a year: not any bilge in a boat kept up like a grand piano. Anyhow, they couldn't possibly need it before to-morrow, and I'll be through with it then. Chances are they wouldn't miss it if I kept it altogether.

The rod came off easily. Plenty of wrenches in the cabinet, and he just unscrewed the nuts at each end of the rod and lifted it out. He paused again, holding the rod in his hand. . . . Suppose he were to injure the rod some way. He hadn't considered that and he stood turning the rod this way and that in his fingers, watching the dull gleams of light on its slender polished length. It was so exactly what he needed. Steel, too; good steel: it cost twelve thousand dollars. And if you can't get good steel for that . . . He put his tongue on it. It tasted principally of machine oil, but it must be good hard steel, costing twelve thousand dollars. I guess I can't hurt anything that cost twelve thousand dollars, specially by just using it one time . . . "If they need it to-morrow, I'll be through with it, anyway," he said aloud.

He replaced the wrenches. His mouth tasted of machine oil and he spat. The captain yet snored, and he passed through the captain's room on his bare feet, closing the door thoughtfully so the light from the passage wouldn't disturb the sleeper. He slipped the rod into his pocket. His hands were greasy and so he wiped them on the seat of his trousers.

He paused again at the galley door, where the steward was still busy over the sink. The steward stopped long enough to find a candle for him, then he returned to his room. He lit the candle, drew Mr. Talliaferro's suitcase from beneath the bunk and dripping a bit of hot wax onto it, he fixed the candle upright. Then he got Mr. Talliaferro's pigskin enclosed shaving kit and propped the rod upon it with one end of the rod in the candle flame. His mouth still tasted of machine oil, so he climbed onto his berth and spat through the port, discovering as he did so that the port was screened. It'll dry, though.

He touched the rod. It was getting warm. But he wanted it red hot. His mouth yet tasted of machine oil and he remembered the other cigarette. It was in the same pocket in which he had had the rod, and it too was slightly reminiscent of machinery, but the burning tobacco would soon kill that.

The rod was getting pretty hot, so he fetched the wooden cylinder from the bunk and laying the cigarette on the edge of the suitcase he picked up the rod and held its heated end firmly against the selected spot on the cylinder; and soon a thin thread of smoke rose curling into the windless air. The smoke had a faint odor like that of scorching leather in it, also. Machine oil, probably.

TEN O'CLOCK

It's being an artist, Mrs. Maurier said to herself with helpless despondence. Mrs. Wiseman, Miss Jameson, Mark and Mr. Talliaferro sat at bridge. She herself did not feel like playing: the strain of her party kept her too nervous and wrought up. "You simply cannot tell what they're going to do," she said aloud in her exasperation, seeing again Major Ayers' vanishing awkward shape and Fairchild leaning over the rail and howling after him like a bullvoiced Druid priest at a sacrifice.

"Yes," Mrs. Wiseman agreed, "it's like an excursion, isn't

it?—all drunkenness and trampling around," she added, attempting to finesse. "Damn you, Mark."

"It's worse than that," the niece corrected, pausing to watch the hissing fall of cards, "it's like a cattle boat—all trampling around."

Mrs. Maurier sighed. "Whatever it is . . ." her sentence died stillborn. The niece drifted away and a tall shape appeared from shadow and joined her, and they went on down the dark deck and from her sight. It was that queer shabby Mr. Gordon, and she knew a sudden sharp stab of conscience, of having failed in her duty as a hostess. She had barely exchanged a word with him since they came aboard. It's that terrible Mr. Fairchild, she told herself. But who could have known that a middleaged man, and a successful novelist, could or would conduct himself so?

The moon was getting up, spreading a silver flare of moonlight on the water. The *Nausikaa* swung gently at her cables motionless but never still, sleeping but not dead, as is the manner of ships on the seas of the world; cradled like a silver dreaming gull on the water . . . her yacht. Her party, people whom she had invited together for their mutual pleasure. . . . Maybe they think I ought to get drunk with them, she thought.

She roused herself, creating conversation. The cardplayers shuffled and dealt interminably, replying Mmmm to her remarks, irrelevant and detached, or pausing to answer sensibly with a patient deference. Mrs. Maurier rose briskly.

"Come, people, I know you are tired of cards. Let's have some music and dance a while."

"I'd rather play bridge with Mark than dance with him," Mrs. Wiseman said. . . . "Whose trick was that?"

"There'll be plenty of men when the music starts," Mrs. Maurier said.

"Mmmm," replied Mrs. Wiseman. . . . "It'll take more than a victrola record to get any men on this party. . . . You'll need extradition papers. . . . Three without and three aces. How much is that, Ernest?"

"Wouldn't you like to dance, Mr. Talliaferro?" Mrs. Maurier persisted.

"Whatever you wish, dear lady," Mr. Talliaferro answered with courteous detachment, busy with his pencil. "That makes—" he totted a column of his neat fingers, then he raised his head. "I beg your pardon: did you say something?"

"Don't bother," Mrs. Maurier said. "I'll put on a record myself: I'm sure our party will gather when they hear it." She wound up the portable victrola and put on a record. "You finish your rubber, and I'll look about and see whom I can find," she added. Mmmm, they replied.

The victrola raised its teasing rhythms of saxophones and drums, and Mrs. Maurier prowled around, peering into the shadows. She found the steward first, whom she dispatched to the gentlemen with a command couched in the form of an invitation. Then further along she discovered Gordon, and her niece sitting on the rail with her legs locked about a stanchion.

"Do be careful," she said, "you might fall. We are going to dance a while," she added happily.

"Not me," her niece answered quickly. "Not to-night, anyway. You have to dance enough in this world on dry land."

"You will certainly not prevent Mr. Gordon dancing, however. Come, Mr. Gordon, we need you."

"I don't dance," Gordon answered shortly.

"You don't dance?" Mrs. Maurier repeated. "You really don't dance at all?"

"Run along, Aunt Pat," the niece answered for him. "We're talking about art."

Mrs. Maurier sighed. "Where's Theodore?" she asked at last. "Perhaps he will help us out."

"He's in bed. He went to bed right after dinner. But you might go down and ask him if he wants to get up and dance."

Mrs. Maurier stared helplessly at Gordon. Then she turned away. The steward met her: the gentlemen were sorry, but they had all gone to bed. They were tired after such a strenuous day. She sighed again and passed on to the companionway. There seemed to be nothing else she could do for them. I've certainly tried, she told herself, taking this thin satisfaction, and stopped again while something shapeless in the dark companionway unblent, becoming two; and after a while Pete said from the darkness:

"It's me and Jenny."

Jenny made a soft meaningless sound, and Mrs. Maurier bent forward suspiciously. Mrs. Wiseman's remark about excursion boats recurred to her.

"You are enjoying the moon, I suppose?" she remarked.

"Yessum," Jenny answered. "We're just sitting here."

"Don't you children want to dance? They have started the victrola," Mrs. Maurier said in a resurgence of optimism.

"Yessum," said Jenny again, after a while. But they made no further move, and Mrs. Maurier sniffed. Quite genteelly, and she said icily:

"Excuse me, please."

They made room for her to pass and she descended without looking back again, and found her door. She snapped the light switch viciously. Then she sighed again.

It's being an artist, she told herself again, helplessly.

*   *   *

"Damn, damn, damn," said Mrs. Wiseman slapping her cards on the table. The victrola record had played itself through and into an endless monotonous rasping. "Mark, stop that thing, as you love God. I'm far enough behind, without being jinxed." The ghostly poet rose obediently and Mrs. Wiseman swept her hand amid the cards on the table, scattering them. "I'm not going to spend any more of my life putting little spotted squares of paper in orderly sequence for three dull people, not to-night, anyway. Gimme a cigarette, some one." She thrust her chair back and Mr. Talliaferro opened his case to her. She took one and lifted her foot to the other knee and scratched a match on the sole of her slipper. "Let's talk a while instead."

"Where on earth did you get those garters?" Miss Jameson asked curiously.

"These?" she flipped her skirt down. "Why? Don't you like 'em?"

"They are a trifle out of the picture, on you."

"What kind would you suggest for me? Pieces of colored string?"

"You ought to have black ones clasped with natural size red roses," Mark Frost told her. "That's what one would expect to find on you."

"Wrrrong, me good man," Mrs. Wiseman answered dramatically. "You have wronged me foully. . . . Where's Mrs. Maurier, I wonder?"

"She must have caught somebody. That Gordon man, perhaps," Miss Jameson replied. "I saw him at the rail yonder a while ago."

"Ah, Mr. Talliaferro!" exclaimed Mrs. Wiseman. "Look out for yourself. Widders and artists, you know. You see how susceptible I am, myself. Wasn't there ever a fortune teller to warn you of a tall red stranger in your destiny?"

"You are a widow only by courtesy," the poet rejoined, "like the serving maids in sixteenth century literature."

"So are some of the artists, my boy," Mrs. Wiseman replied. "But all the men on board are not even artists. What, Ernest?"

Mr. Talliaferro bridled smugly through the smoke of his cigarette. Mrs. Wiseman consumed hers in an unbroken series of deep draughts and flipped it railward: a twinkling scarlet coal. "I said talk," she reminded them, "not a few mild disjointed beans of gossip." She rose. "Come on, let's go to bed, Dorothy."

Miss Jameson sat, a humorless inertia. "And leave that moon?"

Mrs. Wiseman yawned, stretching her arms. The moon spread her silver ceaseless hand on the dark water. Mrs. Wiseman turned, spreading her arms in a flamboyant gesture, in silhouette against it. "Ah, Moon, poor weary one. . . . By yon black moon," she apostrophized.

"No wonder it looks tired," the poet remarked hollowly. "Think of how much adultery it's had to look upon."

"Or assume the blame for," Mrs. Wiseman amended.

She dropped her arms. "I wish I were in love," she said. "Why aren't you and Ernest more . . . more . . . Come on, Dorothy, let's go to bed."

"Have I got to move?" Miss Jameson said. She rose, however. The men rose also, and the two women departed. When they had gone Mr. Talliaferro gathered up the cards Mrs. Wiseman had scattered. Some of them had fallen to the deck.

ELEVEN O'CLOCK

Mr. Talliaferro tapped diffidently at the door of Fairchild's room, was bidden, and opening it he saw the Semitic man sitting in the lone chair and Major Ayers and Fairchild on the bunk, holding glasses. "Come in," Fairchild repeated. "How did you escape? Push her overboard and run?"

Mr. Talliaferro grinned with deprecation, regarding the bottle sitting on a small table, rubbing his hands together with anticipation.

"The human body can stand anything, can't it?" the Semitic man remarked. "But I imagine Talliaferro is just about at the end of his rope, without outside aid," he added. Major Ayers glared at him affably with his china blue eyes.

"Yes, Talliaferro's sure earned a drink," Fairchild agreed. "Where's Gordon? Was he on deck?"

"I think so," Mr. Talliaferro replied. "I believe he's with Miss Robyn."

"Well, more power to him," Fairchild said. "Hope she won't handle him as roughly as she did us, hey, Major?"

"You and Major Ayers deserved exactly what you got," the Semitic man rejoined. "You can't complain."

"I guess so. But I don't like to see a human being arrogating to himself the privileges and pleasures of providence. Quelling nuisances is God's job."

"How about instruments of providence?"

"Oh, take another drink," Fairchild told him. "Stop talking so Talliaferro can have one, anyway. Then we better go up on deck. The ladies might begin to wonder what has become of us."

"Why should they?" the Semitic man asked innocently. Fairchild heaved himself off the bunk and got Mr. Talliaferro a tumbler. Mr. Talliaferro drank it slowly, unctuously; and pressed, accepted another.

He emptied his glass with a flourish. He grimaced slightly.

They had another drink and Fairchild put the bottle away.

"Let's go up a while," he suggested, prodding them to their feet and herding them toward the door. Mr. Talliaferro allowed the others to precede him. Lingering, he touched Fairchild's arm. The other glanced at his meaningful expression, and paused.

"I want your advice," Mr. Talliaferro explained. Major Ayers and the Semitic man halted in the passage, waiting.

"Go on, you fellows," Fairchild told them. "I'll be along in a moment." He turned to Mr. Talliaferro. "Who's the lucky girl this time?"

Mr. Talliaferro whispered a name. "Now, this is my plan of campaign. What do you think—"

"Wait," Fairchild interrupted, "let's have a drink on it."
Mr. Talliaferro closed the door again, carefully.

* * *

Fairchild swung the door open.

"And you think it will work?" Mr. Talliaferro repeated,
quitting the room.

"Sure, sure; I think it's airtight: that she might just as
well make up her mind to the inevitable."

"No: really, I want your candid opinion. I have more
faith in your judgement of people than any one I know."

"Sure, sure," Fairchild repeated solemnly. "She can't
resist you. No chance, no chance at all. To tell the truth, I
kind of hate to think of women and young girls going around
exposed to a man like you."

Mr. Talliaferro glanced over his shoulder at Fairchild,
quickly, doubtfully. But the other's face was solemn, without
guile. Mr. Talliaferro went on again. "Well, wish me luck,"
he said.

"Sure. The admiral expects every man to do his duty,
you know," Fairchild replied solemnly, following Mr. Talliaferro's dapper figure up the stairs.

* * *

Major Ayers and the Semitic man awaited them. There were
no ladies. Nobody at all, in fact. The deck was deserted.

"Are you sure?" Fairchild insisted. "Have you looked
good? I kind of wanted to dance some. Come on, let's look
again."

At the door of the wheelhouse they came upon the helmsman. He wore only an undershirt above his trousers and he was gazing into the sky. "Fine night," Fairchild greeted him.

"Fine now," the helmsman agreed. "Bad weather off there, though." He extended his arm toward the southwest. "Lake may be running pretty high by morning. We're on a lee shore, too." He stared again into the sky.

"Ah, I guess not," Fairchild replied with large optimism. "Hardly on a clear night like this, do you reckon?"

The helmsman stared into the sky, making no answer. They passed on. "I forgot to tell you the ladies had retired," Mr. Talliaferro remarked.

"That's funny," Fairchild said. "I wonder if they thought we were not coming back?"

"Perhaps they were afraid we were," the Semitic man suggested.

"Huh," said Fairchild. . . . "What time is it, anyway?"

It was twelve o'clock, and the sky toward the zenith was hazed over, obscuring the stars. But the moon was still undimmed, bland and chill, affable and bloodless as a successful procuress, bathing the yacht in quiet silver; and across the southern sky went a procession of small clouds, like silver dolphins on a rigid ultramarine wave, like an ancient geographical woodcut.

The Second Day

By three o'clock the storm had blown itself out across the lake and by dawn, when the helmsman waked the captain, the lake, as he had predicted, was running pretty high. The trend was directly inshore; waves came up in endless battalions under a cloudless sky, curling and creaming along the hull, fading and dying as the water shoaled astern of the yacht to a thin white smother against a dark impenetrable band of trees. The *Nausikaa* rose and fell, bows on, dragging at her taut cables. The helmsman roused the captain and returned swiftly to the wheelhouse.

The deckhand got the anchors up and the helmsman rang the telegraph. The *Nausikaa* shivered awake, coming to life again, and pausing for a moment between two waves like a swimmer, she surged ahead. She paid off a little and the helmsman spun the wheel. But she didn't respond, falling off steadily and gaining speed, and as the helmsman put the wheel down hard the *Nausikaa* fell broadside on into the trough of the waves. The helmsman rang the telegraph again and shouted to the deckhand to let go the anchors.

By seven o'clock the *Nausikaa*, dragging her anchors, had touched bottom with a faint jar. She considered a moment, then freed herself and crawling a bit further up the shoaling sand she turned herself a little, and with a barely

perceptible list she sat down like a plump bather waist deep
in the water, taking the waves on her beam.

*   *   *

Dorothy Jameson had a bold, humorless style. She preferred
portraits, though she occasionally painted still life—harsh,
implacable fruit and flowers in dimensionless bowls upon
tables without depth. Her teeth were large and white in the
pale revelation of her gums, and her gray eyes were coldly
effective. Her body was long, loosely articulated and frail,
and while spending in Greenwich Village the two years she
had considered necessary for the assimilation of American
tendencies in painting, she had taken a lover although she
was still a virgin.

She took the lover principally because he owed her
money which he had borrowed of her in order to pay a debt
to another woman. The lover ultimately eloped to Paris
with a wealthy Pittsburgh lady, pawning her—Dorothy's—
fur coat on the way to the dock and mailing the ticket back
to her from shipboard. The lover himself was a musician.
He was quite advanced, what is known as a radical; and in
the intervals of experimenting with the conventional tonal
scale he served as part of an orchestra in an uptown dancing
place. It was here that he met the Pittsburgh lady.

But this episode was complete, almost out of her memory even. She had had a year abroad and had returned to
New Orleans where she settled down to a moderate allow-
ance which permitted her a studio in the vieux carré and her
name several times on the police docket for reckless driving
and a humorless and reasonably pleasant cultivation of her

individuality, with no more than a mild occasional nagging at the hands of her family, like a sound of rain heard beyond a closed window.

She had always had trouble with her men. Principally through habit since that almost forgotten episode she had always tried for artists, but sooner or later they inevitably ran out on her. With the exception of Mark Frost, that is. And in his case, she realized, it was sheer inertia more than anything else. And she admitted with remote perspicuity, who cared one way or the other whether they kept Mark Frost? No one ever cared long for an artist who did nothing save create art, and very little of that.

But other men, men she recognized as having potentialities, all passed through a violent but temporary period of interest which ceased as abruptly as it began, without leaving even the lingering threads of mutually remembered incidence, like those brief thunderstorms of August that threaten and dissolve for no apparent reason, without producing any rain.

At times she speculated with almost masculine detachment on the reason for this. She always tried to keep their relations on the plane which the men themselves seemed to prefer—certainly no woman would, and few women could, demand less of their men than she did. She never made arbitrary demands on their time, never caused them to wait for her nor to see her home at inconvenient hours, never made them fetch and carry for her; she fed them and she flattered herself that she was a good listener. And yet . . . She thought of the women she knew: how all of them had at least one obviously entranced male; she thought of the women she had observed: how they seemed to acquire a man at will, and if he failed to stay acquired, how readily they replaced him.

She thought of the women on board, briefly reviewing them. Eva Wiseman. She had had one husband, practically discarded him. Men liked her. Fairchild, for instance: a man of undisputed ability and accomplishment. Yet this might be due to his friendship with her brother. But no, Fairchild was not that sort: social obligations rested too lightly upon him. It was because he was attracted to her. Because of kindred tastes? But I create, too, she reminded herself.

Then she thought of the two young girls. Of the niece Patricia, with her frank curiosity in things, her childish delight in strenuous physical motion, of her hard unsentimentality and no interest whatever in the function of creating art (I'll bet she doesn't even read) and Gordon aloof and insufferably arrogant, yet intrigued. And Fairchild also interested in his impersonal way. Even Pete, probably.

Pete, and Jenny. Jenny with her soft placidity, her sheer passive appeal to the senses, and Mr. Talliaferro, braving Mrs. Maurier's displeasure to dangle about her, fawning almost. Even she felt Jenny's appeal—an utterly mindless rifeness of young, pink flesh, a supine potential fecundity lovely to look upon: a doll awaiting a quickening and challenging it with neither joy nor sorrow. She had brought one man with her. . . . No, not even brought: he had followed in her blonde troubling orbit as a tide follows the moon, without volition, against his inclination, perhaps. Two women who had no interest whatever in the arts, yet who without effort drew to themselves men, artistic men. Opposites, antitheses . . . perhaps, she thought, I have been trying for the wrong kind of men, perhaps the artistic man is not my type.

SEVEN O'CLOCK

"No, ma'am," the nephew replied courteously, "it's a pipe."

"Oh," she murmured, "a pipe."

He bent over his wooden cylinder, paring at it with a knife, delicately, with care. It was much cooler to-day. The sun had risen from out a serrated miniature sea, into a cloudless sky. For a while the yacht had had a perceptible motion—it was this motion which had roused her—but now it had ceased, although sizable waves yet came in from the lake, creaming whitely along the hull, and spent themselves shoaling up the beach toward a dark cliff of trees. She'd had no idea last night that they were so close to land, either. But distances always confused her by night.

She wished she'd brought a coat: had she anticipated such a cool spell in August . . . She stood huddling her scarf about her shoulders, watching his brown intent forearms and his coarse, cropped head exactly like his sister's, mildly desiring breakfast. I wonder if he's hungry? She thought. She remarked:

"Aren't you rather chilly this morning without a coat?" He carved at his object with a rapt maternal absorption, and after a while she said, louder:

"Wouldn't it be simpler to buy one?"

"I hope so," he murmured . . . then he raised his head and the sun shone full into his opaque yellow-flecked eyes. "What'd you say?"

"I should think you'd wait until we got ashore and buy one instead of trying to make one."

"You can't buy one like this. They don't make 'em."

The cylinder came in two sections, carved and fitted cunningly. He raised one piece, squinting at it, and carved an infinitesimal sliver from it. Then he returned it to its husband. Then he broke them apart again and carved an infinitesimal sliver from the other piece, fitted them together again. Miss Jameson watched him.

"Do you carry the design in your head?" she asked.

He raised his head again. "Huh?" he said in a dazed tone.

"The design you're carving. Are you just carving from memory, or what?"

"Design?" he repeated. "What design?"

It was much cooler to-day.

*　*　*

There was in Pete's face a kind of active alarm not quite yet dispersed, and clutching his sheet of newspaper he rose with belated politeness, but she said, "No, no: I'll get it. Keep your seat." So he stood acutely, clutching his paper, while she fetched a chair and drew it up beside his. "It's quite chilly this morning isn't it?"

"Sure is," he agreed. "When I woke up this morning and felt all that cold wind and the boat going up and down, I didn't know what we were into. I didn't feel so good this morning, anyway, and with the boat going up and down like it was . . . it's still now, though. Looks like they went in closer to the bank and parked it this time."

"Yes, it seems to me we're closer than we were last night." When she was settled he sat also, and presently he forgot and put his feet back on the rail. Then he remembered and removed them.

"Why, how did you manage to get a paper this morning? Did we put in shore somewhere last night?" she asked, raising her feet to the rail.

For some reason he felt uncomfortable about his paper. "It's just an old piece," he explained lamely. "I found it downstairs somewhere. It kind of kept my mind off of how bad I felt." He made a gesture repudiating it.

"Don't throw it away," she said quickly, "go on—don't let me interrupt if you found something interesting in it. I'm sorry you aren't feeling well. Perhaps you'll feel better after breakfast."

"Maybe so," he agreed, without conviction. "I don't feel much like breakfast, waking up like I did and feeling kind of bad, and the boat going up and down too."

"You'll get over that, I'm sure." She leaned nearer to see the paper. It was a single sheet of a Sunday magazine section: a depressing looking article in small print about Romanesque architecture, interspersed with blurred indistinguishable photographs. "Are you interested in architecture?" she asked intensely.

"I guess not," he replied. "I was just looking it over until they get up." He slanted his hat anew: under cover of this movement he raised his feet to the rail, settling down on his spine. She said:

"So many people waste their time over things like architecture and such. It's much better to be a part of life, don't you think? Much better to be in it yourself and make your own mistakes and enjoy making them and suffering for them, than to make your life barren through dedicating it to an improbable and ungrateful posterity. Don't you think so?"

"I hadn't thought about it," Pete said cautiously. He lit a cigarette. "Breakfast is late to-day."

"Of course you hadn't. That's what I admire about a man like you. You know life so well that you aren't afraid of what it might do to you. You don't spend your time thinking about life, do you?"

"Not much," he agreed. "A man don't want to be a fish, though."

"You'll never be a fish, Pete (every one calls you Pete, don't they?—do you mind?) I think the serious things really are the things that make for happiness—people and things that are compatible, love. . . . So many people are content just to sit around and talk about them instead of getting out and attaining them. As if life were a joke of some kind. . . . May I have a cigarette? Thanks. You smoke this brand, too, I see. A m— Thanks. I like your hat: it just suits the shape of your face. You have an extremely interesting face—do you know it? And your eyes. I never saw eyes exactly the color of yours. But I suppose lots of women have told you that, haven't they?"

"I guess so," Pete answered. "They'll tell you anything."

"Is that what love has meant to you, Pete—deception?" she leaned to the match, staring at him with the humorless invitation of her eyes, "Is that your opinion of us?"

"Aw, they don't mean anything by it," Pete said in something like alarm. "What time do they have breakfast on this line?" He rose. "I guess I better run downstairs a minute before it's ready. It oughtn't to be long," he added. Miss Jameson was gazing quietly out across the water. She wore a thin scarf about her shoulders: a webbed brilliant thing that lent her a bloodless fragility, as did the faint bridge of freckles (relict of a single afternoon of sunlight) across her nose. She now sat suddenly quiet, poising the cigarette in her long, delicate fingers; and Pete stood beside her, acutely uncomfortable—why, he knew not. "I guess I'll go downstairs before breakfast," he repeated. "Say"—he extended his newspaper—"why don't you look it over while I'm gone?"

Then she looked at him again, and took the paper. "Ah, Pete, you don't know much about us—for all your experience."

"Sure," he replied. "I'll see you again, see?" and he went away. I'm glad I had a clean collar yesterday, he thought, turning into the companionway. This trip sure ought to be over in a couple of years. . . . Just as he began the descent he looked back at her. The newspaper lay across her lap but she wasn't looking at it. And she had thrown the cigarette away, too. My God, Pete said to himself. Then he was struck by a thought. Pete, my boy, he told himself, it's going to be a hard trip. He descended into the narrow passage. It swept forward on either hand, broken smugly by spaced mute doors with brass knobs. He slowed momentarily, counting doors to find his own, and while he paused the door at his hand opened suddenly and the niece appeared clutching a raincoat about her.

"Hello," she said.

"Don't mention it," Pete replied, raising his hat slightly. "Jenny up, too?"

"Say, I dreamed you lost that thing," the niece told him. "Yes, she'll be out soon, I guess."

"That's good. I was afraid she was going to lay there and starve to death."

"No, she'll be out pretty soon." They stood facing each other in the narrow passage, blocking it completely, and the niece said: "Get on, Pete. I feel too tired to climb over you this morning."

He stood aside for her, and watching her retreat he called after her: "Losing your pants."

She stopped and dragged at her hips as a shapeless fabric descended from beneath the raincoat and wadded slow and lethargic about her feet. She stood on one leg and kicked at the mass, then stooping she picked from amid its folds a man's frayed and shapeless necktie. "Damn that string," she said, kicking out of the garment and picking it up.

Pete turned in the narrow corridor, counting discrete identical doors. He smelled coffee and he added to himself: A hard trip, and, with unction: I'll tell the world it is.

EIGHT O'CLOCK

"It's the steering gear," Mrs. Maurier explained at the breakfast table. "Some—"

"I know," Mrs. Wiseman exclaimed immediately above the grapefruit, "German spies!"

Mrs. Maurier stared at her with patient astonishment.

She said, How cute. "It worked perfectly yesterday. The captain said it worked perfectly yesterday. But this morning, when the storm came up . . . anyway, we're aground, and they are sending some one to get a tug to pull us off. They are trying to find the trouble this morning, but I don't know . . ."

Mrs. Wiseman leaned toward her and patted her fumbling ringed hand. "There, there, don't you feel badly about it: it wasn't your fault. They'll get us off soon, and we can have just as much fun here as we would sailing around. More, perhaps: motion seems to have had a bad effect on the party. I wonder . . ." Fairchild and his people had not yet arrived: before each vacant place its grapefruit, innocent and profound. Surely just the prospect of more grapefruit couldn't have driven them . . . Mrs. Maurier followed her gaze.

"Perhaps it's just as well," she murmured.

"Anyway, I've always wanted to be shipwrecked," Mrs. Wiseman went on. "What do they call it? scuttled the ship, isn't it? But surely Dawson and Julius couldn't have thought of this, though." Mrs. Maurier, brooding above her plate, raised her eyes, cringing. "No, no," the other answered herself hastily, "of course not: that's silly. It just happened, as things do. But let this be a lesson to you children, never to lay yourselves open to suspicion," she added looking from the niece to the nephew. The steward appeared with coffee and Mrs. Maurier directed him to leave the gentlemen's grapefruit until it suited their pleasure to come for it.

"They couldn't have done it if they'd wanted to," the niece replied. "They don't know anything about machinery. Josh could have done it. He knows all about automobile motors. I bet you could fix it for 'em if you wanted to, couldn't you, Gus?"

He didn't seem to have heard her at all. He finished his breakfast, eating with a steady and complete preoccupation, then thrusting his chair back he asked generally for a cigarette. His sister produced a package from somewhere. It bore yet faint traces of pinkish scented powder, and Miss Jameson said sharply:

"I wondered who took my cigarettes. It was you, was it?"

"I thought you'd forgot 'em, so I brought 'em up with me." She and her brother took one each, and she slid the package across the table. Miss Jameson picked it up, stared into it a moment, then put it in her handbag. The nephew had a patent lighter. They all watched with interest, and after a while Mr. Talliaferro with facetious intent offered him a match. But it took fire finally, and he lit his cigarette and snapped the cap down. "Gimme a light too, Gus," his sister said quickly, and from the pocket of his shirt he took two matches, laid them beside her plate. He rose.

He whistled four bars of "Sleepytime Gal" monotonously, ending on a prolonged excruciating note, and from the bed clothing at the foot of his bunk he got the steel rod and stood squinting his eyes against the smoke of his cigarette, examining it. One end of it was kind of blackened, and pinching the cloth of his trouserleg about it, he shuttled it swiftly back and forth. Then he examined it again. It was still kind of black. The smoke of his cigarette was making his eyes water, so he spat it and ground his heel on it.

After a time he found a toothbrush and crossing the passage to a lavatory he scrubbed the rod. A little of the black came off, onto the brush, and he dried the rod on his shirt and scrubbed the brush against the screen in a port, then against a redleaded water pipe, and then against the back of his hand. He sniffed at it . . . a kind of machinery smell yet, but you won't notice it with toothpaste on it. He returned and replaced the brush among Mr. Talliaferro's things.

He whistled four bars of "Sleepytime Gal" monotonously. The engine room was deserted. But he was making no effort toward concealment, anyway. He found the wrenches again and went to the battery room and restored the rod without haste, whistling with monotonous preoccupation. He replaced the wrenches and stood for a while examining the slumbering engine with rapture. Then still without haste he quitted the room.

The captain, the steward and the deckhand sat at breakfast in the saloon. He paused in the door.

"Broke down, have we?" he asked.

"Yes, sir," the captain answered shortly. They went on with their breakfast.

"What's the trouble?" No reply, and after a time he suggested: "Engine play out?"

"Steering gear," the captain answered shortly.

"You ought to be able to fix that. . . . Where is the steering gear?"

"Engine room," the captain replied. The nephew turned away.

"Well, I haven't touched anything in the engine room."

The captain bent above his plate, chewing. Then his

jaws ceased and he raised his head sharply, staring after the nephew retreating down the passage.

TEN O'CLOCK

"The trouble with you, Talliaferro, is that you ain't bold enough with women. That's your trouble."

"But I—" Fairchild wouldn't let him finish.

"I don't mean with words. They don't care anything about words except as little things to pass the time with. You can't be bold with them with words: you can't even shock them with words. Though the reason may be that half the time they are not listening to you. They ain't interested in what you're going to say: they are interested in what you're going to do."

"Yes, but . . . How do you mean, be bold? What must I do to be bold?"

"How do they do it everywhere? Ain't every paper you pick up full of accounts of men being caught in Kansas City or Omaha under compromising conditions with young girls who've been missing from Indianapolis and Peoria and even Chicago for days and days? Surely if a man can get as far as Kansas City with a Chicago girl, without her shooting him through chance or affection or sheer exuberance of spirits or something, he can pretty safely risk a New Orleans girl."

"But why should Talliaferro want to take a New Orleans girl, or any other girl, to Kansas City?" the Semitic man asked. They ignored him.

"I know," Mr. Talliaferro rejoined. "But these men have always just robbed a cigar store. I couldn't do that, you know."

"Well, maybe New Orleans girls won't require that: maybe they haven't got that sophisticated yet. They may not be aware that their favors are worth as high as a cigar store. But I don't know: there are moving pictures, and some of 'em probably even read newspapers, too, so I'd advise you to get busy right away. The word may have already got around that if they just hold off another day or so, they can get a cigar store for practically nothing. And there ain't very many cigar stores in New Orleans, you know."

"But," the Semitic man put in again, "Talliaferro doesn't want a girl and a cigar store both, you know."

"That's right," Fairchild agreed. "You ain't looking for tobacco, are you, Talliaferro?"

ELEVEN O'CLOCK

"No, sir," the nephew answered patiently, "it's a pipe."

"A pipe?" Fairchild drew nearer, interested. "What's the idea? Will it smoke longer than an ordinary pipe? Holds more tobacco, eh?"

"Smokes cooler," the nephew corrected, carving minutely at his cylinder. "Won't burn your tongue. Smoke the tobacco down to the last grain, and it won't burn your tongue. You change gears on it, kind of, like a car."

"Well, I'm damned. How does it work?" Fairchild dragged up a chair, and the nephew showed him how it worked. "Well, I'm damned," he repeated, taking fire. "Say, you ought to make a pile of money out of it, if you make it work, you know."

"It works," the nephew answered, joining his cylinders

again. "Made a little one out of pine. Smoked pretty good for a pine pipe. It'll work all right."

"What kind of wood are you using now?"

"Cherry." He carved and fitted intently, bending his coarse dark head above his work. Fairchild watched him. "Well, I'm damned," he said again in a sort of heavy astonishment. "Funny nobody thought of it before. Say, we might form a stock company, you know, with Julius and Major Ayers. He's trying to get rich right away at something that don't require work, and this pipe is a lot better idea than the one he's got, for I can't imagine even Americans spending very much money for something that don't do anything except keep your bowels open. That's too sensible for us, even though we will buy anything. . . . Your sister tells me you and she are going to Yale college next month."

"I am," he corrected, without raising his head. "She just thinks she's going too. That's all. She kept on worrying dad until he said she could go. She'll be wanting to do something else by then."

"What does she do?" Fairchild asked. "I mean, does she have a string of beaux and run around dancing and buying things like most girls like her do?"

"Naw," the nephew answered. "She spends most of her time and mine too tagging around after me. Oh, she's all right, I guess," he added tolerantly, "but she hasn't got much sense." He unfitted the cylinders, squinting at them.

"That's where she changes gear, is it?" Fairchild leaned nearer again. "Yes, she's a pretty nice sort of a kid. Kind of like a racehorse colt, you know. . . . So you're going up to Yale. I used to want to go to Yale, myself, once. Only I had to go where I could. I guess there is at time in the life of every young American of the class that wants to go to college or accepts the inevitability of education, when he wants to go to Yale or Harvard. Maybe that's the value of Yale and Harvard to our American life: a kind of illusion of an intellectual nirvana that makes the ones that can't go there work like hell where they do go, so as not to show up so poorly alongside of the ones that can go there.

"Still, ninety out of a hundred Yale and Harvard turn out but are reasonably bearable to live with, if they ain't anything else. And that's something to be said for any manufactory, I guess. But I'd like to have gone there. . . ." The nephew was not listening particularly. He shaved and trimmed solicitously at his cylinder. Fairchild said:

"It was a kind of funny college I went to. A denominational college, you know, where they turned out preachers. I was working in a mowing machinery factory in Indiana, and the owner of the factory was a trustee of this college. He was a sanctimonious old fellow with a beard like a goat, and every year he offered a half a scholarship to be competed for by young men working for him. You won it, you know, and he found you a job near the college to pay your board, but not enough to do anything else—to keep you from fleshly temptations, you know—and he had a monthly report on your progress sent to him. And I won it, that year.

"It was just for one year, so I tried to take everything I could. I had about six or seven lectures a day, besides the work I had to do to earn my board. But I kind of got interested in learning things: I learned in spite of the instructors we had. They were a bunch of brokendown preachers: head full of dogma and intolerance and a belly full of big meaningless words. English literature course whittled Shakespeare

down because he wrote about whores without pointing a
moral, and one instructor always insisted that the head devil
in *Paradise Lost* was an inspired prophetic portrait of Dar-
win, and they wouldn't touch Byron with a ten foot pole, and
Swinburne was reduced to his mother and his old standby,
the ocean. And I guess they'd have cut this out had they
worn one piece bathing suits in those days. But in spite of
it, I kind of got interested in learning things. I would like to
have looked inside of my mind, after that year was up. . . ."
He gazed out over the water, over the snoring waves, steady
and windfrothed. He laughed. "And I joined a fraternity, too,
almost."

The nephew bent over his pipe. Fairchild produced
a package of cigarettes. The nephew accepted one with
abstraction. He accepted a light, also. "I guess you've got
your eye on a fraternity, haven't you?" Fairchild suggested.

"Senior club," the nephew corrected shortly. "If I can
make it."

"Senior club," Fairchild repeated. "That means you
won't join for three years, eh? That's a good idea. I like
that idea. But I had to do everything in one year, you see.
I couldn't wait. I never had much time to mix with other
students. Six hours a day at lectures, and the rest of the time
working and studying for next day. But I couldn't help but
hear something about it, about rushing and pledges and
so on, and how so-and-so were after this fellow and that,
because he made the football team or something.

"There was a fellow at my boarding house; a kind of handsome tall fellow he was, always talking about the big athletes
and such in school. He knew them all by their first names.
And he always had some yarn about girls: always showing

you a pink envelope or something—a kind of gentlemanly
innuendo, protecting their good names. He was a senior, he
told me, and he was the first one to talk to me about fraternities. He said he had belonged to one a long time, though
he didn't wear a badge. He had given his badge to a girl
who wouldn't return it. . . . You see," Fairchild explained
again, "I had to work so much. You know: getting into a rut
of work for bread and meat, where chance couldn't touch
me much. Chance and information. That's what they mean
by wisdom, horsesense, you know. . . .

"He was the one that told me he could get me in his
fraternity, if I wanted to." He drew at his cigarette, flipped it
away. "It's young people who put life into ritual by making
conventions a living part of life: only old people destroy life
by making it a ritual. And I wanted to get all I could out of
being at college. The boy that belongs to a secret pirates'
gang and who dreams of defending an abstraction with his
blood, hasn't quite died out before twenty-one, you know.
But I didn't have any money.

"Then he suggested that I get more work to do, temporarily. He pointed out to me other men who belonged to it
or who were going to join—baseball players, and captains
of teams, and prize scholars and all. So I got more work.
He told me not to mention it to anybody, that that was the
way they did it. I didn't know anybody much, you see," he
explained. "I had to work pretty steady all day: no chance to
get to know anybody well enough to talk to 'em." He mused
upon the ceaseless fading battalions of waves. "So I got some
more work to do.

"This had to be night work, so I got a job helping to
fire the college power plant. I could take my books along

and study while the steam was up. Only it cut into my sleep some, and sometimes I would get too drowsy to study. So I had to give up one of my lecture courses, though the instructor finally agreed to let me try to make it up during the Christmas vacation. But I learned how to sleep in a cinder pile or a coal bunker, anyway." The nephew was interested now. His knife was idle in his hand, his cylinder reposed, forgetting the agony of wood.

"It would take twenty-five dollars, but working overtime as I was, I figured it wouldn't be any actual cost at all, except the loss of sleep. And a young fellow can stand that if he has to. I was used to work, you know, and it seemed to me that this was just like finding twenty-five dollars.

"I had been working about a month when this fellow came to me and told me that something had happened and that the fraternity would have to initiate right away, and he asked me how much I had earned. I lacked a little of having twenty-five dollars, so he said he would loan me the difference to make it up. So I went to the power house manager and told him I had to have some money to pay a dentist with, and got my pay up to date and gave it to this fellow, and he told me where to be the following night—behind the library at a certain hour. So I did: I was there, like he said." Fairchild laughed again.

"What'd the bird do?" the nephew asked. "Gyp you?"

"It was cold, that night. Late November, and a cold wind came right out of the north, whistling around that building, among the bare trees. Just a few dead leaves on the trees, making a kind of sad dry sound. We had won a football game that afternoon, and I could hear yelling occasionally, and see lights in the dormitories where the ones that could afford to lived, warm and jolly looking, with the bare trees swaying and waving across the windows. Still celebrating the game we had won.

"So I walked back and forth, stamping my feet, and after a while I went around the corner of the library where it wasn't so cold, and I could stick out my head occasionally in case they came looking for me. From this side of the building I could see the hall where the girl students lived. It was all lighted up, as if for a party, and I could see shadows coming and going upon the drawn shades where they were dressing and fixing their hair and all; and pretty soon I heard a crowd coming across the campus and I thought, here they come at last. But they passed on, going toward the girls' hall, where the party was.

"I walked up and down some more, stamping my feet. Pretty soon I heard a clock striking nine. In half an hour I'd have to be back at the power house. They were playing music at the party: I could hear it even in spite of the closed windows, and I thought maybe I'd go closer. But the wind was colder: there was a little snow in it, and besides I was afraid they might come for me and I wouldn't be there. So I stamped my feet, walking up and down.

"Pretty soon I knew it must be nine thirty, but I stayed a while longer, and soon it was snowing hard—a blizzard. It was the first snow of the year, and somebody came to the door of the party and saw it, and then they all came out to look, yelling: I could hear the girls' voices, kind of high and excited and fresh, and the music was louder. Then they went back, and the music was faint again, and then the clock struck ten. So I went back to the power house. I was already late." He ceased, musing on the glittering battalions of waves and hands of wind slapping them whitely. He laughed again. "But I nearly joined one, though."

"How about the bird?" the nephew asked. "Didn't you hunt him up the next day?"

"He was gone. I never saw him again. I found out later he wasn't even a student in the college. I never did know what became of him." Fairchild rose. "Well, you get it finished, and we'll form a stock company and get rich."

The nephew sat clutching his knife and his cylinder, gazing after Fairchild's stocky back until the other passed from view. "You poor goof," the nephew said, resuming his work again.

TWO O'CLOCK

It was that interval so unbearable to young active people: directly after lunch on a summer day. Every one else was dozing somewhere, no one to talk to and nothing to do. It was warmer than in the forenoon, though the sky was still clear and waves yet came in before a steady wind, slapping the *Nausikaa* on her comfortable beam and creaming on to fade and die frothing up the shoaling beach and its still palisade of trees.

The niece hung over the bows, watching the waves. They were diminishing: by sunset there would be none at all. But occasionally one came in large enough to send up a thin exhilarating spray. Her dress whipped about her bare legs and she gazed downward into the restless water, trying to make up her mind to get her bathing suit. But if I go in now I'll get tired and then when the others go in later, I won't have anything to do. She gazed down into the water, watching it surge and shift and change, watching the slack anchor cables severing the incoming waves, feeling the wind against her back.

Then the wind blew upon her face and she idled along the deck and paused again at the wheelhouse, yawning. Nobody there. But that's so, the helmsman went off early to get word for a tug. She entered the room, examining the control fixtures with interest. She touched the wheel, tentatively. It turned all right: they must have fixed it, whatever was broken about it. She removed her hand and examined the room again, hopefully, and her eyes came upon a binocular suspended from a nail in the wall.

Through the binocular she saw a blur in two colors, but presently under her fingers the blur became trees startlingly distinct and separate leaf by leaf and bough by bough, and pendants of rusty green moss were beards of contemplative goats ruminating among the trees and above a yellow strip of beach and a smother of foam in which the sun hung little fleeting rainbows.

She watched this for a time, entranced, then swinging the glass slowly, waves slid past at arms' length, curling and creaming; and swinging the glass further, the rail of the yacht leapt monstrously into view and upon the rail a nameless object emitting at that instant a number of circular yellow basins. The yellow things fell into the water, seemingly so near, yet without any sound, and swinging the glass again, the thing that had emitted them was gone and in its place the back of a man close enough for her to touch him by extending her hand.

She lowered the glass and the man's back sprang away, becoming that of the steward carrying a garbage pail, and she knew then what the yellow basins were. She raised the glass again and again the steward sprang suddenly and silently within reach of her arm. She called "Hey!" and when he paused and turned, his face was plain as plain. She waved her hand to him, but he only looked at her a moment. Then he went on and around a corner.

She hung the binocular back on its nail and followed along the deck where he had disappeared. Inside the companionway and obliquely through the galley door she could see him moving about, washing the luncheon dishes, and she sat on the top step of the stairs. There was a small round window beside her, and he bent over the sink while light fell directly upon his brown head. She watched him quietly, intently but without rudeness, as a child would, until he looked up and saw her tanned serious face framed roundly in the port. "Hello," she said.

"Hello," he answered as gravely.

"You have to work all the time, don't you?" she asked. "Say, I liked the way you went over after that man, yesterday. With your clothes on, too. Not many have sense enough to dive away from the propeller. What's your name?"

David West, he told her, scraping a stew pan and sloshing water into it. Steam rose from the water and about it bobbed a cake of thick implacable looking yellow soap. The niece sat bent forward to see through the window, rubbing her palms on her bare calves.

"It's too bad you have to work whether we are aground or not," she remarked. "The captain and the rest of them don't have anything to do now, except just lie around. They can have more fun than us, now. Aunt Pat's kind of terrible," she explained. "Have you been with her long?"

"No, ma'am. This is my first trip. But I don't mind light work like this. Ain't much to do, when you get settled down to it. Ain't nothing to what I have done."

"Oh. You don't—You are not a regular cook, are you?"

"No, ma'am. Not regular. It was Mr. Fairchild got me this job with Mrs.—with her."

"He did? Gee, he knows everybody almost, don't he?"

"Does he?"

She gazed through the round window, watching a blackened kettle brighten beneath his brush. Soap frothed, piled like summer clouds, floated in the sink like small reflections of clouds. "Have you known him long?" she asked. "Mr. Fairchild, I mean?"

"I didn't know him any until a couple of days ago. I was in that park where that statue is, down close to the docks, and he came by and we were talking and I wasn't working then, and so he got me this job. I can do any kind of work," he added with quiet pride.

"You can? You don't live in New Orleans, do you?"

"Indiana," he told her. "I'm just traveling around."

"Gee," the niece said, "I wish I were a man, like that. I bet it's all right, going around wherever you want to. I guess I'd work on ships. That's what I'd do."

"Yes," he agreed. "That's where I learned to cook—on a ship."

"Not—"

"Yes'm, to the Mediterranean ports, last trip."

"Gee," she said again. "You've seen lots, haven't you?

What would you do, when the ship got to different places? You didn't just stay on the ship, did you?"

"No'm. I went to a lot of towns. Away from the coast."

"To Paris, I bet."

"No'm," he admitted, with just a trace of apology, "I never seemed to get to Paris. But next—"

"I knew you wouldn't," she said quickly. "Say, men just go to Europe because they say European women are fast, don't they? Are European women like that? Promiscuous, like they say?"

"I don't know," he said. "I nev—"

"I bet you never had time to fool with them, did you? That's what I'd do: I wouldn't waste my time on women, if I went to Europe. They make me sick these little college boys in their balloon pants, and colored stickers all over their suitcases, bringing empty cognac bottles back with 'em and snickering about French girls and trying to make love to you in French. Say, I bet where you went you could see a lot of mountains and little cute towns on the side of 'em, and old gray walls and ruined castles on the mountains, couldn't you?"

"Yes'm. And one place was high over a lake. It was blue as . . . blue like . . . washing water," he said finally. "Water with bluing in it. They put bluing in the water when they wash clothes, country folks do," he explained.

"I know," she said impatiently. "Were there mountains around it?"

"The Alps Mountains, and little white boats on it no bigger than water beetles. You couldn't see 'em moving: you only could see the water kind of spreading out to each side. The water would keep on spreading out until it pretty near touched both shores whenever a boat passed. And you could lay on your back on the mountain where I was and watch eagles flying around way up above the water, until sunset. Then the eagles all went back to the mountains." David gazed through the port, past her sober tanned face mooned there by the round window, not even seeing it any more, seeing instead his washing powder colored lake and his lonely mountains and eagles against the blue.

"And then the sun would go down, and sometimes the mountains would look like they were on fire all over. That was the ice and snow on 'em. It was pretty at night too," he added simply, scrubbing again at his pots.

"Gee," she said with hushed young longing. "And that's what you get for being a woman. I guess I'll have to get married and have a bunch of kids." She watched him with her grave opaque eyes. "No, I'm not, either," she said fiercely, "I'm going to make Hank let me go there next summer. Can't you go back then, too? Say, you fix it up to go back then, and I'll go home and see Hank about it and then I'll come over. Josh'll want to come too, most likely, and you'll know where the places are. Can't you do that?"

"I guess I could," he answered slowly. "Only—"

"Only what?"

"Nothing," he said at last.

"Well, you fix it up to go, then. I'll give you my address, and you can write me when to start and where to meet you . . . I guess I couldn't go over on the same boat you'll be on, could I?"

"I'm afraid not," he answered.

"Well, it'll be all right, anyway. Gee, David, I wish we could go to-morrow, don't you? I wonder if they let people swim in that lake? But I don't know, maybe it's nicer to be away up there where you were, looking down at it. Next summer . . ." her unseeing eyes rested on his brown busy head while her spirit lay on its belly above Maggiore, watching little white boats no bigger than water beetles, and the lonely arrogant eagles aloft in blue sunshot space surrounded and enclosed by mountains cloud brooded, taller than God.

David dried his pots and pans and hung them along the bulkhead in a burnished row. He washed out his dishcloths and hung them to dry upon the wall. The niece watched him.

"It's too bad you have to work all the time," she said with polite regret.

"I'm all done, now."

"Let's go swimming, then. It ought to be good now. I've just been waiting for somebody to go in with me."

"I can't," he answered. "I've got a little more work I better do now."

"I thought you were through. Will it take you very long? If it won't, let's go in then: I'll wait for you."

"Well, you see, I don't go in during the day. I go in early in the morning, before you are up."

"Say, I hadn't thought of that. I bet it's fine then, isn't it? How about calling me in the morning, when you are ready to go in? Will you?" He hesitated again and she added, watching him with her sober opaque eyes, "Is it because you don't like to go swimming with girls? That's all right: I won't bother you. I swim pretty well. You won't have to keep me from drowning."

"It ain't that," he answered lamely. "You see, I—I haven't got a bathing suit," he blurted.

"Oh, is that all? I'll get my brother's for you. It'll be kind of tight, but I guess you can wear it. I'll get it for you now, if you'll go in."

"I can't," he repeated. "I've still got some cleaning up to do."

"Well—" She got to her feet. "If you won't, then. But in the morning? you promised, you know."

"All right," he agreed.

"I'll try to be awake. But you just knock on the door— the second door on the right of the passage, you know." She turned on her silent bare feet. She paused again. "Don't forget you promised," she called back. Then her flat boy's body was gone, and David turned again to his work.

The niece went on up the deck and turned the corner of the deckhouse on her silent feet just in time to see Jenny rout and disperse an attack by Mr. Talliaferro. She stepped back beyond the corner, unseen.

*   *   *

Boldness. But Fairchild had said you can't be bold with words. How, then, to be bold? To try to do anything without words, it seemed to him, was like trying to grow grain without seed. Still, Fairchild had said . . . who knew people, women. . . .

Mr. Talliaferro prowled restlessly, having the boat to himself practically, and presently he found Jenny sleeping placidly in a chair in the shade of the deckhouse. Blonde and pink and soft in sleep was Jenny: a passive soft abandon fitting like water to the sagging embrace of the canvas chair. Mr. Talliaferro envied that chair with a surge of fire like an

adolescent's in his dry bones; and while he stood regarding
the sprawled awkwardness of Jenny's sweet thighs and legs
and one little soiled hand dangling across her hip, that surge
of imminence and fire and desolation seemed to lightly dis-
tend all his organs, leaving a thin salty taste on his tongue.
Mr. Talliaferro glanced quickly about the deck.

He glanced quickly about the deck, then feeling rather
foolish, but strangely and exuberantly young, he came near
and bending he traced with his hand lightly the heavy laxness of Jenny's body through the canvas which supported
her. Then he thought terribly that some one was watching
him, and he sprang erect with an alarm like a nausea, staring at Jenny's closed eyes. But her eyelids lay shadowed, a
faint transparent blue upon her cheeks, and her breath was
a little regular wind come recently from off fresh milk. But
he still felt eyes upon him and he stood acutely, trying to
think of something to do, some casual gesture to perform. A
cigarette his chaotic brain supplied at last. But he had none,
and still spurred by this need, he darted quickly away and to
his cabin.

The nephew slept yet in his berth, and breathing rather
fast, Mr. Talliaferro got his cigarettes and then he stood
before the mirror, examining his face, seeking wildness,
recklessness there. But it bore its customary expression of
polite faint alarm, and he smoothed his hair, thinking of the
sweet passive sag of that deckchair . . . yes, almost directly
over his head. . . . He rushed back on deck in a surge of fear
that she had waked and risen, gone away. He restrained himself by an effort to a more sedate pace, reconnoitering the
deck. All was well.

He smoked his cigarette in short nervous puffs, hearing

his heart, tasting that warm salt. Yes, his hand was actually trembling, and he stood in a casual attitude, looking about at water and sky and shore. Then he moved, and still with casualness he strolled back to where Jenny slept, unchanged her supine abandon, soft and oblivious and terrifying.

Mr. Talliaferro bent over her. Then he got on one knee, then on both knees. Jenny slept ineffably, breathing her sweet regular breath upon his face . . . he wondered if he could rise quickly enough, in an emergency . . . he rose and looked about, then tiptoed across the deck and still on tiptoe he fetched another chair and set it beside Jenny's, and sat down. But it was for reclining, so he tried sitting on the edge of it. Too high, and amid his other chaotic emotions was a harried despair of futility and an implacable passing of opportunity. While all the time it was as though he stood nearby yet aloof, watching his own antics. He lit another cigarette with hands that trembled, took three puffs that he did not taste, and cast it away.

Hard this floor his old knees yes yes Jenny her breath Yes yes her red soft mouth where little teeth but showed parted blondeness a golden pink swirl kaleidoscopic a single blue eye not come fully awake her breath yes yes He felt eyes again, knew they were there, but he cast all things away, and sprawled nuzzling for Jenny's mouth as she came awake.

*   *   *

"Wake sleeping princess Kiss," Mr. Talliaferro jabbered in a dry falsetto. Jenny squealed, moving her head a little. Then she came fully awake and got her hand under Mr. Talliaferro's chin. "Wake princess with kiss," Mr. Talliaferro repeated, laughing a thin hysterical laugh, obsessed with an utter and dreadful need to complete the gesture.

Jenny heaved herself up, thrusting Mr. Talliaferro back on his heels. "Whatcher doing, you old—" Jenny glared at him, and seeking about in that vague pinkish region which was her mind, she brought forth finally an expression such as a steamboat mate or a railroad flagman, heated with wine, might apply to his temporary Saturday night Phillida, who would charge him for it by the letter, like a cablegram.

Jenny watched Mr. Talliaferro's dapper dispersion with soft, blonde indignation. When he had disappeared she flopped back again. Then she snorted, a soft, indignant sound, and turned again onto her side. Once more she expelled her breath with righteous indignation, and soon thereafter she drowsed again and slept.

NINE O'CLOCK

It was a sleazy scrap of slightly soiled applegreen crêpe and its principal purpose seemed to be that of indicating vaguely the shape of Jenny's behind, as she danced, caressing the twin soft points of her thighs with the lingering sterility of an aged lover. It looked as if she might have slept in it recently, and there was also a small hat of pale straw, of no particular shape, ribboned.

Jenny slid about in Mr. Talliaferro's embrace with placid skill. She and Pete had just quarreled bitterly. Pete had, that is. Jenny's bovine troubling placidity had merely dissolved into tears, causing her eyes to be more ineffable than ever, and she had gone calmly about what she had intended all the time: to have as much fun as she could, as long as she was here. Pete couldn't walk out on her: all he could do would be to fuss at her or sulk, or maybe hit her. He had done that once, thereby voluntarily making himself her bond slave. She had rather liked it. . . .

Beyond lights, beyond the sound of the victrola, water was a minor ceaseless sound in the darkness; above, vague drowsy stars. Jenny danced on placidly, untroubled by Mr. Talliaferro's endless flow of soft words against her neck, hardly conscious of his hand sliding a small concentric circle at the small of her back.

"She looks kind of nice, don't she?" Fairchild said to his companion as they stood at the head of the companionway, come up for air. "Kind of soft and stupid and young, you know. Passive, and at the same time troubling, challenging." He watched them for a time, then he added: "Now, there goes the Great Illusion, par excellence."

"What's Talliaferro's trouble?" asked the Semitic man.

"The illusion that you can seduce women. Which you can't. They just elect you."

"And then, Gold help you," the other added.

"And with words, at that," Fairchild continued. "With words," he repeated savagely.

"Well, why not with words? One thing gets along with women as well as another. And you are a funny sort to disparage words; you, a member of that species all of whose actions are controlled by words. It's the word that overturns thrones and political parties and instigates vice crusades, not things: the Thing is merely the symbol for the Word. And more than that, think what a devil of a fix you and I'd be in were it not for words, were we to lose our faith in words. I'd have nothing to do all day long, and you'd have to work or starve to death." He was silent for a while. Jenny yet slid and poised, pleasuring her soft young placidity. "And, after all, his illusion is just as nourishing as yours. Or mine, either."

"I know: but yours or mine ain't quite so ridiculous as his is."

"How do you know they aren't?" Fairchild had no reply, and the other continued: "After all, it doesn't make any difference what you believe. Man is not only nourished by convictions, he is nourished by any conviction. Whatever you believe, you'll always annoy some one, but you yourself will follow and bleed and die for it in the face of law, hell or high water. And those who die for causes will perish for any cause, the more tawdry it is, the quicker they flock to it. And be quite happy at it, too. It's a provision of providence to keep their time occupied." He sucked at his cigar, but it was dead.

"Do you know who is the happiest man in the world today? Mussolini, of course. And do you know who are next? The poor devils he will get killed with his Cæsar illusion. Don't pity them, however: were it not Mussolini and his illusion it would be some one else and his cause. I believe it is some grand cosmic scheme for fertilizing the earth. And it could be so much worse," he added. "Who knows? They might all migrate to America and fall into the hands of Henry Ford.

"So don't you go around feeling superior to Talliaferro. I think his present illusion and its object are rather charming, almost as charming as the consummation of it would be— which is more than you can say for yours." He held a match to his cigar. His sucking, intent face came abruptly out of the darkness, and as abruptly vanished again. He flipped the match toward the rail. "And so do you, you poor emotional eunuch; so do you, despite that bastard of a surgeon and a stenographer which you call your soul, so do you remember with regret kissing in the dark and all the tender and sweet stupidity of young flesh."

"Hell," said Fairchild, "let's have another drink."

His friend was too kind, too tactful to say I told you so.

*   *   *

Mrs. Maurier captured them as they reached the stairs. "Here you are," she exclaimed brightly, prisoning their arms; "come: let's all dance a while. We need men. Eva has taken Mark away from Dorothy, and she has no partner. Come, Mr. Fairchild; Julius."

"We're coming back," Fairchild answered, "we're going now to hunt up Gordon and the Major, and we'll all come right back."

"No, no," she said soothingly, "we'll send the steward for them. Come, now."

"I think we better go," Fairchild objected quickly. "The steward has been working hard all day: he's tired out, I expect. And Gordon's kind of timid; he might not come if you send a servant for him." She released them doubtfully, staring at them with her round, astonished face.

"You will . . . ? Do come back, Mr. Fairchild."

"Sure, sure," Fairchild replied, descending hastily.

"Julius," Mrs. Maurier called after them helplessly.

"I'll bring them up in ten minutes," the Semitic man promised, following. Mrs. Maurier watched them until they had passed from view, then she turned away. Jenny and Mr.

Talliaferro were still dancing, as were Mrs. Wiseman and
the ghostly poet. Miss Jameson, partnerless, sat at the card
table playing solitaire. Mrs. Maurier looked on until the
record played itself through. Then she said firmly:

"I think we'd better change partners among ourselves
until the men come up."

Mr. Talliaferro released Jenny obediently, and Jenny,
released, stood around for a while, then she drifted away and
down the deck, passing that tall ugly man leaning alone at
the rail, and further along the niece spoke from the shadow:

"Going to bed?"

Jenny paused and turning her head toward the voice she
saw the faint glint of Pete's hat. She went on. "Uhuh," she
replied. The moon was getting up, rising out of the dark
water: a tarnished, implacable Venus.

Her aunt came along soon, prowling, peering fretfully
into shadowy chairs and obscure corners, implacable and
tactless as a minor disease.

"My Lord, what've we got to do now?" the niece moaned.
She sighed. "She sure makes life real and earnest for everybody, that woman does."

"Dance, I guess," Pete answered. The vicious serrated
rim of his hat, where the moon fell upon it, glinted dully
like a row of filed teeth, like a gaping lithograph of a charging shark.

"Guess so. Say, I'm going to fade out. Stall her off some
way, or run yourself would be better." The niece rose hurriedly. "So long. See you to-m— Oh, you coming too?"

They stepped behind the companionway housing and
flattened themselves against it, listening to Mrs. Maurier's
fretful prowling, and clutching Pete's hand for caution the

niece craned her head around the corner. "There's Dorothy, too," she whispered and she withdrew her head and they flattened themselves closer yet, clutching hands, while the two searchers passed, pausing to peer into every obscurity.

But they went on, finally, passing from sight, and the niece wriggled her fingers free and moved, and moving found that she had turned into Pete's arm and against his dark shape and the reckless angle of his hat topping it.

An interval like that between two fencers ere they engage, then Pete's arm moved with confidence and his other arm came about her shoulders with a technique that was forcing her face upward. She was so still that he stopped again in a momentary flagging of confidence, and out of this lull a hard elbow came without force but steadily under his chin. "Try it on your saxophone, Pete," she told him without alarm.

His hand moved again and caught her wrist, but she held her elbow jammed against his windpipe, increasing the pressure as he tried to remove her arm, their bodies taut against each other and without motion. Some one approached again and he released her, but before they could dodge again around the corner Miss Jameson saw them.

"Who is that?" she said in her high humorless voice. She drew nearer, peering. "Oh, I recognize Pete's hat. Mrs. Maurier wants you." She peered at them suspiciously. "What are you folks doing here?"

"Hiding from Aunt Pat," the niece answered. "What's she going to make us do, now?"

"Why . . . nothing. She—we ought to be more sociable. Don't you think so? We never are all together, you know. Anyway, she wants to see Pete. Aren't you coming too?"

"I'm going to bed. Pete can go if he wants to risk it,

though." She turned away. Miss Jameson put her hand on Pete's sleeve.

"You don't mind if I take Pete, then?" she persisted intensely.

"I don't if he don't," the niece replied. She went on. "Good night."

"That child ought to be spanked," Miss Jameson said viciously. She slid her hand through Pete's elbow. "Come on, Pete."

* * *

The niece stood and rubbed one bare sole against the other shin, hearing their footsteps retreating toward the lights and the fatuous reiteration of the victrola. She rubbed her foot rhythmically up and down her shin, gazing out upon the water where the moon had begun to spread her pallid and boneless hand. . . . Her foot ceased its motion and she remained motionless for a space. Then she stood on one leg and raised the other one. Under her fingers was a small, hard bump, slightly feverish. Gabriel's pants, she whispered, they've found us again. But there was nothing for it except to wait until the tug came. "And finds a lot of picked bones," she added aloud. She went on across the deck; at the stairs she stopped again.

It was David, standing there at the rail, his shirt blanching in the level moonlight, against the dark shoreline. She went over beside him, silent on her bare feet.

"Hello, David," she said quietly, putting her elbows on the rail beside his and hunching her shoulders and crossing her legs as his were. "This would be a good night to be on our mountain, looking down at the lake and the little boats all lighted up, wouldn't it? I guess this time next summer we'll be there, won't we? And lots of other places, where you went to. You know nice things, don't you? When we come back, I'll know nice things, too." She gazed downward upon the dark, ceaseless water. It was never still, never the same, and on it moonlight was broken into little fleeting silver wings rising and falling and changing.

"Wish I were in it," she said, "swimming around in the moonlight. . . . You won't forget about in the morning, will you?" No, he told her watching her crossed thin arms and the cropped crown of her head. "Say," she looked up at him, "I tell you what: let's go in to-night."

"Now?"

"When the moon gets up more. Aunt Pat wouldn't let me go now, anyway. But about twelve, when they've gone to bed. What do you say?" He looked at her, looked at her in such a strange fashion that she said sharply: "What's the matter?"

"Nothing," he answered at last.

"Well, I'll meet you about twelve o'clock, then. I'll get Gus' bathing suit for you. Don't forget, now."

"No," he repeated. And when she reached the stairs and looked back at him he was still watching her in that strange manner. But she didn't puzzle over it long.

TEN O'CLOCK

Jenny had the cabin to herself. Mrs.—, that one whose name she always forgot, was still on deck. She could hear them talking, and Mr. Fairchild's jolly laugh came from somewhere, though he hadn't been upstairs when she left; and the muted nasal sound of the victrola and thumping of feet just over her head. Still dancing. Should she go back? She sat holding a handglass, staring into it, but the handglass was bland, reminding her that after all this was one night she didn't have to dance any more. And you have to dance so many nights. To-morrow night, perhaps, it said. But I don't have to dance to-morrow night, she thought . . . staring into the glass and sitting utterly motionless. . . . Its thin whine rose keening to an ecstatic point and in the glass she saw it mar her throat with a small gray speck. She slapped savagely. It cluded her with a weary, practiced skill, hanging fuzzily between her and the unshaded light.

My Lord, why do you want to go to Mandeville? she thought. Her palms flashed, smacking cleanly, and Jenny examined her hand with distaste. Where do they carry so much blood she wondered, rubbing her palm on the back of her stocking. And so young, too. I hope that's the last one. It must have been, for there was no sound save a small lapping whisper of water and a troubling faraway suggestion of brass broken by a monotonous thumping of feet over her head. Dancing still. You really don't have to dance at all, thought Jenny, yawning into the glass, examining with interest the pink and seemingly endless curve of her gullet, when the door opened and the girl, Patricia, entered the room. She wore a raincoat over her pajamas and Jenny saw her reflected face in the mirror.

"Hello," she said.

"Hello," the niece replied, "I thought you'd have stayed up there prancing around with 'em."

"Lord," Jenny said, "you don't have to dance all your life, do you? You don't seem to be there."

The niece thrust her hands into the raincoat pockets and stared about the small room. "Don't you close that window when you undress?" She asked. "Standing wide open like that. . . ."

Jenny put the mirror down. "That window? I don't guess there's anybody out there this time of night."

The niece went to the port and saw a pale sky bisected laterally by a dark rigidity of water. The moon spread her silver hand on it; a broadening path of silver, and in the path the water came alive ceaselessly, no longer rigid. "I guess not," she murmured. "The only man who could walk on water is dead. . . . Which one is yours?" She threw off the raincoat and turned toward the two berths. The lower garment of her pajamas was tied about her waist with a man's frayed necktie.

"Is he?" Jenny murmured with detachment. "That one," she answered vaguely, twisting her body to examine the back of one reverted leg. After a while she looked up. "That ain't mine. That's Mrs. What's-her-name's you are in."

"Well, it don't make any difference." The niece lay flat, spreading her arms and legs luxuriously. "Gimme a cigarette. Have you got any?"

"I haven't got any. I don't smoke." Jenny's leg was satisfactory, so she unwrithed herself.

"You don't smoke? Why don't you?"

"I don't know," Jenny replied, "I just don't."

"Look around and see if Eva's got some somewhere." The niece raised her head. "Go on: look in her things, she won't mind."

Jenny hunted for cigarettes in a soft blonde futility. "Pete's got some," she remarked after a time. "He bought twenty packages just before we left town, to bring on the boat."

"Twenty packages? Good Lord, where'd he think we were going? He must have been scared of shipwreck or something."

"I guess so."

"Gabriel's pants," the niece said. "That's all he brought, was it? Just cigarettes? What did you bring?"

"I brought a comb," Jenny dragged her little soiled dress over her head. Her voice was muffled, "and some rouge." She shook out her drowsy gold hair and let the dress fall to the floor. "Pete's got some, though," she repeated, thrusting the dress beneath the dressing table with her foot.

"I know," the niece rejoined, "and so has Mr. Fairchild. And so has the steward, if Mark Frost hasn't borrowed 'em all. And I saw the captain smoking one, too. But that's not doing me any good."

"No," agreed Jenny placidly. Her undergarment was quite pink, enveloping her from shoulder to knee with ribbons and furbelows. She loosened a few of these and stepped sweetly and rosily out of it, casting it also under the table.

"You aren't going to leave 'em there, are you?" the niece asked. "Why don't you put 'em on the chair?"

"Mrs.—Mrs. Wiseman puts hers on the chair."

"Well, you got here first: why don't you take it? Or hang 'em on those hooks behind the door?"

"Hooks?" Jenny looked at the door. "Oh. . . . They'll be all right there, I guess." She stripped off her stockings and laid them on the dressing table. Then she turned to the mirror again and picked up her comb. The comb passed through her fair, soft hair with a faint sound, as of silk, and her hair lent to Jenny's divine body a halo like an angel's. The remote victrola, measured feet, a lapping of water, came into the room.

"You've got a funny figure," the niece remarked after a while, calmly, watching her.

"Funny?" repeated Jenny, looking up with soft belligerence. "It's no funnier than yours. At least my legs don't look like birds' legs."

"Neither do mine," the other replied with complacence, flat on her back. "Your legs are all right. I mean, you are kind of thick through the middle for your legs; kind of big behind for them."

"Well, why not? I didn't make it like that, did I?"

"Oh, sure. I guess it's all right if you like it to be that way."

Without apparent effort Jenny dislocated her hip and stared downward over her shoulder. Then she turned sideways and accepted the mute proffering of the mirror. Reassured, she said: "Sure, it's all right. I expect to be bigger than that, in front, some day."

"So do I . . . when I have to. But what do you want one for?"

"Lord," said Jenny, "I guess I'll have a whole litter of 'em. Besides, I think they're kind of cute, don't you?"

The sound of the victrola came down, melodious and nasal, and measured feet marked away the lapping of waves. The light was small and inadequate, sunk into the ceiling, and Jenny and the niece agreed that they were kind of cute

and pink. Jenny was quite palpably on the point of coming
to bed and the other said:

"Don't you wear any nightclothes?"

"I can't wear that thing Mrs. What's-her-name lent me,"
Jenny replied. "You said you were going to lend me something, only you didn't. If I'd depended on you on this trip,
I guess I'd be back yonder about ten miles, trying to swim
home."

"That's right. But it doesn't make any difference what
you sleep in, does it? . . . Turn off the light." Light followed
Jenny rosily as she crossed the room, it slid rosily upon
her as she turned obediently toward the switch beside the
door. The niece lay flat on her back gazing at the unshaded
globe. Jenny's angelic nakedness went beyond her vision
and suddenly she stared at nothing with a vague orifice
vaguely in the center of it, and beyond the orifice a pale
moonfilled sky.

Jenny's bare feet hissed just a little on the uncarpeted
floor and she came breathing softly in the dark, and her hand
came out of the dark. The niece moved over against the wall.
The round orifice in the center of the dark was obscured,
then it reappeared, and breathing with a soft blonde intentness Jenny climbed gingerly into the berth. But she bumped
her head anyway, lightly, and she exclaimed "ow" with
placid surprise. The bunk heaved monstrously, creaking;
the porthole vanished again, then the berth became still and
Jenny sighed with a soft explosive sound.

Then she changed her position again and the other said:
"Be still, can't you?" thrusting at Jenny's boneless, naked
abandon with her elbow.

"I'm not fixed yet," Jenny replied without rancor.

"Well, get in then, and quit flopping around."

Jenny became lax. "I'm fixed now," she said at last. She sighed again, a frank yawning sound.

Those slightly dulled feet thudthudded monotonously overhead. Outside, in the pale darkness, water lapped at the hull of the yacht. The close cabin emptied slowly of heat: heat ebbed steadily away now that the light was off, and in it was no sound save that of their breathing. No other sound at all. "I hope that was the last one, the one I killed," Jenny murmured.

"God, yes," the niece agreed. "This party is wearing enough with just people on it. . . . Say, how'd you like to be on a party with a boatful of Mr. Talliaferros?"

"Which one is he?"

"Why, don't you remember him? You sure ought to. He's that funny talking little man that puts his hands on you—that dreadful polite one. I don't see how you could forget a man as polite as him."

"Oh, yes," said Jenny, remembering, and the other said:

"Say, Jenny, how about Pete?"

Jenny became utterly still for a moment. Then she said innocently: "What about him?"

"He's mad at you about Mr. Talliaferro, isn't he?"

"Pete's all right, I guess."

"You keep yourself all cluttered up with men, don't you?" the other asked curiously.

"Well, you got to do something," Jenny defended herself.

"Bunk," the niece said roughly, "bunk. You like petting. That's the reason. Don't you?"

"Well, I don't mind," Jenny answered. "I've kind of got

used to it," she explained. The niece expelled her breath in a thin snorting sound and Jenny repeated: "You've got to do something, haven't you?"

"Oh, sweet attar of bunk," the niece said. In the darkness she made a gesture of disgust. "You women! That's the way Dorothy Jameson thinks about it too, I bet. You better look out: I think she's trying to take Peter away from you."

"Oh, Pete's all right," Jenny repeated placidly. She lay perfectly still again. The water was a cool dim sound. Jenny spoke, suddenly confidential.

"Say, you know what she wants Pete to do?"

"No: What?" asked the niece quickly.

"Well— Say, what kind of a girl is she? Do you know her very good?"

"What does she want Pete to do?" the other insisted.

Jenny was silent. Then she blurted in prim disapproval: "She wants Pete to let her paint him."

"Yes? And then what?"

"That's it. She wants Pete to let her paint him in a picture."

"Well, that's the way she usually goes about getting men, I guess. What's wrong with it?"

"Well, it's the wrong way to go about getting Pete. Pete's not used to that," Jenny replied in that prim tone.

"I don't blame him for not wanting to waste his time that way. But what makes you and Pete so surprised at the idea of it? Pete won't catch lead poisoning just from having his portrait painted."

"Well, it may be all right for folks like you all. But Pete says he wouldn't let any strange woman see him without any clothes on. He's not used to things like that."

"Oh," remarked the niece. Then: "So that's the way she wants to paint him, is it?"

"Why, that's the way they always do it, ain't it? In the nude?" Jenny pronounced it nood.

"Good Lord, didn't you ever see a picture of anybody with clothes on? Where'd you get that idea from? From the movies?"

Jenny didn't reply. Then she said suddenly: "Besides, the ones with clothes on are all old ladies, or mayors or something. Anyway, I thought . . ."

"Thought what?"

"Nothing," Jenny answered, and the other said:

"Pete can get that idea right out of his head. Chances are she wants to paint him all regular and respectable, not to shock his modesty at all. I'll tell him so, to-morrow."

"Never mind," Jenny said quickly, "I'll tell him. You needn't to bother about it."

"All right. Whatever you like. . . . Wish I had a cigarette." They lay quiet for a time. Outside water whispered against the hull. The victrola was hushed temporarily and the dancers had ceased. Jenny moved again, onto her side, facing the other in the darkness.

"Say," she asked, "what's your brother making?"

"Gus? Why don't you ask him yourself?"

"I did, only . . ."

"What?"

"Only he didn't tell me. At least, I don't remember."

"What did he say when you asked him?"

Jenny mused briefly. "He kissed me. Before I knew it, and he kind of patted me back here and told me to call again later, because he was in conference or something like that."

"Gabriel's pants," the niece murmured. Then she said sharply: "Look here, you leave Josh alone, you hear? Haven't you got enough with Pete and Mr. Talliaferro, without fooling with children?"

"I'm not going to fool with any children."

"Well, please don't. Let Josh alone, anyway." She moved her arm, arching her elbow against Jenny's soft nakedness. "Move over some. Gee, woman, you sure do feel indecent. Get over on your side a little, can't you?"

Jenny moved away, rolling onto her back again, and they lay quiet, side by side in the dark. "Say," remarked Jenny presently, "Mr.—that polite man—" "Talliaferro," the other prompted. "—Talliaferro. I wonder if he's got a car?"

"I don't know. You better ask him. What do you keep on asking me what people are making or what they've got, for?"

"Taxicabbers are best, I think," Jenny continued, unruffled. "Sometimes when they have cars they don't have anything else. They just take you riding."

"I don't know," the niece repeated. "Say," she said suddenly, "what was that you said to him this afternoon?"

Jenny said, "Oh." She breathed placidly and regularly for a while. Then she remarked: "I thought you were there, around that corner."

"Yes. What was it? Say it again." Jenny said it again. The niece repeated it after her. "What does it mean?"

"I don't know. I just happened to remember it. I don't know what it means."

"It sounds good," the other said. "You didn't think it up yourself, did you?"

"No. It was a fellow told it to me. There was two couples of us at the Market one night, getting coffee: me and Pete and a girl friend of mine and another fellow. We had been to Mandeville on the boat that day, swimming and dancing. Say, there was a man drownded at Mandeville that day. Pete and Thelma, my girl friend, and Roy, this girl friend of mine's fellow, saw it. I didn't see it because I wasn't with them. I didn't go in bathing with them: it was too sunny. I don't think blondes ought to expose themselves to hot sun like brunettes, do you?"

"Why not? But what about—"

"Oh, yes. Anyway, I didn't go in swimming where the man got drowned. I was waiting for them, and I got to talking to a funny man. A little kind of black man—"

"A nigger?"

"No. He was a white man, except he was awful sunburned and kind of shabby dressed—no necktie and hat. Say, he said some funny things to me. He said I had the best digestion he ever saw, and he said if the straps of my dress was to break I'd devastate the country. He said he was a liar by profession, and he made good money at it, enough to own a Ford as soon as he got it paid out. I think he was crazy. Not dangerous: just crazy."

The niece lay quiet. She said, contemplatively: "You do look like they feed you on bread and milk and put you to bed at sunset every day. . . . What was his name? Did he tell you?" she asked suddenly.

"Yes. It was . . ." Jenny pondered a while. "I remembered it because he was such a funny kind of man. It was . . . Walker or Foster or something."

"Walker or Foster? Well, which one was it?"

"It must be Foster because I remembered it by it began with a F like my girl friend's middle name—Frances. Thelma

Frances, only she don't use both of them. Only I don't think it was Foster, because—"

"You don't remember it, then."

"Yes, I do. Wait. . . . Oh, yes: I remember—Faulkner, that was it."

"Faulkner?" the niece pondered in turn. "Never heard of him," she said at last, with finality. "And he was the one that told you that thing?"

"No. It was after that, when we had come back to N.O. That crazy man was on the boat coming back. He got to talking to Pete and Roy while me and Thelma was fixing up downstairs, and he danced with Thelma. He wouldn't dance with me because he said he didn't dance very well, and so he had to keep his mind on the music while he danced. He said he could dance with either Roy or Thelma or Pete, but he couldn't dance with me. I think he was crazy. Don't you?"

"It all sounds crazy, the way you tell it. But what about the one that said that to you?"

"Oh, yes. Well, we was at the Market. There was a big crowd there because it was Sunday night, see, and these other fellows was there. One of them was a snappy looking fellow, and I kind of looked at him. Pete had stopped in a place to get some cigarettes, and me and Thelma and Roy was crowded in with a lot of folks, having coffee. So I kind of looked at this goodlooking fellow."

"Yes. You kind of looked at him. Go on."

"All right. And so this goodlooking fellow crowded in behind me and started talking to me. There was a man in between me and Roy, and this fellow that was talking to me said, Is he with you? talking about the man sitting next to me, and I said, No, I didn't know who he was. And this fellow said, How about coming out with him because he had his car parked outside . . . Pete's brother has a lot of cars. One of them is the same as Pete's . . . And then . . . Oh, yes, and I said, where will we go, because my old man didn't like for me to go out with strangers, and the fellow said he wasn't a stranger, that anybody could tell me who some name was, I forgot what it was he said his name was. And I said he better ask Pete if I could go, and he said, Who was Pete? Well, there was a big man standing near where we was. He was big as a stevedore, and just then this big man happened to look at me again. He looked at me a minute, and I kind of knew that he'd look at me again pretty soon, so I told this fellow talking to me that he was Pete, and when the big man looked somewheres else a minute this fellow said that to me. And then the big man looked at me again, and the fellow that said that to me kind of went away. So I got up and went to where Thelma and Roy was, and pretty soon Pete came back. And that's how I learned it."

"Well, it sure sounds good. I wonder . . . Say, let me say it sometimes, will you?"

"All right," Jenny agreed. "You can have it. Say, what's that you keep telling your aunt? Something about pulling up the sheet or something?" The niece told her. "That sounds good, too," Jenny said magnanimously.

"Does it? I tell you what: You let me use yours some-time, and you can take mine. How about it?"

"All right," Jenny agreed again, "it's a trade."

Water lapped and whispered ceaselessly in the pale darkness. The curve of the low ceiling directly over the berth lent a faint sense of oppression to the cabin, but this sense of oppression faded out into the comparatively greater spa-

ciousness of the room, of the darkness with a round orifice
vaguely in the center of it. The moon was higher and the
lower curve of the brass rim of the port was now a thin silver
sickle, like a new moon.

Jenny moved again, turning against the other's side,
breathing ineffably across the niece's face. The niece lay
with Jenny's passive nakedness against her arm, and moving her arm outward from the elbow she slowly stroked the
back of her hand along the swell of Jenny's flank. Slowly,
back and forth, while Jenny lay supine and receptive as a cat.
Slowly, back and forth and back . . . "I like flesh," the niece
murmured. "Warm and smooth. Wish I'd lived in Rome . . .
oiled gladiators. . . . Jenny," she said abruptly, "are you a virgin?"

"Of course I am," Jenny answered immediately in a
startled tone. She lay for a moment in lax astonishment. "I
mean," she said, "I—yes. I mean, yes, of course I am." She
brooded in passive surprise, then her body lost its laxness.
"Say—"

"Well," the niece agreed judicially, "I guess that's about
what I'd have said, myself."

"Say," demanded Jenny, thoroughly aroused, "what did
you ask me that for?"

"Just to see what you'd say. It doesn't make any difference, you know, whether you are or not. I know lots of
girls that say they're not. I don't think all of 'em are lying,
either."

"Maybe it don't to some folks," Jenny rejoined primly,
"but I don't approve of it. I think a girl loses a man's respect
by pom—prom—I don't approve of it, that's all. And I don't
think you had any right to ask me."

"Good Lord, you sound like a girl scout or something. Don't Pete ever try to persuade you otherwise?"

"Say, what're you asking me questions like that for?"

"I just wanted to see what you'd say. I don't think it's anything to tear your shirt over. You're too easily shocked, Jenny," the niece informed her.

"Well, who wouldn't be? If you want to know what folks say when you ask 'em things like that, why don't you ask 'em to yourself? Did anybody ever ask you if you were one?"

"Not that I know of. But I wou—"

"Well, are you?"

The niece lay perfectly still a moment. "Am I what?"

"Are you a virgin?"

"Why, of course I am," she answered sharply. She raised herself on her elbow. "I mean— Say, look here—"

"Well, that's what I'd 'a' said, myself," Jenny responded with placid malice from the darkness.

The niece poised on her tense elbow above Jenny's sweet regular breathing. "Anyway, what bus—I mean— You asked me so quick," she rushed on, "I wasn't even thinking about being asked something like that."

"Neither was I. You asked me quicker than I asked you."

"But that was different. We were talking about you being one. We were not even thinking about me being one. You asked it so quick I had to say that. It wasn't fair."

"So did I have to say what I said. It was as fair for you as it was for me."

"No, it was different. I had to say I wasn't: quick, like that."

"Well, I'll ask it when you're not surprised, then. Are you?"

The niece lay quiet for a time. "You mean, sure enough?"

"Yes." Jenny breathed her warm intent breath across the other's face.

The niece lay silent again. After a time she said: "Hell," and then: "Yes, I am. It's not worth lying about."

"That's what I think," Jenny agreed smugly. She became placidly silent in the darkness. The other waited a moment, then said sharply:

"Well? Are you one?"

"Sure I am."

"I mean, sure enough. You said sure enough, didn't you?"

"Sure, I am," Jenny repeated.

"You're not playing fair," the niece accused, "I told you."

"Well, I told you, too."

"Honest? You swear?"

"Sure, I am," Jenny said again with her glib and devastating placidity.

The niece said, "Hell." She snorted thinly.

They lay quiet, side by side. They were quiet on deck, too, but it seemed as though there still lingered in the darkness a thin stubborn ghost of syncopation and thudding tireless feet. Jenny wiggled her free toes with pleasure. Presently she said:

"You're mad, ain't you?" No reply. "You've got a good figure, too," Jenny offered, conciliatory. "I think you've got a right sweet little shape."

But the other refused to be cajoled. Jenny sighed again ineffably, her milk-and-honey breath. She said: "Your brother's a college boy, ain't he? I know some college boys. Tulane. I think college boys are cute. They don't dress as well as Pete . . . sloppy." She mused for a time. "I wore a frat pin once, for a couple of days. I guess your brother belongs to it, don't he?"

"Gus? Belong to one of these jerkwater clubs? I guess not. He's a Yale man—he will be next month, that is. I'm going with him. They don't take every Tom, Dick and Harry that shows up in up there. You have to wait until sophomore year. But Gus is going to work for a senior society, anyhow. He don't think much of fraternities. Gee, you'd sure give him a laugh if he could hear you."

"Well, I didn't know. It seems to me one thing you join is about like another. What's he going to get by joining the one he's going to join?"

"You don't get anything, stupid. You just join it."

Jenny pondered this a while. "And you have to work to join it?"

"Three years. And only a few make it, then."

"And if you do make it, you don't get anything except a little button or something? Good Lord . . . Say, you know what I'm going to tell him to-morrow? I'm going to tell him he better hold up the sheet: he's—he's— What's the rest of it?"

"Oh, shut up and get over on your side," the niece said sharply, turning her back. "You don't understand anything about it."

"I sure don't," Jenny agreed, rolling away and onto her other side, and they lay with their backs to each other and their behinds just touching, as children do. . . . "Three years . . . Good Lord."

*   *   *

Fairchild had not returned. But she had known they would not: she was not even surprised, and so once more her party had evolved into interminable cards. Mrs. Wiseman, herself, Mr. Talliaferro and Mark. By craning her neck she could see Dorothy Jameson's frail humorless intentness and the tawdry sophistication of Jenny's young man where they swung their legs from the roof of the wheelhouse. The moon was getting up and Pete's straw hat was a dull implacable gleam slanted above the red eye of his eternal cigarette. And, yes, there was that queer, shy, shabby Mr. Gordon, mooning alone, as usual; and again she felt a stab of reproof for having neglected him. At least the others seemed to be enjoying the voyage, however trying they might be to one another. But what could she do for him? He was so difficult, so ill at ease whenever she extended herself for him . . . Mrs. Maurier rose.

"For a while," she explained; "Mr. Gordon . . . the trials of a hostess, you know. You might play dummy until I—no: wait." She called Dorothy with saccharine insistence and presently Miss Jameson responded. "Won't you take my hand for a short time? I'm sure the young gentleman will excuse you."

"I'm sorry," Miss Jameson called back. "I have a headache. Please excuse me."

"Go on, Mrs. Maurier," Mrs. Wiseman said, "we can pass the time until you come back: we've got used to sitting around."

"Yes, do," Mr. Talliaferro added, "we understand."

Mrs. Maurier looked over to where Gordon still leaned his tall body upon the rail. "I really must," she explained again. "It's such a comfort to have a few on whom I can depend."

"Yes, do," Mr. Talliaferro repeated.

When she had gone Mrs. Wiseman said: "Let's play red dog for pennies. I've got a few dollars left."

*   *   *

She joined him quietly. He glanced his gaunt face at her, glanced away. "How quiet, how peaceful it is," she began, undeterred, leaning beside him and gazing also out across the restless slumber of water upon which the worn moon spread her ceaseless peacock's tail like a train of silver sequins. In the yet level rays of the moon the man's face was spare and cavernous, haughty and inhuman almost. He doesn't get enough to eat, she knew suddenly and infallibly. It's like a silver faun's face, she thought. But he is so difficult, so shy. . . . "So few of us take time to look inward and contemplate ourselves, don't you think? It's the life we lead, I suppose. Only he who creates has not lost the art of this: of making his life complete by living within himself. Don't you think so, Mr. Gordon?"

"Yes," he answered shortly. Beyond the dimensionless curve of the deck on which he stood he could see, forward and downward, the stem of the yacht: a pure triangle of sheer white with small waves lapping at its horizontal leg, breaking and flashing each with its particle of shattered moonlight, making a ceaseless small whispering. Mrs. Maurier moved her hands in a gesture: moonlight smoldered greenly amid her rings.

"To live within yourself, to be sufficient unto yourself. There is so much unhappiness in the world . . ." she sighed again with astonishment. "To go through life, keeping yourself from becoming involved in it, to gather inspiration for your Work—ah, Mr. Gordon, how lucky you who create are. As for we others, the best we can hope is that sometime, somewhere, somehow we may be fortunate enough to furnish that inspiration, or the setting for it, at least. But, after all, that would be an end in itself, I think. To know that one had given her mite to Art, no matter how humble the mite or the giver . . . The humble laborer, Mr. Gordon: she, too, has her place in the scheme of things; she, too, has given something to the world, has walked where gods have trod. And I do so hope that you will find on this voyage something to compensate you for having been taken away from your Work."

"Yes," said Gordon again, staring at her with his arrogant uncomfortable stare. The man looks positively uncanny, she thought with a queer cold feeling within her. Like an animal, a beast of some sort. Her own gaze fluttered away and despite herself she glanced quickly over her shoulder to the reassuring group at the card table. Dorothy's and Jenny's young man's legs swung innocent and rhythmic from the top of the wheelhouse, and as she looked Pete snapped his cigarette outward and into the dark water, twinkling.

"But to be a world in oneself, to regard the antics of man as one would a puppet show—ah, Mr. Gordon, how happy you must be."

"Yes," he repeated. Sufficient unto himself in the city of his arrogance, in the marble tower of his loneliness and pride, and . . . She coming into the dark sky of his life like a star, like a flame . . . O bitter and new . . . Somewhere within him was a far dreadful laughter, unheard; his whole life was become toothed with jeering laughter, and he faced the old woman again, putting his hand on her and turning her face upward into the moonlight. Mrs. Maurier knew utter fear. Not fright, fear: a passive and tragic condition like a dream. She whispered Mr. Gordon, but made no sound.

"I'm not going to hurt you," he said harshly, staring at her face as a surgeon might. "Tell me about her," he commanded. "Why aren't you her mother, so you could tell me how conceiving her must have been, how carrying her in your loins must have been?"

Mr. Gordon! she implored through her dry lips, without making a sound. His hand moved over her face, learning the bones of her forehead and eyesockets and nose through her flesh.

"There's something in your face, something behind all this silliness," he went on in his cold level voice while an interval of frozen time refused to pass. His hand pinched the loose sag of flesh around her mouth, slid along the fading line of her cheek and jaw. "I suppose you've had what you call your sorrows, too, haven't you?"

"Mr. Gordon!" she said at last, finding her voice. He released her as abruptly and stood over her, gaunt and ill nourished and arrogant in the moonlight while she believed she was going to faint, hoping vaguely that he would make some effort to catch her when she did, knowing that he would not do so. But she didn't faint, and the moon spread her silver and boneless hand on the water, and the water lapped and lapped at the pure dreaming hull of the *Nausi-kaa* with a faint whispering sound.

ELEVEN O'CLOCK

"Do you know," said Mrs. Wiseman rising and speaking across her chair, "what I'm going to do if this lasts another night? I'm going to ask Julius to exchange with me and let me get drunk with Dawson and Major Ayers in his place. And so, to one and all: Good night."

"Aren't you going to wait for Dorothy?" Mark Frost asked. She glanced toward the wheelhouse.

"No. I guess Pete can look out for himself," she replied, and left them. The moon cast a deep shadow on the western side of the deck, and near the companionway some one lay in a chair. She slowed, passing. "Mrs. Maurier?" she said. "We wondered what had become of you. Been asleep?"

Mrs. Maurier sat up slowly, as a very old person moves. The younger woman bent down to her, quickly solicitous. "You don't feel well, do you?"

"Is it time to go below?" Mrs. Maurier asked, raising herself more briskly. "Our bridge game . . ."

"You all had beat us too badly. But can't I—"

"No, no," Mrs. Maurier objected quickly, a trifle testily. "It's nothing: I was just sitting here enjoying the moonlight."

"We thought Mr. Gordon was with you." Mrs. Maurier shuddered.

"These terrible men," she said with an attempt at lightness. "These artists!"

"Gordon, too? I thought he had escaped Dawson and Julius."

"Gordon, too," Mrs. Maurier replied. She rose. "Come, I think we'd better go to bed." She shuddered again, as with cold: her flesh seemed to shake despite her, and she took the younger woman's arm, clinging to it. "I do feel a little tired," she confessed. "The first few days are always trying, don't you think? But we have a very nice party, don't you think so?"

"An awfully nice party," the other agreed without irony. "But we are all tired: we'll all feel better to-morrow, I know."

Mrs. Maurier descended the stairs slowly, heavily. The other steadied her with her strong hand, and opening Mrs. Maurier's door she reached in and found the light button. "There. Would you like anything before you go to bed?"

"No, no," Mrs. Maurier answered, entering and averting her face quickly. She crossed the room and busied herself at the dressing table, keeping her back to the other. "Thank you, nothing. I shall go to sleep at once, I think. I always sleep well on the water. Good night."

Mrs. Wiseman closed the door. I wonder what it is, she thought, I wonder what happened to her? She went on along the passage to her own door. Something did, something happened to her, she repeated, putting her hand on the door and turning the knob.

TWELVE O'CLOCK

The moon had got higher, that worn and bloodless one, old and a little weary and shedding her tired silver on yacht and water and shore; and the yacht, the deck and its fixtures, was passionless as a dream upon the shifting silvered wings of water when she appeared in her bathing suit. She stood for a moment in the doorway until she saw movement and his white shirt where he half turned on the coil of rope where he sat. Her lifted hand blanched slimly in the hushed treachery of the moon: a gesture, and her bare feet made no sound on the deck.

"Hello, David. I'm on time, like I said. Where's your bathing suit?"

"I didn't think you would come," he said, looking up at her, "I didn't think you meant it."

"Why not?" she asked. "Good Lord, what'd I want to tell you I was for, if I wasn't?"

"I don't know. I just thought . . . You sure are brown, seeing it in the moonlight."

"Yes, I've got a good one," she agreed. "Where's your bathing suit? Why haven't you got it on?"

"You were going to get one for me, you said."

She stared at his face in consternation. "That's right: I sure was. I forgot it. Wait, maybe I can wake Josh up and get it. It won't take long. You wait here."

He stopped her. "It'll be all right. Don't bother about it to-night. I'll get it some other time."

"No, I'll get it. I want somebody to go in with me. You wait."

"No, never mind: I'll row the boat for you."

"Say, you still don't believe I meant it, do you?" She examined him curiously. "All right, then. I guess I'll have to go in by myself. You can row the boat, anyway. Come on."

He fetched the oars and they got in the tender and

cast off. "Only I wish you had a bathing suit," she repeated
from the stern. "I'd rather have somebody to go in with me.
Couldn't you go in in your clothes or something? Say, I'll
just turn my back, and you take off your clothes and jump
in: how about that?"

"I guess not," he answered in alarm. "I guess I better not
do that."

"Shucks, I wanted somebody to go swimming with me.
It's not any fun, by myself. . . . Take off your shirt and pants,
then, and go in in your underclothes. That's almost like a
bathing suit. I went in yesterday in Josh's."

"I'll row the boat for you while you go in," he repeated.
The niece said Shucks again. David pulled steadily on upon
the mooned and shifting water. Little waves slapped the bottom of the boat lightly as it rose and fell, and behind them
the yacht was pure and passionless as a dream against the
dark trees.

"I just love to-night," the niece said. "It's like we owned
everything." She lay flat on her back on the stern seat, propping her heels against the gunwale. David pulled rhythmically, the motion of the boat was a rhythm that lent to the
moon and stars swinging up and down beyond the tapering
simplicity of her propped knees a motion slow and soothing
as a huge tree in a wind.

"How far do you want to go?" he asked presently.

"I don't care," she answered, gazing into the sky. He
rowed on, the oarlocks thumping, and measured, and she
turned onto her belly, dragging her arm in the water while
small bubbles of silver fire clung to her arm, broke away
reluctantly and swam slowly to the surface, disappeared. . . .
Little casual swells slapped the bottom of the boat, lightly,

and slid along beside the hull, mooned with bubbling fire. She slid her legs overside and swung from the stern of the boat, dragging through the water. He pulled on a few strokes.

"I can't row with you hanging there," he said. Her two hands vanished from the gunwale and her dark head vanished, but when he slewed the boat sharply and half rose, she reappeared, whipping a faint shower of silver drops from her head. The moon slid and ran on her alternate arms and before her spread a fan of silver lines, shifting and spreading and fading.

"Gee," she said. Her voice came low along the water, not loud but still distinct: little waves lapped at it. "It's grand: warm as warm. You better come in." Her head vanished again, he saw her sickling legs as they vanished, and once more she rayed shattered silver from her flung head. She swam up to the boat. "Come on in, David," she insisted. "Take off your shirt and pants and jump in. I'll swim out and wait for you. Come on, now," she commanded.

So he removed his outer garments, sitting in the bottom of the boat, and slid quickly and modestly into the water. "Isn't it grand?" she called to him. "Come on out here."

"We better not get too far from the boat," he said cautiously, "she ain't got any anchor, you know."

"We can catch it. It won't drift fast. Come on out here, and I'll race you back to it."

He swam out to where her dark wet head awaited him. "I bet I beat you," she challenged. "Are you ready? One. Two. Three—Go!" And she did beat him and with a single unceasing motion she slid upward and into the tender, and stood erect for the moonlight to slide over her in hushed silver.

"I'll plunge for distance with you," she now challenged. David hung by his hands, submerged to his neck. She waited for him to get into the skiff, then she said: "You can dive, can't you?" But he still clung to the gunwale, looking up at her. "Come on, David," she said sharply. "Are you timid, or what? I'm not going to look at you, if you don't want me to." So he got into the boat, modestly keeping his back to her, but even his wet curious garment could not make ridiculous the young lean splendor of him.

"I don't see what you are ashamed of. You've got a good physique," she told him. "Tall and hard looking. . . . Are you ready? One. Two. Three—Go!"

But soon she was content to float on her back and recover breath, while he trod water beside her. Little hands of water lapped at her, in her hair and upon her face, and she breathed deeply, closing her eyes against the bland waning moon.

"I'll hold you up a while," he offered, putting his hand under the small of her back.

"You sure can," she said, holding herself motionless. "Is it hard to do? Let me see if I can hold you up. This water is different from seawater: you don't hardly sink in seawater if you want to." She let her legs sink and he lay obediently on his back. "I can hold you up, can't I? Say, can you carry somebody in the water, like lifesavers?"

"A little," he admitted and she rolled again onto her back and he showed her how it was done. Then she must try it herself, and he submitted with dubious resignation. Her hard young arm gripped him chokingly across his throat, jamming his windpipe, and she plunged violently forward, threshing her legs. He jerked up his arms to remove her strangling elbow and his head went under, openmouthed. He fought free of her and reappeared gasping. Her concerned face came to him and she tried to hold him up, unnecessarily.

"I'm so sorry: I didn't mean to duck you."

"It's all right," he said, coughing and strangling.

"I didn't do it right, did I? Are you all right now?" She watched him anxiously, trying to support him.

"I'm all right," he repeated. "You had the wrong hold," he explained, treading water. "You had me around the neck."

"Gee, I thought I was doing it right. I'll do it right this time."

"I guess we better wait and practice it in shallow water sometime," he demurred quickly.

"Why . . . all right," she agreed. "I think I know how, now. I guess I had better learn good, first, though. I'm awful sorry I strangled you."

"It don't hurt any more. I don't notice it."

"But it was such a dumb thing to do. I'll learn it good next time."

"You know how now, all right. You just got the wrong hold that time. Try it again: see if you don't know it."

"You don't mind?" she said with quick joy. "I won't catch you wrong this time. . . . No, no: I might duck you again. I'd better learn it first."

"Sure you won't," he said. "You know how now. You won't hurt me. Try it." He turned onto his back.

"Gee, David," she said. She slid her arm carefully across his chest and beneath his opposite arm. "That's right? Now, I'm going."

She held him carefully, intent on doing it correctly,

while he encouraged her. But their progress was maddeningly slow: the boat seemed miles away, and so much of her effort was needed to keep her own head above water. Soon she was breathing faster, gulping air and then closing her mouth against the water her thrusting arm swirled up against her face. I will do it, I will do it, she told herself, but it was so much harder than it had looked. The skiff rose and fell against the stars, and mooned water bubbled about her. It would take more effort or she'd have to give up. And she'd drown before that.

The arm that held him was numb, and she swam harder, shifting her grip and again her hard elbow shut with strangling force upon his windpipe. But he was expecting it and without moving his body he twisted his head aside and filled his lungs and shut his mouth and eyes. . . . Soon she ceased swimming and her arm slid down again, holding him up, and he emptied his lungs and opened his eyes to remark the gunwale of the tender rising and falling against the sky above his head.

"I did make it," she gasped, "I did make it. Are you all right?" she asked, panting. "I sure did it, David. I knew I could." She clung to the skiff, resting her head upon her hands. "I thought for a while, when I had to change my hold, that I was doing it wrong again. But I did it right, didn't I?" The remote chill stars swung over them, and the decaying disc of the moon, over the empty world in which they clung by their hands, side by side. "I'm pretty near all in," she admitted.

"It's pretty hard," he agreed, "until you've practiced a lot. I'll hold you up until you get your breath." He put his arm around her under the water.

"I'm not all the way winded," she protested, but by degrees she relaxed until he supported her whole weight, feeling her heart thumping against his palm, while she clung to the gun-wale resting her bowed head upon her hands; and it was like he had been in a dark room and all of a sudden the lights had come on: simple, like that.

It was like one morning when he was in a bunch of hoboes riding a freight into San Francisco and the bulls had jumped them and they had had to walk in. Along the water front it was, and there were a lot of boats in the water, kind of rocking back and forth at anchor: he could see reflections of boats and of the piles of the wharves in the water, wavering back and forth; and after a while dawn had come up out of the smoke of the city, like a sound you couldn't hear, and a lot of yellow and pink had come onto the water where the boats were rocking, and around the piles of the wharf little yellow lines seemed to come right up out of the water; and pretty soon there were gulls looking like they had pink and yellow feathers, slanting and wheeling around.

And it was like there was a street in a city, a street with a lot of trash in it, but pretty soon he was out of the street and in a place where trees were. It must be spring because the trees were not exactly bare, and yet they didn't exactly have leaves on them, and there was a wind coming through the trees and he stopped and heard music somewhere; it was like he had just waked up and a wind with music in it was coming across green hills brave in a clean dawn. Simple, like that.

She moved at last against his arm. "Maybe I can climb in now. You better gimme a push, I guess." His hand found her knee, slid down, and she raised her foot to his palm. He saw her flat boy's body against the stars rising, and she was in the boat, leaning down to him. "Catch my hands," she said, extending them, but for a time he didn't move at all, but only clung to the gunwale and looked up at her with an utter longing, like that of a dog.

*   *   *

Mrs. Maurier lay in bed in her darkened room. There was a port just over the bed and a long pencil of moonlight came slanting through it, shattering upon the floor and filling the room with a cold, disseminated radiance. Upon the chair, vaguely, her clothes: a shapeless, familiar mass, comforting; and about her the intimate familiarity of her own possessions—her toilet things, her clothing, her very particular odor with which she had grown so familiar that she no longer noticed it at all.

She lay in bed—her bed, especially built for her, was the most comfortable on board—surrounded, lapped in security and easeful things, walled and secure within the bland, hushed planes of the bulkheads. A faint, happy sound came in to her: little tongues of water lapping ceaselessly alongside the yacht, against her yacht—that island of security that was always waiting to transport her comfortably beyond the rumors of the world and its sorrows; and beyond the yacht, space: water and sky and darkness and silence; a worn cold moon neither merry nor sad. . . . Mrs. Maurier lay in her easy bed, within her comfortable room, weeping long shuddering sobs: a passive terrible hysteria without a sound.

The Third Day

This morning waked in a quiet fathomless mist. It was upon the world of water unstirred; soon the first faint wind of morning would thin it away, but now it was about the *Nausikaa* timelessly: the yacht was a thick jewel swaddled in soft gray wool, while in the wool somewhere dawn was like a suspended breath. The first morning of Time might well be beyond this mist, and trumpets preliminary to a golden flourish; and held in suspension in it might be heard yet the voices of the Far Gods on the first morning saying, It is well: let there be light. A short distance away, a shadow, a rumor, a more palpable thickness: this was the shore. The water fading out of the mist became as a dark metal in which the *Nausikaa* was rigidly fixed, and the yacht was motionless, swaddled in mist like a fat jewel.

FIVE O'CLOCK

Up from the darkness of the companionway the niece came, naked and silent as a ghost. She stood for a space, but there was no sound from anywhere, and she crossed the deck and stopped again at the rail, breathing the soft chill mist into her lungs, feeling the mist swaddling her firm simple body with a faint lingering chillness. Her legs and arms were so tan that naked she appeared to wear a bathing suit of a startling white. She climbed the rail. The tender rocked a little under her, causing the black motionless water to come alive, making faint sounds. Then she slid over the stern and swam out into the mist.

The water divided with oily reluctance, closing again behind her with scarce a ripple. Here, at the water level, she could see nothing save a grayness and flaccid disturbed tongues of water lapping into it, leaving small fleeting gaps between mist and water before the mist filled them again silently as settling wings. The hull of the yacht was a vague thing, a thing felt, known, rather than seen. She swam slowly, circling the place where she knew it should be.

She swam slowly and steadily, trying to keep her approximate distance from the yacht by instinct. But, consciously this was hard to do; consciously in this vague restricted immensity, this limitless vagueness whose center was herself, the yacht could be in any direction from her. She paused and trod water while little tongues of water kissed her face, lapping against her lips. It's on my right, she told herself. It's on my right, over there. Not fear: merely a faint unease, an exasperation; but to reassure herself she swam a few strokes in that direction. The mist neither thickened nor thinned.

She trod water again and water licked at her face soundlessly. Damn your fool soul, she whispered, and at that moment a round huge thing like a dead lidless eye watched her suddenly from the mist and there came a faint sound from somewhere in the mist above her head. In two strokes she touched the hull of the yacht: a vindication, and she knew a faint pride and a touch of relief as she swam along the hull and circled the stern. She grasped the gunwale of the tender and hung there for a while, getting her wind back.

That faint sound came again from the deck; a movement, and she spoke into the mist: "David?" The mist took the word, sweeping it lightly against the hull, then it rebounded again and the mist absorbed it. But he had heard and he appeared vaguely above her at the rail, looking down at her where she hung in the water. "Go away, so I can get out," she said. He didn't move, and she added: "I haven't got on a bathing suit. Go away a minute, David."

But he didn't move. He leaned over the rail, looking at her with a dumb and utter longing and after a while she slid quickly and easily into the tender, and still he remained motionless, making no move to help her as her grave simple body came swiftly aboard the yacht. "Be back in a minute," she said over her shoulder and her startling white bathing suit sped across the deck and out of the ken of his dog's eyes. The mist without thinning was filling with light: an imminence of dawn like a glory, a splendor of trumpets unheard.

Her minute was three minutes. She reappeared in her little colored linen dress, her dark coarse hair still damp, carrying her shoes and stockings in her hand. He hadn't moved at all.

"Well, let's get going," she said. She looked at him impatiently. "Aren't you ready yet?" He stirred at last, watching her with the passive abjectness of a dog. "Come on," she said sharply. "Haven't you got the stuff for breakfast yet? What's the matter with you, David? Snap out of your trance." She examined him again, with a sober impersonality. "You didn't believe I was going to do it—is that it? Or are you backing out yourself? Come on, say so now, if you want to call it off."

She came nearer, examining his face with her grave opaque eyes. She extended her hand. "David?"

He took her hand slowly, looking at her, and she grasped his hand and shook his arm sharply. "Wake up. Say, you haven't—Come on, let's get some stuff for breakfast, and beat it. We haven't got all day."

He followed her and in the galley she switched on the light and chose a flat box of bacon and a loaf of bread, putting them on a table and delving again among boxes and lockers and shelves. "Have you got matches? A knife?" she asked over her shoulder. "And—where are oranges? Let's take some oranges. I love oranges, don't you?" She turned her head to look at him. His hand was just touching her sleeve, so diffidently that she had not felt it. She turned suddenly, putting the oranges down, and put her arms about him, hard and firm and sexless, drawing his cheek down to her sober moist kiss. She could feel his hammering erratic heart against her breast, could hear it surging in the silence almost as though it were in her own body. His arms tightened and he moved his head, seeking her mouth, but she evaded him with a quick movement, without reproof.

"No, no, not that. Everybody does that." She strained him against her hard body again, then released him. "Come on, now. Have you got everything?" She examined the shelves again, finding at last a small basket. It was filled with damp lettuce but she dumped the lettuce out and put her things in it. "You take my shoes. They'll go in your pocket, won't they?" She crumpled her limp blonde stockings into her slippers and gave them to him. Then she picked up the basket and snapped off the light.

Day was a nearer thing yet, though it was not quite come. Though the mist had not thinned, the yacht was visible from stem to stern, asleep like a gull with folded wings; and against the hull the water sighed a long awakening sigh. The shoreline was darker, a more palpable vagueness in the mist.

"Say," she remarked, stopping suddenly, "how are we going to get ashore? I forgot that. We don't want to take the tender."

"Swim," he suggested. Her dark damp head came just to his chin and she mused for a time in a sober consternation. "Isn't there some way we can go in the tender and then pull it back to the yacht with a rope?"

"I . . . Yes. Yes, we can do that."

"Well, you get a rope then. Snap into it."

When he returned with a coiled line she was already in the tender with the oars, and she watched with interest while he passed the rope around a stanchion and brought both ends into the boat with him and made one of the ends fast to the ringbolt in the stem of the skiff. Then she caught the idea and she sat and paid out the line while he pulled away for shore. Soon they beached and she sprang ashore, still holding the free end of the rope. "How're we going to keep the tender from pulling the rope back around that post and getting aloose?" she asked.

"I'll show you," he answered, and she watched him while he tied the oars and the rowlocks together with the free end of the line and wedged them beneath the thwarts. "That'll hold, I guess. Somebody'll be sure to see her pretty soon," he added, and prepared to draw the skiff back to the yacht.

"Wait a minute," she said. She mused gravely, gazing at the dim shadowy yacht, then she borrowed matches from him, and sitting on the gunwale of the tender she tore a strip of paper from the bacon box and with a charred match printed Going to— She looked up. "Where are we going?" He looked at her and she added quickly: "I mean, what town? We'll have to go to a town somewhere, you know, to get back to New Orleans so I can get some clothes and my seventeen dollars. What's the name of a town?"

After a while he said: "I don't know. I never—"

"That's right, you never were over here before, either, were you? Well, what's that town the ferries go to? The one Jenny's always talking about you have fun at?" She stared again at the vague shape of the *Nausikaa*, then she suddenly printed Mandeville. "That's the name of it—Mandeville. Which way is Mandeville from here?" He didn't know, and she added: "No matter, we'll find it, I guess." She signed the note and laid it on the sternseat, weighting it with a small rock. "Now, pull her off," she commanded, and soon there came back to them across the motionless water a faint thud.

"Good-by, *Nausikaa*," she said. "Wait," she added, "I better put my shoes on, I guess." He gave her her slippers and she sat flat on the narrow beach and put them on, returning the crumpled stockings to him. "Wait," she said again, taking the stockings again and flipping them out. She slid one of them over her brown arm and withdrew a crumpled wad—the money she had been able to rake up by ransacking her aunt's and Mrs. Wiseman's and Miss Jameson's things. She reached her hand and he drew her to her feet. "You'd better carry the money," she said, giving it to him. "Now, for breakfast," she said, clutching his hand.

SIX O'CLOCK

Trees heavy and ancient with moss loomed out of it hugely and grayly: the mist might have been a sluggish growth between and among them. No, this mist might have been the first prehistoric morning of time itself; it might have been the very substance in which the seed of the beginning of things fecundated; and these huge and silent trees might have been the first of living things, too recently born to know either fear or astonishment, dragging their sluggish umbilical cords from out the old miasmic womb of a nothingness latent and dreadful. She crowded against him, suddenly quiet and subdued, trembling a little like a puppy against the reassurance of his arm. "Gee," she said in a small voice.

That small sound did not die away. It merely dissolved into the moist gray surrounding them, and it was as if at a movement of any sort the word might repeat itself somewhere between sky and ground as a pebble is shaken out of cotton batting. He put his arm across her shoulders and at his touch she turned quickly beneath his armpit, hiding her face.

"I'm hungry," she said at last, in that small voice. "That's what's the matter with me," she added with more assurance. "I want something to eat."

"Want me to build a fire?" he asked of the dark coarse crown of her head.

"No, no," she answered quickly, holding to him. "Besides, we are too close to the lake, here. Somebody might see it. We ought to get farther from the shore." She clung to him, inside his arm. "I guess we'd better wait here until the fog goes away, though. A piece of bread will do." She reached her brown hand. "Let's sit down somewhere. Let's sit down and eat some bread," she decided. "And when the fog goes away we can find the road. Come on, let's find a log or something."

She drew him by the hand and they sat at the foot of a huge tree, on the damp ground, while she delved into the basket. She broke a bit from the loaf and gave it to him, and a fragment for herself. Then she slid further down against her propped heels until her back rested against him, and bit from her bread. She sighed contentedly.

"There now. Don't you just love this?" she raised her grave chewing face to look at him. "All gray and lonesome. Makes you feel kind of cold on the outside and warm inside, doesn't it?—say, you aren't eating your bread. Eat your bread, David. I love bread, don't you?" She moved again, inward upon herself: in some way she seemed to get herself yet closer against him.

The mist was already beginning to thin, breaking with heavy reluctance before a rumor of motion too faint to be called wind. The mist broke raggedly and drifted in sluggish wraiths that seemed to devour all sound, swaying and swinging like huge spectral apes from tree to tree, rising and falling, revealing somber patriarchs of trees, hiding them again. From far, far back in the swamp there came a hoarse homely sound—an alligator's lovesong.

"Chicago," she murmured. "Didn't know we were so near home." Soon the sun; and she sprawled against him, contentedly munching her bread.

SEVEN O'CLOCK

They hadn't found the road, but they had reached a safe distance from the lake. She had discovered a butterfly larger than her two hands clinging to a spotlight of sun on the ancient trunk of a tree, moving its damp lovely wings like laboring exposed lungs of glass or silk; and while he gathered firewood—a difficult feat, since neither of them had thought of a hatchet—she paused at the edge of a black stream to harry a sluggish thick serpent with a small switch. A huge gaudy bird came up and cursed her, and the snake ignored her with a sort of tired unillusion and plopped heavily into the thick water. Then, looking around, she saw thin fire in the somber equivocal twilight of the trees.

They ate again: the oranges; they broiled bacon, scorched it, dropped it on the ground, retrieved it and wiped it and chewed it down; and the rest of the loaf. "Don't you just love camping?" She sat crosslegged and wiped a strip of bacon on her skirt. "Let's always do this, David: let's don't ever have a house where you've always got to stay in one place. We'll just go around like this, camping . . . David?" She raised the strip of bacon and met his dumb yearning eyes. She poised her bacon.

"Don't look at me like that," she told him sharply. Then,

more gently: "Don't ever look at anybody like that. You'll never get anybody to run away with you if you look at 'em like that, David." She extended her hand. His hand came out, slowly and diffidently, but her grip was hard, actual. She shook his arm for emphasis.

"How was I looking at you?" he asked after a while, in a voice that didn't seem to him to be his voice at all. "How do you want me to look at you?"

"Oh—you know how. Not like that, though. Like that, you look at me just like a—a man, that's all. Or a dog. Not like David." She writhed her hand free and ate her strip of bacon. Then she wiped her fingers on her dress. "Gimme a cigarette."

The mist had gone, and the sun came already sinister and hot among the trees, upon the miasmic earth. She sat on her crossed legs, replete, smoking. Abruptly she poised the cigarette in a tense cessation of all movement. Then she moved her head quickly and stared at him in consternation. She moved again, suddenly slapping her bare leg.

"What is it?" he asked.

For reply she extended her flat tan palm. In the center of it was a dark speck and a tiny splash of crimson. "Good Lord, gimme my stockings," she exclaimed. "We'll have to move. Gee, I'd forgotten about them," she said, drawing her stockings over her straightening legs. She sprang to her feet. "We'll soon be out, though. David, stop looking at me that way. Look like you were having a good time, at least. Cheer up, David. A man would think you were losing your nerve already. Buck up: I think it's grand, running off like this. Don't you think it's grand?" She turned her head and saw again that diffident still gesture of his hand touching her dress. Across the hot morning there came the high screech of the *Nausikaa's* whistle.

EIGHT O'CLOCK

"No, sir," the nephew answered patiently. "It's a pipe."

"A pipe, eh?" repeated Major Ayers, glaring at him with his hard affable little eyes. "You make pipes, eh?"

"I'm making this one," the nephew replied with preoccupation.

"Came away and left your own ashore, perhaps?" Major Ayers suggested after a time.

"Naw. I don't smoke 'em. I'm just making a new kind."

"Ah, I see. For the market." Major Ayers' mind slowly took fire. "Money in it, eh? Americans would buy a new kind of pipe, too. You've made arrangements for the marketing of it, of course?"

"No, I'm just making it. For fun," the nephew explained in that patient tone you use with obtuse children. Major Ayers glared at his bent preoccupied head.

"Yes," he agreed. "Best to say nothing about it until you've completed all your computations regarding the cost of production. Don't blame you at all." Major Ayers brooded with calculation. He said: "Americans really would buy a new sort of pipe. Strange no one had thought of that." The nephew carved minutely at his pipe. Major Ayers said secretly: "No, I don't blame you at all. But when you've done, you'll require capital: that sort of thing, you know. And then . . . a word to your friends at the proper time, eh?"

The nephew looked up. "A word to my friends?" he

repeated. "Say, I'm just making a pipe, I tell you. A pipe. Just to be making it. For fun."

"Right you are," Major Ayers agreed suavely. "No offense, dear lad. I don't blame you, don't blame you at all. Experienced the same situation myself."

NINE O'CLOCK

They had found the road at last—two faint scars and a powder of unbearable dust upon a raised levee traversing the swamp. But between them and the road was a foul sluggish width of water and vegetation and biology. Huge cypress roots thrust up like weathered bones out of a green scum and a quaking neither earth nor water, and always those bearded eternal trees like gods regarding without alarm this puny desecration of a silence of air and earth and water ancient when hoary old Time himself was a pink and dreadful miracle in his mother's arms.

It was she who found the fallen tree, who first essayed its oozy treacherous bark and first stood in the empty road stretching monotonously in either direction between battalioned patriarchs of trees. She was panting a little, whipping a broken green branch about her body, watching him as he inched his way across the fallen trunk.

"Come on, David," she called impatiently. "Here's the road: we're all right now." He was across the ditch and he now struggled up the rank reluctant levee bank. She leaned down and reached her hand to him. But he would not take it, so she leaned further and clutched his shirt. "Now, which way is Mandeville?"

"That way," he answered immediately, pointing.

"You said you never were over here before," she accused.

"No. But we were west of Mandeville when we went aground, and the lake is back yonder. So Mandeville must be that way."

"I don't think so. It's this way: see, the swamp isn't so thick this way. Besides, I just know it's this way."

He looked at her a moment. "All right," he agreed. "I guess you are right."

"But don't you know which way it is? Isn't there any way you could tell?" She bent and whipped her legs with the broken branch.

"Well, the lake is over yonder, and we were west of Mandeville last night—"

"You're just guessing," she interrupted harshly.

"Yes," he answered. "I guess you are right."

"Well, we've got to go somewhere. We can't stand here." She twitched her shoulders, writhing her body beneath her dress. "Which way, then?"

"Well, we w—"

She turned abruptly in the direction she had chosen. "Come on, I'll die here." She strode on ahead.

TEN O'CLOCK

She was trying to explain it to Pete. The sun had risen sinister and hot, climbing into a drowsy haze, and up from a low vague region neither water nor sky clouds like fat little girls in starched frocks marched solemnly.

"It's a thing they join at that place he's going to. Only

they have to work to join it, and sometimes you don't even get to join it then. And the ones that do join it don't get anything except a little button or something."

"Pipe down and try it again," Pete told her, leaning with his elbows and one heel hooked backward on the rail, his hat slanted across his reckless dark face, squinting his eyes against the smoke of his cigarette. "What're you talking about?"

"There's something in the water," Jenny remarked with placid astonishment, creasing her belly over the rail and staring downward into the faintly rippled water while the land breeze molded her little green dress. "It must of fell off the boat. . . . Oh, I'm talking about that college he's going to. You work to join things there. You work three years, she says. And then maybe you—"

"What college?"

"I forgot. It's the one where they have big football games in the papers every year. He's—"

"Yale and Harvard?"

"Uhuh, that's the one she said. He's—"

"Which one? Yale, or Harvard?"

"Uhuh. And so he—"

"Come on, baby. You're talking about two colleges. Was it Yale she said, or Harvard? Or Sing Sing or what?"

"Oh," Jenny said. "It was Yale. Yes, that's the one she said. And he'll have to work three years to join it. And even then maybe he won't."

"Well, what about it? Suppose he does work three years: what about it?"

"Why, if he does, he won't get anything except a little

button or something, even if he does join it, I mean." Jenny brooded softly, creasing herself upon the rail. "He's going to have to work for it," she recurred again in a dull soft amazement. "He'll have to work three years for it, and even then he may not—"

"Don't be dumb all your life, kid," Pete told her.

Wind and sun were in Jenny's drowsing hair. The deck swept trimly forward, deserted. The others were gathered on the deck above. Occasionally they could hear voices, and a pair of masculine feet were crossed innocently upon the rail directly over Pete's head. A half-smoked cigarette spun in a small twinkling arc astern. Jenny watched it drop lightly onto the water, where it floated amid the other rubbish that had caught her attention. Pete spun his own cigarette backward over his shoulder, but this one sank immediately, to her placid surprise.

"Let the boy join his club, if he wants," Pete added. "What kind of a club is it? What do they do?"

"I don't know. They just join it. You work for it three years, she said. Three years. . . . Gee, by that time you'd be too old to do anything if you got to join it. . . . Three years. My Lord."

"Sit down and give your wooden leg a rest," Pete said. "Don't be a dumbbell forever." He examined the deck a moment, then without changing his position against the rail he turned his head toward Jenny. "Give papa a kiss."

Jenny also glanced briefly up the deck. Then she came with a sort of wary docility, raising her ineffable face . . . presently Pete withdrew his face. "What's the matter?" he asked.

"The matter with what?" said Jenny innocently.

Pete unhooked his heel and he put his arm around Jenny. Their faces merged again and Jenny became an impersonal softness against his mouth and a single blue eye and a drowsing aura of hair.

ELEVEN O'CLOCK

The swamp did not seem to end, ever. On either side of the road it brooded, fetid and timeless, somber and hushed and dreadful. The road went on and on through a bearded tunnel, beneath the sinister brass sky. The dew was long departed and dust puffed listlessly to her fierce striding. David tramped behind her, watching two splotches of dead blood on her stockings. Abruptly there were three of them and he drew abreast of her. She looked over her shoulder, showing him her wrung face.

"Don't come near me!" she cried. "Don't you see you make 'em worse?"

He dropped behind again and she stopped suddenly, dropping the broken branch and extending her arms. "David," she said. He went to her awkwardly, and she clung to him, whimpering. She raised her face, staring at him. "Can't you do something? They hurt me, David." But he only looked at her with his unutterable dumb longing.

She tightened her arms, released him quickly. "We'll be out soon." She picked up the branch again. "It'll be different then. Look! There's another big butterfly!" Her squeal of delight became again a thin whimpering sound. She strode on.

*   *   *

Jenny found Mrs. Wiseman in their room, changing her dress.

"Mr. Ta—Talliaferro," Jenny began. Then she said: "He's an awful refined man, I guess. Don't you think so?"

"Refined?" the other repeated. "Exactly that. Ernest invented that word."

"He did?" Jenny went to the mirror and looked at herself a while. "Her brother's refined, too, ain't he?"

"Whose brother, honey?" Mrs. Wiseman paused and watched Jenny curiously.

"The one with that saw."

"Oh. Yes, fairly so. He seems to be too busy to be anything else. Why?"

"And that popeyed man. All English men are refined, though. There was one in a movie I saw. He was awful refined." Jenny looked at her reflected face, timelessly and completely entertained. Mrs. Wiseman gazed at Jenny's fine minted hair, at her sleazy little dress revealing the divine inevitability of her soft body.

"Come here, Jenny," she said.

TWELVE O'CLOCK

When he reached her she sat huddled in the road, crouching bonelessly upon herself, huddling her head in her crossed thin arms. He stood beside her, and presently he spoke her name. She rocked back and forth, then wrung her body in an ecstasy. "They hurt me, they hurt me," she wailed, crouching again in that impossible spasm of agony. David knelt beside her and spoke her name again, and she sat up.

"Look," she said wildly, "on my legs—look, look," staring with a sort of fascination at a score of great gray specks hovering about her blood-flecked stockings, making no effort to brush them away. She raised her wild face again. "Do you see them? They are everywhere on me—my back, my back, where I can't reach." She lay suddenly flat, writhing her back in the dust, clutching his hand. Then she sat up again and against his knees she turned wringing her body from the hips, trying to draw her bloody legs beneath her brief skirt. He held her while she writhed in his grasp, staring her wild bloodless face up at him. "I must get in water," she panted. "I must get in water. Mud, anything. I'm dying, I tell you."

"Yes, yes: I'll get you some water. You wait here. Will you wait here?"

"You'll get me some water? You will? You promise?"

"Yes, yes," he repeated. "I'll get you some. You wait here. You wait here, see?" he repeated idiotically. She bent again inward upon herself, moaning and writhing in the dust, and he plunged down the bank, stripping his shirt off and dipped it into the foul warm ditch. She had dragged her dress up about her shoulders, revealing her startling white bathing suit between her knickers and the satin band binding her breasts. "On my back," she moaned, bending forward again, "quick! Quick!"

He laid the wet shirt on her back and she caught the ends of it and drew it around her, and presently she leaned back against his knees with a long shuddering sigh. "I want a drink. Can't I have a drink of water, David?"

"Soon," he promised with despair. "You can have one soon as we get out of the swamp."

She moaned again, a long whimpering sound, lowering her head between her arms. They crouched together in the dusty road. The road went on shimmering before them, endless beneath bearded watching trees, crossing the implacable swamp with a puerile bravado like a thin voice cursing in a cathedral. Needles of fire darted about them, about his bare shoulders and arms. After a while she said:

"Wet it again, please, David."

He did so, and returned, scrambling up the steep rank levee side.

"Now, bathe my face, David." She raised her face and closed her eyes and he bathed her face and throat and brushed her damp coarse hair back from her brow.

"Let's put the shirt on you," he suggested.

"No," she demurred against his arm, without opening her eyes, drowsily. "They'll eat you alive without it."

"They don't bother me like they do you. Come on, put it on." She demurred again and he tried awkwardly to draw the shirt over her head. "I don't need it," he repeated.

"No. . . . Keep it, David. . . . You ought to keep it. Besides, I'd rather have it underneath. . . . Oooo, it feels so good. You're sure you don't need it?" She opened her eyes, watching him with that sober gravity of hers. He insisted and she sat up and slipped her dress over her head. He helped her to don the shirt, then she slipped her dress on again. "I wouldn't take it, only they hurt me so damn bad. I'll do something for you some day, David. I swear I will."

"Sure," he repeated. "I don't need it."

He rose, and she came to her feet in a single motion, before he could offer to help her. "I swear I wouldn't take it if they didn't hurt me so much, David," she persisted, putting her hand on his shoulder and raising her tanned serious face.

"Sure, I know."

"I'll pay you back somehow. Come on: let's get out of here."

ONE O'CLOCK

Mrs. Wiseman and Miss Jameson drove Mrs. Maurier moaning and wringing her hands, from the galley and prepared lunch—grapefruit again, disguised thinly.

"We have so many of them," the hostess apologized helplessly. "And the steward gone. . . . We are aground, too, you see," she explained.

"Oh, we can stand a little hardship, I guess," Fairchild reassured her jovially. "The race hasn't degenerated that far. In a book, now, it would be kind of terrible; if you forced characters in a book to eat as much grapefruit as we do, both the art boys and the humanitarians would stand on their hind legs and howl. But in real life— In life, anything might happen; in actual life people will do anything. It's only in books that people must function according to arbitrary rules of conduct and probability; it's only in books that events must never flout credulity."

"That's true," Mrs. Wiseman agreed. "People's characters, when writers delineate them by revealing their likings and dislikings, always appear so perfect, so inevitably consistent, but in li—"

"That's why literature is art and biology isn't," her brother interrupted. "A character in a book must be consistent in all things, while man is consistent in one thing only: he is consistently vain. It's his vanity alone which keeps his particles damp and adhering one to another, instead of like any other handful of dust which any wind that passes can disseminate."

"In other words, he is consistently inconsistent," Mark Frost recapitulated.

"I guess so," the Semitic man replied. "Whatever that means. . . . But what were you saying, Eva?"

"I was thinking of how book people, when you find them in real life, have such a perverse and disconcerting way of liking and disliking the wrong things. For instance, Dorothy here. Suppose you were drawing Dorothy's character in a novel, Dawson. Any writer would give her a liking for blue jewelry: white gold, and platinum, and sapphires in dull silver—you know. Wouldn't you do that?"

"Why, yes, so I would," Fairchild agreed with interest. "She would like blue things, sure enough."

"And then," the other continued, "music. You'd say she would like Grieg, and those other cold mad northern people with icewater in their veins, wouldn't you?"

"Yes," Fairchild agreed again, thinking immediately of Ibsen and the Peer Gynt legend and remembering a sonnet of Siegfried Sassoon's about Sibelius that he had once read in a magazine. "That's what she would like."

"Should like," Mrs. Wiseman corrected. "For the sake of esthetic consistency. But I bet you are wrong. Isn't he, Dorothy?"

"Why, yes," Miss Jameson replied. "I always liked Chopin."

Mrs. Wiseman shrugged: a graceful dark gesture. "And there you are. That's what makes art so discouraging. You come to expect anything associated with and dependent on the actions of man to be discouraging. But it always shocks me to learn that art also depends on population, on the herd instinct just as much as manufacturing automobiles or stockings does—"

"Only they can't advertise art by means of women's legs yet," Mark Frost interrupted.

"Don't be silly, Mark," Mrs. Wiseman said sharply. "That's exactly how art came to the attention of the ninety-nine who don't produce it and so have any possible reason for buying it—postcards and lithographs barely esoteric enough to escape police persecution. Ask any man on the street what he understands by the word art: he'll tell you it means a picture. Won't he?" she appealed to Fairchild.

"That's so," he agreed. "And it's a wrong impression. Art means anything consciously done well, to my notion. Living, or building a good lawn mower, or playing poker. I don't like this modern idea of restricting the word to painting, at all."

"The art of Life, of a beautiful and complete existence of the Soul," Mrs. Maurier put in. "Don't you think that is Art's greatest function, Mr. Gordon?"

"Of course you don't, child," Mrs. Wiseman told Fairchild, ignoring Mrs. Maurier. "As rabidly American as you are, you can't stand that, can you? And there's the seat of your bewilderment, Dawson—your belief that the function of creating art depends on geography."

"It does. You can't grow corn without something to plant it in."

"But you don't plant corn in geography: you plant it in soil. It not only does not matter where that soil is, you can even move the soil from one place to another—around the world, if you like—and it will still grow corn."

"You'd have a different kind of corn, though—Russian corn, or Latin or Anglo-Saxon corn."

"All corn is the same to the belly," the Semitic man said.

"Julius!" exclaimed Mrs. Maurier. "The Soul's hunger: that is the true purpose of Art. There are so many things to satisfy the grosser appetites. Don't you think so, Mr. Talliaferro?"

"Yes," Mrs. Wiseman took her brother up. "Dawson clings to his conviction for the old reason: it's good enough to live with and comfortable to die with—like a belief in immortality. Insurance against doubt or alarm."

"And laziness," her brother added. Mrs. Maurier exclaimed "Julius" again. "Clinging spiritually to one little spot of the earth's surface, so much of his labor is performed for him. Details of dress and habit and speech which entail no hardship in the assimilation and which, piled one on another, become quite as imposing as any single startling stroke of originality, as trivialities in quantities will. Don't you agree? But then, I suppose that all poets in their hearts consider prosewriters shirkers, don't they?"

"Yes," his sister agreed. "We do think they are lazy—just a little. Not mentally, but that their . . . not hearts—"

"Souls?" her brother suggested. "I hate that word, but it's the nearest thing. . . ." She met her brother's sad quizzical eyes and exclaimed: "Oh, Julius! I could kill you, at times. He's laughing at me, Dawson."

"He's laughing at us both," Fairchild said. "But let him have his fun, poor fellow." He chuckled, and lit a cigarette. "Let him laugh. I always did want to be one of those old time eunuchs, for one night. They must have just laughed themselves to death when those sultans and things would come visiting."

"Mister Fairchild! Whatever in the world!" exclaimed Mrs. Maurier.

"It's a good thing there's some one to see something amusing in that process," the other rejoined. "The husbands, the active participants, never seem to."

"That's a provision of nature's for racial survival," Fairchild said. "If the husbands ever saw the comic aspect of it. . . . But they never do, even when they have the opportunity, no matter how white and delicate the hand that decorates their brows."

"It's not lovely ladies nor dashing strangers," the Semitic man said, "it's the marriage ceremony that disfigures our foreheads."

Fairchild grunted. Then he chuckled again. "There'd sure be a decline in population if a man were twins and had to stand around and watch himself making love."

"Mister Fairchild!"

"Chopin," Mrs. Wiseman interrupted. "Really, Dorothy, I'm disappointed in you." She shrugged again, flashing her hands. Mrs. Maurier said with relief:

"How much Chopin has meant to me in my sorrows"—

she looked about in tragic confiding astonishment—"no one will ever know."

"Surely," agreed Mrs. Wiseman, "he always does." She turned to Miss Jameson. "Just think how much better Dawson would have done you than God did. With all deference to Mrs. Maurier, so many people find comfort in Chopin. It's like having a pain that aspirin will cure, you know. I could have forgiven you even Verdi, but Chopin! Chopin," she repeated, then with happy inspiration: "Snow rotting under a dead moon."

Mark Frost sat staring at his hands on his lap, beneath the edge of the table, moving his lips slightly. Fairchild said:

"What music do you like, Eva?"

"Oh—Debussy, George Gershwin, Berlioz perhaps—why not?"

"Berlioz," repeated Miss Jameson mimicking the other's tone: "Swedenborg on a French holiday." Mark Frost stared at his hands on his lap, moving his lips slightly.

"Forget your notebook, Mark?" Fairchild asked quizzically.

"It's very sad," the Semitic man said. "Man gets along quite well until that unhappy day on which some one else discovers him thinking. After that, God help him: he doesn't dare leave home without a notebook. It's very sad."

"Mark's not such an accomplished buccaneer as you and Dawson," his sister answered quickly. "At least he requires a notebook."

"My dear girl," the Semitic man murmured in his lazy voice, "you flatter yourself."

"So do I," Fairchild said. "I always—"

"Whom?" the Semitic man asked. "Yourself, or me?"

"What?" said Fairchild, staring at him.

"Nothing. Excuse me: you were saying—?"

"I was saying that I always carry my portfolio with me because it's the only comfortable thing I ever found to sit on."

*   *   *

Talk, talk, talk: the utter and heartbreaking stupidity of words. It seemed endless, as though it might go on forever. Ideas, thoughts, became mere sounds to be bandied about until they were dead.

Noon was oppressive as a hand, as the ceaseless blow of a brass hand: a brass blow neither struck nor withheld; brass rushing wings that would not pass. The deck blistered with it, the rail was too hot to touch and the patches of shadow about the deck were heavy and heat soaked as sodden blankets. The water was an unbearable glitter, the forest was a bronze wall cast at a fearful heat and not yet cooled, and no breeze was anywhere under the world's heaven.

But the unbearable hiatus of noon passed at last and the soundless brazen wings rushed westward. The deck was deserted as it had been on that first afternoon when he had caught her in midflight like a damp swallow, a swallow hard and passionate with flight; and it was as though he yet saw upon the deck the wet and simple prints of her naked feet, and he seemed to feel about him like an odor that young hard graveness of hers. No wonder she was gone out of it: she who here was as a flame among stale ashes, a little tanned flame; who, gone, was a pipe blown thinly and far away, as a remembered surf on a rocky coast at dawn . . . ay ay strangle

your heart o israfel winged with loneliness feathered bitter
with pride.

*   *   *

Dust spun from their feet, swirling sluggish and lazy in the
brooding dreadful noon. Beside them always and always
those eternal bearded trees, bearded and brooding, older
and stiller than eternity. The road ran on like a hypnotism:
a dull and endless progression from which there was no
escape.

After a while he missed her from her position at his
shoulder and he stopped and looked back. She was kneeling
beside the foul ditch. He watched her stupidly, then he suddenly realized what she was about and he ran back to her,
grasping her by the shoulder. "Here, you can't do that! That
stuff is poison: you can't drink it!"

"I can't help it! I've got to have some water, I've got to!"
She strained against his hands. "Please, David. Just one
mouthful. Please, David. Please, David."

He got his hands under her arms, but his feet slid in the
rank sloping grass and he went up to his knees in thick reluctant water. She twisted in his hands. "Please, oh, please! Just
enough to wet my mouth. Look at my mouth." She raised
her face: her broad pale lips were parched, rough. "Please,
David."

But he held her. "Put your feet in it, like mine. That'll
help some," he said through his own dry harsh throat. "Here,
let me take off your shoes."

She sat whimpering like a dog while he removed her
slippers. Then she slid her legs into the water and moaned

with partial relief. The sunlight was beginning to slant at last, slanting westward like a rushing of unheard golden wings across the sky; though the somber twilight under the trees was unchanged—somber and soundless, brooding, and filled with a vicious darting of invisible fire.

"I must have water," she said at last. "You'll have to find me some water, David."

"Yes." He climbed heavily out of the hot ooze, out of the mud and slime. He bent and slid his hands under her arms. "Get up. We must go on."

TWO O'CLOCK

Jenny yawned, frankly, then she did something to the front of her dress, drawing it away from her to peer down into her bosom. It seemed to be all right, and she settled her dress again with a preening motion, lifting her shoulders and smoothing it over her hips. She went upstairs and presently she saw them, sitting around like always. Mrs. Maurier wasn't there.

She drifted over to the rail and laxed herself against it and stood there, placidly waiting until Mr. Talliaferro became aware of her presence.

"I was watching these things in the water," she said when he came to her like a tack to a magnet, volitionless and verbose.

"Where?" He also stared overside.

"That stuff there," she answered, looking forward to the group of chairs.

"Why, that's just refuse from the galley," Mr. Talliaferro said with surprise.

"Is it? It's kind of funny looking. . . . There's some more of it down here a ways." Mr. Talliaferro followed her, intrigued and curious. She stopped and glanced back over her shoulder and beyond him: Mr. Talliaferro aped her but saw no living thing except Mark Frost on the edge of the group. The others were out of sight beyond the deckhouse. "It's farther on," Jenny said.

Further along she stopped again and again she looked forward. "Where?" Mr. Talliaferro asked.

"Here." Jenny stared at the lake a moment. Then she examined the deck again. Mr. Talliaferro was thoroughly puzzled now, even a trifle alarmed. "It was right here, that funny thing I saw. I guess it's gone, though."

"What was it you saw?"

"Some kind of a funny thing," she answered with detachment. . . . "The sun is hot here." Jenny moved away and went to where an angle of the deckhouse wall formed a shallow niche. Mr. Talliaferro followed her in amazement. Again Jenny peered around him, examining that part of the deck which was in sight and the immediate approaches to it. Then she became utterly static beside him and without moving at all she seemed to envelop him, giving him to think of himself surrounded, enclosed by the sweet cloudy fire of her thighs, as young girls can.

Mr. Talliaferro saw her as through a blonde mist. A lightness was moving down his members, a lightness so exquisite as to be almost unbearable, while above it all he listened to the dry interminable incoherence of his own voice. That unbearable lightness moved down his arms to his hands, and down his legs, reaching his feet at last, and Mr. Talliaferro fled.

Jenny looked after him. She sighed.

*　　*　　*

After a while the white dusty road left the swamp behind. It ran now through a country vaguely upland: sand and pines and a crisp thick undergrowth sunburnt and sibilant.

"We're out of it at last," she called back to him. Her pace quickened and she called over her shoulder: "It can't be much further now. Come on, let's run a while." He shouted to her, but she trotted on, drawing away from him. He followed her splotched flashing legs at a slower pace, steadily losing distance.

Her legs twinkled on ahead in the shimmering forgotten road. Heat wavered and shimmered above the road and the sky was a metallic intolerable bowl and the tall pines in the windless afternoon exuded a thin exhilarating odor of resin and heat, casting sparse patches of shade upon the shimmering endless ribbon of the road. Lizards scuttled in the dust before them, hissing abruptly amid the dusty brittle undergrowth beside the road. The road went on and on, endless and shimmering ahead of them. He called to her again, but she trotted on unheeding.

Without faltering in her pace she turned and ran from the road and when he reached her she leaned against a tree, panting. "I ran too much," she gasped through her pale open mouth. "I feel funny—all gone. Better hold me up," she said, staring at him. "No: let me lie down." She slumped against him. "My heart's going too fast. Feel how it's going." He felt her heart leaping against his hand. "It's too fast, isn't it? What'll I do now?" she asked soberly. "Do something quick, David," she told him, staring at him, and he lowered her awkwardly and knelt beside her, supporting her head. She closed her eyes against the implacable sky, but opened them immediately and struggled to rise. "No, no: I mustn't stay here. I want to get up again. Help me up."

He did so, and had to hold her on her feet. "I must go on," she repeated. "Make me go on, David. I don't want to die here. Make me go on, I tell you." Her face was flushed: he could see blood pumping in her throat, and holding her so he knew sharp and utter terror. "What must I do?" she was saying. "You ought to know. Don't you know what to do? I'm sick, I tell you. They've given me hydrophobia or something."

She closed her eyes and all her muscles relaxed at once and she slipped to the ground and he knelt again beside her in terror and despair. "Raise my head a little," she muttered and he sat and drew her across his legs and raised her head against his breast, smoothing her damp hair from her forehead. "That's right." She opened her eyes. "Cheer up, David. . . . I told you once about looking at me like that." Then she closed her eyes again.

THREE O'CLOCK

"If we were only afloat," Mrs. Maurier moaned for the twelfth time. "They can't be further than Mandeville: I know they can't. What will Henry say to me!"

"Why don't they start her up and try to get off again?" Fairchild asked. "Maybe the sand has settled or something by now," he added vaguely.

"The captain says they can't, that we'll have to wait for the tug. They sent for the tug yesterday, and it hasn't come yet," she added in a sort of stubborn astonishment. She rose and went to the rail and stared up the lake toward Mandeville.

"You wouldn't think it'd take a tug to pull us off," Fairchild remarked. "She ain't such a big boat, you know. Seems like any sort of a boat would pull us off. I've seen little launches hauling bigger boats than this around. And a river tug can haul six or eight of these steel barges, upstream, too."

Mrs. Maurier returned hopefully. "It really doesn't seem necessary to have a tug to move this yacht, does it? You'd think that sailors could think of some way, something with ropes and things," she added, also vaguely.

"What would they stand on while they pulled the ropes?" Mark Frost wanted to know. "They couldn't pull from the shore. That isn't the way we want to go."

"They might row out in the tender and anchor," the Semitic man offered as his mite.

"Why, yes," Mrs. Maurier agreed, brightening. "If they could just anchor the tender securely, they might . . . if there were something to pull the rope with. The men themselves. . . . Do you suppose the sailors themselves could move a boat like this by hand?"

"I've seen a single river tug not much bigger than a Ford hauling a whole string of loaded steel barges up the river," Fairchild repeated. He sat and stared from one to another of his companions and a strange light came into his eyes. "Say," he said suddenly, "I bet that if all of us were to . . ."

The Semitic man and Mark Frost groaned in simultane-
ous alarm, and Pete sitting on the outskirt of the group rose
hastily and unostentatiously and headed for the companionway. He ducked into his room and stood listening.

Yes, they were really going to try it. He could hear Fairchild's burly voice calling for all the men, and also one or
two voices raised in protest; and above all of them the voice
of the old woman in an indistinguishable senseless excitement. Jesus Christ, he whispered, clutching his hat.

People descending the stairs alarmed him and he sprang
behind the open door. It was Fairchild and the fat Jew, but
they passed his door and entered the room next to his, from
which he heard immediately sounds of activity that culmi-
nated in a thin concussion of glass and glass.

"My God, man"—the fat Jew's voice—"what have you
done? Do you really think we can move this boat?"

"Naw. I just want to stir 'em up a little. Life's getting
altogether too tame on this boat: nothing's happened at all
to-day. I did it principally to see Talliaferro and Mark Frost
sweat some." Fairchild laughed. His laughter died into
chuckles, heavily. "But I have seen a little river tug no bigger than a Ford hauling a st—"

"Good Lord," the other man said again. "Finish your
drink. O immaculate cherubim," he said, going on down
the passage. Fairchild followed. Pete heard their feet on
the stairs, then crossing the deck. He returned to the
port.

Yes, sir, they were going to try it, sure as hell. They
were now embarking in the tender: he could hear them,
thumping and banging around and talking; a thin shriek of
momentary alarm. Women, too (Damn to hell, I bet Jenny's

with 'em, Pete whispered to himself). And somebody that didn't want to go at all.

Voices without; alarums and excursions, etc:

Come on, Mark, you've got to go. All the men will be needed, hey, Mrs. Maurier?

Yes, indeed; indeed, yes. All the men must help.

Sure: all you brave strong men have got to go.

I'm a poet, not an oarsman. I can't—

So is Eva: look at her, she's going.

Shelley could row a boat.

Yes, and remember what happened to him, too.

I'm going to keep you all from drowning, Jenny. That's (Damn to hell, Pete whispered) why I'm going.

Aw, come on, Mark; earn your board and keep.

Oooo, hold the boat still, Dawson.

Come on, come on. Say, where's Pete?

Pete!

Pete! (Feet on the deck.)

Pete! Oh, Pete! (At the companionway.) Pete! (Jesus Christ, Pete whispered, making no sound.)

Never mind, Eva. We've got a boatload now. If anybody else comes, they'll have to walk.

There's somebody missing yet. Who is it?

Ah, we've got enough. Come on.

But somebody ain't here. I don't guess he fell overboard while we were not looking, do you?

Oh, come on and let's go. Shove off, you Talliaferro (a scream).

Look out, there: catch her! Y'all right, Jenny? Let's go, then. Careful, now.

Ooooooo!

"Damn to hell, she's with 'em," Pete whispered again, trying to see through the port. More thumping, and presently the tender came jerkily and lethargically into sight, loaded to the gunwales like a nigger excursion. Yes, Jenny was in it, and Mrs. Wiseman and five men, including Mr. Talliaferro. Mrs. Maurier leaned over the rail above Pete's head, waving her handkerchief and shrieking at them as the tender drew uncertainly away, trailing a rope behind it. Almost every one had an oar: the small boat bristled with oars beating the water vainly, so that it resembled a tarantula with palsy and no knee joints. But they finally began to get the knack of it and gradually the boat began to assume something like a definite direction. As Pete watched it there came again feet on the stairs and a voice said guardedly:

"Ed."

An indistinguishable response from the captain's room and the voice added mysteriously: "Come up on deck a minute." Then the footsteps withdrew, accompanied.

*   *   *

The tender evinced a maddening inclination to progress in any fashion save that for which it was built. Fairchild turned his head and glanced comprehensively about his small congested island enclosed with an unrhythmic clashing of blades. The oars clashed against each other, jabbing and scuttering at the tortured water until the tender resembled an ancient stiffjointed horse in a state of mad unreasoning alarm.

"We've got too many rowers," Fairchild decided. Mark Frost drew in his oar immediately, striking the Semitic man across the knuckles with it. "No, no: not you," Fairchild said. "Julius, you quit: you ain't doing any good, anyhow; you're the one that's holding us back. Gordon, and Mark, and Talliaferro and me—"

"I want to row," Mrs. Wiseman said. "Let me have Julius' oar. Ernest will have to help Jenny watch the rope."

"Take mine," Mark Frost offered quickly, extending his oar and clashing it against some one else's. The boat rocked alarmingly. Jenny squealed.

"Look out," Fairchild exclaimed. "Do you want to have us all in the water? Julius, pass your oar along—that's it. Now, you folks sit still back there. Dammit, Mark, if you hit anybody else with that thing, we'll throw you out. Shelley could swim, too, you know."

Mrs. Wiseman got fixed at last with her oar, and at last the tender became comparatively docile. Jenny and Mr. Talliaferro sat in the stern, paying out the line. "Now," Fairchild glanced about at his crew and gave the command: "Let's go."

"Give way, all," Mrs. Wiseman corrected with inspiration. They dipped their oars anew. Mark Frost drew his oar in once more, clashing it against Gordon's.

"Let me get my handkerchief," he said. "My hands are tender."

"That's what I want, too," Mrs. Wiseman decided. "Gimme your handkerchief, Ernest."

Mark Frost released his oar and it leapt quickly overboard. "Catch that paddle!" Fairchild shouted. Mrs. Wiseman and Mr. Talliaferro both reached for it and Gordon and the Semitic man trimmed the boat at the ultimate instant. It became stable presently and Jenny closed her mouth upon her soundless scream.

The oar swam away and stopped just beyond reach, raising and falling on the faint swells. "We'll have to row over and get it," Mrs. Wiseman said. So they did, but just before they reached it the oar swam on again, slowly and maddeningly. The rowers clashed and churned. Mr. Talliaferro sat in a taut diffident alarm.

"I really think," he said, "we'd better return to the yacht. The ladies, you know." But they didn't heed him.

"Now, Ernest," Mrs. Wiseman directed sharply, "reach out and grab it." But it eluded them again, and Fairchild said:

"Let's let the damn thing go. We've got enough left to row with, anyway." But at that moment the oar, rocking sedately, swung slowly around and swam docilely up alongside.

"Grab it! grab it!" Mrs. Wiseman cried.

"I really think—" Mr. Talliaferro offered again. Mark Frost grabbed it and it came meekly and unresistingly out of the water.

"I've got it," he said, and as he spoke it leapt viciously at him and struck him upon the mouth. Then it became docile again.

They got started again, finally; and after a few false attempts they acquired a vague sort of rhythm though Mark Frost, favoring his hands, caught a crab at every stroke for a while, liberally wetting Mr. Talliaferro and Jenny where they sat tensely in the stern. Jenny's eyes were quite round and her mouth was a small red O: a continuous soundless squeal. Mr. Talliaferro's expression was that of a haggard anticipatory alarm. He said again: "I really think—"

"I suspect we had better try to go another way," the Semitic man suggested without emphasis from the bows, "or we'll be aground ourselves."

They all scuttered their oars upon the water, craning their necks. The shore was only a few yards away and immediately, as though they had heard the Semitic man speak, needles of fire assailed the crew with fierce joy.

They bent to their oars again, flapping their spare frantic hands about their heads, and after a few minutes of violent commotion the tender acquiesced and crept slowly and terrifically seaward again. But their presence was now known, the original scouting party was reinforced and offing could not help them.

"I really think," Mr. Talliaferro said, "for the ladies' sake, that we'd better return."

"So do I," Mark Frost abetted quickly.

"Don't lose your nerve, Mark," Mrs. Wiseman told him. "Just a little more and we can take a nice long boatride this afternoon."

"I've had enough boatriding in the last half hour to do me a long time," the poet answered. "Let's go back. How about it, you fellows back there? How about it, Jenny? Don't you want to go back?"

Jenny answered "Yes, sir," in a small frightened voice, clutching the seat with both hands. Her green dress was splotched and stained with water from Mark Frost's oar. Mrs. Wiseman released one hand and patted Jenny's knee.

"Shut up, Mark. Jenny's all right. Aren't you, darling? It'll be such a good joke if we really were to get the yacht afloat. Look sharp, Ernest. Isn't that rope almost tight?"

It was nearly taut, sliding away into the water in a lovely slender arc and rising again to the bow of the yacht. Mrs. Maurier stood at the rail, waving her handkerchief at intervals. On the farther wall sat three people in attitudes studiedly casual: these were the captain, the helmsman and the deckhand.

"Now," Fairchild said, "let's all get started at the same time. Talliaferro, you keep the rope straight, and Julius—" he glanced over his shoulder, sweating, marshaling his crew. "Durn that shore," he exclaimed in an annoyed tone, "there it is again." They were nearly ashore a second time. Commotion, and more sweat and a virulent invisible fire; and after a while the tender acquiesced reluctantly and again they attained the necessary offing.

"Give way, all!" Mrs. Wiseman cried. They dug their oars anew.

"Mine hurts my hands," Mark Frost complained. "Is it moving, Ernest?" The tender was off the yacht's quarter: the bows of the yacht pointed inshore of them. Mr. Talliaferro rose cautiously and knelt on the seat, putting his hand on Jenny's shoulder to steady himself.

"Not yet," he replied.

"Pull all you know, men," Fairchild panted, releasing one hand momentarily and batting it madly about his face. The crew pulled and sweated, goaded unto madness with invisible needles of fire, clashing one another's fingers with their oars, and presently the tender acquired a motion reminiscent of the rocking horses of childhood.

"The rope's becoming loose," Mr. Talliaferro called in a warning tone.

"Pull," Fairchild urged them, gritting his teeth. Mark Frost groaned dismally and released one hand to fan it across his face.

"It's still loose," Mr. Talliaferro said after a time.

"She must be moving then," Fairchild panted.

"Maybe it's because we aren't singing," Mrs. Wiseman suggested presently, resting on her oar. "Don't you know any deep sea chanteys, Dawson?"

"Let Julius sing: he ain't doing anything," Fairchild answered. "Pull, you devils!"

Mr. Talliaferro shrieked suddenly: "She's moving! She's moving!"

They all ceased rowing to stare at the yacht. Sure enough, she was swinging slowly across their stern. "She's moving!" Mr. Talliaferro screamed again, waving his arms. Mrs. Maurier responded madly from the deck of the yacht with her handkerchief; beyond her, the three men sat motionless and casual. "Why don't the fools start the engine?" Fairchild gasped. "Pull!" he roared.

They dipped their oars with new life, flailing the water like mad. The yacht swung slowly; soon she was pointing her prow seaward of them, and continued to swing slowly around. "She's coming off, she's coming off," Mr. Talliaferro chanted in a thin falsetto, his voice breaking, fairly dancing up and down. Mrs. Maurier was shrieking also, waving her handkerchief. "She's coming off," Mr. Talliaferro chanted, standing erect and clutching Jenny's shoulder. "Pull! Pull!"

"All together," Fairchild gasped and the crew repeated it, flailing the water. The yacht was almost broadside to them, now. "She's coming!" Mr. Talliaferro screamed in an ecstasy. "She's co—"

A faint abrupt shock. The tender stopped immediately. They saw the sweet blonde entirety of Jenny's legs and the pink seat of her ribboned undergarment as with a wild despairing cry Mr. Talliaferro plunged overboard, taking Jenny with him, and vanished beneath the waves.

All but his buttocks, that is. They didn't quite vanish, and presently all of Mr. Talliaferro rose in eighteen inches of water and stared in shocked amazement at the branch of a tree directly over his head. Jenny, yet prone in the water, was an indistinguishable turmoil of blondeness and green crêpe and fright. She rose, slipped and fell again, then the Semitic man stepped into the water and picked her up bodily and set her in the boat where she sat and gazed at them with abject beseeching eyes, strangling.

Only Mrs. Wiseman had presence of mind to thump her between the shoulders, and after a dreadful trancelike interval during which they sat clutching their oars and gazing at her while she beseeched them with her eyes, she caught her breath, wailing. Mrs. Wiseman mothered her, holding her draggled unhappy wetness while Jenny wept dreadfully. "He—he sc-scared me so bad," Jenny gasped after a time, shuddering and crying again, utterly abject, making no effort to hide her face.

Mrs. Wiseman made meaningless comforting sounds, holding Jenny in her arms. She borrowed a handkerchief and wiped Jenny's streaming face. Mr. Talliaferro stood in the lake and dripped disconsolately, peering his harried face across Mrs. Wiseman's shoulder. The others sat motionless, holding their oars.

Jenny raised her little wet hands futilely about her face. Then she remarked her hand and she held it before her face, gazing at it. On it was a thinly spreading crimson stain that grew as she watched it, and Jenny wept again with utter and hopeless misery.

"Oh, you've cut your poor hand! Dawson," Mrs. Wiseman said, "you are the most consummate idiot unleashed. You take us right back to that yacht. Don't try to row back: we'll never get there. Can't you pull us back with the rope?"

They could, and Mrs. Wiseman helped Jenny into the bows and the men took their places again. Mr. Talliaferro flitted about in the water with his despairing face. "Jump in," Fairchild told him. "We ain't going to maroon you."

They pulled the tender back to the yacht with chastened expedition. Mrs. Maurier met them at the rail, shrieking with alarm and astonishment. Pete was beside her. The sailors had decreetly vanished.

"What is it? What is it?" Mrs. Maurier chanted, mooning her round alarmed face above them. They brought the tender alongside and held it steady while Mrs. Wiseman helped Jenny across the thwarts and to the rail. Mr. Talliaferro flitted about in a harried distraction, but Jenny shrank from him. "You scared me so bad," she repeated.

Pete leaned over the rail, reaching his hands while Mr. Talliaferro flitted about his victim. The tender rocked, scraping against the hull of the yacht. Pete caught Jenny's hands.

"Hold the boat still, you old fool," he told Mr. Talliaferro fiercely.

*   *   *

His legs were completely numb beneath her weight, but he would not move. He swished the broken branch about her, and at intervals he whipped it across his own back. Her face wasn't so flushed, and he laid his hand again above her heart. At his touch she opened her eyes.

"Hello, David. I dreamed about water. . . . Where've you been all these years?" She closed her eyes again. "I feel better," she said after a while. And then: "What time is it?" He looked at the sun and guessed. "We must go on," she said. "Help me up."

She sat up and a million red ants scurried through the arteries of his legs. She stood, dizzy and swaying, holding to him. "Gee, I'm not worth a damn. Next time you elope you'd better make her stand a physical examination, David. Do you hear? . . . But we must go on: come on, make me walk." She took a few unsteady steps and clutched him again, closing her eyes. "Jesus H, if I ever get out of this alive . . ." She stopped again. "What must we do?" she asked.

"I'll carry you a ways," he said.

"Can you? I mean, aren't you too tired?"

"I'll carry you a ways, until we get somewhere," he repeated.

"I guess you'll have to. . . . But if you were me, I'd leave you flat. That's what I'd do."

He squatted before her and reached back and slid his hands under her knees, and as he straightened up she leaned forward onto his back and put her arms around his neck, clasping the broken branch against his chest. He rose slowly, hitching her legs further around his hips as the constriction of her skirt lessened.

"You're awful nice to me, David," she murmured against his neck, limp upon his back.

*   *   *

Mrs. Wiseman washed and bound Jenny's hand, interestingly; then she scrubbed Jenny's little soft wormlike fingers and cleaned her fingernails while Jenny, naked, dried rosily in the cabined air. Underthings were not difficult, and stockings were simple also. But Jenny's feet were short rather than small, and shoes were a problem. Though Jenny insisted that Mrs. Wiseman's shoes were quite comfortable.

But she was clothed at last and Mrs. Wiseman gathered up the two wet garments gingerly and went to lean her hip against the bunk. The dress Jenny now wore belonged to the girl Patricia and Jenny stood before the mirror, bulging it divinely, examining herself in the mirror, smoothing the dress over her hips with a slow preening motion.

I had no idea there was that much difference between them, the other thought. It's far more exciting than a bathing suit. . . . "Jenny," she said, "I think—really, I— Darling, you simply must not go where men can see you, like that. For Mrs. Maurier's sake, you know; she's having enough trouble as it is, without any rioting."

"Don't it look all right? It feels all right," Jenny answered, trying to see as much of herself as possible in a twelve-inch glass.

"I don't doubt it. You must be able to feel every stitch in it. But we'll have to get something else for you to wear. Slip it off, darling."

Jenny obeyed. "It feels all right to me," she repeated. "It don't feel funny."

"It doesn't look funny, not at all. On the contrary, in fact. That's the trouble with it," the other answered delving busily in her bag.

"I always thought I had the kind of figure that could wear anything," Jenny persisted, holding the dress regretfully in her hands.

"You have," the other told her, "exactly that kind. Terribly like that. Simple and inevitable. Devastating."

"Devastating," Jenny repeated with interest. "There was a kind of funny little man at Mandeville that day . . ." She turned to the mirror again, trying to see as much of herself as possible. "I've been told I have a figure like Dorothy Mackaill's, only not too thin. . . . I think a little flesh is becoming to a girl. Don't you?"

"Devastating," the other agreed again. She rose and held a dark colored dress between her hands. "You'll look worse than ever in this . . . terrible as young widow." . . . She went to Jenny and held the dress against her, contemplative; then still holding the dress between her hands she put her arms around Jenny. "A little flesh is worse than a little dynamite, Jenny," she said soberly, looking at Jenny with her dark, sad eyes. . . . "Does your hand still hurt?"

"It's all right now." Jenny craned her neck, peering downward along her flank. "It's a little long, ain't it?"

"Yours will dry soon." She raised Jenny's face and kissed

her on the mouth. "Slip it on, and we'll hang your things in the sun."

FOUR O'CLOCK

He strode on in the dust, along the endless shimmering road between pines like fixed explosions on the afternoon. The afternoon was an endless unbearable brightness. Their shapeless, merged shadow moved on: two steps more and he would tread upon it and through it as he did the sparse shadows of pines, but it moved on just ahead of him between the faded forgotten ruts, keeping its distance effortlessly in the uneven dust. The dust was fine as powder and unbroken; only an occasional hoofprint, a fading ghost of a forgotten passage. Above, the metallic implacable sky resting upon his bowed neck and her lax, damp weight upon his back and her cheek against his neck, rubbing monotonously against it. Thin fire darted upon him constantly. He strode on.

The dusty road swam into his vision, passed beneath his feet and so behind like an endless ribbon. He found that his mouth was open, drooling, though no moisture came, and his gums took a thin dry texture like cigarette paper. He closed his mouth, trying to moisten his gums.

Trees without tops passed him, marched up abreast of him, topless, and fell behind; the rank roadside grass approached and became monstrous and separate, blade by blade: lizards hissed in it sibilantly ere it faded behind him. Thin unseen fire darted upon him but he didn't even feel it, for in his shoulders and arms there was no longer any sensation at all save that of her lax weight upon his back and the brass sky resting against his neck and her moist cheek rubbing against his neck monotonously. He found that his mouth was open again, and he closed it.

"That's far enough," she said, presently rousing. "Let me down." Their merged shadow blended at intervals with the shadows of the tall topless trees, but beyond the shadow of the trees their blended shadow appeared again, two paces ahead of him. And the road went on ahead of him shimmering and blistered and whiter than salt. "Put me down, David," she repeated.

"No," he said between his dry, rough teeth, above the remote, imperturbable tramping of his heart, "not tired." His heart made a remote sound. Each beat seemed to be somewhere in his head, just behind his eyes; each beat was a red tide that temporarily obscured his vision. But it always ended, then another dull surge blinded him for a moment. But remote, like a tramping of soldiers in red uniforms stepping endlessly across the door of a room where he was, where he crouched trying to look out the door. It was a dull, heavy sound, like a steamer's engines, and he found that he was thinking of water, of a blue monotony of seas. It was a red sound, just back of his eyes.

The road came on, an endless blistering ribbon between worn ruts where nothing had passed for a long time. The sea makes a swishing sound in your ears. Regular. Swish. Swish. Not against your eyes, though. Not against the backs of your eyes. The shadow came out of a blotch of larger shadows cast by trees that had no tops. Two steps more. No, three steps now. Three steps. Getting to be afternoon, getting to be later than it was once. Three steps, then. All right. Man walks on his hind legs; a man can take three steps, a monkey can take three steps, but there is water in a monkey's cage, in a pan. Three steps. All right. One. Two. Three. Gone. Gone. Gone. It's a red sound. Not behind your eyes. Sea. See. Sea. See. You're in a cave, you're in a cave of dark sound, the sound of the sea is outside the cave. Sea. See. See. See. Not when they keep stepping in front of the door.

There was another sound in his ears now, a faint annoying sound, and the weight on his back was shifting of its own volition, thrusting him downward toward the blistering, blanched dust in which he walked, took three steps a man can take three steps and he staggered, trying to shift his numb arms and get a new grip. His mouth was open again and when he tried to shut it, it made a dry, hissing sound. One. Two. Three. One. Two. Three.

"Let me down, I tell you," she repeated, thrusting herself backward. "Look, there's a signboard. Let me down, I tell you. I can walk now."

She thrust herself away from him, twisting her legs from his grasp and forcing him down, and he stumbled and went to his knees. Her feet touched the ground and still astride of his body she braced herself and held him partially up by his shoulders. He stopped at last, on all fours like a beast, his head hanging between his shoulders; and kneeling beside him in the dust she slid her hand under his forehead to lessen the tension on his neck and raised her eyes to the signboard. Mandeville. Fourteen miles, and a crude finger pointing in the direction from which they had come. The front of her dress was damp, blotched darkly with his sweat.

* * *

After the women had hovered Jenny's draggled helpless-ness below decks Fairchild removed his hat and mopped his face, looking about upon his fatuous Frankenstein with a sort of childlike astonishment. Then his gaze came to rest on Mr. Talliaferro's haggard damp despair and he laughed and laughed.

"Laugh you may," the Semitic man told him, "but much more of this sort of humor and you'll be doing your laugh-ing ashore. I think now, if Talliaferro'd start an active protest with you as its immediate object, that we'd all be inclined to support him." Mr. Talliaferro dripped forlornly: an utter and hopeless dejection. The Semitic man looked at him, then he too looked about at the others and upon the now peaceful scene of their recent activities. "One certainly pays a price for art," he murmured, "one really does."

"Talliaferro's the only one who has suffered any actual damage," Fairchild protested. "And I'm just going to buy him off now. Come on, Talliaferro, we can fix you up."

"That won't be sufficient," the Semitic man said, still ominous. "The rest of us have been assailed enough in our vanities to rise from principle."

"Well, then, if I have to, I'll buy you all off," Fairchild answered. He led the way toward the stairs. But he halted again and looked back at them. "Where's Gordon?" he asked. Nobody knew. "Well, no matter. He knows where to come." He went on. "After all," he said, "there are compen-sations for art, ain't there?"

The Semitic man admitted that there were. "Though," he added, "it's a high price to pay for whisky." He descended in his turn. "Yes, we really must get something out of it. We spend enough time on it and suffer enough moral and mental turmoil because of it."

"Sure," Fairchild agreed. "The ones that produce it get a lot from it. They get the boon of keeping their time pretty well filled. And that's a whole lot to expect in this world," he said profoundly, fumbling at his door. It opened at last and he said: "Oh, here you are. Say, you just missed it."

Major Ayers, his neglected tumbler beside him and clutching a book, came up for air when they entered, festooned yet with a kind of affable bewilderment. "Missed what?" he repeated.

They all began to tell him about it at once, producing Mr. Talliaferro as evidence from where he lurked unhappily in their midst, for Major Ayers' inspection and commiseration; and still telling him about it they found seats while Fairchild again assumed the ritual of his hidden suitcase. Major Ayers already had the chair, but the Semitic man attempted the book anyway. "What have you got there?" he asked.

Major Ayers' hearty bewilderment descended upon him again. "I was passing the time," he explained quickly. He stared at the book. "It's quite strange," he said. Then he added: "I mean, the way . . . The way they get their books up nowadays. I like the way they get their books up. Jolly, with colors, y'know. But I—" He considered a moment. "I rather lost the habit of reading at Sandhurst," he explained in a burst of confidence. "And then, on active service constantly . . ."

"War is bad," the Semitic man agreed. "What were you reading?"

"I rather lost the habit of reading at Sandhurst," Major Ayers explained again. He raised the book again.

Fairchild opened a fresh bottle. "Somebody'll have to dig up some more glasses. Mark, see if you can slip back to the kitchen and get one or two more. Let's see the book," he said reaching his hand. The Semitic man forestalled him.

"You go ahead and give us some whisky. I'd rather forget my grief that way, just now."

"But look," Fairchild insisted. The other fended him off.

"Give us some whisky, I tell you," he repeated. "Here's Mark with the glasses. What we need in this country is protection from artists. They even want to annoy us with each other's stuff."

"Go ahead," Fairchild replied equably, "have your joke. You know my opinion of smartness." He passed glasses among them.

"He can't mean that," the Semitic man said, "Just because the *New Republic* gives him hell—"

"But the *Dial* once bought a story of him," Mark Frost said with hollow envy.

"And what a fate for a man in all the lusty pride of his Ohio valley masculinity: immolation in a home for old young ladies of either sex. . . . That atmosphere was too rare for him. Eh, Dawson?"

Fairchild laughed. "Well, I ain't much of an Alpinist. What do you want to be in there for, Mark?"

"It would suit Mark exactly," the Semitic man said, "that vague polite fury of the intellect in which they function. What I can't see is how Mark has managed to stay out of it. . . . But then, if you'll look close enough, you'll find an occasional grain of truth in these remarks which Mark and I make and which you consider merely smart. But you utter things not quite clever enough to be untrue, and while we are marveling at your profundity, you lose courage and flatly contradict yourself the next moment. Why, only that tactless and well meaning God of yours alone knows. Why any one should worry enough about the temporary meaning or construction of words to contradict himself consciously or to feel annoyed when he has done it unconsciously, is beyond me."

"Well, it is a kind of sterility—Words," Fairchild admitted. "You begin to substitute words for things and deeds, like the withered cuckold husband that took the Decameron to bed with him every night, and pretty soon the thing or the deed becomes just a kind of shadow of a certain sound you make by shaping your mouth a certain way. But you have a confusion, too. I don't claim that words have life in themselves. But words brought into a happy conjunction produce something that lives, just as soil and climate and an acorn in proper conjunction will produce a tree. Words are like acorns, you know. Every one of 'em won't make a tree, but if you just have enough of 'em, you're bound to get a tree sooner or later."

"If you just talk long enough, you're bound to say the right thing some day. Is that what you mean?" the Semitic man asked.

"Let me show you what I mean." Fairchild reached again for the book.

"For heaven's sake," the other exclaimed, "let us have this one drink in peace. We'll admit your contention, if that's what you want. Isn't that what you say, Major?"

"No, really," Major Ayers protested, "I enjoyed the book. Though I rather lost the habit of reading at Sa—"

"I like the book myself," Mark Frost said. "My only criticism is that it got published."

"You can't avoid that," Fairchild told him. "It's inevitable; it happens to every one who will take the risk of writing down a thousand coherent consecutive words."

"And sooner than that," the Semitic man added, "if you've murdered your husband or won a gold championship."

"Yes," Fairchild agreed. "Cold print. Your stuff looks so different in cold print. It lends a kind of impersonal authority even to stupidity."

"That's backward," the other said. "Stupidity lends a kind of impersonal authority even to cold print."

Fairchild stared at him. "Say, what did you just tell me about contradicting myself?"

"I can afford to," the other answered. "I never authenticate mine." He drained his glass. "But as for art and artists, I prefer artists: I don't even object to paying my pro rata to feed them, so long as I am not compelled to listen to them."

"It seems to me," Fairchild rejoined, "that you spend a lot of time listening to them, for a man who professes to dislike it and who don't have to."

"That's because I'd have to listen to somebody—artist or shoe clerk. And the artist is more entertaining because he knows less about what he is trying to do. . . . And besides, I talk a little, myself. I wonder what became of Gordon?"

FIVE O'CLOCK

Evening came sad as horns among the trees. The road had dropped downward again into the swamp where amid rank, impenetrable jungle dark streams wallowed aimless and obscene, and against the hidden flame of the west huge trees brooded bearded and ancient as prophets out of Genesis. David lay at full length at the roadside. He had lain there a long time, but at last he sat up and looked about for her.

She stood beside a cypress, up to her knees in thick water, her arms crossed against the tree trunk and her face hidden in her arms, utterly motionless. About them, a moist green twilight filled with unseen fire.

"David." Her voice was muffled by her arms, and after it, there was no sound in this fecund, timeless twilight of trees. He sat beside the road, and presently she spoke again. "It's a mess, David. I didn't know it was going to be like this." He made a harsh, awkward sound, as though it were some one else's voice he was trying to speak with. "Hush," she said. "It's my fault: I got you into this. I'm sorry, David."

These trees were thicker, huger, more ancient than any yet, amid the brooding twilight of their beards. "What must we do now, David?" After a while she raised her head and looked at him and repeated the question.

He answered slowly: "Whatever you want to do."

She said: "Come here, David." And he got slowly to his feet and stepped into the black, thick water and went to her, and for a while she looked at him soberly, without moving. Then she turned from the tree and came nearer and they stood in the foul, black water, embracing. Suddenly she clasped him fiercely. "Can't you do something about it? Can't you make it different? Must it be like this?"

"What do you want me to do?" he asked slowly in that voice which was not his. She loosed her arms, and he repeated as though prompted: "You do whatever you want to."

"I'm damn sorry, David, for getting you into this. Josh is right: I'm just a fool." She writhed her body beneath her dress, whimpering again. "They hurt me so damn bad," she moaned.

"We must get out of this," he said. "You tell me what you want to do."

"It will be all right, if I do what I think is best?" she asked quickly, staring at him with her grave opaque eyes. "You swear it will?"

"Yes," he answered with utter weariness. "You do whatever you want to."

She became at once passive, a submissive docility in his embrace. But he stood holding her loosely, not even looking at her. As abruptly her passiveness faded and she said: "You're all right, David. I'd like to do something for you. Pay you back, some way." She looked at him again and found that he was looking at her. "David! Why, David! Don't feel that way about it!" But he continued to look at her with his quiet utter yearning. "David, I'm sorry, sorry, sorry. What can I do about it? Tell me: I'll do it. Anything, just anything."

"It's all right," he said.

"But it isn't. I want to make it up to you, some way, for getting you into this." His head was averted: he seemed to be listening. Then the sound came again across the afternoon, among the patriarchal trees—a faint, fretful sound.

"There's a boat," he said. "We are close to the lake."

"Yes," she agreed. "I heard it a while ago. I think it's coming in near here." She moved, and he released her. She listened again, touching his shoulder lightly. "Yes, it's coming this way. You'd better take your shirt again. Turn your back, please, David."

SIX O'CLOCK

"Sure, I know where your boat is, seen her hove to when I come along. In mighty shaller water, too. Ain't more'n three miles down the lake," the man told them, setting a galvanized pail of water on the edge of the veranda. His house stood on piles driven into the moist earth at the edge of the jungle. Before it a dark broad stream was seemingly without any movement at all between rigid palisades of trees.

The man stood on the veranda and watched her while she poured dippersful of heavenly water on her head. The water ran through her hair and dripped down her face, sopping her dress, while the man stood and watched her. His blue collarless shirt was fastened at the throat by a brass collar button, his sweat-stained suspenders drew his faded cotton trousers snugly over his paunch. His loose jowls moved rhythmically and he spat brownly upon the earth at their feet, barely averting his head.

"You folks been wandering around in the swamp all day?" he asked staring at her with his pale, heavy eyes, roving his gaze slowly up her muddy stockings and her stained dress. "What you want to go back fer, now? Feller got enough, huh?" He spat again, and made a heavy sound of disparagement and disgust. "Ain't no such thing as enough. Git a real man, next time." He looked at David and asked him a question, using an unprintable verb.

Anger, automatic and despite his weariness, fired him slowly, but she forestalled him. "Let's get back to the boat, first," she said to him. She looked at the man again, meeting his pale heavy stare. "How much?" she asked briskly.

"Five dollars." He glanced at David again. "In advance."

David put his hand to his waist. "With my money," she said quickly, watching him as he dug into his watch pocket and extracted a single bill, neatly folded. "No, no: with mine," she insisted peremptorily, staying his hand. "Where's mine?" she asked, and he drew from his trousers her crumpled mass of notes, and she took it.

The man accepted the bill and spat again. He descended heavily from the porch and led the way down to the water where his launch was moored. They got in and he cast off and thrust the boat away from the shore and bent heavily over the engine. "Yes, sir, that's the way with these town fellers. No guts. Next time, come over to this side and git you a real man. I kin git off most any day. And I won't be honing to git home by sundown, neither," he added, looking back over his shoulder.

"Shut your mouth," she told him sharply. "Make him shut up, David." The man paused, staring at her with his pale sleepy eyes.

"Now, look-a-here," he began heavily.

"Shut up and start your flivver," she repeated. "You've got your money, so let's go if we are going."

"Well, that's all right, too. I like 'em to have a little git-up-and-git to 'em." He stared at her with his lazy drooping eyes, chewing rhythmically, then he called her a name.

David rose from his seat, but she restrained him with one hand and she cursed the man fluently and glibly. "Now get started," she finished. "If he opens his head again, David, just knock him right out of the boat."

The man snarled his yellow teeth at them, then he bent again over the engine. Its fretful clamor rose soon and the boat slid away circling, cutting the black motionless water. Ahead, soon, there was a glint of space beyond the trees, a glint of water; and soon they had passed from the bronze nave of the river onto the lake beneath the rushing soundless wings of sunset and a dying glory of day under the cooling brass bowl of the sky.

*   *   *

The *Nausikaa* was more like a rosy gull than ever in the sunset, squatting sedately upon the darkening indigo of the water, against the black metallic trees. The man shut off his fussy engine and the launch slid up alongside and the man caught the rail and held his boat stationary, watching her muddy legs as she climbed aboard the yacht.

No one was in sight. They stood at the rail and looked downward upon his thick backside while he spun the fly-wheel again. The engine caught at last and the launch circled away from the yacht and headed again into the sunset while the fussy engine desecrated the calm of water and sky and trees. Soon the boat was only a speck in the fading path of the sunset.

"David?" she said, when it had gone. She turned and put her firm tanned hand on his breast, and he turned his head also and looked at her with his beastlike longing.

"It's all right," he said after a time. She put her arms

round him again, sexless and hard, drawing his cheek down
to her sober moist kiss. This time he didn't move his head.

"I'm sorry, David."

"It's all right," he repeated. She laid her hands flat on his
chest and he released her. For a time they gazed at each other.
Then she left him and crossed the deck and descended the
companionway without looking back, and so left him and
the evening from which the sun had gone suddenly and into
which night was as suddenly come, and across which the
fretful thin sound of the launch came yet faintly along the
dreaming water, beneath the tarnished sky where stars were
already pricking like a hushed magical blooming of flowers.

*   *   *

She found the others at dinner in the saloon, since what
breeze there was was still offshore and the saloon was
screened. They greeted her with various surprise, but she
ignored them and her aunt's round suffused face, going
haughtily to her place.

"Patricia," Mrs. Maurier said at last, "where have you
been?"

"Walking," the niece snapped. In her hand she carried a
small crumpled mass and she put this on the table, separating the notes and smoothing them into three flat sheaves.

"Patricia," said Mrs. Maurier again.

"I owe you six dollars," she told Miss Jameson, putting
one of the sheaves beside her plate. "You only had a dollar,"
she informed Mrs. Wiseman, passing a single note across
the table to her. "I'll pay you the rest of yours when we get

home," she told her aunt, reaching across Mr. Talliaferro's shoulder with the third sheaf. She met her aunt's apoplectic face again. "I brought your steward back, too. So you haven't got anything to kick about."

"Patricia," Mrs. Maurier said. She said, chokingly: "Mr. Gordon, didn't he come back with you?"

"He wasn't with me. What would I want to take him along for? I already had one man."

Mrs. Maurier's face became dreadful, and as the blood died swooning in her heart she had again that brief vision of floating inert buttocks, later to wash ashore with that inopportune and terrible implacability of the drowned. "Patricia," she said dreadfully.

"Oh, haul in your sheet," the niece interrupted wearily. "You're jibbing. Gosh, I'm hungry." She sat down and met her brother's cold gaze. "And you too, Josh," she added, taking a piece of bread.

The nephew glanced briefly at his aunt's wrung face. "You ought to beat hell out of her," he said calmly, going on with his dinner.

NINE O'CLOCK

"But I saw him about four o'clock," Fairchild argued. "He was in the boat with us. Didn't you see him, Major? But that's so: you were not with us. You saw him, Mark, didn't you?"

"He was in the boat when we started. I remember that. But I don't remember seeing him after Ernest fell out."

"Well, I do. I know I saw him on deck right after we got back. But I can't remember seeing him in the boat after

Jenny and Talliaferro . . . Ah, he's all right, though. He'll
show up soon. He ain't the sort to get drowned."

"Don't be too sure of that," Major Ayers said. "There are
no women missing, you know."

Fairchild laughed his burly appreciative laugh. Then he
met Major Ayers' glassy solemn stare, and ceased. Then he
laughed once more, somewhat after the manner of one feeling his way into a dark room, and ceased again, turning on
Major Ayers his trustful baffled expression. Major Ayers said:

"This place to which these young people went to-day—"
"Mandeville," the Semitic man supplied. "—what sort of a
place is it?" They told him. "Ah, yes. They have facilities for
that sort of thing, eh?"

"Well, not more than usual," the Semitic man answered,
and Fairchild said, still watching Major Ayers with a sort of
cautious bafflement:

"Not any more than you can carry along with you. We
Americans always carry our own facilities with us. It's living
high tension go-getting lives like we do in this country, you
see."

Major Ayers glared at him politely. "Somewhat like the
Continent," he suggested after a time.

"Not exactly," the Semitic man said. "In America you
often find an H in caste." Fairchild and Major Ayers stared
at the Semitic man.

"As well as a cast in chaste," Mark Frost put in. Fairchild
and Major Ayers now stared at him, watching him while he
lit a fresh cigarette from the stub of his present one, and left
his chair and went to lie at full length on the deck.

"Why not?" the Semitic man took him up. "Love itself
is stone blind."

"It has to be," Mark Frost answered. Major Ayers stared from one to the other for a while. He said:

"This Mandeville, now. It is a convention, eh? A local convention?"

"Convention?" Fairchild repeated.

"I mean, like our Gretna Green. You ask a lady there, and immediately there is an understanding: saves unnecessary explanations and all that."

"I thought Gretna Green was a place where they used to go to get marriage licenses in a hurry," Fairchild said suspiciously.

"It was, once," Major Ayers agreed. "But during the Great Fire all the registrars' and parsons' homes were destroyed. And in those days communication was so poor that word didn't get about until a fortnight or so later. In the meantime quite a few young people had gone there in all sincerity, you know, and were forced to return the next day without benefit of clergy. Of course the young ladies durst not tell until matters were remedied, which, during those unsettled times, might be any time up to a month or so. But by that time, of course, the police had heard of it—London police always hear of things in time, you know."

"And so, when you go to Gretna Green now, you get a policeman," the Semitic man said.

"You've Yokohama in mind," Major Ayers answered as gravely. "Of course, they are native policemen," he added.

"Like whitebait," the Semitic man suggested.

"Or sardines," Mark Frost corrected.

"Or sardines," Major Ayers agreed suavely. He sucked violently at his cold pipe while Fairchild stared at him with intrigued bewilderment.

"But this young lady, the one who popped off with the steward. And came back the same day. . . . Is this customary with your young girls? I ask for information," he added quickly. "Our young girls don't do that, you know; with us, only decayed countesses do that—cut off to Italy with chauffeurs and second footmen. And they never return before nightfall. But our young girls . . ."

"Art," the Semitic man explained succinctly. Mark Frost elaborated: -

"In Europe, being an artist is a form of behavior; in America, it's an excuse for a form of behavior."

"Yes. But, I say—" Major Ayers mused again, sucking violently at his cold pipe. Then: "She's not the one who did that tweaky little book, is she? The syphilis book?"

"No. That was Julius' sister; the one named Eva," Fairchild said. "This one that eloped and then came back ain't an artist at all. It's just the artistic atmosphere of the boat, I guess."

"Oh," said Major Ayers. "Strange," he remarked. He rose and thumped his pipe against his palm. Then he blew through the stem and put it in his pocket. "I think I shall go below and have a whisky. Who'll come along?"

"I guess I won't, right now," Fairchild decided. The Semitic man said later on. Major Ayers turned to the prone poet.

"And you, old thing?"

"Bring it up to us," Mark Frost suggested. But Fairchild vetoed this. The Semitic man supported him and Major Ayers departed.

"I wish I had a drink," Mark Frost said.

"Go down and have one, then," Fairchild told him. The poet groaned.

The Semitic man lighted his cigar again and Fairchild spoke from his tentative bewilderment. "That was interesting, about Gretna Green, wasn't it? I didn't know about that. Never read it anywhere, I mean. But I guess there's lots of grand things in the annals of all the people that never get into the history books." The Semitic man chuckled. Fairchild tried to see his face in the obscurity. Then he said:

"Englishmen are funny folks: always kidding you at the wrong time. Things just on the verge of probability, and just when you have made up your mind to take it one way, you find they meant it the other." He mused a while in the darkness.

"It was kind of nice, wasn't it? Young people, young men and girls caught in that strange hushed magic of sex and the mystery of intimate clothing and functions and all, and of lying side by side in the darkness, telling each other things . . . that's the charm of virginity: telling each other things. Virginity don't make any difference as far as the body's concerned. Young people running away together in a flurry of secrecy and caution and desire, and getting there to find" . . . again he turned his kind, baffled face toward his friend. He continued after a while.

"Of course the girls would be persuaded, after they'd come that far, wouldn't they? You know—strange surroundings, a strange room like an island in an uncharted sea full of monsters like landlords and strangers and such; the sheer business of getting their bodies from place to place and feeding 'em and caring for 'em; and your young man thwarted and lustful and probably fearful that you'd change your mind and back out altogether, and a strange room all secret and locked and far away from familiar things and you young and soft and nice to look at and knowing it, too. . . . Of course they'd be persuaded.

"And, of course, when they got back home they wouldn't tell, not until another parson turned up and everything was all regular again. And maybe not then. Maybe they'd whisper it to a friend some day, after they'd been married long enough to prefer talking to other women to talking to their husbands, while they were discussing the things women talk about. But they wouldn't tell the young unmarried ones, though. And if they, even a year later, ever got wind of another one being seen going there or coming away . . . They are such practical creatures, you know: only men hold to conventions for moral reasons."

"Or from habit," the Semitic man added.

"Yes," Fairchild agreed. . . . "I wonder what became of Gordon."

* * *

Jenny remarked his legs, tweeded. How can he stand them heavy clothes in this weather, she thought with placid wonder, calling him soundlessly as he passed. His purposeful stride faltered and he came over beside her.

"Enjoying the evening, eh?" he suggested affably, glaring down at her in the darkness. Inside her borrowed clothes she was rife as whipped cream, blonde and perishable as an expensive pastry.

"Kind of," she admitted. Major Ayers leaned his elbows on the rail.

"I was on my way below," he told her.

"Yes, sir," Jenny agreed, passive in the darkness, like an

erotic lightning bug projecting that sense of himself surrounded, enclosed by the sweet, cloudy fire of her thighs, as young girls will. Major Ayers looked down at her vague, soft head. Then he jerked his head sharply, glaring about.

"Enjoying the evening, eh?" he asked again.

"Yes, sir," Jenny repeated. She bloomed like a cloying heavy flower. Major Ayers moved restively. Again he jerked his head as if he had heard his name spoken. Then he looked at Jenny again.

"Are you a native of New Orleans?"

"Yes, sir. Esplanade."

"I beg pardon?"

"Esplanade. Where I live in New Orleans," she explained. "It's a street," she added after a while.

"Oh," Major Ayers murmured. . . . "Do you like living there?"

"I don't know. I always lived there." After a time she added: "It's not far."

"Not far, eh?"

"No, sir." She stood motionless beside him and for the third time Major Ayers jerked his head quickly, as though some one were trying to attract his attention.

"I was on my way below," he repeated. Jenny waited a while. Then she murmured:

"It's a fine night for courting."

"Courting?" Major Ayers repeated.

"With dates." Major Ayers stared down upon her hushed, soft hair. "When boys come to see you," she explained. "When you go out with the boys."

"Go out with boys," Major Ayers repeated. "To Mandeville, perhaps?"

"Sometimes," she agreed. "I've been there."

"Do you go often?"

"Why . . . sometimes," she repeated.

"With boys, eh? With men, too, hey?"

"Yes, sir," Jenny answered with mild surprise. "I don't guess anybody would just go there by herself."

Major Ayers calculated heavily. Jenny stood docile and rife, projecting her little enticing aura, doing her best. "I say," he said presently, "suppose we pop down there to morrow—you and I?"

"To-morrow?" Jenny repeated with soft astonishment.

"To-night, then," he amended. "What d'ye say?"

"To-night? Can we get there to-night? It's kind of late, ain't it? How'll we get there?"

"Like those people who went this morning did. There's a tram or a bus, isn't there? Or a train at the nearest village?"

"I don't know. They come back in a boat."

"Oh, a boat." Major Ayers considered a moment. "Well, no matter: we'll wait until to-morrow, then. We'll go to-morrow, eh?"

"Yes, sir," Jenny repeated tirelessly, passive and rife, projecting her emanation. Once more Major Ayers looked about him. Then he moved his hand from the rail and as Jenny, seeing the movement, turned to him with a slow unreluctance, he chucked her under the chin.

"Right, then," he said briskly, moving away. "To-morrow it is." Jenny gazed after him in passive astonishment and he turned and came back to her, and giving her an intimate inviting glare he chucked her again under her soft surprised chin. Then he departed permanently.

Jenny gazed after his tweedclad dissolving shape, watching him out of sight. He sure is a foreigner, she told herself. She sighed.

*   *   *

The water lapped at the hull of the yacht with little sounds, little hushed sounds like boneless hands might make, and she leaned again over the rail, gazing downward into the dark water.

He would be refined as anybody, she mused to herself. Being her brother . . . more refined, because she had been away all day with that waiter in the dining room. . . . But maybe the waiter was refined, too. Except I never found many boys that . . . I guess her aunt must have jumped on her. I wonder what she'd 'a' done when they come back, if we'd got the boat started and went away . . . and now that redheaded man and She says he's drowned. . . .

Jenny gazed into the dark water, thinking of death, of being helpless in that terrible suffocating resilience of water, feeling again that utter and dreadful helpfulness of terror and fear. So when Mr. Talliaferro was suddenly and silently beside her, touching her, she recognized him by instinct. And feeling again her world become unstable and shifting beneath her, feeling all familiar solid things fall away from under her and seeing familiar faces and objects are swooping away from her as she plunged from glaring sunlight through a timeless interval into Fear like a green lambence straying to receive her, she was stark and tranced. But at last she could move again, screaming.

"You scared me so bad," she gasped piteously, shrinking

from him. She turned and ran, ran toward light, toward the
security of walls.

*   *   *

The room was dark: no sound within it, and after the dim
spaciousness of the deck it seemed close and hot. But here
were comfortable walls and Jenny snapped on the light and
entered, entered into an atmosphere of familiarity. Here
was a vague ghost of the scent she liked and with which
she had happily been impregnated when she came aboard
and which had not yet completety died away, and the thin
sharp odor of lilacs which she had come to associate with
Mrs. Wiseman and which lingered also in the room, and the
other's clothing, and her own comb on the dressing table
and the bright metal cylinder of her lipstick beside it.

Jenny looked at her face in the mirror for a while. Then
she removed a garment and returned to gaze at her stain-
less pink-and-whiteness, ineffable, unmarred by any thought
at all. Then she removed the rest of her clothes, and again
before the glass she passed her comb through thc drowsing
miniature Golconda of her hair, then she got her naked
body placidly into bed, as was her habit since three nights.

But she didn't turn out the light. She lay in her berth,
gazing up at the smug glare of light upon the painted unbroken sweep of the ceiling. Time passed while she lay rosy
and motionless, measured away by the small boneless hands
of water lapping against the hull beyond the port; and she
could hear feet also, and people moving about and making
sounds.

She didn't know what it was she wanted, except it was something. So she lay on her back rosy and quiet beneath the unshaded glare of the inadequate light, and after a while she thought that maybe she was going to cry. Maybe that was it, so she lay naked and rosy and passive on her back, waiting to begin.

She could still hear people moving about: voices and feet, and she kept waiting for that first taste of crying that comes into your throat before you really get started—that feeling that there are two little salty canals just under your ears when you feel sorry for yourself, and that other kind of feeling you have at the base of your nose. Only my nose don't get red when I cry, she thought, in a placid imminent misery of sadness and meaningless despair, waiting passive and still and without dread for it to begin. But before it began, Mrs. Wiseman entered the room.

She came over to Jenny and Jenny looked up and saw the other's dark small head, like a deer's head, against the light, and that dark intent way the other had of looking at her; and presently Mrs. Wiseman said:

"What is it, Jenny? What's the matter?"

But she had forgotten what it was, almost: all she could remember was that there had been something; but now that the other had come Jenny could hardly remember that she had forgotten anything even, and so she just lay and looked up at the other's dark slender head against the unshaded light.

"Poor child, you have had a hard day, haven't you?" She put her hand on Jenny's brow, smoothing back the fine hushed gold of Jenny's hair, stroking her hand along Jenny's cheek. Jenny lay quiet under the hand, drowsing her eyes like a stroked kitten, and then she knew she could cry all right, whenever she wanted to. Only it was almost as much fun just lying here and knowing you could cry whenever you got ready to, as the crying itself would be. She opened her blue ineffable eyes.

"Do you suppose he's really drowned?" she asked. Mrs. Wiseman's hand stroked Jenny's cheek, pushing her hair upward and away from her brow.

"I don't know, darling," she answered soberly. "He's a luckless man. And anything may happen to a luckless man. But don't you think about that any more. Do you hear?" She leaned her face down to Jenny's. "Do you hear?" she said again.

*   *   *

"No," Fairchild said, "he ain't the sort to get drowned. Some people just ain't that sort. . . . I wonder," he broke off suddenly and gazed at his companions. "Say, do you suppose he went off because he thought that girl was gone for good?"

"Drowned himself for love?" Mark Frost said. "Not in this day and time. People suicide because of money and disease: not for love."

"I don't know about that," Fairchild objected. "They used to die because of love. And human nature don't change. Its actions achieve different results under different conditions, but human nature don't change."

"Mark is right," the Semitic man said. "People in the old books died of heartbreak also, which was probably merely some ailment that any modern surgeon or veterinarian could cure out of hand. But people do not die of love. That's the reason love and death in conjunction have such an undying appeal in books: they are never very closely associated anywhere else."

"But as for a broken heart in this day of general literacy and facilities for disseminating the printed word—" he made a sound of disparagement. "Lucky he who believes that his heart is broken: he can immediately write a book and so take revenge (what is more terrible than the knowledge that the man you just knocked down discovered a coin in the gutter while getting up?) on him or her who damaged his or her ventricles. Besides cleaning up in the movies and magazines. No, no," he repeated, "you don't commit suicide when you are disappointed in love. You write a book."

"I don't know about that," repeated Fairchild stubbornly. "People will do anything. But I suppose it takes a fool to believe that and act on that principle." Beyond the eastern horizon was a rumor of pale silver, pallid and chill and faint, and they sat for a while in silence, thinking of love and death. The red eye of a cigarette twelve inches from the deck: this was Mark Frost. Fairchild broke the silence.

"The way she went off with Da—the steward. It was kind of nice, wasn't it? And came back. No excuses, no explanations—'think no evil' you know. That's what these postwar young folks have taught us. Only old folks like Julius and me would ever see evil in what people, young people, do. But then, I guess folks growing up into the manner of looking at life that we inherited, would find evil in anything where inclination wasn't subservient to duty. We were taught to believe that duty is infallible, or it wouldn't be . duty, and if it were just unpleasant enough, you got a mark in heaven, sure. . . . But maybe it ain't so different, taken one generation by another. Most of our sins are vicarious, anyhow. I guess when you are young you have too much fun just being, to sin very much. But it's kind of nice, being young in this generation."

"Surely. We all think that, when our arteries begin to harden," the Semitic man rejoined. "Not only are most of our sins vicarious, but most of our pleasures are too. Look at our books, our stage, the movies. Who supports 'em? Not the young folks. They'd rather walk around or just sit and hold each other's hands."

"It's a substitute," Fairchild said. "Don't you see?"

"Substitute for what? When you are young and in love yesterday and out to-day and in again to-morrow, do you know anything about love? Is it anything to you except a rather dreadful mixture of jealousy and thwarted desires and interference with that man's world which after all, we all prefer, and nagging and maybe a little pleasure like a drug? It's not the women you sleep with that you remember, you know."

"No, thank God," Fairchild said. The other continued:

"It's the old problem of the aristocracy over and over: a natural envy of that minority which is at liberty to commit all the sins which the majority cannot stop earning a living long enough to commit." He lit his cigar again. "Young people always shape their lives as the preceding generation requires of them. I don't mean exactly that they go to church when they are told to, for instance, because their elders expect it of them—though God only knows what other reason they could possibly have for going to church as it is conducted nowadays, with a warden to patrol the building in the urban localities and in the rural districts squads of K.K.K.'s beating the surrounding copses and all those traditional retreats that in the olden days enabled the church to produce a soul for every one it saved. But youth in general lives unquestioningly according to the arbitrary precepts of its elders.

"For instance, a generation ago higher education was not considered so essential, and young people grew up at home into the convention that the thing to do was to get married at twenty-one and go to work immediately, regardless of one's equipment or inclination or aptitude. But now they grow up into the convention that youth, that being under thirty years of age, is a protracted sophomore course without lectures, in which one must spend one's entire time dressed like a caricature, drinking homemade booze and pawing at the opposite sex in the intervals of being arrested by traffic policemen.

"A few years ago a so called commercial artist (groan, damn you) named John Held began to caricature college life, cloistered and otherwise, in the magazines; ever since then college life, cloistered and otherwise, has been busy caricaturing John Held. It is expected of them by their elders, you see. And the young people humor them: young people are far more tolerant of the inexplicable and dangerous vagaries of their elders than the elders ever were or ever will be of the natural and harmless foibles of their children. . . . But perhaps they both enjoy it."

"I don't know," Fairchild said. "Not even the old folks would like to be surrounded by people making such a drama of existence. And the young folks wouldn't like it, either: young people have so many other things to do, you know. I think . . ." His voice ceased, died into darkness and a faint lapping sound of water. The moon had swum up out of the east again, that waning moon of decay, worn and affable and cold. It was a magic on the water, a magic of pallid and fleshless things. The red eye of Mark Frost's cigarette arced slow and lateral in his invisible hand, returned to its station twelve inches above the deck, and glowed and faded like a pulse. "You see," Fairchild added like an apology, "I believe in young love in the spring, and things like that. I guess I'm a hopeless sentimentalist."

The Semitic man grunted. Mark Frost said: "Virtue through abjectness and falsification: immolation of insincerity." Fairchild ignored him, wrapped in this dream of his own.

"When youth goes out of you, you get out of it. Out of life, I mean. Up to that time you just live; after that, you are aware of living and living becomes a conscious process. Like thinking does in time, you know. You become conscious of thinking, and then you start right off to think in words. And first thing you know, you don't have thoughts in your mind at all: you just have words in it. But when you are young, you just be. Then you reach a stage where you do. Then a stage where you think, and last of all, where you remember. Or try to."

"Sex and death," said Mark Frost sepulchrally, arcing the red eye of his cigarette, "a blank wall on which sex casts a shadow, and the shadow is life." The Semitic man grunted again, immersed in one of his rare periods of uncommunicativeness. The moon climbed higher, the pallid unmuscled belly of the moon, and the *Nausikaa* dreamed like a silver gull on the dark restless water.

"I don't know," Fairchild said again. "I never found anything shadowy about life, people. Least of all, about my own doings. But it may be that there are shadowy people in the world, people to whom life is a kind of antic shadow. But people like that make no impression on me at all, I can't seem to get them at all. But this may be because I have a kind of firm belief that life is all right." Mark Frost had cast away his final cigarette and was now a long prone shadow. The Semitic man was motionless also, holding his dead cigar.

"I was spending the summer with my grandfather, in Indiana. In the country. I was a boy then, and it was a kind of family reunion, with aunts and cousins that hadn't seen each other in years. Children, too, all sizes.

"There was a girl that I remember, about my age, I reckon. She had blue eyes and a lot of long, prim, golden curls. This girl, Jenny, must have looked like her, when she was about twelve. I didn't know the other children very well, and besides I was used to furnishing my own diversion anyway; so I just kind of hung around and watched them doing the things children do. I didn't know how to go about getting acquainted with them. I'd seen how the other newcomers would do it, and I'd kind of plan to myself how I'd go about it: what I'd say when I went up to them. . . ." He ceased and mused for a time in a kind of hushed surprise. "Just like Talliaferro," he said at last, quietly. "I hadn't thought of that before." He mused for a time. Then he spoke again.

"I was kind of like a dog going among strange dogs. Scared, kind of, but acting haughty and aloof. But I watched them. The way she made up to them, for instance. The day after she came she was the leader, always telling them what to do next. She had blue dresses, mostly." Mark Frost snored in the silence. The *Nausikaa* dreamed like a gull on the dark water.

"This was before the day of water works and sewage systems in country homes, and this one had the usual outhouse. It was down a path from the house. In the late summer there were tall burdocks on either side of the path, taller than a twelve-year-old boy by late August. The outhouse was a small square frame box kind of thing, with a partition separating the men from the women inside.

"It was a hot day, in the middle of the afternoon. The others were down in the orchard, under the trees. From where I had been, in a big tree in the yard, I could see them, and the girls' colored dresses in the shade; and when I climbed down from the tree and went across the back yard and through the gate and along the path toward the privy I could still see them occasionally through gaps in the burdocks. They were sitting around in the shade, playing some game, or maybe just talking.

"I went on down the path and went inside, and when I turned to shut the door to the men's side, I looked back. And I saw her blue dress kind of shining, coming along the path between the tall weeds. I couldn't tell if she had seen me or not, but I knew that if I went back I'd have to pass her, and I was ashamed to do this. It would have been different if I'd already been there and was coming away: or it seemed to me that it would have. Boys are that way, you know," he added uncertainly, turning his bewilderment again toward his friend. The other grunted. Mark Frost snored in his shadow.

"So I shut the door quick and stood right quiet, and soon I heard her enter the other side. I didn't know yet if she'd seen me, but I was going to stay quiet as I could until she went away. I just had to do that, it seemed to me.

"Children are much more psychic than adults. More of a child's life goes on in its mind than other people believe. A child can distil the whole gamut of experiences it has never actually known, into a single instant. Anthropology explains a little of it. But not much, because the gaps in human knowledge that have to be bridged by speculation are too large. The first thing a child is taught is the infallibility and necessity of precept, and by the time the child is old enough to add anything to our knowledge of the mind, it has forgotten. The soul sheds every year, like snakes do, I believe. You can't recall the emotions you felt last year: you remember only that an emotion was associated with some physical fact of experience. But all you have of it now is a kind of ghost of happiness and a vague and meaningless regret. Experience: why should we be expected to learn wisdom from experience? Muscles only remember, and it takes repetition and repetition to teach a muscle anything. . . ."

Arcturus, Orion swinging head downward by his knees, in the southern sky an electric lobster fading as the moon rose. Water lapped at the hull of the *Nausikaa* with little sounds.

"So I tiptoed across to the seat. It was hot in there, with the sun beating down on it: I could smell hot resin, even above the smell of the place itself. In a corner of the ceiling there was a dirt dobber's nest—a hard lump of clay with holes in it, stuck to the ceiling, and big green flies made a steady droning sound. I remember how hot it was in there, and that feeling places like that give you—a kind of letting down of the bars of pretense, you know; a kind of submerg-

ing of civilized strictures before the grand implacability of
nature and the physical body. And I stood there, feeling this
feeling and the heat, and hearing the drone of those big flies,
holding my breath and listening for a sound from beyond
the partition. But there wasn't any sound from beyond it, so
I put my head down through the seat."

Mark Frost snored. The moon, the pallid belly of the
moon, inundating the world with a tarnished magic not of
living things, laying her silver fleshless hand on the water
that whispered and lapped against the hull of the yacht. The
Semitic man clutched his dead cigar and he and Fairchild
sat in the implacable laxing of muscles and softening tissue
of their forty odd years, seeing two wide curious blue eyes
into which an inverted surprise came clear as water, and
long golden curls swinging downward above the ordure; and
they sat in silence, remembering youth and love, and time
and death.

ELEVEN O'CLOCK

Mark Frost had roused and with a ghostly epigram had taken
himself off to bed. Later the Semitic man rose and departed,
leaving him with a cigar; and Fairchild sat with his stock-
inged feet on the rail, puffing at the unfamiliar weed. He
could see the whole deck in the pallid moonlight, and presently he remarked some one sitting near the afterrail. How
long this person had been there Fairchild could not have
told, but he was there now, alone and quite motionless, and
there was something about his attitude that unleashed Fairchild's curiosity, and at last he rose from his chair.

It was David, the steward. He sat on a coiled rope and he held something in his hands, between his knees. When Fairchild stopped beside him David raised his head slowly into the moonlight and gazed at the older man, making no effort to conceal that which he held. Fairchild leaned nearer to see. It was a slipper, a single slipper, cracked and stained with dried mud and disreputable, yet seeming still to hold in its mute shape something of that hard and sexless graveness of hers.

After a while David looked away, gazing again out across the dark water and its path of shifting silver, holding the slipper between his hands; and without speaking Fairchild turned and went quietly away.

The Fourth Day

Fairchild waked and lay for a while luxuriously on his back. After a time he turned on his side to doze again, and when he turned he noticed the square of paper lying on the floor, as though it had been thrust under the door. He lay watching it for a while, then he came fully awake, and he rose and crossed the room and picked it up.

> Dear Mr. Fairchild: I am leaveing the boat to day
> I have got a better job I have got 2 days comeing to
> me I will not claim it I am leaveing the boat be fore
> the trip is over tell Mrs. More I have got a better job
> ask her she will pay you $5 dollars of it you loned me
> yours truly
>
> *David West.*

He reread the note, brooding over it, then he folded it and put it in the pocket of his pajama jacket, and poured himself a drink. The Semitic man in his berth snored, profound, defenseless on his back.

Fairchild sat again in his berth, his drink untasted beside him, and he unfolded the note and read it through again, remembering youth, thinking of age and slackening flesh like an old thin sorrow everywhere in the world.

EIGHT O'CLOCK

"Now, don't you worry at all," they reassured Mrs. Maurier, "we can do just as we did yesterday: it will be more fun than ever, that way. Dorothy and I can open cans and warm things. We can get along just as well without a steward as with one. Can't we, Dorothy?"

"It will be like a picnic," Miss Jameson agreed. "Of course, the men will have to help, too," she added, looking at Pete with her pale humorless eyes.

Mrs. Maurier submitted, dogging them with her moaning fatuousness while Mrs. Wiseman and Miss Jameson and the niece opened cans and heated things, smearing dreadfully about the galley with grease and juices and blood from the niece's thumb; opening, at Mark Frost's instigation, a can labeled Beans, which turned out to be green string beans.

But they got coffee made at last, and breakfast was finally not very late. As they had said, it was like a picnic, though there were no ants, as the Semitic man pointed out just before he was ejected from the kitchen.

"We'll open a can of them for you," his sister offered briskly.

Besides, there was still plenty of grapefruit.

AT BREAKFAST

Fairchild—But I saw him after we got back to the yacht. I know I did.

Mark—No, he wasn't in the boat when we came back: I remember now. I never saw him after we changed places, just after Jenny and Ernest fell out.

Julius—That's so. . . . Was he in the boat with us at all? Does anybody remember seeing him in the boat at all?

Fairchild—Sure he was: don't you remember how Mark kept hitting him with his oar? I tell you I saw—

Mark—He was in the boat at first. But after Jenny and—

Fairchild—Sure he was. Don't you remember seeing him after we came back, Eva?

Eva—I don't know. My back was toward all of you while we were rowing. And after Ernest threw Jenny out, I don't remember who was there and who wasn't.

Fairchild—Talliaferro was facing us. Didn't you see him, Talliaferro? And Jenny, Jenny ought to remember. Don't you remember seeing him, Jenny?

Mr. Talliaferro—I was watching the rope, you know.

Fairchild—How about you, Jenny? Don't you remember?

Eva—Now, don't you bother Jenny about it. How could she be expected to remember anything about it? How could anybody be expected to remember anything about such an idiotic—idiotic—

Fairchild—Well, I do. Don't you all remember him going below with us, after we got back?

Mrs. Maurier (wringing her hands)—Doesn't some one remember something about it? It's terrible. I don't know what to do: you people don't seem to realize what a position it puts me in, with such a dreadful thing hanging over me. You people have nothing to lose, but I live here, I have a certain . . . And now a thing like this—

Fairchild—Ah, he ain't drowned. He'll turn up soon: you watch what I say.

The Niece—And if he is drowned, we'll find him all right. The water isn't very deep between here and the shore. (Her aunt gazed at her dreadfully.)

The Nephew—Besides, a dead body always floats after forty-eight hours. All we have to do is wait right here until tomorrow morning: chances are he'll be bumping alongside, ready to be hauled back on board. (Mrs. Maurier screamed. Her scream shuddered and died among her chins and she gazed about at her party in abject despair.)

Fairchild—Aw, he ain't drowned. I tell you I saw—

The Niece—Sure. Cheer up, Aunt Pat. We'll get him back, even if he is. It's not like losing him altogether, you know. If you send his body back, maybe his folks won't even claim your boat or anything.

Eva—Shut up, you children.

Fairchild—But I tell you I saw—

NINE O'CLOCK

Forward, Jenny, the niece, her brother come temporarily out of his scientific shell, and Pete stood in a group; Pete in his straw hat and the nephew with his lean young body and the two girls in their little scanty dresses and awkward with a sort of terrible grace. So flagrantly young they were that it served as a barrier between them and the others, causing even Mr. Talliaferro to lurk nearby without the courage to join them.

"These young girls," Fairchild said. He watched the group, watched the niece and Jenny as they clung to the rail and swung aimlessly back and forth, pivoting on their heels, in a sheer wantonness of young muscles. "They scare me," he admitted. "Not as a possible or probable chastity, you know. Chastity ain't . . ."

"A bodiless illusion multiplied by lack of opportunity," Mark Frost said.

"What?" he asked, looking at the poet. "Well, maybe so." He resumed his own tenuous thought. "Maybe we all have different ideas of sex, like all races do. . . . Maybe us three sitting here are racially unrelated to each other, as regards sex. Like a Frenchman and an Anglo-Saxon and a Mongol, for instance."

"Sex," said the Semitic man, "to an Italian is something like a firecracker at a children's party; to a Frenchman, a business the relaxation from which is making money; to an Englishman, it is a nuisance; to an American, a horserace. Now, which are you?"

Fairchild laughed. He watched the group forward a while. "Their strange sexless shapes, you know," he went on. "We, you and I, grew up expecting something beneath a woman's dress. Something satisfying in the way of breasts and hips and such. But now . . .

"Do you remember the pictures you used to get in packages of cigarettes, or that you saw in magazines in barber shops? Anna Held and Eva Tanguay with shapes like elegant parlor lamp chimneys? Where are they now? Now, on the street, what do you see? Creatures with the uncomplex awkwardness of calves or colts, with two little knobs for breasts and indicated buttocks that, except for their soft look, might well belong to a boy of fifteen. Not satisfying any more; just exciting and monotonous. And mostly monotonous."

"Where," he continued, "are the soft bulging rabbitlike things women used to have inside their clothes? Gone, with the poor Indian and ten cent beer and cambric drawers. But still, they are kind of nice, these young girls: kind of like a thin monotonous flute music or something."

"Shrill and stupid," the Semitic man agreed. He, too, gazed at the group forward for a time. "Who was the fool who said that our clothing, our custom in dress, does not affect the shape of our bodies and our behavior?"

"Not stupid," the other objected. "Women are never stupid. Their mental equipment is too sublimely sufficient to do what little directing their bodies require. And when your mentality is sufficient to your bodily needs, where there is such a perfect mating of capability and necessity, there can't be any stupidity. When women have more intelligence than that, they become nuisances sooner or later. All they need is enough intelligence to move and eat and observe the cardinal precautions of existence—"

"And recognize the current mode in time to standardize themselves," Mark Frost put in.

"Well, yes. And I don't object to that, either," Fairchild said. "As a purely lay brother to the human race, I mean. After all they are merely articulated genital organs with a kind of aptitude for spending whatever money you have; so when they get themselves up to look exactly like all the other ones, you can give all your attention to their bodies."

"How about the exceptions?" Mark Frost asked. "The ones that don't paint or bob their hair?"

"Poor things," Fairchild answered, and the Semitic man said:

"Perhaps there is a heaven, after all."

"You believe they have souls, then?" Fairchild asked.

"Certainly. If they are not born with them, it's a poor creature indeed who can't get one from some man by the time she's eleven years old."

"That's right," Fairchild agreed. He watched the group forward for a time. Then he rose. "I think I'll go over and hear what they're talking about."

*   *   *

Mrs. Wiseman came up and borrowed a cigarette of Mark Frost, and they watched Fairchild's burly retreating back. The Semitic man said: "There's a man of undoubted talent, despite his fumbling bewilderment in the presence of sophisticated emotions."

"Despite his lack of self-assurance, you mean," Mark Frost corrected.

"No, it isn't that," Mrs. Wiseman put in. "You mean the same thing that Julius does: that having been born an American of a provincial midwestern lower middle class family, he has inherited all the lower middle class's awe of Education with a capital E, an awe which the very fact of his difficulty in getting to college and staying there, has increased."

"Yes," her brother agreed. "And the reaction which sheer accumulated years and human experience has brought about in him has swung him to the opposite extreme without destroying that ingrained awe or offering him anything to replace it with, at all. His writing seems fumbling, not because life is unclear to him, but because of his innate humorless belief that, though it bewilder him at times, life at bottom is sound and admirable and fine; and because hovering over this American scene into which he has been thrust, the ghosts of the Emersons and Lowells and other exemplifiers of Education with a capital E who, 'seated on chairs in handsomely carpeted parlors' and surrounded by an atmosphere of half calf and security, dominated American letters in its most healthy American phase 'without heat or vulgarity,' simper yet in a sort of ubiquitous watchfulness. A sort of puerile bravado in flouting while he fears," he explained.

"But," his sister said, "for a man like Dawson there is no better American tradition than theirs—if he but knew it. They may have sat among their objects, transcribing their Greek and Latin and holding correspondences across the Atlantic, but they still found time to put out of their New England ports with the Word of God in one hand and a belaying pin in the other and all sails drawing aloft; and whatever they fell foul of was American. And it was American. And is yet."

"Yes," her brother agreed again. "But he lacks what they had at command among their shelves of discrete books and their dearth of heat and vulgarity—a standard of literature that is international. No, not a standard, exactly: a belief, a conviction that his talent need not be restricted to delineating things which his conscious mind assures him are American reactions."

"Freedom?" suggested Mark Frost hollowly.

"No. No one needs freedom. We cannot bear it. He need only let himself go, let himself forget all this fetich of culture and education which his upbringing and the ghosts of those whom circumstance permitted to reside longer at college than himself, and whom despite himself he regards with awe, assure him that he lacks. For by getting himself and his own bewilderment and inhibitions out of the way by describing, in a manner that even translation cannot injure (as Balzac did) American life as American life is, it will become eternal and timeless despite him.

"Life everywhere is the same, you know. Manners of living it may be different—are they not different between adjoining villages? Family names, profits on a single field or orchard, work influences—but man's old compulsions, duty and inclination: the axis and the circumference of his squirrel cage, they do not change. Details don't matter, details only entertain us. And nothing that merely entertains us can matter, because the things that entertain us are purely speculative: prospective pleasures which we probably will not achieve. The other things only surprise us. And he who has stood the surprise of birth can stand anything."

TEN O'CLOCK

"Gabriel's pants," the nephew said, raising his head. "I've already told you once what I'm making, haven't I?" He had repaired to his retreat in the lee of the wheelhouse, where he would be less liable to interruption. Or so he thought.

Jenny stood beside his chair and looked at him placidly. "I wasn't going to ask you again," she replied without rancor, "I just happened to be walking by here." Then she examined the visible deck space with a brief comprehensive glance. "This is a fine place for courting," she remarked.

"Is, huh?" the nephew said. "What's the matter with Pete?" His knife ceased and he raised his head again. Jenny answered something vaguely. She moved her head again and stood without exactly looking at him, placid and rife, giving him to think of himself surrounded enclosed by the sweet cloudy fire of her thighs, as young girls do. The nephew laid his pipe and his knife aside.

"Where'm I going to sit?" Jenny asked, so he moved over in his canvas chair, making room, and she came with slow unreluctance and squirmed into the sagging chair. "It's a kind of tight fit," she remarked.

. . . Presently the nephew raised his head. "You don't put much pep into your petting," he remarked. So Jenny placidly put more pep into it. . . . After a time the nephew raised his head and gazed out over the water. "Gabriel's pants," he murmured in a tone of hushed detachment, stroking his hand slowly over the placid points of Jenny's thighs, "Gabriel's pants." . . . After a while he raised his head.

"Say," he said abruptly, "where's Pete?"

"Back yonder, somewheres," Jenny answered. "I saw him just before you stopped me."

The nephew craned his neck, looking aft along the deck. Then he uncraned it, and after a while he raised his head. "I guess that's enough," he said. He pushed at Jenny's blonde abandon. "Get up, now. I got my work to do. Beat it, now."

"Gimme time to," Jenny said placidly, struggling out of the chair. It was a kind of tight fit, but she stood erect finally, smoothing at her clothes. The nephew resumed his tools, and so after a while Jenny went away.

ELEVEN O'CLOCK

It was a thin volume bound in dark blue boards and a narrow orange arabesque of esoteric design unbroken across front and back near the top, and the title, in orange, *Satyricon in Starlight*.

"Now, here," said Fairchild, flattening a page under his hand, his heavy hornrimmed spectacles riding his blobby benign face jauntily, "is the Major's syphilis poem. After all, poetry has accomplished something when it causes a man like the Major to mull over it for a while. Poets lack business judgment. Now, if I—"

"Perhaps that's what makes one a poet," the Semitic man suggested, "being able to sustain a fine obliviousness of the world and its compulsions."

"You're thinking of oyster fishermen," Mrs. Wiseman said. "Being a successful poet is being just glittering and obscure and imminent enough in your public life to excuse whatever you might do privately."

"If I were a poet—" Fairchild attempted.

"That's right," the Semitic man said. "Nowadays the gentle art has attained that state of perfection where you don't have to know anything about literature at all to be a poet; and the time is coming when you won't even have to write to be one. But that day hasn't quite arrived yet: you still have to write something occasionally; not very often of course, but still occasionally. And if it's obscure enough every one is satisfied and you have vindicated yourself and are immediately forgotten and are again at perfect liberty to dine with whoever will invite you."

"But listen," repeated Fairchild, "if I were a poet, you know what I'd do? I'd—"

"You'd capture an unattached but ardent wealthy female. Or, lacking that, some other and more fortunate poet would divide a weekend or so with you: there seems to be a noblesse oblige among them," the other answered. "Gentleman poets, that is," he added.

"No," said Fairchild, indefatigable, "I'd intersperse my book with photographs and art studies on ineffable morons in bathing suits or clutching imitation lace window curtains across their middles. That's what I'd do."

"That would damn it as Art," Mark Frost objected.

"You're confusing Art with Studio Life, Mark," Mrs. Wiseman told him. She forestalled him and accepted a cigarette. "I'm all out, myself. Sorry. Thanks."

"Why not?" Mark Frost responded. "If studio life costs you enough, it becomes art. You have to have a good reason to give to your people back home in Ohio or Indiana or somewhere."

"But everybody wasn't born in the Ohio valley, thank God," the Semitic man said. Fairchild stared at him, kind and puzzled, a trifle belligerent. "I speak for those of us who read books instead of write them," he explained. "It's bad enough to grow into the conviction after you reach the age of discretion that you are to spend the rest of your life writing books, but to have your very infancy darkened by the possibility that you may have to write the Great American Novel . . ."

"Oh," Fairchild said. "Well, maybe you are like me, and prefer a live poet to the writings of any man."

"Make it a dead poet, and I'll agree."

"Well . . ." He settled his spectacles. "Listen to this": Mark Frost groaned, rising, and departed. Fairchild read implacably:

> "'On rose and peach their droppings bled,
>   Love a sacrifice has lain,
>   Beneath his hand his mouth is slain,
>   Beneath his hand his mouth is dead—'

"No: wait." He skipped back up the page. Mrs. Wiseman listened restively, her brother with his customary quizzical phlegm.

> "'The Raven bleak and Philomel
>   Amid the bleeding trees were fixed,
>   His hoarse cry and hers were mixed
>   And through the dark their droppings fell

> "'Upon the red erupted rose,
>   Upon the broken branch of peach
>   Blurred with scented mouths, that each
>   To another sing, and close—'"

He read the entire poem through. "What do you make of it?" he asked.

"Mostly words," the Semitic man answered promptly, "a sort of cocktail of words. I imagine you get quite a jolt from it, if your taste is educated to cocktails."

"Well, why not?" Mrs. Wiseman said with fierce protectiveness. "Only fools require ideas in verse."

"Perhaps so," her brother admitted. "But there's no nourishment in electricity, as you poets nowadays seem to believe."

"Well, what would you have them write about, then?" she demanded. "There's only one possible subject to write anything about. What is there worth the effort and despair of writing about, except love and death?"

"That's the feminine of it. You'd better let art alone and stick to artists, as is your nature."

"But women have done some good things," Fairchild objected. "I've read—"

"They bear geniuses. But do you think they care anything about the pictures and music their children produce? That they have any other emotion than a fierce tolerance of the vagaries of the child? Do you think Shakespeare's mother was any prouder of him than, say, Tom o' Bedlam's?"

"Certainly she was," Mrs. Wiseman said. "Shakespeare made money."

"You made a bad choice for comparison," Fairchild said. "All artists are kind of insane. Don't you think so?" he asked Mrs. Wiseman.

"Yes," she snapped. "Almost as insane as the ones that sit around and talk about them."

"Well—" Fairchild stared again at the page under his hand. He said slowly: "It's a kind of dark thing. It's kind of like somebody brings you to a dark door. Will you enter that room, or not?"

"But the old fellows got you into the room first," the

Semitic man said. "Then they asked you if you wanted to go out or not."

"I don't know. There are rooms, dark rooms, that they didn't know anything about at all. Freud and these other—"

"Discovered them just in time to supply our shelterless literati with free sleeping quarters. But you and Eva just agreed that subject, substance, doesn't signify in verse, that the best poetry is just words."

"Yes . . . infatuation with words," Fairchild agreed. "That's when you hammer out good poetry, great poetry. A kind of singing rhythm in the world that you get into without knowing it, like a swimmer gets into a current. Words. . . . I had it once."

"Shut up, Dawson," Mrs. Wiseman said. "Julius can afford to be a fool."

"Words," repeated Fairchild. "But it's gone out of me now. That first infatuation, I mean; that sheer infatuation with and marveling over the beauty and power of words. That has gone out of me. Used up, I guess. So I can't write poetry any more. It takes me too long to say things, now."

"We all wrote poetry, when we were young," the Semitic man said. "Some of us even put it down on paper. But all of us wrote it."

"Yes," repeated Fairchild, turning slowly onward through the volume. "Listen:

"'. . . O spring O wanton O cruel
   baring to the curved and hungry hand
   of march your white unsubtle thighs . . .'"

And listen." He turned onward. Mrs. Wiseman was gazing aft where Jenny and Mr. Talliaferro had come into view and now leaned together upon the rail. The Semitic man listened with weary courtesy.

> "'. . . above unsapped convolvulæ of hills
>   april a bee sipping perplexed with pleasure . . .'

"It's a kind of childlike faith in the efficacy of words, you see, a kind of belief that circumstance somehow will invest the veriest platitude with magic. And, darn it, it does happen at times, let it be historically or grammatically incorrect or physically impossible; let it even be trite: there comes a time when it will be invested with a something not of this life, this world, at all. It's a kind of fire, you know. . . ." He fumbled himself among words, staring at them, at the Semitic man's sad quizzical eyes and Mrs. Wiseman's averted face.

"Somebody, some drug clerk or something, has shredded the tender—and do you know what I believe? I believe that he's always writing it for some woman, that he fondly believes he's stealing a march on some brute bigger or richer or handsomer than he is; I believe that every word a writing man writes is put down with the ultimate intention of impressing some woman that probably don't care anything at all for literature, as is the nature of women. Well, maybe she ain't always a flesh and blood creature. She may be only the symbol of a desire. But she is feminine. Fame is only a by-product. . . . Do you remember, the old boys never even bothered to sign their things. . . . But, I don't know. I suppose nobody ever knows a man's reasons for what he does: you can only generalize from results."

"He very seldom knows his reasons, himself," the other said. "And by the time he has recovered from his astonishment at the unforeseen result he got, he has forgotten what reason he once believed he had. . . . But how can you generalize from a poem? What result does a poem have? You say that substance doesn't matter, has no proper place in a poem. You have," the Semitic man continued with curious speculation, "the strangest habit of contradicting yourself, of fumbling around and then turning tail and beating your listener to the refutation. . . . But God knows, there is plenty of room for speculation in modern verse. Fumbling, too, though the poets themselves do most of this. Don't you agree, Eva?"

His sister answered "What?" turning upon him her dark, preoccupied gaze. He repeated the question. Fairchild interrupted in full career:

"The trouble with modern verse is, that to comprehend it you must have recently passed through an emotional experience identical with that through which the poet himself has recently passed. The poetry of modern poets is like a pair of shoes that only those whose feet are shaped like the cobbler's feet, can wear; while the old boys turned out shoes that anybody who can walk at all can wear—"

"Like overshoes," the other suggested.

"Like overshoes," Fairchild agreed. "But, then, I ain't disparaging. Perhaps the few that the shoes fit can go a lot further than a whole herd of people shod alike could go."

"Interesting, anyway," the Semitic man said, "to reduce the spiritual progress of the race to terms of an emotional migration; esthetic Israelites crossing unwetted a pink sea of dullness and security. What about it, Eva?"

Mrs. Wiseman, thinking of Jenny's soft body, came out of her dream. "I think you are both not only silly, but dull." She rose. "I want to bum another cigarette, Dawson."

He gave her one, and a match, and she left them. Fairchild turned a few pages. "It's kind of difficult for me to reconcile her with this book," he said slowly. "Does it strike you that way?"

"Not so much that she wrote this," the other answered, "but that she wrote anything at all. That anybody should. But there's no puzzle about the book itself. Not to me, that is. But you, straying trustfully about this park of dark and rootless trees which Dr. Ellis and your Germans have recently thrown open to the public . . . You'll always be a babe in that wood, you know. Bewildered, and slightly annoyed; restive, like Ashurbani-pal's stallion when his master mounted him."

"Emotional bisexuality," Fairchild said.

"Yes. But you are trying to reconcile the book and the author. A book is the writer's secret life, the dark twin of a man: you can't reconcile them. And with you, when the inevitable clash comes, the author's actual self is the one that goes down, for you are of those for whom fact is the one that goes down, for you are of those for whom fact and fallacy gain verisimilitude by being in cold print."

"Perhaps so," Fairchild said, with detachment, brooding again on a page. "Listen:

> "*Lips that of thy weary all seem weariest,*
>   *Seem wearier for the curled and pallid sly*
>   *Still riddle of thy secret face, and thy*

Sick despair of its own ill obsessed;
Lay not to heart thy boy's hand, to protest
That smiling leaves thy tired mouth reconciled,
For swearing so keeps thee but ill beguiled
With secret joy of thine own woman's breast.

" 'Weary thy mouth with smiling; canst thou bride
Thyself with thee and thine own kissing slake?
Thy virgin's waking doth itself deride
With sleep's sharp absence, coming so awake,
And near thy mouth thy twinned heart's grief doth hide
For there's no breast between: it cannot break.'

" 'Hermaphroditus,' " he read. "That's what it's about. It's a kind of dark perversion. Like a fire that don't need any fuel, that lives on its own heat. I mean, all modern verse is a kind of perversion. Like the day for healthy poetry is over and done with, that modern people were not born to write poetry any more. Other things, I grant. But not poetry. Kind of like men nowadays are not masculine and lusty enough to tamper with something that borders so close to the unnatural. A kind of sterile race: women too masculine to conceive, men too feminine to beget. . . ."

He closed the book and removed his spectacles slowly. "You and me sitting here, right now, this is one of the most insidious things poetry has to combat. General education has made it too easy for everybody to have an opinion on it. On everything else, too. The only people who should be allowed an opinion on poetry should be poets. But as it is . . . But then, all artists have to suffer it, though: oblivion and scorn and indignation and, what is worse, the adulation of fools."

"And," added the Semitic man, "what is still worse: talk."

TWELVE O'CLOCK

"You must get rather tired of bothering about it," Fairchild suggested as they descended toward lunch. (There was an offshore breeze and the saloon was screened. And besides, it was near the galley.) "Why don't you leave it in your stateroom? Major Ayers is pretty trustworthy, I guess."

"It'll be all right," Pete replied. "I've got used to it. I'd miss it, see?"

"Yes," the other agreed. "New one, eh?"

"I've had it a while." Pete removed it and Fairchild remarked its wanton gay band and the heavy plaiting of the straw.

"I like a panama, myself," he murmured. "A soft hat. . . . This must have cost five or six dollars, didn't it?"

"Yeh," Pete agreed, "but I guess I can look out for it."

"It's a nice hat," the Semitic man said. "Not everybody can wear a stiff straw hat. But it rather suits the shape of Pete's face, don't you think?"

"Yes, that's so," Fairchild agreed. "Pete has a kind of humorless reckless face that a stiff hat just suits. A man with a humorous face should never wear a stiff straw hat. But then, only a humorless man would dare buy one."

Pete preceded them into the saloon. The man's intent was kindly, anyway. Funny old bird. Easy. Easy. Somebody's gutting. Anybody's. Fairchild spoke to him again with a kind of tactful persistence.

"Look here, here's a good place to leave it while you eat. You hadn't seen this place, I reckon. Slip it under here, see? It'll be safe as a church under here until you want it again. Look, Julius, this place was made for a stiff straw hat, wasn't it?" This place was a collapsible serving table of two shelves that let shallowly into the bulkhead: it operated by a spring and anything placed on the lower shelf would be inviolate until some one came along and lowered the shelves again.

"It don't bother me any," Pete said.

"All right," the other answered. "But you might as well leave it here: it's such a grand place to leave a hat. Lots better than the places in theaters. I kind of wish I had a hat to leave there, don't you, Julius?"

"I can hold it all right," Pete said again.

"Sure," agreed Fairchild readily, "but just try it a moment." Pete did so, and the other two watched with interest. "It just fits, don't it? Why not leave it there, just for a trial?"

"I guess not. I guess I'll hold onto it," Pete decided. He took his hat again and when he had taken his seat he slid it into its usual place between the chairback and himself.

Mrs. Maurier was chanting: "Sit down, people," in an apologetic, hopeless tone. "You must excuse things. I had hoped to have lunch on deck, but with the wind blowing from the shore . . ."

"They've found where we are and that we are good to eat, so it doesn't make any difference where the wind blows from," Mrs. Wiseman said, businesslike with her tray.

"And with the steward gone, and things so unsettled," the hostess resumed in antistrophe, roving her unhappy gaze. "And Mr. Gordon—"

"Oh, he's all right," Fairchild said heavily helpful, taking his seat. "He'll show up all right."

"Don't be a fool, Aunt Pat," the niece added. "What would he want to get drowned for?"

"I'm so unlucky," Mrs. Maurier moaned, "things— things happen to me, you see," she explained, haunted with that vision of a pale implacability of water, and sodden pants, and a red beard straying amid the slanting green regions of the sea in a dreadful simulation of life.

"Aw, shucks," the niece protested, "ugly like he is, and so full of himself. . . . He's got too many good reasons for getting drowned. It's the ones that don't have any excuse for it that get drowned and run down by taxis and things."

"But you never can tell what people will do," Mrs. Maurier rejoined, becoming profound through the sheer disintegration of comfortable things. "People will do anything."

"Well, if he's drowned, I guess he wanted to be," the niece said bloodlessly. "He certainly can't expect us to fool around here waiting for him, anyway. I never heard of anybody fading out without leaving a note of some kind. Did you, Jenny?"

Jenny sat in a soft anticipatory dread. "Did he get drownded?" she asked. "One day at Mandeville, I saw . . ." Into Jenny's heavenly eyes there welled momentarily a selfless emotion, temporarily pure and clean. Mrs. Wiseman looked at her, compelling her with her eyes. She said:

"Oh, forget about Gordon for a while. If he's drowned

(which I don't believe) he's drowned; if he isn't, he'll show up again, just as Dawson says."

"That's what I say," the niece supported her quickly. "Only he'd better show up soon, if he wants to go back with us. We've got to get back home."

"You have?" her aunt said with heavy astonished irony, "How are you going, pray?"

"Perhaps her brother will make us a boat with his saw," Mark Frost suggested.

"That's an idea," Fairchild agreed. "Say, Josh, haven't you got a tool of some sort that'll get us off again?" The nephew regarded Fairchild solemnly.

"Whittle it off," he said. "Lend you my knife if you bring it back right away." He resumed his meal.

"Well, we've got to get back," his sister repeated. "You folks can stay around here if you want to, but me and Josh have got to get back to New Orleans."

"Going by Mandeville?" Mark Frost asked.

"But the tug should be here at any time," Mrs. Maurier insisted, reverting again to her hopeless amaze. The niece gave Mark Frost a grave speculative stare.

"You're smart, aren't you?"

"I've got to be," Mark Frost answered equably, "or, I'd—"

"—have to work, huh? It takes a smart man to sponge off of Aunt Pat, don't it?"

"Patricia!" her aunt exclaimed.

"Well, we have got to get back. We've got to get ready to go up to New Haven next month."

Her brother came again out of his dream. "We have?" he repeated heavily.

"I'm going, too," she answered quickly. "Hank said I could."

"Look here," her brother said, "are you going to follow me around all your life?"

"I'm going to Yale," she repeated stubbornly. "Hank said I could go."

"Hank?" Fairchild repeated, watching the niece with interest.

"It's what she calls her father," her aunt explained. "Patricia—"

"Well, you can't go," her brother answered violently. "Dam'f I'm going to have you tagging around behind me forever. I can't move, for you. You ought to be a bill collector."

"I don't care: I'm going," she repeated stubbornly. Her aunt said vainly:

"Theodore!"

"Well, I can't do anything, for her," he complained bitterly. "I can't move, for her. And now she's talking about going— She worried Hank until he had to say she could go. God knows, I'd 'a' said that too: I wouldn't want her around me all the time."

"Shut your goddam mouth," his sister told him. Mrs. Maurier chanted "Patricia, Patricia." "I'm going, I'm going, I'm going!"

"What'll you do up there?" Fairchild asked. The niece whirled, viciously belligerent. Then she said:

"What'd you say?"

"I mean, what'll you do to pass the time while he's at classes and things? Are you going to take some work, too?"

"Oh, I'll just go around with balloon pants. To night

clubs and things. I won't bother him: I won't hardly see him, he's such a damn crum."

"Like hell you will," her brother interrupted, "you're not going, I tell you."

"Yes, I am. Hank said I could go. He said I could. I—"

"Well, you won't ever see me: I'm not going to have you tagging around after me up there."

"Are you the only one in the world that's going up there next year? Are you the only one that'll be there? I'm not going up there to waste my time hanging around the entrance to Dwight or Osborne hall just to see you. You won't catch me sitting on the rail of the Green with freshmen. I'll be going to places that maybe you'll get into in three years, if you don't bust out or something. Don't you worry about me. Who was it," she rushed on, "got invited up for Prom Week last year, only Hank wouldn't let me go? Who was it saw the game last fall, while you were perched up on the top row with a bunch of newspaper reporters, in the rain?"

"You didn't go up for Prom Week."

"Because Hank wouldn't let me. But I'll be there next year, and you can haul out the family sock on it."

"Oh, shut up for a while," her brother said wearily. "Maybe some of these ladies want to talk some."

TWO O'CLOCK

And there was the tug, squatting at her cables, breaking the southern horizon with an effect of abrupt magic, like a stereopticon slide flashed on the screen while you had turned your head for a moment.

"Look at that boat," said Mark Frost, broaching. Mrs. Maurier directly behind him, shrieked:

"It's the tug!" She turned and screamed down the companionway: "It's the tug: the tug has come!" The others all chanted "The tug! The tug!" Major Ayers exclaimed dramatically and opportunely:

"Ha, gone away!"

"It has come at last," Mrs. Maurier shrieked. "It came while we were at lunch. Has any one—" She roved her eyes about. "The captain— Has he been notified? Mr. Talliaferro—?"

"Surely," Mr. Talliaferro agreed with polite alacrity, mounting the stairs and disintegrating his members with expedition, "I'll summon the captain."

So he rushed forward and the others came on deck and stared at the tug, and a gentle breeze blew offshore and they slapped intermittently at their exposed surfaces. Mr. Talliaferro shouted: "Captain! oh, Captain!" about the deck: he screamed it into the empty wheelhouse and returned. "He must be asleep," he told them.

"We are off at last," Mrs. Maurier intoned, "we can get off at last. The tug has come: I sent for it days and days ago. But we can get off, now. But the captain. . . . Where is the captain? He shouldn't be asleep—Mr. Talliaferro—"

"But Gordon," Mark Frost said, "how about—"

Miss Jameson clutched his arm. "Let's get off, first," she said.

"I called him," Mr. Talliaferro reminded them. "He must be asleep in his room."

"He must be asleep," Mrs. Maurier repeated. "Will some gentleman—"

Mr. Talliaferro took his cue. "I'll go," he said.

"If you will be so kind," Mrs. Maurier screamed after him. She stared again at the tug. "He should have been here, so we could be all ready to start," she said fretfully. She waved her handkerchief at the tug: it ignored her.

"We might be getting everything ready, though," Fairchild suggested. "We ought to have everything ready when they pull us off."

"That's so," Mark Frost agreed. "We'd better run down and pack, hadn't we?"

"Ah, we ain't going back home yet. We've just started the cruise. Are we, folks?"

They all looked at the hostess. She roved her stricken eyes, but she said at last, bravely: "Why, no. No, of course not, if you don't want to. . . . But the captain: we ought to be ready," she repeated.

"Well, let's get ready," Mrs. Wiseman said.

"Nobody knows anything about boats except Fairchild," Mark Frost said. Mr. Talliaferro returned, barren.

"Me?" Fairchild repeated. "Mr. Talliaferro's been across the whole ocean. And there's Major Ayers. All Britishers cut their teeth on anchor chains and marlinspikes."

"And draw their toys with lubbers' lines," Mrs. Wiseman chanted. "It's almost a poem. Finish it, some one."

Mr. Talliaferro made a sound of alarm. "No: really, I—" Mrs. Maurier turned to Fairchild.

"Will you assume charge until the captain appears, Mr. Fairchild?"

"Mr. Fairchild," Mr. Talliaferro parroted. "Mr. Fairchild is temporary captain, people. The captain doesn't seem to be on board," he whispered to Mrs. Maurier.

Fairchild glanced about with a sort of ludicrous helplessness. "What am I supposed to do?" he asked. "Jump overboard with a shovel and shovel the sand away?"

"A man who has reiterated his superiority as much as you have for the last week should never be at a loss for what to do," Mrs. Wiseman told him. "We ladies have already thought of that. You are the one to think of something else."

"Well, I've already thought of not jumping overboard and shoveling her off," Fairchild answered, "but that don't seem to help much, does it?"

"You ought to coil ropes or something like that," Miss Jameson suggested. "That's what they were always doing on all the ships I ever read about."

"All right," Fairchild agreed equably. "We'll coil ropes, then. Where are the ropes?"

"That's your trouble," Mrs. Wiseman said. "You're captain now."

"Well, we'll find some ropes and coil 'em." He addressed Mrs. Maurier. "We have your permission to coil ropes?"

"No: really," said Mrs. Maurier in her helpless astonished voice. "Isn't there something we can do? Can't we signal to them with a sheet? They may not know that this is the right boat."

"Oh, they know, I guess. Anyway, we'll coil ropes and be ready for them. Come on here, you men." He named over his depleted watch and herded it forward. He herded it down to his cabin and nourished it with stimulants.

"We may coil the right rope, at that," the Semitic man suggested. "Major Ayers ought to know something about boats: it should be in his British blood."

Major Ayers didn't think so. "American boats have

amphibious traits that are lacking in ours," he explained. "Half the voyage on land, you know," he explained tediously.

"Sure," Fairchild agreed. He brought his watch above again and forward, where instinct told him the ropes should be. "I wonder where the captain is. Surely he ain't drowned, do you reckon?"

"I guess not," the Semitic man answered. "He gets paid for this. . . . There comes a boat."

The boat came from the tug, and soon it came alongside and the captain came over the rail. A stranger followed him and they went below without haste, leaving Mrs. Maurier's words like vain unmated birds in the air. "Let's get ready, then," Fairchild ordered his crew. "Let's tie a rope to something."

So they tied a rope to something, knotting it intricately, then Major Ayers discovered that they had tied it to a winch handle which fitted loosely into a socket and which would probably come out quite easily, once a strain came onto the rope. So they untied it and found something attached firmly to the deck, and they tied the rope to this, and after a while the captain and the stranger, clutching a short evil pipe, came back on deck and stood and watched them. "We've got the right rope," Fairchild told his watch in an undertone, and they knotted the rope intricately and straightened up.

"How's that, Cap?" Fairchild asked.

"All right," the captain answered. "Can we trouble you for a match?"

Fairchild gave them a match. The stranger fired his pipe and they got into the tender and departed. They hadn't got far when the one called Walter came out and called them, and they put about and returned for him. Then they went back to the tug. Fairchild's watch had ceased work, and it gazed after the tender. After a time Fairchild said: "He said that was the right rope. So I guess we can quit."

So they did, and went aft to where the ladies were, and presently the tender came bobbing back across the water. It came alongside again and a negro, sweating gently and regularly, held it steady while the one called Walter and yet another stranger got aboard, bringing a rope that trailed away into the water behind them.

Every one watched with interest while Walter and his companion made the line fast in the bows, after having removed Fairchild's rope. Then Walter and his friend went below.

"Say," Fairchild said suddenly, "do you reckon they've found our whisky?"

"I guess not," the Semitic man assured him. "I hope not," he amended; and they all returned in a body to stare down into the tender where the negro sat without selfconsciousness, eating of a large grayish object. While they watched the negro Walter and his companion returned, and the stranger bawled at the tug through his hands. A reply at last, and the other end of the line which they had recently brought aboard the yacht and made fast, slid down from the deck of the tug and plopped heavily into the water; and Walter and his companion drew it aboard the yacht and coiled it down, wet and dripping. Then they elbowed themselves to the rail, cast the rope into the tender and got in themselves, and the negro stowed his strange edible object temporarily away and rowed back to the tug.

"You guessed wrong again," Mark Frost said with sepulchral irony. He bent and scratched his ankles. "Try another rope."

"You wait," Fairchild retorted, "wait ten minutes, then talk. We'll be under full stream in ten minutes. . . . Where did that boat come from?"

This boat was a skiff, come when and from where they knew not; and beneath the drowsy afternoon there came faintly from somewhere up the lake the fretful sound of a motor boat engine. The skiff drew alongside, manned by a malaria-ridden man wearing a woman's dilapidated hat of black straw that lent him a vaguely bereaved air.

"Whar's the drownded feller?" he asked, grasping the rail.

"We don't know," Fairchild answered. "We missed him somewhere between here and the shore." He extended his arm. The newcomer followed his gesture sadly.

"Any reward?"

"Reward?" repeated Fairchild.

"Reward?" Mrs. Maurier chimed in, breathlessly. "Yes, there is a reward: I offer a reward."

"How much?"

"You find him first," the Semitic man put in. "There'll be a reward, all right."

The man clung yet to the rail. "Have you drug fer him yet?"

"No, we've just started hunting," Fairchild answered. "You go on and look around, and we'll get our boat and come out and help you. There'll be a reward."

The man pushed his skiff clear and engaged his oars. The sound of the motor boat grew clearer steadily; soon it came into view, with two men in it, and changed its course and bore down on the skiff. The fussy little engine ceased its racket and it slid up to the skiff, pushing a dying ripple under its stem. The two boats clung together for a time, then they parted, and at a short distance from each other they moved slowly onward while their occupants prodded at the lake bottom with their oars.

"Look at them," the Semitic man said, "just like buzzards. Probably be a dozen boats out there in the next hour. How do you suppose they learned about it?"

"Lord knows," Fairchild answered. "Let's get our crew and go out and help look. We better get the tug's men."

They shouted in turn for a while, and presently one came to the rail of the tug and gazed apathetically at them, and went away; and after a while the small boat came away from the tug and crossed to them. A consultation, assisted by all hands, while the man from the tug moved unhurriedly about the business of making fast another and dirtier rope to the *Nausikaa's* bows. Then he and Walter went back to the tug, paying out the line behind them while Mrs. Maurier's insistence wasted itself upon the somnolent afternoon. The guests looked at one another helplessly. Then Fairchild said with determination:

"Come on, we'll go in our boat." He chose his men, and they gathered all the available oars and prepared to embark.

"Here comes the tug's boat again," Mark Frost said.

"They forgot and tied one end of that rope to something." Mrs. Wiseman said viciously. The boat came alongside without haste and it and the yacht's tender lay rubbing noses, and Walter's companion asked, without interest:

"Wher's the feller y'all drownded?"

"I'll go along in their boat and show 'em," Fairchild decided. Mark Frost got back aboard the yacht with alacrity. Fairchild stopped him. "You folks come on behind us in this boat. The more to hunt, the better."

Mark Frost groaned and acquiesced. The others took their places, and under Fairchild's direction the two tenders retraced the course of yesterday. The first two boats were some distance ahead, moving slowly, and the tenders separated also and the searchers poled along, prodding with their oars at the lake floor. And such is the influence of action on the mind that soon even Fairchild's burly optimism became hushed and uncertain before the imminence of the unknown, and he too was accepting the possible for the probable, unaware.

The sun was hazed, as though wearied of its own implacable heat, and the water—that water which might hold, soon to be revealed, the mute evidence of ultimate flouting of all man's strife—lapped and plopped at the mechanical fragilities that supported them: a small sound, monotonous and without rancor—it could well wait! They poled slowly on.

Soon the four boats, fanwise, had traversed the course, and they turned and quartered back and forth again, slowly and in silence. Afternoon drew on, drowsing and somnolent. Yacht and tug lay motionless in a blinding shimmer of water and sun. . . .

Again the course of yesterday was covered foot by foot, patiently and silently and in vain; and the four boats as without volition drew nearer each other, drifting closer together as sheep huddle, while water lapped and plopped beneath their hulls, sinister and untroubled by waiting . . . soon the motor boat drifted up and scraped lightly along the hull in which Fairchild sat, and he raised his head, blinking against the glare. After a while he said:

"Are you a ghost, or am I?"

"I was about to ask you that," Gordon, sitting in the motor boat, replied. They sat and stared at each other. The other boats came up, and presently the one called Walter spoke.

"Is this all you wanted out here," he asked in a tone of polite disgust, breaking the spell, "or do you want to row around some more?"

Fairchild went immoderately into hysterical laughter.

FOUR O'CLOCK

The malarial man had attached his skiff to the fat man's motor boat and they had puttered away in a morose dejection, rewardless; the tug had whistled a final derisive blast, showed them her squat, unpretty stern, where the negro leaned eating again of his grayish object, and as dirty a pair of heels as it would ever be their luck to see, and sailed away. The *Nausikaa* was free once more and she sped quickly onward, gaining offing, and the final sharp concussion of flesh and flesh died away beneath the afternoon.

Mrs. Maurier had gazed at him, raised her hands in a fluttering cringing gesture, and cut him dead.

"But I saw you on the boat right after we came back," Fairchild repeated with a sort of stubborn wonder. He opened a fresh bottle.

"You couldn't have," Gordon answered shortly. "I got out of the boat in the middle of Talliaferro's excitement." He waved away the proffered glass. The Semitic man said triumphantly, "I told you so," and Fairchild essayed again, stubbornly:

"But I saw—"

"If you say that again," the Semitic man told him, "I'll kill you." He addressed Gordon. "And you thought Dawson was drowned?"

"Yes. The man who brought me back—I stumbled on his house this morning—he had already heard of it, some way. It must have spread all up and down the lake. He didn't remember the name, exactly, and when I named over the party and said Dawson Fairchild, he agreed. Dawson and Gordon—you see? And so I thought—"

Fairchild began to laugh again. He laughed steadily, trying to say something. "And so—and so he comes back and sp-spends—" Again that hysterical note came into his laughter and his hands trembled, clinking the bottle against the glass and sloshing a spoonful of the liquor onto the floor "—and spends . . . He comes back, you know, and spends half a day looking—looking for his own bububod—"

The Semitic man rose and took the bottle and glass from him and half led, half thrust him into his bunk. "You sit down and drink this." Fairchild drank the whisky obediently. The Semitic man turned to Gordon again. "What made you come back? Not just because you heard Dawson was drowned, was it?"

Gordon stood against the wall, mudstained and silent. He raised his head and stared at them, and through them, with his harsh, uncomfortable stare. Fairchild touched the Semitic man's knee warningly.

"That's neither here nor there," he said. "The question is, Shall we or shall we not get drunk? I kind of think we've got to, myself."

"Yes," the other agreed. "It looks like it's up to us. Gordon ought to celebrate his resurrection, anyway."

"No," Gordon answered, "I don't want any." The Semitic man protested, but again Fairchild gripped him silent, and when Gordon turned toward the door, he rose and followed him into the passage.

"She came back too, you know," he said.

Gordon looked down at the shorter man with his lean bearded face, his lonely hawk's face arrogant with shyness and pride. "I know it," he answered (your name is like a little golden bell hung in my heart). "The man who brought me back was the same one who brought them back yesterday."

"He was?" said Fairchild. "He's doing a landoffice business with deserters, ain't he?"

"Yes," Gordon answered. And he went on down the passage with a singing lightness in his heart, a bright silver joy like wings.

* * *

The deck was deserted, as on that other afternoon. But he waited patiently in the hushed happiness of his dream and his arrogant bitter heart was young as any yet, as forgetful of yesterday and to-morrow; and soon, as though in answer to it, she came barelegged and molded by the wind of motion, and her grave surprise ebbed and she thrust him a hard tanned hand.

"So you ran away," she said.

"And so did you," he answered after an interval filled with a thing all silver and clean and fine.

"That's right. We're sure the herrings on this boat, aren't we?"

"Herrings?"

"Guts, you know," she explained. She looked at him gravely from beneath the coarse dark bang of her hair. "But you came back," she accused.

"And so did you," he reminded her from amid his soundless silver wings.

FIVE O'CLOCK

"But we're moving again, at last," Mrs. Maurier repeated at intervals, with a detached air, listening to a sound somehow vaguely convivial that welled at intervals up the companionway. Presently Mrs. Wiseman remarked the hostess' preoccupied air and she too ceased, hearkening.

"Not again?" she said with foreboding.

"I'm afraid so," the other answered unhappily.

Mr. Talliaferro hearkened also. "Perhaps I'd better . . ." Mrs. Maurier fixed him with her eye, and Mrs. Wiseman said:

"Poor fellows. They have had to stand a great deal in the last few days."

"Boys will be boys," Mr. Talliaferro added with docile

regret, listening with yearning to that vaguely convivial sound. Mrs. Maurier listened to it, coldly detached and speculative. She said:

"But we are moving again, anyway."

SIX O'CLOCK

The sun was setting across the scudding water: the water was shot goldenly with it, as was the gleaming mahogany-and-brass elegance of the yacht, and the silver wings in his heart were touched with pink and gold while he stood and looked downward upon the coarse crown of her head and at her body's grave and sexless replica of his own attitude against the rail—an unconscious aping both comical and heart-shaking.

"Do you know," he asked, "what Cyrano said once?" *Once there was a king who possessed all things. All things were his: power, and glory, and wealth, and splendor and ease. And so he sat at dusk in his marble court filled with the sound of water and of birds and surrounded by the fixed gesturing of palms, looking out across the hushed fading domes of his city and beyond, to the dreaming lilac barriers of his world.*

"No: what?" she asked. But he only looked down upon her with his cavernous uncomfortable eyes. "What did he say?" she repeated. And then: "Was he in love with her?"

"I think so. . . . Yes, he was in love with her. She couldn't leave him, either. Couldn't go away from him at all."

"She couldn't? What'd he done to her? Locked her up?"

"Maybe she didn't want to," he suggested.

"Huh." And then: "She was an awful goof, then. Was he fool enough to believe she didn't want to?"

"He didn't take any chances. He had her locked up. In a book."

"In a book?" she repeated. Then she comprehended. "Oh. . . . That's what you've done, isn't it? With that marble girl without any arms and legs you made? Hadn't you rather have a live one? Say, you haven't got any sweetheart or anything, have you?"

"No," he answered. "How did you know?"

"You look so bad. Shabby. But that's the reason: no woman is going to waste time on a man that's satisfied with a piece of wood or something. You ought to get out of yourself. You'll either bust all of a sudden some day, or just dry up . . . How old are you?"

"Thirty-six," he told her. She said:

"Gabriel's pants. Thirty-six years old, and living in a hole with a piece of rock, like a dog with a dry bone. Gabriel's pants. Why don't you get rid of it?" But he only stared down at her. "Give it to me, won't you?"

"No."

"I'll buy it from you, then."

"No."

"Give you—" she looked at him with sober detachment. "Give you seventeen dollars for it. Cash."

"No."

She looked at him with a sort of patient exasperation. "Well, what are you going to do with it? Have you got any reason for keeping it? You didn't steal it, did you? Don't tell me you haven't got any use for seventeen dollars, living like you do. I bet you haven't got five dollars to your name, right now. Bet you came on this party to save food. I'll give you twenty dollars, seventeen in cash." He continued to gaze at her as though he had not heard.—*and the king spoke to a slave crouching at his feet—Halim—Lord?—I possess all things, do I not?—Thou art the Son of Morning, Lord—Then listen, Halim: I have a desire—* "Twenty-five," she said, shaking his arm.

"No."

"No, no, no, no!" she hammered both brown fists on the rail. "You make me so damn mad! Can't you say anything except No? You—you—" she glared at him with her angry tanned face and her grave opaque eyes, and used that phrase Jenny had traded her.

He took her by the elbows, and she became taut, still watching his face: he could feel the small hard muscles in her arms. "What are you going to do?" she asked. He raised her from the floor, and she began to struggle. But he carried her implacably across the deck and sat on a deckchair and turned her face downward across his knees. She clawed and kicked in a silent fury, but he held her, and she ceased to struggle, and set her teeth into his leg through the gritty cloth of his trousers, and clung like a raging puppy while he drew her skirt tight across her thighs and spanked her, good.

"I meant it!" she cried, raging and tearless, when he had dragged her teeth loose and set her upright on his lap. There was a small wet oval on his trouserleg. "I meant it!" she repeated, taut and raging.

"I know you meant it. That's why I spanked you. Not because you said it: what you said doesn't mean anything because you've got the genders backward. I spanked you because you meant it, whether you knew what to say or not."

Suddenly she became lax, and wept, and he held her against his breast. But she ceased crying as abruptly, and lay quiet while he moved his hand over her face, slowly and firmly, but lightly. *It is like a thing heard, not as a music of brass and plucked strings is heard and a pallid voluption of dancing girls among the strings; nay, Halim, it is no pale virgin from Tal with painted fingernails and honey and myrrh cunningly beneath her tongue. Nor is it a scent as of myrrh and roses to soften and make to flow like water the pith in a man's bones, nor yet—Stay, Halim: Once I was . . . once I was? Is not this a true thing? It is dawn, in the high cold hills, dawn is like a wind in the clean hills, and on the wind comes the thin piping of shepherds, and the smell of dawn and of almond trees on the wind. Is not that a true thing?—Ay, Lord. I told thee that. I was there.*

"Are you a petter, as well as a he-man?" she asked, becoming taut again and rolling upward her exposed eye. His hand moved slowly along her cheekbone and jaw, pausing, tracing a muscle, moving on. *Then hark thee, Halim: I desire a thing that, had I not been at all, becoming aware of it I would awake; that, dead, remembering it I would cling to this world though it be as a beggar in a tattered robe; yea, rather that would I than a king among kings amid the soft and scented sounds of paradise. Find me this, O Halim.* "Say," she said curiously, no longer alarmed, "what are you doing that for?"

"Learning your face."

"Learning my face? Are you going to make me in marble?" she asked quickly, raising herself. "Can you do a marble of my head?"

"Yes."

"Can I have it?" she thrust herself away, watching his face. "Make two of them, then," she suggested. And then: "If you won't do that, give me the other one, the one you've got, and I'll pose for this one without charging you anything. How about that?"

"Maybe."

"I'd rather do that than to have this one. Have you learned my face good?" She moved again, quickly, returning to her former position. She turned her face up. "Learn it good." *Now, this Halim was an old man, so old that he had forgotten much. He had held this king on his first pony, walking patiently beside him through the streets and paths; he had stood between the young prince and all those forms of sudden and complete annihilation which the young prince had engendered after the ingenuous fashion of boys; he had got himself between the young prince and the inevitable parental admonishment which these entailed. And he sat with his gray hands on his thin knees and his gray head bent above his hands while dusk came across the simple immaculate domes of the city and into the court, stilling the sound of birds so that the lilac silence of the court was teased only by the plashing of water, and on among the grave restlessness of the palms. After a while Halim spoke.—Ah, Lord, in the Georgian hills I loved this maid myself, when I was a lad. But that was long ago, and she is dead.*

She lay still against his breast while sunset died like brass horns across the water. She said, without moving:

"You're a funny man. . . . I wonder if I could sculp? Suppose I learn your face? . . . Well, don't, then. I'd just as soon lie still. You're a lot more comfortable to lie on than you look. Only I'd think you'd be getting tired now—I'm no humming bird. Aren't you tired of holding me?" she persisted. He moved his head at last and looked at her again with his caverned uncomfortable eyes, and she tried to do something with her eyes, assuming at the same time an attitude, a kind of leering invitation, so palpably theatrical and false that it but served to emphasize that grave, hard sexlessness of hers.

"What are you trying to do?" he asked quietly, "vamp me?"

She said "Shucks." She sat up, then squirmed off his lap and to her feet. "So you won't give it to me? You just won't?"

"No," he told her soberly. She turned away, but presently she stopped again and looked back at him.

"Give you twenty-five dollars for it."

"No."

She said "Shucks" again, and she went on on her brown silent feet, and was gone. (Your name is like a little golden bell hung in my heart, and when I think of you . . .) The *Nausikaa* sped on. It was twilight abruptly; soon, a star.

SEVEN O'CLOCK

The place did appear impregnable, but then he had got used to feeling it behind him in his chair, where he knew nothing was going to happen to it. Besides, to change now, after so many days, would be like hedging on a bet. . . . Still, to let those two old bums kid him about it . . . He paused in the door of the saloon.

The others were seated and well into their dinner, but

before four vacant places that bland eternal grapefruit, sinister and bland as taxes. Some of them hadn't arrived: he'd have time to run back to his room and leave it. And let one of them drunkards throw it out the window for a joke?

Mrs. Wiseman carrying a tray said briskly: "Gangway, Pete," and he crowded against the wall for her to pass, and then the niece turned her head and saw him. "Belly up," she said, and he heard a further trampling drawing near. He hesitated a second, then he thrust his hat into the little cubbyhole between the two shelves. He'd risk it to-night, anyway. He could still sort of keep an eye on it. He took his seat.

Fairchild's watch surged in: a hearty joviality that presently died into startled consternation when it saw the grapefruit. "My God," said Fairchild in a hushed tone.

"Sit down, Dawson," Mrs. Wiseman ordered sharply. "We've had about all that sort of humor this voyage will stand."

"That's what I think," he agreed readily. "That's what Julius and Major Ayers and me think at every meal. And yet, when we come to the table, what do we see?"

"My first is an Indian princess," said Mark Frost in a hollow lilting tone. "But it's a little early to play charades yet, isn't it?"

Major Ayers said "Eh?" looking from Mark Frost to Fairchild. Then he ventured: "It's grapefruit, isn't it?"

"But we have so many of them," Mrs. Maurier explained. "You are supposed to never tire of them."

"That's it," said Fairchild solemnly. "Major Ayers guessed it the first time. I wasn't certain what it was, myself. But you can't fool Major Ayers; you can't fool a man that's traveled as much as he has, with just a grapefruit. I guess you've shot lots of grapefruit in China and India, haven't you, Major?"

"Dawson, sit down," Mrs. Wiseman repeated. "Make them sit down, Julius, or go out to the kitchen if they just want to stand around and talk."

Fairchild sat down quickly. "Never mind," he said. "We can stand it if the ladies can. The human body can stand anything," he added owlishly. "It can get drunk and stay up and dance all night, and consume crate after crate of gr—" Mrs. Wiseman leaned across his shoulder and swept his grapefruit away. "Here," he exclaimed.

"They don't want 'em," she told Miss Jameson across the table. "Get his, too." So they reft Major Ayers of his also, and Mrs. Wiseman clashed the plates viciously onto her tray. In passing behind Mrs. Maurier she struck the collapsible serving table with her hip and said "Damn!" pausing to release the catch and slam it back into the bulkhead. Pete's hat slid onto the floor and she thrust it against the wall with her toe.

"Yes, sir," Fairchild repeated, "the human body can stand lots of things. But if I have to eat another grapefruit . . . Say, Julius, I was examining my back to-day, and do you know, my skin is getting dry and rough, with a kind of yellowish cast. If it keeps on, first thing I know I won't any more dare undress in public than Al Jack—"

Mark Frost made a sound of sharp alarm. "Look out, people," he exclaimed, rising. "I'm going to get out of here."

"—son would take off his shoes in public," Fairchild continued unperturbed. Mrs. Wiseman returned and she stood with her hands on her hips, regarding Fairchild's unkempt head with disgust. Mrs. Maurier gazed helplessly at him.

"Every one's finished," Mrs. Wiseman said. "Come on, let's go on deck."

"No," Mrs. Maurier protested. She said firmly: "Mr. Fairchild."

"Go on," the niece urged him. "What about Al Jackson?"

"Shut up, Pat," Mrs. Wiseman commanded. "Come on, you all. Let 'em stay here and drivel to each other. Let's lock 'em in here: what do you say?"

Mrs. Maurier asserted herself. She rose. "Mr. Fairchild, I simply will not have—if you continue in this behavior, I shall leave the room. Don't you see how trying—how difficult—how difficult"—beneath the beseeching helplessness of her eyes her various chins began to quiver a little—"how difficult—"

Mrs. Wiseman touched her arm. "Come: it's useless to argue with them now. Come, dear." She drew Mrs. Maurier's chair aside and the old woman took a step and stopped abruptly, clutching the other's arm.

"I've stepped on something," she said, peering blindly.

Pete rose with a mad inarticulate cry.

* * *

"Old man Jackson"—Fairchild continued—"claims to be a lineal descendant of Old Hickory. A fine old southern family with all a fine old southern family's pride. Al has a lot of that pride, himself: that's why he won't take off his shoes in company. I'll tell you the reason later.

"Well, old man Jackson was a bookkeeper or something,

drawing a small salary with a big family to support, and he wanted to better himself with the minimum of labor, like a descendant of any fine old southern family naturally would, and so he thought up the idea of taking up some of this Louisiana swamp land and raising sheep on it. He'd noticed how much ranker vegetation grows on trees in swampy land, so he figured that wool ought to grow the same rank way on a sheep raised in a swamp. So he threw up his bookkeeping job and took up a few hundred acres of Tchufuncta river swamp and stocked it with sheep, using the money his wife's uncle, a member of an old aristocratic Tennessee moonshining family, had left 'em.

"But his sheep started right in to get themselves drowned, so he made lifebelts for 'em out of some small wooden kegs that had been part of the heritage from that Tennessee uncle, so that when the sheep strayed off into deep water they would float until the current washed 'em back to land again. This worked all right, but still his sheep kept on disappearing—the ewes and lambs did, that is. Then he found that the alligators were—"

"Yes," murmured Major Ayers, "Old Hickory."

"—getting them. So he made some imitation rams' horns out of wood and fastened a pair to each ewe and to every lamb when it was born. And that reduced his losses by alligators to a minimum scarcely worth notice. The rams' flesh seemed to be too rank even for alligators.

"After a time the lifebelts wore out, but the sheep had learned to swim pretty well by then, so old man Jackson decided it wasn't worth while to put any more lifebelts on 'em. The fact is, the sheep had got to like the water: the first crop of lambs would only come out of the water at feeding time; and when the first shearing time came around, he and his boys had to round up the sheep with boats.

"By the next shearing time, those sheep wouldn't even come out of the water to be fed. So he and his boys would go out in boats and set floating tubs of feed around in the bayous for them. This crop of lambs could dive, too. They never saw one of them on land at all: they'd only see their heads swimming across the bogues and sloughs.

"Finally another shearing time came around. Old man Jackson tried to catch one of them, but the sheep could swim faster than he and his boys could row, and the young ones dived under water and got away. So they finally had to borrow a motor boat. And when they finally tired one of those sheep down and caught it and took it out of the water, they found that only the top of its back had any wool on it. The rest of its body was scaled like a fish. And when they finally caught one of the spring lambs on an alligator hook, they found that its tail had broadened out and flattened like a beaver's, and that it had no legs at all. They didn't hardly know what it was, at first."

"I say," murmured Major Ayers.

"Yes, sir, completely atrophied away. Time passed, and they never saw the next crop of lambs at all. The food they set out the birds ate, and when the next shearing time came, they couldn't even catch one with the motor boat. They hadn't even seen one in three weeks. They knew they were still there, though, because they would occasionally hear 'em baa-ing at night way back in the swamp. They caught one occasionally on a trotline of shark hooks baited with ears of corn. But not many.

"Well, sir, the more old man Jackson thought about that

swampful of sheep, the madder he got. He'd stamp around the house and swear he'd catch 'em if he had to buy a motor boat that would run fifty miles an hour, and a diving suit for himself and every one of his boys. He had one boy named Claude—Al's brother, you know. Claude was kind of wild: hell after women, a gambler and a drunkard—a kind of handsome humorless fellow with lots of dash. And finally Claude made a trade with his father to have half of every sheep he could catch, and he got to work right away. He never bothered with boats or trotlines: he just took off his clothes and went right in the water and grappled for 'em."

"Grappled for 'em?" Major Ayers repeated.

"Sure: run one down and hem him up under the bank and drag him out with his bare hands. That was Claude, all over. And then they found that this year's lambs didn't have any wool on 'em at all, and that its flesh was the best fish eating in Louisiana; being partly cornfed that way giving it a good flavor, you see. So that's where old man Jackson quit the sheep business and went to fish ranching on a large scale. He knew he had a snap as long as Claude could catch 'em, so he made arrangements with the New Orleans markets right away, and they began to get rich."

"By Jove," Major Ayers said tensely, his mind taking fire.

"Claude liked the work. It was an adventurous kind of life that just suited him, so he quit everything and gave all his time to it. He quit drinking and gambling and running around at night, and there was a marked decrease in vice in that neighborhood, and the young girls pined for him at the local dances and sat on their front porches of a Sunday evening in vain.

"Pretty soon he could outswim the old sheep, and having

to dive so much after the young ones, he got to where he could stay under water longer and longer at a time. Sometimes he'd stay under for a half an hour or more. And pretty soon he got to where he'd stay in the water all day, only coming out to eat and sleep; and then they noticed that Claude's skin was beginning to look funny and that he walked kind of peculiar, like his knees were stiff or something. Soon after that he quit coming out of the water at all, even to eat, so they'd bring his dinner down to the water and leave it, and after a while he'd swim up and get it. Sometimes they wouldn't see Claude for days. But he was still catching those sheep, herding 'em into a pen old man Jackson had built in a shallow bayou and fenced off with hog wire, and his half of the money was growing in the bank. Occasionally half eaten pieces of sheep would float ashore, and old man Jackson decided alligators were getting 'em again. But he couldn't put horns on 'em now because no one but Claude could catch 'em, and he hadn't seen Claude in some time.

"It had been a couple of weeks since anybody had seen Claude, when one day there was a big commotion in the sheep pen. Old man Jackson and a couple of his other boys ran down there, and when they got there they could see the sheep jumping out of the water every which way, trying to get on land again; and after a while a big alligator rushed out from among 'em, and old man Jackson knew what had scared the sheep.

"And then, right behind the alligator he saw Claude. Claude's eyes had kind of shifted around to the side of his head and his mouth had spread back a good way, and his teeth had got longer. And then old man Jackson knew what had scared that alligator. But that was the last they ever saw of Claude.

"Pretty soon after that, though, there was a shark scared at the bathing beaches along the Gulf coast. It seemed to be a lone shark that kept annoying women bathers, especially blondes; and they knew it was Claude Jackson. He was always hell after blondes."

Fairchild ceased. The niece squealed and jumped up and came to him, patting his back. Jenny's round ineffable eyes were upon him, utterly without thought. The Semitic man was slumped in his chair: he may have slept.

Major Ayers stared at Fairchild a long time. At last he said: "But why does the alligator one wear congress boots?"

Fairchild mused a moment. Then he said dramatically: "He's got webbed feet."

"Yes," Major Ayers agreed. He mused in turn. "But this chap that got rich—" The niece squealed again. She sat beside Fairchild and regarded him with admiration.

"Go on, go on," she said, "about the one that stole the money, you know."

Fairchild looked at her kindly. Into the silence there came a thin saccharine strain. "There's the victrola," he said. "Let's go up and start a dance."

"The one who stole the money," she insisted. "Please." She put her hand on his shoulder.

"Some other time," he promised, rising. "Let's go up and dance now." The Semitic man yet slumped in his chair, and Fairchild shook him. "Wake up, Julius. I'm safe now."

The Semitic man opened his eyes and Major Ayers said: "How much did they gain with their fish ranching?"

"Not as much as they would have with a patent nice-tasting laxative. All Americans don't eat fish, you know. Come on, let's go up and hold that dance they've been worrying us about every night."

NINE O'CLOCK

"Say," the niece said as she and Jenny mounted to the deck, "remember that thing we traded for the other night? the one you let me use for the one I let you use?"

"I guess so," Jenny answered. "I remember trading."

"Have you used it yet?"

"I never can think of it," Jenny confessed. "I never can remember what it was you told me. . . . Besides, I've got another one, now."

"You have? Who told it to you?"

"The popeyed man. That Englishman."

"Major Ayers?"

"Uhuh. Last night we was talking and he kept on saying for us to go to Mandeville to-day. He kept on saying it. And so this morning he acted like he thought I meant we was going. He acted like he was mad."

"What was it he said?" Jenny told her—a mixture of pidgin English and Hindustani that Major Ayers must have picked up along the Singapore water front, or mayhap at some devious and doubtful place in the Straits, but after Jenny had repeated it, it didn't sound like anything at all.

"What?" the niece asked. Jenny said it again.

"It don't sound like anything, to me," the niece said. "Is that the way he said it?"

"That's what it sounded like to me," Jenny replied.

The niece said curiously: "Men sure do swear at you a lot. They're always cursing you. What do you do to them, anyway?"

"I don't do anything to them," Jenny answered. "I'm just talking to them."

"Well, they sure do. . . . Say, you can have that one back you loaned me."

"Have you used it on anybody?" Jenny asked with interest.

"I tried it on that redheaded Gordon."

"That drownded man? What'd he say?"

"He beat me." The niece rubbed herself with a tanned retrospective hand. "He just beat hell out of me," she said.

"Gee," said Jenny.

TEN O'CLOCK

Fairchild gathered his watch, nourished it, and brought it on deck again. The ladies hailed its appearance with doubtful pleasure. Mr. Talliaferro and Jenny were dancing, and the niece and Pete with his damaged hat, were performing together with a skillful and sexless abandon that was almost professional, while the rest of the party watched them.

"Whee," Fairchild squealed, watching the niece and Pete with growing childish admiration. At the moment they faced each other at a short distance, their bodies rigid as far as the waist. But below this they were as amazing jointless toys, and their legs seemed to fly in every direction at once until their knees seemed to touch the floor. Then they caught hands and whirled sharply together, without a break in that dizzy staccato of heels. "Say, Major, look there! Look there, Julius! Come on, I believe I can do that."

He led his men to the assault. The victrola ran down at the moment; he directed the Semitic man to attend to it, and went at once to where Pete and the niece stood. "Say, you folks are regular professionals. Pete, let me have her this time, will you? I want her to show me how you do that. Will you show me? Pete won't mind."

"All right," the niece agreed, "I'll show you. I owe you something for that yarn at dinner to-night." She put her hand on Pete's arm. "Don't go off, Pete. I'll show him and then he can practise on the others. Don't you go off; you are all right. You might take Jenny for a while. She must be tired: he's been leaning on her for a half an hour. Come on, Dawson. Watch me now." She had no bones at all.

Major Ayers and the Semitic man had partners, though more sedately. Major Ayers galloped around in a heavy dragoonish manner: when that record was over Miss Jameson was panting. She offered to sit out the next one, but Fairchild overruled her. He believed he had the knack of it. "We'll put the old girl's dance over in style," he told them.

Major Ayers, inflamed by Fairchild's example, offered for the niece himself. Mr. Talliaferro, reft of Jenny, acquired Mrs. Wiseman; the Semitic man was cajoling the hostess. "We'll put her dance over for her," Fairchild chanted. They were off.

Gordon had come up from somewhere and he stood in shadow, watching. "Come on, Gordon," Fairchild shouted to him. "Grab one!" When the music ceased Gordon cut in on Major Ayers. The niece looked up in surprise, and Major Ayers departed in Jenny's direction.

"I didn't know you danced," she said.

"Why not?" Gordon asked.

"You just don't look like you did. And you told Aunt Pat you couldn't dance."

"I can't," he answered, staring down at her. "Bitter," he said slowly. "That's what you are. New. Like bark when the sap is rising."

"Will you give it to me?" He was silent. She couldn't see his face distinctly: only the bearded shape of his tall head. "Why won't you give it to me?" Still no answer, and his head was ugly as bronze against the sky. Fairchild started the victrola again: a saxophone was a wailing obscenity, and she raised her arms. "Come on."

*   *   *

When that one was finished Fairchild's watch rushed below again, and presently Mr. Talliaferro saw his chance and followed surreptitiously. Fairchild and Major Ayers were ecstatically voluble: the small room fairly moiled with sound. Then they rushed back on deck.

"Watch your step, Talliaferro," Fairchild cautioned him as they ascended. "She's got her eye on you. Have you danced with her yet?" Mr. Talliaferro had not. "Better kind of breathe away from her when you do."

He led his men to the assault. The ladies demurred, but Fairchild was everywhere, cajoling, threatening, keeping life in the party. Putting the old girl's dance over. Mrs. Maurier was trying to catch Mr. Talliaferro's eye. The niece had peremptorily commandeered Pete again, and again Gordon stood in his shadow, haughty and aloof. They were off.

ELEVEN O'CLOCK

"I say," said Mr. Talliaferro, popping briskly and cautiously into the room, accepting his glass, "we'd better slow up a bit, hadn't we?"

"What for?" asked the Semitic man, and Fairchild said:

"Ah, it's all right. She expects it of us. Somebody's got to be the hoi polloi, you know. Besides, we want to make this cruise memorable in the annals of deep water. Hey, Major? Talliaferro'd better go easy, though."

"Oh, we'll look out for Talliaferro," the Semitic man said.

"No damned fear," Major Ayers assured him. "Have a go eh?" They all had a go. Then they rushed back on deck.

* * *

"What do you do in New Orleans, Pete?" Miss Jameson asked intensely.

"One thing and another," Pete answered cautiously. "I'm in business with my brother," he added.

"You have lots of friends, I imagine? Girls would all like to dance with you. You are one of the best dancers I ever saw—almost professional. I like dancing."

"Yeh," Pete agreed. He was restive. "I guess—"

"I wonder if you and I couldn't get together some evening and dance again? I don't go to night clubs much, because none of the men I know dance very well. But I'd enjoy it, with you."

"I guess so," Pete answered. "Well, I—"

"I'll give you my phone number and address, and you call me soon, will you? You might come out to dinner, and we'll go out afterward, you know."

"Sure," Pete answered uncomfortably. He removed his hat and examined the crown. Then he slanted it once more across his dark reckless head. Miss Jameson said:

"Do you ever make dates ahead of time, Pete?"

"Naw," he answered quickly. "I wouldn't have a date over a day old. I just call 'em up and take 'em out and bring 'em back in time to go to work next day. I wouldn't have one I had to wait until to-morrow on."

"Neither do I. So I tell you what: let's break the rule one time, and make a date for the first night we are ashore— what do you say? You come out to dinner at my house, and we'll go out later to dance. I've got a car."

"I—Well, you see—"

"We'll just do that," Miss Jameson continued remorselessly. "We won't forget that; it's a promise, isn't it?"

Pete rose. "I guess we—I guess I better not promise. Something might turn up so I—we couldn't make it. I guess . . ." She sat quietly, looking at him. "Maybe it'll be better to wait and fix it up when we get back. I might have to be out of town or something that day, see? Maybe we better wait and see how things shape up." Still she said nothing, and presently she removed her patient humorless eyes and looked out across the darkling water, and Pete stood uncomfortably with his goading urge to keep on saying something. "I guess we better wait and see later, see?"

Her head was turned away, so he departed unostentatiously. He paused again and looked back at her. She gazed still out over the water: an uncomplaining abjectness of passivity, quiet in her shadowed chair.

*   *   *

As he embraced her, Jenny removed his hat slanted viciously upon his reckless head, and examined the broken crown with a recurrence of soft astonishment; and still holding the hat in her hand she came to him in a flowing enveloping movement, without seeming to move at all. Their faces merged and Jenny was immediately utterly boneless, seeming to suspend her merging rifeness by her soft mouth, then she opened her mouth against his . . . after a while Pete raised his head, Jenny's face was a passive drowsing blur rich, ineffably rich, in the dark; and Pete got out his unfresh handkerchief and wiped her mouth, quite gently.

"Got over it without leaving a scar, didn't you?" he said. Without volition they swung in a world unseen and warm as water, unseen and rife and beautiful, strange and hushed and grave beneath that waning moon of decay and death. . . . "Give your old man a kiss, kid. . . ."

*   *   *

The niece entered her aunt's room, without knocking. Mrs. Maurier raised her astonished, shrieking face and dragged a garment shapelessly across her recently uncorseted breast, as women do. When she had partially recovered from the shock she ran heavily to the door and locked it.

"It's just me," the niece said. "Say, Aunt Pat—"

Her aunt gasped: her breast and chins billowed unconfined. "Why don't you knock? You should never enter a room like that. Doesn't Henry ever—"

"Sure he does," the niece interrupted, "all the time. Say, Aunt Pat, Pete thinks you ought to pay him for his hat. For stepping on it, you know."

Her aunt stared at her. "What?"

"You stepped through Pete's hat. He and Jenny think you ought to pay for it. Or offer to, anyway. I expect if you'd offer to, he wouldn't take it."

"Thinks I ought to p—" Mrs. Maurier's voice faded into a shocked, soundless amazement.

"Yes, they think so. . . . I mentioned it because I promised them I would. You don't have to unless you want to, you know."

"Thinks I ought to p—" Again Mrs. Maurier's voice failed her, and her amazement became a chaotic thing that filled her round face interestingly. Then it froze into something definite: a coldly determined displeasure, and she recovered her voice.

"I have lodged and fed these people for a week," she said without humor. "I do not feel that I am called upon to clothe them also."

"Well, I just mentioned it because I promised," the niece repeated soothingly.

*　　*　　*

Mrs. Maurier, Jenny and the niece had disappeared, to Mr. Talliaferro's mixed relief. They still had two left, however. They took turn about with them.

Major Ayers, Fairchild and the Semitic man rushed below again. Mr. Talliaferro following openly this time, and a trifle erratically.

"How's it coming along?" Fairchild asked, poising the bottle. Mr. Talliaferro made a wet deprecating sound, glancing at the other two. They regarded him with kindly interest. "Oh, they're all right," Fairchild reassured him. "They are as anxious to see you put it over as I am." He set the bottle down well within reach, and gulped at his glass. "I tell you what, it's boldness that does the trick with women, ain't it, Major?"

"Right you are. Boldness: dash in; take 'em by storm."

"Sure. That's what you want to do. Have another drink." He filled Mr. Talliaferro's glass.

"That's my plan, exactly. Boldness. Boldness. Boldness." Mr. Talliaferro stared at the other glassily. He tried to wink. "Didn't you see me dancing with her?"

"Yes, but that ain't bold enough. If I were you, if I were doing it, I'd turn the trick to-night, now. Say, Julius, you know what I'd do? I'd go right to her room: walk right in. He's been dancing with her and talking to her: ground already broken, you see. I bet she's in there right now, waiting for him, hoping he is bold enough to come in to her. He'll feel pretty cheap to-morrow when he finds he missed his chance, won't he? You never have but one chance with a woman, you know. If you fail her then, she's done with you—the next man that comes along gets her without a struggle. It ain't the man a woman cares for that reaps the harvest of passion, you know: it's the next man that comes along after she's lost the other one. I'd sure hate to think I'd been doing work for somebody else to get the benefit of. Wouldn't you?"

Mr. Talliaferro stared at him. He swallowed twice. "But suppose, just suppose, that she isn't expecting me."

"Oh, sure. Of course, you've got to take that risk. It would take a bold man, anyway, to walk right in her room, walk right in without knocking and go straight to the bed. But how many women would resist? I wouldn't, if I were a woman. If you were her, Talliaferro, would you resist? I've found," he went on, "that boldness gets pretty near anything, in this world, especially women. But it takes a bold man. . . . Say, I bet Major Ayers would do it."

"Right you are. I'd walk right in, by Jove. . . . I say, I think I shall, anyway. Which one is it? Not the old one?"

"All right. That is, if Talliaferro don't want to do it. He has first shot, you know: he's done all the heavy preparatory work. But it takes a bold man."

"Oh, Talliaferro's bold as any man," the Semitic man said.

"But, really," Mr. Talliaferro repeated, "suppose she isn't expecting me. Suppose she were to call out—No, no."

"Yes, Talliaferro ain't bold enough. We better let Major Ayers go, after all. No necessity for disappointing the girl, at least."

"Besides," Mr. Talliaferro added quickly, "she is in a room with some one else."

"No, she ain't. She's in a room to herself, now; that one at the end of the hall."

"That's Mrs. Maurier's room," Mr. Talliaferro said, staring at him.

"No, no; she changed. That room has a broken screen, so she changed. Julius and I were helping her move this afternoon. Weren't we, Julius? That's how I happen to know Jenny's in there now."

"But, really—" Mr. Talliaferro swallowed again. "Are you sure that's her room? This is a serious matter, you know."

"Have another drink," Fairchild said.

TWELVE O'CLOCK

The deck was deserted. Fairchild and Major Ayers halted and gazed about in pained astonishment. The victrola was hooded and mute, smugly inscrutable. They held a hurried council, then they set forth to beat up stragglers. There were no stragglers.

"Put on a record," Fairchild suggested at last. "Maybe that'll get 'em up here. They must have thought we'd gone to bed."

The Semitic man started the victrola again, and again Major Ayers and Fairchild combed the deck in vain. The moon had risen, its bony erstwhile disc was thumbed into the sky like a coin after too much handling.

* * *

Mrs. Maurier routed out the captain and together they repaired to Fairchild's room. "Find it all," she directed, "every single one." The captain found it all. "Now, open that window."

She gave the captain further directions, when they had finished, and she returned to her room and sat again on the edge of her bed. Moonlight came into the room level as a lance through the port, like a marble pencil shattering and filling the room with a thin silver dust, as of marble. "It has come, at last," she whispered, aware of her body, heavy and soft with years. I should feel happy, I should feel happy, she told herself, but her limbs felt chill and strange to her and within her a terrible thing was swelling, a thing terrible and poisonous and released, like water that has been dammed too long: it was as though there were waking within her comfortable, long familiar body a thing that abode there dormant and which she had harbored unaware.

She sat on the edge of her bed, feeling her strange chill limbs, while that swelling thing within her unfolded like an intricate poisonous flower, an intricate slow convolvulæ of petals that grew and faded, died and were replaced by other petals huger and more implacable. Her limbs were strange and cold: they were trembling. That dark flower of laughter, that secret hideous flower grew and grew until that entire world which was herself was become a slow implacable swirling of hysteria that rose in her throat and shook it as though with a myriad small hands while from overhead there came a thin saccharine strain spaced off by a heavy thumping of feet, where Fairchild was teaching Major Ayers the Charleston.

And soon, another sound; and the *Nausikaa* trembled and pulsed, girding herself with motion.

* * *

Mr. Talliaferro stood in the bows, letting the wind blow upon his face, amid his hair. The worn moon had risen and she spread her boneless hand upon the ceaseless water, and the cold remote stars swung overhead, cold and remote and incurious: what cared they for the haggard despair in his face, for the hushed despair in his heart? They had seen too much of human moiling and indecision and astonishments to be concerned over the fact that Mr. Talliaferro had got himself engaged to marry again.

. . . Soon, a sound; and the *Nausikaa* trembled and pulsed, girding herself with motion.

* * *

Suddenly Fairchild stopped, raising his hand for silence. "What's that?" he asked.

"What's what?" he responded Major Ayers, pausing also and staring at him.

"I thought I heard something fall into the water." He crossed to the rail and leaned over it. Major Ayers followed him and they listened. But the dark restless water was untroubled by any foreign sound, the night was calm, islanding the worn bland disc of the moon.

"Steward throwing out grapefruit," Major Ayers suggested at last. They turned away.

"Hope so," Fairchild said. "Start her up again, Julius."

And, soon, another sound; and the *Nausikaa* trembled and pulsed, girding herself with motion.

Epilogue

1

Lake water had done strange things to Jenny's little green dress. It was rough-dried and draggled, and it had kind of sagged here and drawn up there. The skirt in the back, for instance; because now between the gracious miniature ballooning of its hem and the tops of her dingy stockings, you saw pink flesh.

But she was ineffably unaware of this as she stood on Canal street waiting for her car to come along, watching Pete's damaged hat slanting away amid the traffic, clutching the dime he had given her for carfare in her little soiled hand. Soon her car came along and she got in it and gave the conductor her dime and received change and put seven cents in the machine while men, unshaven men and coatless men and old men and spruce young men and men that smelled of toilet water and bay rum and sweat and men that smelled of just sweat, watched her with the moist abjectness of hounds. Then she went on up the aisle, rife, placidly unreluctant, and then the car jolted forward and she sat partly upon a fat man in a derby and a newspaper, who looked up at her and then hunched over to the window and dived again into his newspaper with his derby on.

The car hummed and spurted and jolted and stopped and jolted and hummed and spurted between croaching

walls and old iron lovely as dingy lace, and shrieking children from south Europe once removed and wild and soft as
animals and cheerful with filth; and old rich food smells,
smells rich enough to fatten the flesh through the lungs; and
women screaming from adjacent door to door in bright dirty
shawls. Her three pennies had got warm and moist in her
hand, so she changed them to the other hand and dried her
palm on her thigh.

Soon it was a broader street at right angles—a weary
green spaciousness of late August foliage and civilization
again in the shape of a filling station; and she descended
and passed between houses possessing once and long ago
individuality, reserve, but now become somehow vaguely
and dingily identical: reaching at last an iron gate through
which she went and on up a shallow narrow concrete walk
bordered on either side by beds in which flowers for some
reason never seemed to grow well, and so on across the
veranda and into the house.

Her father was on the night force and he now sat in his
sock feet and with his galluses down, at his supper of mack-
erel (it is Friday) and fried potatoes and coffee and an early
afternoon edition. He wiped his mustache with two sweeps
of the back of his hand.

"Where you been?"

Jenny entered the room removing her hat. She dropped
it to the floor and came up in a flanking movement. "On
a boat ride," she answered. Her father drew his feet under
his chair to rise and his face suffused slowly with relief and
anger.

"And you think you can go off like that, without a word
to nobody, and then walk back into this house—" But Jenny

captured him and she squirmed onto his rising lap and though he tried to defend himself, kissed him through his mackerelish mustache, and held him speechless so while she delved amid that vague pinish region which was her mind. After a while she remembered it.

"Haul up your sheet," she said. "You're jibbing."

2

Pete was the baby: he was too young to have been aware of it, of course, but that electric sign with the family name on it had marked a climacteric: the phœnix-like rise of the family fortunes from the dun ashes of respectability and a small restaurant catering to Italian working people, to the final and ultimate Americanization of the family, since this fortune, like most American ones, was built on the flouting of a statutory impediment.

Prior to nineteen-nineteen you entered a dingy room fecund with the rich heavy odor of Italian cooking, you sat surrounded by Italian faces and frank Italian eating sounds, at oilcloth of a cheerful red-and-white check and cunningly stained, impermeated with food, where you were presently supplied with more food. Perhaps old lady Ginotta herself came bustling out with soup and one thumb in a thick platter and a brisk word for you, or by Joe, anyway, barearmed and skilful and taciturn, while Mr. Ginotta himself in his stained apron stood talking to a table of his intimates. Perhaps if you lingered long enough over your banana or overripe ofthandled grapes you would see Pete in his ragged corduroy knickers and faded clean shirt, with his curling shock of hair and his queer golden eyes, twelve years old and beautiful as only an Italian lad can be.

But now, all this was changed. Where was once a dingy food-laden room, wooden floored and not too clean, was now a tiled space cleared and waxed for dancing and enclosed on one side by mirrors and on the other by a row of booths containing each a table and two chairs and lighted each by a discreet table lamp of that surreptitious and unmistakable shade of pink and curtained each with heavy maroon rep. And where you once got food good and Italian and cheap, you now paid so much for it that you were not required to eat it at all: and platters of spaghetti and roasted whole fowls, borne not by Joe, barearmed and skilful if taciturn, but by dinner-coated waiters with faces ironed and older than sin;—platters which served as stage properties for the oldest and weariest comedy in the world, were served you and later removed by the waiters with a sort of clairvoyant ubiquity and returned to the kitchen practically intact. And from the kitchen there came no longer any odor of cooking at all.

Joe's idea, it was. Joe, five-and-twenty and more American than any of them, had seen the writing on the wall, had argued, prevailed, and proven himself right. Mr. Ginotta had not stood prosperity. He was afraid of the new floor, to begin with. It was too slick, dangerous for a man of his age and bulk; and to look out of his kitchen, that kitchen into which he no longer dared bring his stained apron, upon a room once crowded with his friends and noisy and cheerful with eating and smells of food . . .

But all that was changed now. The very waiters themselves he did not know, and the food they bore back and forth was not food; and the noise was now a turgid pandemonium of saxophones and drums and, riding above it like distracted birds, a shrill and metallic laughter of women, ceaseless and without joy; and the smells a blending of tobacco and alcohol and unchaste scent. And from the kitchen there came no longer any odor of cooking at all: even his range was gone, replaced by an oil stove.

So he died, fairly full of years and with more money to his name in the bank than most Italian princes have. Mrs. Ginotta had the flu at the same time. It had settled in her ears and as time passed she became quite deaf; and because of the fact that her old friends now went elsewhere to dine and the people who came now arrived quite late, after she was in bed mostly, and her old man was dead and her sons were such Americans now, busy and rich and taciturn, and because the strange waiters frightened her a little, the old lady had got out of the habit of talking at all. She prepared food for her sons on the new stove of which she was afraid, but they were in and out so much it was hard to anticipate their mealtimes; and her eyes being no longer good enough for sewing, she spent her time puttering about their living quarters overhead or in a corner of the kitchen where she would be out of the way, preparing vegetables and such— things that didn't require keenness of sight or attention.

The room itself she would not enter, though from her accustomed corner in the kitchen she could on occasion watch the boneless sophistication of the saxophone player and the drummer's flapping elbows, and years ago she had heard the noise they made. But that was long ago and she had forgotten it, and now she accepted their antics as she accepted the other changes, associating no sound with them at all. Joe had several automobiles now: big noticeable ones, and he used to try to persuade her to ride in them. But she refused stubbornly always, though it was a matter of neighborhood comment, how good the Ginotta boys were to the old lady.

But Joe, with his shrewd taciturn face and his thinning hair and his shirt of heavy striped silk smoothly taut across his tight embryonic paunch—Joe, standing with his headwaiter at the desk, paused in his occupation to glance down that room with its every modern fixture, its tiled floor and lights and mirrors, with commendable pride. With the quiet joy of ownership his gaze followed its mirrored diminishing tunnel and passed on to the discreetly curtained entrance beneath that electric sign, that ultimate accolade of Americanization, flashing his name in golden letters in rain or mist or against the remote insane stars themselves; and to his brother slanting his damaged hat defiantly, turning in beneath it.

Joe held his sheaf of banknotes in one hand and his poised wetted finger over it and watched Pete traverse the mirrored length of the room.

"Where in hell you been?" he demanded.

"To the country," Pete answered shortly. "Anything to eat?"

"Eat, hell," his brother exclaimed. "Here I've had to pay a man two days just because you were off helling around somewheres. And now you come in talking about something to eat. Here—" he put aside his sheaf of money and from a drawer he took a pack of small slips of paper and ran through them. The headwaiter counted money undisturbed, methodically. "I promised this stuff to her by noon. You get busy and run it out there—here's the address—and no more foolishness, see? Eat, hell." But Pete had brushed past the other without even pausing. His brother followed him. "You get right at it, you hear?" He raised his voice. "You think you can walk out of here and stay as long as you want, huh? You think you can come strolling back after a week, huh? You think you own this place?"

The old lady was waiting inside the kitchen. She didn't hardly talk at all any more: only made sounds, wet sounds of satisfaction and alarm; and she saw her older son's face and she made these sounds now, looking from one to the other but not offering to touch them. Pete entered the room and his brother stopped at the door, and the old lady shuffled across to the stove and fetched Pete a plate of warmed-over spaghetti and fish and set it before him at a zinc-covered table. His brother stood in the door and glared at him.

"Get up from there, now, like I told you. Come on, come on, you can eat when you get back."

But the old lady bustled around, getting between them with the stubborn barrier of her deafness, and her alarmed sounds rose again, then fell and became a sort of meaningless crooning while she kept herself between them, pushing Pete's plate nearer, patting his knife and fork into his hands. "Look out," Pete said at last, pushing her hands away. Joe glared from the door, but he humored her, as he always did.

"Make it snappy," he said gruffly, turning away. When he had gone the old lady returned to her chair and her discarded bowl of vegetables.

Pete ate hungrily. Sounds came back to him: a broom, and indistinguishable words, and then the street door opened and closed and above a swift tapping of heels he heard a woman's voice. It spoke to his brother at the desk, but the brittle staccato came on without stopping, and as Pete raised his head the girl entered on her high cheap heels and an unbelievable length of pale stocking severed sharply by her skimpy dark frock. Within the small bright bell of her hat, her painted passionate face, and her tawdry shrillness was jointless and poised as a thin tree.

"Where you been?" she asked.

"Off with some women." He resumed his meal.

"More than one?" she asked quickly, watching him.

"Yeh. Five or six. Reason it took me so long."

"Oh," she said. "You're some little poppa, ain't you?" He continued to eat and she came over beside him. "Whatcher so glum about? Somebody take your candy away from you?" She removed his hat. "Say, look at your hat." She stared at it, then laid it on the table and sliding her hand into his thickly curling hair she tugged his face up, and his queer golden eyes. "Wipe your mouth off," she said. But she kissed him anyway, and raised her head again. "You better wipe it off now, sure enough," she said with contemplation. She released his hair. "Well, I got to go." And she turned, but paused again at the old lady's chair and screamed at her in Italian. The old lady looked up, nodding her head, then bent over her beans again.

Pete finished his meal. He could still hear her shrill voice from the other room, and he lit a cigarette and strolled out. The old lady hadn't been watching him, but as soon as he was gone, she got up and removed the plate and washed it and put it away, and then sat down again and picked up her bowl.

"Ready to go, huh?" his brother looked up from the desk. "Here's the address. Snap it up, now: I told her I'd have it out there by noon." The bulk of Joe's business was outside, like this. He had a name for reliability of which he was proud. "Take the Studebaker," he added.

"That old hack?" Pete paused, protesting. "I'll take your Chrysler."

"Damn if you will," his brother rejoined, heating again. "Get on, now; take that Studebaker like I told you," he said violently. "If you don't like it, buy one of your own."

"Ah, shut up." Pete turned away. Within one of the booths, beyond a partly drawn curtain, he saw her facing the mirror, renewing the paint on her mouth. Beside her stood one of the waiters in his shirtsleeves, holding a mop. She made a swift signal with her hand to his reflection in the glass. He slanted his hat again, without replying.

She was an old hack, beside the fawn-and-nickel splendor of the new Chrysler, but she would go and she'd carry six or seven cases comfortably—the four cases he now had were just peas in a matchbox. He followed the traffic to Canal street, crossed it and fell into the line waiting to turn out St. Charles. The line inched forward, stopped, inched forward again when the bell rang. The policeman at the curb held the line again and Pete sat watching the swarming darting newsboys, and the loafers and shoppers and promenaders, and little colt-like girls with their monotonous blonde legs. The bell rang, but the cop still held them. Pete leaned out, jazzing his idling engine. "Come on, come on, you blue-bellied bastard," he called. "Let's go."

At last the cop lowered his glove and Pete whipped skilfully into St. Charles, and presently the street widened and became an avenue picketed with palms, and settling onto his spine and slanting his damaged straw hat to a swaggering slant on his dark reckless head, he began to overhaul the slow ones, passing them up.

3

Fairchild's splitting head ultimately roused him and he lay for some time submerged in the dull throbbing misery of his body before he discovered that the boat was stationary again and, after an effort of unparalleled stoicism, that it was eleven o'clock. No sound anywhere, yet there was something in the atmosphere of his surroundings, something different. But trying to decide what it was only made his head pound the worse, so he gave it up and lay back again. The Semitic man slumbered in his berth.

After a while Fairchild groaned, and rose and wavered blundering across the cabin and drank deeply of water. Then he saw land through the port: a road and a weathered board wall, and beyond it, trees. Mandeville he decided. He tried to rouse the Semitic man, but the other cursed him from slumber and rolled over to face the wall.

He hunted again for a bottle, but there were not even any empty ones: who ever did it had made a clean sweep. Well, a cup of coffee, then. So he got into his trousers and crossed the passage to a lavatory and held his head beneath a tap for a while. Then he returned and finished dressing and sallied forth.

Some one slumbered audibly in Major Ayers' room. It was Major Ayers himself, and Fairchild closed the door and went on, struck anew with that strange atmosphere which the yacht seemed to have gained overnight. The saloon was empty also, and a broken meal offended his temporarily refined sensibilities with partially emptied cups and cold soiled plates. But still no sound, no human sound, save Major Ayers and the Semitic man in slumber's strophe and antistrophe. He stood in the door of the saloon and groaned again. Then he took his splitting head on deck.

Here he blinked in the light, shutting his eyes against it while hot brass hammers beat against his eyeballs. Three men dangled their legs over the edge of the quay and regarded him, and he opened his eyes again and saw the three men.

"Good morning," he said. "What town's this? Mandeville?"

The three men looked at him. After a time one said: "Mandeville? Mandeville what?"

"What town is it, then?" he asked, but as he spoke awareness came to him and looking about he saw a steel bridge and a trolley on the bridge, and further still, a faint mauve smudge on the sky, and in the other direction the flag that floated above the yacht club, languorous in a faint breeze. The three men sat and swung their legs and watched him. Presently one of them said:

"Your party went off and left you."

"Looks like it," Fairchild agreed. "Do you know if they said anything about sending a car back for us?"

"No, she ain't going to send back to-day," the man

answered. Fairchild cleared his aching eyes: it was the captain. "Trolley track over yonder a ways," he called after Fairchild as he turned and descended the companionway.

4

Major Ayers' appointment was for three o'clock. His watch
corroborated and commended him as he stepped from the
elevator into a long cool corridor glassed on either hand by
opaque plate from beyond which came a thin tapping of
typewriters. Soon he found the right door and entered it,
and across a low barrier he gave his card to a thin scented
girl, glaring at her affably, and stood in the ensuing interval gazing out the window across diversified rectangles of
masonry, toward the river.

The girl returned. "Mr. Reichman will see you now,"
she said across her chewing gum, swinging the gate open
for him.

Mr. Reichman shook his hand and offered him a chair
and a cigar. He asked Major Ayers for his impressions of
New Orleans and immediately interrupted the caller's confused staccato response to ask Major Ayers, for whom the
war had served as the single possible condition under which
he could have returned to England at all, and to whom for
certain private reasons London had been interdict since
the Armistice, how affairs compared between the two cities.
Then he swung back in his patent chair and said:

"Now, Major, just what is your proposition?"

"Ah, yes," said Major Ayers, flicking the ash from his
cigar. "It's a salts. Now, all Americans are constipated—"

5

Beneath him, on the ground floor, where a rectangle of light fell outward across the alley, a typewriter was being hammered by a heavy and merciless hand. Fairchild sat with a cigar on his balcony just above the unseen but audible typist, enjoying the cool darkness and the shadowed treefilled spaciousness of the cathedral close beneath his balcony. An occasional trolley clanged and crashed up Royal street, but this was but seldom, and when it had died away there was no sound save the monotonous merging clatter of the typewriter. Then he saw and recognized Mr. Talliaferro turning the corner and with an exclamation of alarm he sprang to his feet, kicking his chair over backward. Ducking quickly into the room redolent of pennyroyal he snapped off the reading lamp and leaped upon a couch, feigning sleep.

Mr. Talliaferro walked dapperly, swinging his stick, his goal in sight. Yes, Fairchild was right, he knew women, the feminine soul—? No, not soul: they have no souls. Nature, the feminine nature: that substance, that very substance of their being, impalpable as moonlight, challenging and retreating at the same time; inconsistent, nay, incomprehensible, yet serving their ends with such a devastating practicality. As though the earth, the world, man and his very desires and impulses themselves, had been invented for the sole purpose of hushing their little hungry souls by filling their time through serving their biological ends. . . .

Yes, boldness. And propinquity. And opportunity, that happy conjunction of technique and circumstance, being with the right one in the right place at the right time. Yes, yes, Opportunity, Opportunity—more important than all, perhaps. Mr. Talliaferro put up Opportunity: he called for a ballot. The ayes had it.

He stopped utterly still in the flash of his inspiration. At last he had it, had the trick, the magic Word. It was so simple that he stood in amaze at the fact that it had not occurred to him before. But then he realized that its very simplicity was the explanation. And my nature is complex, he told himself, gazing at stars in the hot dark sky, in a path of sky above the open coffin of the street. It was so devastatingly simple that he knew a faint qualm. Was it—was it exactly sporting? Wasn't it like shooting quail on the ground? But no, no: now that he had the key, now that he had found the Word, he dared admit to himself that he had suffered. Not so much in his vanity, not physically—after all, man can do without the pleasures of love: it will not kill him; but because each failure seemed to put years behind him with far more finality than the mere recurrence of natal days. Yes, Mr. Talliaferro owed himself reparation, let them suffer who must. And was not that woman's part from time immemorial?

Opportunity, create your opportunity, prepare the ground by overlooking none of those small important trivialities which mean so much to them, then take advantage of it. And I can do that, he told himself. Indifference, perhaps, as though women were no rare thing with me; that there is perhaps another woman I had rather have seen, but circumstances over which neither of us had any control intervened. They like a man who has other women, for some reason. Can it be that love to them is half adultery and half jealousy? . . . Yes, I can do that sort of thing, I really can. . . . "She would have one suit of black underthings," Mr. Talliaferro said aloud with a sort of exultation.

He struck the pavement with his stick, lightly. "By God, that's it," he exclaimed in a hushed tone, striding on. . . . "Create the opportunity, lead up to it delicately but firmly Drop a remark about coming to-night only because I had promised. . . . Yes, they like an honorable man: it increases their latitude. She'll say, 'Please take me to dance,' and I'll say 'No, really, I don't care to dance to-night,' and she'll say, 'Won't you take me?' leaning against me, eh?—let's see— yes, she'll take my hand. But I shan't respond at once. She'll tease and then I'll put my arm around her and raise her face in the dark cab and kiss her, coldly, and I'll say, 'Do you really want to dance to-night?' and then she'll say, 'Oh, I don't know. Suppose we just drive around a while? . . .' Will she say that at this point? Well, should she not . . . Let's see, what would she say?"

Mr. Talliaferro strode on, musing swiftly. Well, anyway, if she says that, if she does say that, then I'll say 'No, let's dance.' Yes, yes, something like that. Though perhaps I'd better kiss her again, not so coldly, perhaps? . . . But should she say something else . . . But then, I shall be prepared for any contingency, eh? Half the battle. . . . Yes, something like that, delicately but firmly done, so as not to alarm the quarry. Some walls are carried by storm, but all walls are reduced by siege. There is also the fable of the wind and the sun and the man in a cloak. "We'll change the gender, by Jove," Mr. Talliaferro said aloud, breaking suddenly from his revery to discover that he had passed Fairchild's door. He retraced his steps and craned his neck to see the dark window.

"Fairchild!"

No reply.

"Oh, Fairchild!"

The two dark windows were inscrutable as two fates. He pressed the bell, then stepped back to complete his aria. Beside the door was another entrance. Light streamed across a half length lattice blind like a saloon door; beyond it a typewriter was being thumped viciously. Mr. Talliaferro knocked diffidently upon the blind.

"Hello," a voice boomed above the clattering machine, though the machine itself did not falter. Mr. Talliaferro pondered briefly, then he knocked again.

"Come in, damn you." The voice drowned the typewriter temporarily. "Come in: do you think this is a bathroom?" Mr. Talliaferro opened the blind and the huge collarless man at the typewriter raised his sweating leonine head, and regarded Mr. Talliaferro fretfully. "Well?"

"Pardon me, I'm looking for Fairchild."

"Next floor," the other snapped, poising his hands. "Good night."

"But he doesn't answer. Do you happen to know if he is in to-night?"

"I do not."

Mr. Talliaferro pondered again, diffidently. "I wonder how I might ascertain? I'm pressed for time—"

"How in hell do I know? Go up and see, or stand out there and call him."

"Thanks, I'll go up, if you've no objection."

"Well, go up, then," the big man answered, leaping again upon his typewriter. Mr. Talliaferro watched him for a time.

"May I go through this way?" he ventured at last, mildly and politely.

"Yes, yes. Go anywhere. But for God's sake, don't bother me any longer."

Mr. Talliaferro murmured Thanks and sidled past the large frenzied man. The whole small room trembled to the man's heavy hands and the typewriter leaped and chattered like a mad thing.

He went on and into a dark corridor filled with a thin vicious humming, and mounted lightless stairs into an acrid region scented with pennyroyal. Fairchild heard him stumble in the darkness, and groaned. I'll have your blood for this! he swore at the thundering oblivious typewriter beneath him. After a time his door opened and the caller hissed Fairchild! into the room. Fairchild swore again under his breath. The couch complained to his movement, and he said:

"Wait there until I turn up the light. You'll break everything I've got, blundering around in the dark."

Mr. Talliaferro sighed with relief. "Well, well, I had just about given you up and gone away when that man beneath you kindly let me come through his place." The light came on under Fairchild's hand. "Oh, you were asleep, weren't you? So sorry to have disturbed you. But I want your advice, as I failed to see you this morning. . . . You got home all right?" he asked with thoughtful tact.

Fairchild answered "Yes" shortly, and Mr. Talliaferro laid his hat and stick on a table, knocking therefrom a vase of late summer flowers. With amazing agility he caught the vase before it crashed, though not before its contents had liberally splashed him. "Ah, the devil!" he ejaculated. He replaced the vase and quickly fell to mopping at his sleeves and coat front with his handkerchief. "And this suit fresh from the presser, too!" he added with exasperation.

Fairchild watched him with ill-suppressed vindictive glee. "Too bad," he commiserated insincerely, lying again on the couch. "But she won't notice it: she'll be too interested in what you're saying to her."

Mr. Talliaferro looked up quickly, a trifle dubiously. He spread his handkerchief across the corner of the table to dry. Then he smoothed his hands over his neat pale hair.

"Do you think so? Really? That's what I stopped in to discuss with you." For a while Mr. Talliaferro sat neatly and gazed at his host from beyond a barrier of a polite and hopeless despair. Fairchild remarked his expression with sudden curiosity, but before he could speak Mr. Talliaferro reassimilated himself and became again his familiar articulated mild alarm.

"What's the matter?" Fairchild asked.

"I? Nothing. Nothing at all, my dear fellow. Why do you ask?"

"You looked like you had something on your mind, just then."

The guest laughed artificially. "Not at all. You imagined it, really." His hidden dark thing lurked behind his eyes yet, but he vanquished it temporarily. "I will ask a favor, however, before I . . . before I ask your advice. That you don't mention our—conversation. The general trend of it, you know." Fairchild watched him with curiosity. "To any of our mutual women friends," he added further, meeting his host's curious gaze.

"All right" Fairchild agreed. "I never mention any of the conversations we have on this subject. I don't reckon I'll start now."

"Thank you." Mr. Talliaferro was again his polite smug self. "I have a particular reason, this time, which I'll divulge

to you as soon as I consider myself . . . You will be the first
to know."

"Sure," said Fairchild again. "What is it to be this time?"

"Ah, yes," said the guest with swift optimism, "I really
believe that I have discovered the secret of success with
them: create the proper setting beforehand, indifference
to pique them, then boldness—that is what I have always
overlooked. Listen: to-night I shall turn the trick. But I want
your advice." Fairchild groaned and lay back. Mr. Talliaferro picked his handkerchief from the table and whipped it
about his ankles. He continued:

"Now, I shall make her jealous to begin with, by speaking of another woman in—ah—quite intimate terms. She
will doubtless wish to dance, but I shall pretend indifference, and when she begs me to take her to dance, perhaps
I'll kiss her, suddenly but with detachment—you see?"

"Yes?" murmured the other, cradling his head on his
arms and closing his eyes.

"Yes. So we'll go and dance, and I'll pet her a bit, still
impersonally, as if I were thinking of some one else. She'll
naturally be intrigued and she'll say, 'What are you thinking
of?' and I'll say, 'Why do you want to know?' She'll plead
with me, perhaps dancing quite close to me, cajoling; but
I'll say, 'I'd rather tell you what you are thinking of,' and she
will say 'What?' immediately, and I'll say, 'You are thinking
of me.' Now, what do you think of that? What will she say
then?"

"Probably tell you you've got a swelled head."

Mr. Talliaferro's face fell. "Do you think she'll say that?"

"Don't know. You'll find out soon enough."

"No," Mr. Talliaferro said after a while, "I don't believe she will. I rather fancied she'd think I knew a lot about women." He mused deeply for a time. Then he burst out again: "If she does, I'll say 'Perhaps so. But I am tired of this place. Let's go.' She'll not want to leave, but I'll be firm. And then—" Mr. Talliaferro became smug, bursting with something he withheld. "No, no: I shan't tell you—it's too excruciatingly simple. Why some one else has not . . ." He sat gloating.

"Scared I'll run out and use it myself before you have a chance?" Fairchild asked.

"No, really; not at all. I—" He considered a moment, then he leaned to the other. "It's not that at all, really; I only feel that . . . Being the discoverer, that sort of thing, eh? I trust you, my dear fellow," he added swiftly in a burst of confidence. "Merely my own scruples— You see?"

"Sure," said Fairchild drily. "I understand."

"You will have so many opportunities, while I . . ." Again that dark thing came up behind Mr. Talliaferro's eyes and peered forth a moment. He drove it back. "And you really think it will work?"

"Sure. Provided that final coup is as deadly as you claim. And provided she acts like she ought to. It might be a good idea to outline the plot to her, though, so she won't slip up herself."

"You are pulling my leg now," Mr. Talliaferro bridled slightly. "But don't you think this plan is good?"

"Airtight. You've thought of everything, haven't you?"

"Surely. That's the only way to win battles, you know. Napoleon taught us that."

"Napoleon said something about the heaviest artillery, too," the other said wickedly. Mr. Talliaferro smiled with deprecatory complacence.

"I am as I am," he murmured.

"Especially when it hasn't been used in some time," Fairchild added. Mr. Talliaferro looked like a struck beast and the other said quickly: "But are you going to try this scheme to-night, or are you just describing a hypothetical case?"

Mr. Talliaferro produced his watch and glanced at it in consternation. "Good gracious. I must run!" He sprang to his feet and thrust his handkerchief into his pocket. "Thanks for advising me. I really think I have the system at last, don't you?"

"Sure," the other agreed. At the door Mr. Talliaferro turned and rushed back to shake hands. "Wish me luck," he said turning again. He paused once more. "Our little talk: you'll not mention it?"

"Sure, sure," repeated Fairchild. The door closed upon the caller and his descending feet sounded on the stairs. He stumbled again, then the street door closed behind him, and Fairchild rose and stood on the balcony and watched him out of sight.

Fairchild returned to the couch and reclined again, laughing. Abruptly he ceased chuckling and lay for a time in alarmed concern. Then he groaned again, and rose and took his hat.

As he stepped into the alley, the Semitic man pausing at the entrance spoke to him. "Where are you going?" he asked.

"I don't know," Fairchild replied. "Somewhere. The Great Illusion has just called," he explained. "He has an entirely new scheme to-night."

"Oh. Slipping out, are you?" the other asked, lowering his voice.

"No, he just dashed away. But I don't dare stay in this evening. He'll be back inside of two hours to tell me why this one didn't work. We'll have to go somewhere else." The Semitic man mopped his handkerchief across his bald head. Beyond the lattice blind beside them the typewriter still chattered. Fairchild chuckled again. Then he sighed. "I wish Talliaferro could find him a woman. I'm tired of being seduced. . . . Let's go over to Gordon's."

6

The niece had already yawned elaborately several times at the lone guest: she was prepared, and recognized the pre-liminary symptoms indicating that her brother was on the point of his customary abrupt and muttered departure from the table. She rose also, with alacrity.

"Well," she said briskly, "I've enjoyed knowing you a lot, Mark. Next summer maybe we'll be back here, and we'll have to do it again, won't we?"

"Patricia," her aunt said, "sit down."

"I'm sorry, Aunt Pat. But Josh wants me to sit with him to-night. He's going away to-morrow," she explained to the guest.

"Aren't you going, too?" Mark Frost asked.

"Yes, but this is our last night here, and Gus wants me to—"

"Not me," her brother denied quickly. "You needn't come away on my account."

"Well, I think I'd better, anyway."

Her aunt repeated "Patricia."

But the niece ignored her. She circled the table and shook the guest's hand briskly, before he could rise. "Goodby," she repeated. "Until next summer." Her aunt said "Patricia" again, firmly. She turned again at the door and said politely: "Good-night, Aunt Pat."

Her brother had gone on up the stairs. She hurried after him, leaving her aunt to call "Patricia!" from the dining room, and reached the head of the stairs in time to see his door close behind him. When she tried the knob, the door was locked, so she came away and went quietly to her room.

She stripped off her clothes in the darkness and lay on her bed, and after a while she heard him banging and splashing in the connecting bathroom. When these sounds had ceased she rose and entered the bathroom quietly from her side, and quietly she tried his door. Unlocked.

She snapped on the light and spun the tap of the shower until needles of water drummed viciously into the bath. She thrust her hand beneath it at intervals: soon it was stinging and cold; and she drew her breath as for a dive and sprang beneath it, clutching a cake of soap, and cringed shuddering and squealing while the water needled her hard simple body in its startling bathing suit of white skin, matting her coarse hair, stinging and blinding her.

She whirled the tap again and the water ceased its antiseptic miniature thunder, and after toweling herself vigorously she found that she was hot as ever, though not sticky any longer; so moving more slowly she returned to her room and donned fresh pajamas. This suit had as yet its original cord. Then she went on her bare silent feet and stood again at the door of her brother's room, listening.

"Look out, Josh," she called suddenly, flinging open the door, "I'm coming in."

His room was dark, but she could discern the shape of him on the bed and she sped across the room and plumped jouncing onto the bed beside him. He jerked himself up sharply.

"Here," he exclaimed. "What do you want to come in here worrying me, for?" He raised himself still further: a brief violent struggle, and the niece thudded solidly on the floor. She said Ow in a muffled surprised tone. "Now, get out and stay out," her brother added. "I want to go to sleep."

"Aw, lemme stay a while. I'm not going to bother you."

"Haven't you been staying under my feet for a week, without coming in here where I'm trying to go to sleep? Get out, now."

"Just a little while," she begged. "I'll lie still if you want to go to sleep."

"You won't keep still. You go on, now."

"Please, Gus. I swear I will."

"Well," he agreed at last, grudgingly. "But if you start flopping around—"

"I'll be still," she promised. She slid quickly onto the bed and lay rigidly on her back. Outside, in the hot darkness, insects scraped and rattled and droned. The room, however, was a spacious quiet coolness, and the curtains at the windows stirred in a ghost of a breeze.

"Josh." She lay flat, perfectly still.

"Huh."

"Didn't you do something to that boat?"

After a while he said: "What boat?" She was silent, taut with listening. He said: "Why? What would I want to do anything to the boat for? What makes you think I did?"

"Didn't you, now? Honest?"

"You're crazy. I never hurt—I never was down there except when you came tagging down there, that morning. What would I want to do anything to it, for?" They lay motionless, a kind of tenseness. He said, suddenly: "Did you tell her I did something to it?"

"Aw, don't be a goof. I'm not going to tell on you."

"You're damn right you won't. I never did anything to it."

"All right, all right: I'm not going to tell if you haven't got guts to. You're yellow, Josh," she told him calmly.

"Look here, I told you that if you wanted to stay in here, you'd have to keep quiet, didn't I? Shut up, then. Or get out."

"Didn't you break that boat, honest?"

"No, I told you. Now, you shut up or get out of here."

They lay quiet for a time. After a while she moved carefully, turning onto her belly by degrees. She lay still again for a time, then she raised her head. He seemed to be asleep, so she lowered her head. He seemed to be asleep, so she lowered her head and relaxed her muscles, spreading her arms and legs to where the sheet was still cool.

"I'm glad we're going to-morrow," she murmured, as though to herself. "I like to ride on the train. And moun-

tains again. I love mountains, all blue and . . . blue. . . .
We'll be seeing mountains day after to-morrow. Little towns
on 'em that don't smell like people eating all the time . . .
and mountains. . . ."

"No mountains between here and Chicago," her brother
said gruffly. "Shut up."

"Yes, there are." She raised herself to her elbow. "There
are some. I saw some coming down here."

"That was in Virginia and Tennessee. We don't go
through Virginia to Chicago, dumbbell."

"We go through Tennessee, though."

"Not that part of Tennessee. Shut up, I tell you. Here,
you get up and go back to your room."

"No. Please, just a little while longer. I'll lie still. Come
on, Gus, don't be so crummy."

"Get out, now," he repeated implacably.

"I'll be still: I won't say a w—"

"No. Outside, now. Go on. Go on, Gus, like I tell you."
She heaved herself over nearer. "Please, Josh. Then I'll
go."

"Well. Be quick about it." He turned his face away and
she leaned down and took his ear between her teeth, biting
it just a little, making a kind of meaningless maternal sound
against his ear. "That's enough," he said presently, turning
his head and his moistened ear. "Get out, now."

She rose obediently and returned to her room. It seemed
to be hotter in here than in his room, so she got up and
removed her pajamas and got back in bed and lay on her
back, cradling her dark grave head in her arms and gazing
into the darkness; and after a while it wasn't so hot and it was
like she was on a high place looking away out where moun-

tains faded dreaming and blue and on and on into a purple haze under the slanting and solemn music of the sun. She'd see 'em day after to-morrow. Mountains . . .

7

Fairchild went directly to the marble and stood before it, clasping his hands at his burly back. The Semitic man sat immediately on entering the room, preempting the single chair. The host was busy beyond the rep curtain which constituted his bedroom, from where he presently reappeared with a bottle of whisky. He had removed both shirt and undershirt now, and beneath a faint reddish fuzz his chest gleamed with heat, like an oiled gladiator's.

"I see," Fairchild remarked as the host entered, "that you too have been caught by this modern day fetich of virginity. But you have this advantage over us: yours will remain inviolate without your having to shut your eyes to its goings-on. You don't have to make any effort to keep yours from being otherwise. Very satisfactory. And very unusual. The greatest part of man's immolation of virginity is, I think, composed of an alarm and a suspicion that some one else may be, as the term is, getting it."

"Perhaps Gordon's alarm regarding his own particular illusion of it is, that some one else may not get it," the Semitic man suggested.

"No, I guess not," Fairchild said. "He don't expect to sell this to anybody, you know. Who would pay out good money for a virginity he couldn't later violate, if only to assure himself it was the genuine thing?"

"Leda clasping her duck between her thighs could yet be carved out of it, however," the other pointed out; "it is large enough for that. Or—"

"Swan," corrected Fairchild.

"No. Duck," the Semitic man insisted. "Americans would prefer a duck. Or udders and a fig leaf might be added to the thing as it stands. Isn't that possible, Gordon?"

"Yes. It might be restored," Gordon admitted drily. He disappeared again beyond the curtain and returned with two heavy tumblers and a shaving mug bearing a name in Gothic lettering of faded gilt. He drew up the bench on which his enamel water pitcher rested, and Fairchild came and sat upon it. Gordon took the shaving mug and went to lean his tall body against the wall. His intolerant hawk's face was like bronze in the unshaded glare of the light. The Semitic man puffed at his cigar. Fairchild raised his glass, squinting through it.

"Udders, and a fig leaf," he repeated. He drank, and set his tumbler down to light a cigarette. "After all, that is the end of art. I mean—"

"We do get something out of art," the Semitic man agreed. "We all admit that."

"Yes," said Fairchild. "Art reminds us of our youth, of that age when life don't need to have her face lifted every so often for you to consider her beautiful. That's about all the virtue there is in art: it's a kind of Battle Creek, Michigan, for the spirit. And when it reminds us of youth, we remember grief and forget time. That's something."

"Something, if all a man has to do is forget time," the Semitic man rejoined. "But one who spends his days trying to forget time is like one who spends his time forgetting death or digestion. That's another instance of your unshakable faith in words. It's like morphine, language is. A fearful habit to form: you become a bore to all who would otherwise cherish you. Of course, there is the chance that you may be hailed as a genius after you are dead long years, but what is that to you? There will still be high endeavor that ends, as always, with kissing in the dark, but where are you? Time? Time? Why worry about something that takes care of itself so well? You were born with the habit of consuming time. Be satisfied with that. Tom-o'-Bedlam had the only genius for consuming time: that is, to be utterly unaware of it.

"But you speak for the artists. I am thinking of the majority of us who are not artists and who need protection from artists, whose time the artists insist on passing for us. We get along quite well with our sleeping and eating and procreating, if you artists only let us alone. But you accursed who are not satisfied with the world as it is and so must try to rebuild the very floor you are standing on, you keep on talking and shouting and gesturing at us until you get us all fidgety and alarmed. So I believe that if art served any purpose at all, it would at least keep the artists themselves occupied."

Fairchild raised his glass again. "It's more than that. It's getting into life, getting into it and wrapping it around you, becoming a part of it. Women can do it without art—old biology takes care of that. But men, men . . . A woman conceives: does she care afterward whose seed it was? Not she. And bears, and all the rest of her life—her young troubling years, that is—is filled. Of course the father can look at it occasionally. But in art, a man can create without any assistance at all: what he does is his. A perversion, I grant you, but a perversion that builds Chartres and invents Lear is a pretty good thing." He drank, and set his tumbler down.

"Creation, reproduction from within. . . . Is the dominating impulse in the world feminine, after all, as aboriginal peoples believe? . . . There is a kind of spider or something. The female is the larger, and when the male goes to her he goes to death: she devours him during the act of conception. And that's man: a kind of voraciousness that makes an artist stand beside himself with a notebook in his hand always, putting down all the charming things that ever happen to him, killing them for the sake of some problematical something he might or he might not ever use. Listen," he said, "love, youth, sorrow and hope and despair—they were nothing at all to me until I found later some need of a particular reaction to put in the mouth of some character of whom I wasn't at that time certain, and that I don't yet consider very admirable. But maybe it was because I had to work all the time to earn a living, when I was a young man."

"Perhaps so," the Semitic man agreed. "People still believe they have to work to live."

"Sure you have to work to live," Fairchild said quickly.

"You'd naturally say that. If a man has had to deny himself any pleasures during his pleasuring years, he always likes to believe it was necessary. That's where you get your Puritans from. We don't like to see any one violate laws we observed, and get away with it. God knows, heaven is a dry reward for abnegation."

Fairchild rose and went to stand again before the fluid, passionate fixity of the marble. "The end of art," he repeated. "I mean, to the consumer, not to us: we have to do it, they don't. They can take it or leave it. Probably Gordon feels the same way about stories that I do about sculpture, but for me . . ." He mused upon the marble for a time. "When the statue is completely nude, it has only a coldly formal significance, you know. But when some foreign matter like a leaf or a fold of drapery (kept there in defiance of gravity by God only knows what) draws the imagination to where the organs of reproduction are concealed, it lends the statue a warmer, a—a—more—"

"Speculative significance," supplied the Semitic man.

"—speculative significance which I must admit I require in my sculpture."

"Certainly the moralists agree with you."

"Why shouldn't they? The same food nourishes everybody's convictions alike. And a man that earns his bread in a glue factory must get some sort of pleasure from smelling cattle hooves, or he'd change his job. There's your perversion, I think."

"And," the Semitic man said, "if you spend your life worrying over sex, it's an added satisfaction to get paid for your time."

"Yes. But if I earned my bread by means of sex, at least I'd have enough pride about it to be a good honest whore." Gordon came over and filled the glasses again. Fairchild returned and got his, and prowled aimlessly about the room, examining things. The Semitic man sat with his handkerchief spread over his bald head. He regarded Gordon's naked torso with envious wonder. "They don't seem to bother you at all," he stated fretfully.

"Look here," Fairchild called suddenly. He had unswaddled a damp cloth from something and he now bent over his find. "Come here, Julius." The Semitic man rose and joined him.

It was clay, yet damp, and from out its dull, dead grayness Mrs. Maurier looked at them. Her chins, harshly, and her flaccid jaw muscles with savage verisimilitude. Her eyes were caverns thumbed with two motions into the dead familiar astonishment of her face; and yet, behind them, somewhere within those empty sockets, behind all her familiar surprise, there was something else—something that exposed her face for the mask it was, and still more, a mask unaware. "Well, I'm damned," Fairchild said slowly, staring at it. "I've known her for a year, and Gordon comes along after four days . . . Well, I'll be damned," he said again.

"I could have told you," the Semitic man said. "But I wanted you to get it by yourself. I don't see how you missed it; I don't see how any one with your faith in your fellow man could believe that any one could be as silly as she, without reason."

"An explanation for silliness?" Fairchild repeated. "Does her sort of silliness require explanation?"

"It shouts it," the other answered. "Look how Gordon got it, right away."

"That's so," Fairchild admitted. He gazed at the face again, then he looked at Gordon with envious admiration. "And you got it right away, didn't you?"

Gordon was replenishing the glasses again. "He couldn't have missed it," the Semitic man repeated. "I don't see how you missed it. You are reasonably keen about people— sooner or later."

"Well, I guess I missed her," Fairchild returned, and

extended his tumbler. "But it's the usual thing, ain't it? Plantations and things? First family, and all that?"

"Something like that," the Semitic man agreed. He returned to his chair and Fairchild sat again beside the water pitcher. "She's a northerner, herself. Married it. Her husband must have been pretty old when they married. That's what explains her, I think."

"What does? Being a northerner, or marriage? Marriage starts and explains lots of things about us, just like singleness or widowhood does. And I guess the Ohio river can affect your destiny, too. But how does it explain her?"

"The story is, that her people forced her to marry old Maurier. He had been overseer on a big place before the Civil War. He disappeared in '63, and when the war was over he turned up again riding a horse with a Union Army cavalry saddle and a hundred thousand dollars in uncut Federal notes for a saddle blanket. Lord knows what the amount really was, or how he got it, but it was enough to establish him. Money. You can't argue against money: you only protest.

"Everybody expected him to splurge about with his money: show up the penniless aristocracy, that sort of thing; work out some of the inhibitions he must have developed during his overseer days. But he didn't. Perhaps he'd got rid of his inhibitions during his sojourn at the war. Anyway, he failed to live up to character, so people decided that he was a moral coward, that he was off somewhere in a hole with his money, like a rat. And this was the general opinion until a rumor got out about several rather raw land deals in which he was assisted by a Jew named Julius Kauffman who was acquiring a fortune and an unsavory name during those years immediately following General Butler's assumption of the local purple.

"And when the smoke finally cleared somewhat, he had more money than ever rumor could compute and he was the proprietor of that plantation on which he had once been a head servant, and within a decade he was landed gentry. I don't doubt but that he had dug up some blueblood émigré ancestry. He was a small shrewd man, a cold and violent man; just the sort to have an unimpeachable genealogy. Humorless and shrewd, but I don't doubt that he sat at times in the halls of his newly adopted fathers, and laughed.

"The story is that her father came to New Orleans on a business trip, with a blessing from Washington. She was young, then; probably a background of an exclusive school, and a social future, the taken-for-granted capital letter kind, but all somehow rather precarious—cabbage, and a footman to serve it; a salon in which they sat politely, surrounded by objects, and spoke good French; and bailiff's men on the veranda and the butcher's bill in the kitchen—gentility: evening clothes without fresh linen underneath. I imagine he—her father—was pretty near at the end of his rope. Some government appointment, I imagine, brought him south: hijacking privileges with official sanction, you know.

"The whole family seemed to have found our climate salubrious, though, what with hibiscus and mimosa on the lawn instead of bailiffs, and our dulcet airs after the rigors of New England; and she cut quite a figure among the jeunesse dorée of the nineties; fell in love with a young chap, penniless but real people, who led cotillions and went

without gloves to send her flowers and glacé trifles from
the rue Vendôme and sang to a guitar among the hibiscus
and mimosa when stars were wont to rise. Old Maurier had
made a bid, himself, in the meantime. Maurier was not yet
accepted by the noblesse. But you can't ignore money, you
know: you can only protest. And tremble. It took my people to teach the world that. . . . And so—" the Semitic man
drained his glass. He continued:

"You know how it is, how there comes a certain moment
in the course of human events during which everything—
public attention, circumstance, even destiny itself—is
caught at the single possible instant, and the actions of
certain people, for no reason at all, become of paramount
interest and importance to the rest of the world? That's
how it was with these people. There were wagers laid; a
famous gambler even made a book on it. And all the
time she went about her affairs, her parties and routs and
balls, behind that cold Dresden china mask of hers. She
was quite beautiful then, they say. People always painting
her, you know. Her face in every exhibition, her name
a byword in the street and a toast at Antoine's or the St.
Charles. . . . But then, perhaps nothing went on behind that
mask at all."

"Of course there was," said Fairchild quickly. "For the
sake of the story, if nothing else."

"Pride, anyway, I guess. She had that." The Semitic man
reached for the bottle. Gordon came and refilled his mug.
"It must have been pretty hard for her, even if there was only
pride to suffer. But women can stand anything—"

"And enjoy it," Fairchild put in. "But go on."

"That's all. They were married in the Cathedral. She

wasn't a Catholic—Ireland had yet to migrate in any sizable quantities when her people established themselves in
New England. That was another thing, mind you. And her
horseless Lochinvar was present. Bets had been made that
if he stayed away or passed the word, no one would attend
at all. Maurier was still regarded—Well, imagine for yourself a situation like that: a tradition of ease unassailable and
unshakable gone to pieces right under you, and out of the
wreckage rising a man who once held your stirrup while you
mounted. . . . Thirty years is barely the adolescence of bit-
terness, you know.

"I'd like to have seen her, coming out of the church
afterward. They would have had a canopy leading from the
door to the carriage: there must have been a canopy, and
flowers, heavy ones—Lochinvar would have sent gardenias;
and she, decked out in all the pagan trappings of innocence
and her beautiful secret face beside that cold, violent man,
graying now, but you have remarked how it takes the harle-
quinade of aristocracy to really reveal peasant blood, haven't
you? And her Lochinvar to wish her godspeed, watching her
ankles as she got into the carriage.

"They never had any children. Maurier may have been
too old; she herself may have been barren. Often that type
is. But I don't think so. I believe . . . But who knows? I don't.
Anyway, that explains her, to me. At first you think it's just
silliness, lack of occupation—a tub of washing, to be exact.
But I see something thwarted back of it all, something sti-
fled, yet which won't quite die."

"A virgin," Fairchild said immediately. "That's what it is,
exactly. Fooling with sex, kind of dabbing at it, like a kitten

at a ball of string. She missed something: her body told her so, insisted, forced her to try to remedy it and fill the vacuum. But now her body is old; it no longer remembers that it missed anything, and all she has left is a habit, the ghost of a need to rectify something the lack of which her body has long since forgotten about."

The Semitic man lit his cold cigar again. Fairchild gazed at his glass, turning it this way and that slowly in his hand. Gordon stood yet against the wall, looking beyond them and watching something not in this room. The Semitic man slapped his other wrist, then wiped his palm on his handkerchief. Fairchild spoke.

"And I missed it, missed it clean," he mused. "And then Gordon . . . Say," he looked up suddenly, "how did you happen to learn all this?"

"Julius Kauffman was my grandfather," the Semitic man replied.

"Oh . . . Well, it's a good thing you told me about it. I guess I won't have another chance to get anything from her at first hand." He chuckled without mirth.

"Oh, yes, you will," the other told him. "She won't hold this boat party against us. People are far more tolerant of artists than artists are of people." He puffed at his cigar for a time. "The trouble with you," he said, "is that you don't act right at all. You are the most disappointing artist I know. Mark Frost is much nearer the genuine thing than you are. But then, he's got more time to be a genius than you have: you spend too much time writing. And that's where Gordon is going to fall down. You and he typify genius décolleté. And people who own motor cars and food draw the line just at negligé—somewhere about the collarbone. And remind me to give that to Mark to-morrow: it struck me several times these last few days that he needs a new one."

"Speaking of décolleté—" Fairchild mopped his face again. "What is it that makes a man drink whisky on a night like this, anyway?"

"I don't know," the other answered. "Perhaps it's a scheme of nature's to provide for our Italian immigrants. Or of Providence. Prohibition for the Latin, politics for the Irish, invented He them."

Fairchild filled his glass again, unsteadily. "Might as well make a good job of it," he said. Gordon yet leaned against the wall, motionless and remote. Fairchild continued: "Italians and Irish. Where do we homegrown Nordics come in? What has He invented for us?"

"Nothing," the Semitic man answered. "You invented Providence." Fairchild raised his tumbler, gulping, and a part of the liquor ran over thinly and trickled from both corners of his mouth down his chin. Then he set the glass down and stared at the other with a mild astonishment.

"I am afraid," he enunciated carefully, "that that one is going to do the business for me." He wiped his chin unsteadily, and moving he struck his empty glass to the floor. The Semitic man groaned.

"Now we'll have to move again, just when I had become inured to them. Or perhaps you'd like to lie down for a while?"

Fairchild sat and mused a moment. "No, I don't," he stated thickly. "If I lie down, I wouldn't get up again. Little air, fresh air. I'll go outside." The Semitic man rose and helped him to his feet. Fairchild pulled himself together. "Come along, Gordon. I've got to get outside for a while."

Gordon came out of his dream. He came and raised the bottle to the light, and divided it between his mug and the Semitic man's tumbler, and supporting Fairchild between them they drank. Then Fairchild must examine the marble again.

"I think it's kind of nice." He stood before it, swaying, swallowing the hot salty liquid that continued to fill his throat. "You kind of wish she could talk, don't you? It would be sort of like wind through trees. . . . No . . . not talk: you'd like to watch her from a distance on a May morning, bathing in a pool where there were a lot of poplar trees. Now, this is the way to forget your grief."

"She is not blonde," Gordon said harshly, holding the empty bottle in his hand. "She is dark, darker than fire. She is more terrible and beautiful than fire." He ceased and stared at them. Then he raised the bottle and hurled it crashing into the huge littered fireplace.

"Not—?" murmured Fairchild, trying to focus his eyes.

"Marble, purity," Gordon said in his harsh, intolerant voice. "Pure because they have yet to discover some way to make it unpure. They would if they could, God damn them!" He stared at them for a moment from beneath his caverned bronze brows. His eyes were pale as two bits of steel. "Forget grief," he repeated harshly. "Only an idiot has no grief; only a fool would forget it. What else is there in this world sharp enough to stick to your guts?"

He took the thin coat from behind the door and put it on over his naked torso, and they helped Fairchild from the room and down the dark stairs, abruptly subdued and quiet.

8

Mark Frost stood on the corner, frankly exasperated. The street light sprayed his tall ghostly figure with shadows of bitten late August leaves, and he stood in indecision, musing fretfully. His evening was spoiled: too late to instigate anything on his own hook or to join any one else's party, too soon to go home. Mark Frost depended utterly upon other people to get his time passed.

He was annoyed principally with Mrs. Maurier. Annoyed and unpleasantly shocked and puzzled. At her strange . . . not coldness: rather, detachment, aloofness . . . callousness. If you were at all artistic, if you had any taint of art in your blood, dining with her filled the evening. But now, to-night . . . Never saw the old girl so bloodless in the presence of genius, he told himself. Didn't seem to give a damn whether I stayed or not. But perhaps she doesn't feel well, after the recent excitement, he added generously. Being a woman, too. . . . He had completely forgotten about the niece: the sepulchral moth of his heart had completely forgotten that temporary flame.

His car (owned and operated by the city) came along presently, and instinct got him aboard. Instinct also took the proper transfer for him, but a crumb of precaution (or laziness) at the transfer point haled him amid automobiles bearing the young enchanted of various ages swiftly toward nowhere or less, to and within a corner drug store where was a telephone. His number cost him a nickel.

"Hello . . . It's me . . . Thought you were going out to night . . . Yes, I did. Very stupid party, though. I couldn't stick it . . . So you decided to stay in, did you? . . . No, I just

thought I'd call you up . . . you're welcome. I have another
button off . . . Thanks. I'll bring it next time I am out that
way. . . . Tonight? We—ll . . . huh? . . . all right. I'll come on
out. G'bye."

His very ghostliness seemed to annihilate space: he
invariably arrived after you had forgotten about him and
before you expected him. But she had known him for a long
time and ere he could ring she appeared in a window overhead and dropped the latchkey, and he retrieved its forlorn
clink and let himself into the dark hall. A light gleamed
dimly from the stairhead where she leaned to watch the thin
evaporation of his hair as he mounted.

"I'm all alone to-night," she remarked. "The folks are
gone for the weekend. They didn't expect me back until
Sunday."

"That's good," he answered. "I don't feel up to talking to
your mother to-night."

"Neither do I. Not to anybody, after these last four days.
Come in."

It was a vaguely bookish room, in the middle of which
a heavy, hotlooking champagne shaded piano lamp cast an
oasis of light upon a dull blue brocaded divan. Mark Frost
went immediately to the divan and lay at full length upon it.
Then he moved again and extracted a package of cigarettes
from his jacket. Miss Jameson accepted one and he relaxed
again and groaned with hollow relief.

"I'm too comfortable," he said. "I'm really ashamed to
be so comfortable."

Miss Jameson drew up a chair, just without the oasis of
light. "Help yourself," she replied. "There's nobody here but
us. The family won't be back until Sunday night."

"Elegant," Mark Frost murmured. He laid his arm across his face, shading his eyes. "Whole house to yourself. You're lucky. Lord, I'm glad to be off that boat. Never again for me."

"Don't mention that boat," Miss Jameson shuddered. "I think it'll be never again for any of that party. From the way Mrs. Maurier talked this morning. Not for Dawson and Julius, anyway."

"Did she send a car back for them?"

"No. After yesterday, they could have fallen overboard and she wouldn't even have notified the police. . . . But let's don't talk about that trip any more," she said wearily. She sat just beyond the radius of light: a vague humorless fragility. Mark Frost lay on his back, smoking his cigarette. She said: "While I think of it: Will you be sure to lock the door after you? I'll be here alone, to-night."

"All right," he promised from beneath his arm. His pale, prehensile mouth released the cigarette and his arm swung it outward to where he hoped there was an ash tray. The ash tray wasn't there and his hand made a series of futile dabbing motions until Miss Jameson leaned forward and moved the ash tray into the automatic ellipsis of his hand. After a while she leaned forward again and crushed out her cigarette.

A clock somewhere behind him tapped monotonously at silence and she moved restlessly in her chair, and presently she leaned and took another cigarette from his pack. Mark Frost removed his arm long enough to raise the pack to his vision and count the remaining cigarettes. Then he replaced his arm.

"You're quiet to-night," she remarked. He grunted and once more she leaned forward and ground out her half-smoked cigarette with decision. She rose. "I'm going to take off some clothes and get into something cooler. Nobody here to object. Excuse me a moment."

He grunted again beneath his arm, and she went away from the oasis of light. She opened the door of her room and stood in the darkness just within the door a moment. Then she closed the door audibly, stood for a moment, then opened it again slightly and pressed the light switch.

She went to her dressing table and switched on two small, shaded electric candles there, and returned and switched off the ceiling light. She considered for a while; then she returned to the door and stood with the knob in her hand, then without closing it she went back to the dressing table and turned off one of the lights there. This left the room filled with a soft, pinkish glow in which a hushed gleaming of crystal on the dressing-table was the only distinguishable feature. She removed her dress hastily and stood in her underthings with a kind of cringing, passive courage, but there was still no sound of movement beyond the door, and she switched on the other light again and examined herself in the mirror.

She mused again, examining her frail body in its intimate garment. Then she ran swiftly and silently to a chest of drawers and in a locked drawer she sought feverishly among a delicate neat mass of sheer fabric, coming at last upon an embroidered night dress, neatly folded and unworn and scented faintly. Then, standing where the door, should it be opened, would conceal her for a moment, she slipped the gown over her head and from beneath it she removed the undergarment. Then she took her reckless troubled heart and the fragile and humorless calmness in which it beat, back to the dressing table; and sitting before the mirror she assumed a studied pose, combing and combing out her long, uninteresting hair.

*   *   *

Mark Frost lay at length on the divan, as was his habit, shading his eyes with his arm. At intervals he roused himself to light a fresh cigarette, at each time counting the diminishing few that remained, with static alarm. A clock ticked regularly somewhere in the room. The soft light from the lamp bathed him in a champagne colored and motionless sea. . . . He raised a fresh cigarette: his pale, prehensile mouth wrapped about it as though his mouth were a separate organism.

But after a while there were no more cigarettes. And roused temporarily, he remarked his hostess' prolonged absence. But he lay back again, luxuriating in quiet and the suave surface on which he rested. But before long he raised the empty cigarette package and groaned dismally and rose and prowled quietly about the room, hoping perhaps to find one cigarette some one had forgotten. But there was none.

The couch drew him and he returned to the oasis of light, where he discovered and captured the practically whole cigarette which Miss Jameson had discarded. "Snipe," he murmured with sepulchral humorlessness and he fired it, averting his head lest he lose his eyelashes in doing so, and he lay once more, shading his eyes with his arm. The clock ticked on in the silence. It seemed to be directly behind him: if he could just roll his eyes a bit further back into his skull. . . . He'd better look, anyhow, after a while. After midnight only one trolley to the hour. If he missed the twelve o'clock car . . .

So, after a while he did look, having to move to do so, and he immediately rose from the divan in a mad, jointless haste. Fortunately he remembered where he had left his hat and he caught it up and plunged down the stairs and on through the dark hall. He blundered into a thing or so, but the pale rectangle of the glass door guided him and after a violent struggle he opened it, and leaping forth he crashed it behind him. It failed to catch and in midflight down the steps he glanced wildly back at the growing darkness of its gap that revealed at the top edge a vague gleam from the light at the head of the stairs.

The corner was not far, and as he ran loosely and frantically toward it there came among the grave gesturing of tall palms a worn and bloodless rumor of the dying moon, and the rising hum of the street car crashed among the trees. He saw its lighted windows halt, heard its hum cease, saw the windows move again and heard its hum rise swelling, drowning his hoarse reiterated cries. But the conductor saw him at last and pulled the cord again and the car halted once more, humming impatiently; and Mark Frost plunged his long ungovernable legs across the soft slumbrous glare of polished asphalt and clawed his panting, ghostly body through the opened doors out of which the conductor leaned, calling to him:

"Come on, come on: this ain't a taxi."

9

Three gray, softfooted priests had passed on, but in an interval hushed by windowless old walls there lingers yet a thin celibate despair. Beneath a high stone gate with a crest and a device in carven stone, a beggar lies, nursing in his hand a crust of bread.

(Gordon, Fairchild and the Semitic man walked in the dark city. Above them, the sky: a heavy, voluptuous night and huge, hot stars like wilting gardenias. About them, streets: narrow, shallow canyons of shadow rich with decay and laced with delicate ironwork, scarcely seen.)

Spring is in the world somewhere, like a blown keen reed, high and fiery cold—he does not yet see it; a shape which he will know—he does not yet see it. The three priests pass on: the walls have hushed their gray and unshod feet.

(In a doorway slightly ajar were women, their faces in the starlight flat and pallid and rife, odorous and exciting and unchaste. Gordon hello dempsey loomed hatless above his two companions. He strode on, paying the women no heed. Fairchild lagged, the Semitic man perforce also. A woman laughed, rife and hushed and rich in the odorous dark come in boys lots of girls cool you off come in boys. The Semitic man drew Fairchild onward, babbling excitedly.)

That's it, that's it! You walk along a dark street, in the dark. The dark is close and intimate about you, holding all things, anything—you need only put out your hand to touch life, to feel the beating heart of life. Beauty: a thing unseen, suggested: natural and fecund and foul—you don't stop for it; you pass on.

(The Semitic man drew him onward after Gordon's tall striding.) I love three things. *Rats like dull and cunning silver, keen and plump as death, steal out to gnaw the crust held loosely by the beggar beneath the stone gate. Unreproved they swarm about his still recumbent shape, exploring his clothing in an obscene silence, dragging their hot bellies over his lean and agechilled body, sniffing his intimate parts.* I love three things.

(He drew Fairchild onward, babbling in an ecstasy.) A voice, a touch, a sound: life going on about you unseen in the close dark, beyond these walls, these bricks—(Fairchild stopped, laying his hand against the heatdrunken wall beside him, staring at his friend in the starlight. Gordon strode on ahead)—in this dark room or that dark room. You want to go into all the streets of all the cities men live in. To look into all the darkened rooms in the world. Not with curiosity, not with dread nor doubt nor disapproval. But humbly, gently, as you would steal in to look at a sleeping child, not to disturb it.

Then as one rat they flash away, and, secure again and still, they become as a row of cigarettes unwinking at a single level. The beggar, whose hand yet shapes his stolen crust, sleeps beneath the stone gate.

(Fairchild babbled on. Gordon striding on ahead turned and passed through a door. The door swung open, letting a sheet of light fall outward across the pavement, then the door swung to, snatching the sheet of light again. The Semitic man grasped Fairchild's arm, and he halted. About him the city swooned in a voluption of dark and heat, a sleep which was not sleep; and dark and heat lapped his burly short body about with the hidden eternal pulse of the world. Above him, above the shallow serrated canyon of the street, huge hot stars burned at the heart of things.)

Three more priests, barefoot, in robes the color of silence, appear from nowhere. They are speeding after the first three, when they spy the beggar beneath the stone gate. They pause

above him: the walls hush away their gray and sibilant foot-
steps. The rats are motionless as a row of cigarettes. (Gordon
reappeared, looming above the other two in the hushed starlight. He held in his hand a bottle.) *The priests draw nearer,*
touching one another, leaning diffidently above the beggar in
the empty street while silence comes slow as a procession of
nuns with breathing blent. Above the hushing walls, a thing
wild and passionate, remote and sad; shrill as pipes, and yet
unheard. Beneath it, soundless shapes amid which, vaguely,
a maiden in an ungirdled robe and with a thin bright chain
between her ankles, and a sound of far lamenting.

(They went on around a corner and into a darker street.
Gordon stopped again, brooding and remote. He raised the
bottle against the sky.) Yes, bitter and new as fire. Fueled
close now with sleep. Hushed her strange and ardent fire. A
chrysalis of fire whitely. Splendid and new as fire. (He drank,
listening to the measured beat of his wild, bitter heart. Then
he passed the bottle to his companions, brooding his hawk's
face above them against the sky. The others drank. They
went on through the dark city.)

The beggar yet sleeps, shaping his stolen crust, and one
of the priests says, Do you require aught of man, Brother?
Just above the silence, amid the shapes, a young naked boy
daubed with vermilion, carrying casually a crown. He moves
erratic with senseless laughter; and the headless naked body
of a woman carved of ebony, surrounded by women wearing
skins of slain beasts and chained one to another, lamenting.
The beggar makes no reply, he does not stir; and the second
priest leans nearer his pale half-shadowed face. Beneath his
high white brow he is not asleep, for his eyes stare quietly past

the three priests without remarking them. The third priest leans down, raising his voice. Brother

(They stopped and drank again. Then they went on, the Semitic man carrying the bottle, nursing it against his breast.) I love three things. (Fairchild walked erratically beside him. Above him, among the mad stars, Gordon's bearded head. The night was full and rich, smelling of streets and people, of secret beings and things.)

The beggar does not move and the priest's voice is a dark bird seeking its way from out a cage. Above the silence, between it and the antic sky, there grows a sound like that of the sea heard afar off. The three priests gaze at one another. The beggar lies motionless beneath the stone gate. The rats stare their waiting cigarettes upon the scene.

I love three things: gold, marble and purple. *The sound grows. Amid shadows and echoes it becomes a wind thunderous from hills with the clashing hooves of centaurs. The headless black woman is a carven agony beyond the fading placidity of the ungirdled maiden, and as the shadows and echoes blend the chained women raise their voices anew, lamenting thinly.* (They were accosted. Whispers from every doorway, hands unchaste and importunate and rife in the tense wild darkness. Fairchild wavered beside him, and Gordon stopped again. "I'm going in here," he said. "Give me some money." The Semitic man gave him a nameless bill.) *The wind rushes on, becoming filled with leaping figures antic as flames, and a sound of pipes fiery cold carves the world darkly out of space. The centaurs' hooves clash, storming; shrill voices ride the storm like gusty birds, wild and passionate and sad.* (A door opened in the wall. Gordon entered and before the door closed again they saw him in a narrow passageway lift a woman from the shadow and raise her against the mad stars, smothering her squeal against his tall kiss.) *Then voices and sounds, shadows and echoes change form swirling, becoming the headless, armless, legless torso of a girl, motionless and virginal and passionately eternal before the shadows and echoes whirl away.*

(They went on. The Semitic man nursed the bottle against his breast.) I love three things. . . . Dante invented Beatrice, creating himself a maid that life had not had time to create, and laid upon her frail and unbowed shoulders the whole burden of man's history of his impossible heart's desire. . . . *At last one priest, becoming bolder, leans yet nearer and slips his hand beneath the beggar's sorry robe, against his heart. It is cold.* (Suddenly Fairchild stumbled heavily beside him and would have fallen. He held Fairchild up and supported him to the wall, and Fairchild leaned against the wall, his head tilted back, hatless, staring into the sky, listening to the dark and measured beating of the heart of things. "That's what it is. Genius." He spoke slowly, distinctly, staring into the sky. "People confuse it so, you see. They have got it now to where it signifies only an active state of the mind in which a picture is painted or a poem is written. When it is not that at all. It is that Passion Week of the heart, that instant of timeless beatitude which some never know, which some, I suppose, gain at will, which others gain through an outside agency like alcohol, like to-night—that passive state of the heart with which the mind, the brain, has nothing to do at all, in which the hackneyed accidents which make up this world—love and life and death and sex and sorrow— brought together by chance in perfect proportions, take on

a kind of splendid and timeless beauty. Like Yseult of the
White Hands and her Tristan with that clean, highhearted
dullness of his; like that young Lady Something that some
government executed, asking permission and touching with
a kind of sober wonder the edge of the knife that was to cut
her head off; like a redhaired girl, an idiot, turning in a white
dress beneath a wistaria covered trellis on a late sunny afternoon in May. . . ." He leaned against the wall, staring into
the hushed mad sky, hearing the dark and simple heart of
things. From beyond a cornice there came at last a cold and
bloodless rumor of the dying moon.)

   (The Semitic man nursed the bottle against his breast.
"I love three things: gold, marble and purple—") *The priests
cross themselves while the nuns of silence blend anew their
breath, and pass on: soon the high windowless walls have
hushed away their thin celibate despair. The rats are arrogant
as cigarettes. After a while they steal forth again climbing
over the beggar, dragging their hot bellies over him, exploring unreproved his private parts. Somewhere above the dark
street, above the windcarved hills, beyond the silence; thin
pipes unheard, wild and passionate and sad.* ("—form solid-
ity color," he said to his own dark and passionate heart and to
Fairchild beside him, leaning against a dark wall, vomiting.)

10

The rectangle of light yet fell outward across the alleyway;
beyond the halflength lattice blind the typewriter yet leaped
and thundered.

   "Fairchild."

The manipulator of the machine felt a vague annoyance, like knowing that some one is trying to waken you from a pleasant dream, knowing that if you resist the dream will be broken.

"Oh, Fairchild."

He concentrated again, trying to exorcise the ravisher of his heart's beatitude by banging louder on the keyboard. But at last there came a timid knock at the blind.

"Damn!" He surrendered. "Come in," he bellowed, raising his head. "My God, where did you come from? I just let you in about ten minutes ago, didn't I?" Then he saw his caller's face. "What's the matter, friend?" he asked quickly, "sick?"

Mr. Talliaferro stood blinking in the light. Then he entered slowly and drooped upon a chair. "Worse than that," he answered with utter despondence. The large man wheeled heavily to face him.

"Need a doctor or anything?"

The caller buried his face in his hands. "No, no, a doctor can't help me."

"Well, what do you want, then? I'm busy. What is it?"

"I believe I want a drink of whisky," Mr. Talliaferro said at last. "If it's no trouble," he added with his customary polite diffidence. He raised a stricken face for a moment. "A terrible thing happened to me to-night." He lowered his face to his hands again, and the other rose and returned presently with a tumbler half full of liquor. Mr. Talliaferro accepted it gratefully. He took a swallow, then lowered the glass shakily. "I simply must talk to some one. A terrible thing happened to me . . ." He brooded for a moment. "It was my last opportunity, you see," he burst out suddenly. "For Fairchild now,

or you, it would be different. But for me—" Mr. Talliaferro
hid his face in his free hand. "A terrible thing happened to
me," he repeated.

"Well, spit it out, then. But be quick about it."

Mr. Talliaferro fumbled his handkerchief and weakly
mopped his face. The other sat watching him impatiently.
"Well, just as I'd planned, I pretended indifference; said that
I didn't care to dance to-night. But she said, 'Ah, come along:
do you think I came out just to sit in the park or something?'
Like that. And when I put my arm around her—"

"Around who?"

"Around her. And when I tried to kiss her, she just put—"

"But where was this?"

"In the cab. I haven't a car, you see. Though I am plan-
ning to buy one next year. And she just put her elbow under
my chin and choked me until I had to move back to my side
of the seat, and she said, 'I never dance in private or without
music, mister man.' And the—"

"In God's name, friend, what are you raving about?"

"About J——, about that girl I was with this evening. And
so we went to dance, and I was petting her a bit, just as I had
done on the boat: no more, I assure you; and she told me
immediately to stop. She said something about not having
lumbago. And yet, all the time we were on the yacht she
never objected once." Mr. Talliaferro looked at his host with
polite uncomprehending astonishment. Then he sighed
and finished the whisky and set the glass near his feet.

"Good Lord," the other murmured in a hushed tone.

Mr. Talliaferro continued more briskly: "And quite soon
I remarked that her attention was engaged by something or
some one behind me. She was dodging her head this way

and that as we danced and getting out of step and saying, 'Pardon me,' but when I tried to see what it was I could discover nothing at all to engage her like that. So I said, 'What are you thinking of?' and she said 'Huh?' like that, and I said, 'I can tell you what you are thinking of,' and she said 'Who? me? What am I thinking of?' still trying to see something behind me, mind you. Then I saw that she was smiling also, and I said, 'You are thinking of me,' and she said 'Oh. Was I?'"

"Good God," the other murmured.

"Yes," agreed Mr. Talliaferro unhappily. He continued briskly however: "And so I said, as I'd planned, 'I'm tired of this place. Let's go.' She demurred, but I was firm, and so at last she consented and told me to run down and engage a cab and she would join me on the street."

"I should have suspected something then, but I didn't. I ran down and engaged a cab. I gave the driver ten dollars and he agreed to drive out on some unfrequented road and to stop and pretend that he had lost something back along the road, and to wait there until I blew the horn for him.

"So I waited and waited. She didn't appear, so at last I ordered the cab to wait and I ran back upstairs. I didn't see her in the anteroom, so I went back to the dancing floor." He ceased, and sat for a while in a brooding dejection.

"Well?" the other prompted.

Mr. Talliaferro sighed. "I swear, I think I'll give it up: never have anything to do with them any more. When I returned to the dancing floor I looked for her at the table where we had been sitting. She was not there, and for a moment I couldn't find her, but presently I saw her, dancing. With a man I had never seen before. A large man, like

you. I didn't know what to think. I decided finally he was
a friend of hers with whom she was dancing until I should
return, having misunderstood our arrangement about meeting below. Yet she had told me herself to await her on the
street. That's what confused me.

"I waited at the door until I finally caught her eye, and I
signaled to her. She flipped her hand in reply, as though she
desired that I wait until the dance was finished. So I stood
there. Other people were entering and leaving, but I kept
my place near the door, where she could find me without
difficulty. But when the music ceased, they went to a table
and sat down and called to a waiter. And she didn't even
glance toward me again!

"I began to get angry, then. I walked over to them. I didn't
want every one to see that I was angry, so I bowed to them,
and she looked up at me and said, 'Why hello, I thought
you'd left me and so this kind gentleman was kind enough
to take me home.' 'You damn right I will,' the man said,
popping his eyes at me. 'Who's he?' You see," Mr. Talliaferro
interpolated, "I'm trying to talk as he did. I can't imitate his
execrable speech. You see, it wouldn't have been so—so— I
wouldn't have felt so helpless had he spoken proper English.
But the way he said things—there seemed to be no possible
rejoinder— You see?"

"Go on, go on," the other said.

"And she said, 'Why, he's a little friend of mine' and the
man said, 'Well, it's time little boys like him was in bed.'
He looked at me, hard, but I ignored him and said firmly,
'Come, Miss Steinbauer, our taxi is waiting.' Then he said,
'Herb, you ain't trying to take my girl, are you?' I told him
that she had come with me, firmly, you know; and then she

said, 'Run along. You are tired of dancing: I ain't. So I'm going to stay and dance with this nice man. Good night.'

"She was smiling again: I could see that they were ridiculing me; and then he laughed—like a horse. 'Beat it, brother,' he said, 'she's gave you the air. Come back to-morrow.' Well, when I saw his fat red face all full of teeth I wanted to hit him. But I remembered myself in time—my position in the city and my friends," he explained, "so I just looked at them and turned and walked away. Of course every one had seen and heard it all: as I went through the door a waiter said to me: 'Hard luck, fellow, but they will do it.'"

Mr. Talliaferro mused again in a sort of polite incomprehension, more of bewilderment than anger or even dejection. He sighed again. "And on top of all that, the cab driver had gone off with my ten dollars."

The other man looked at Mr. Talliaferro with utter admiration. "O Thou above the thunder and above the excursions and alarms, regard Your masterpiece! Balzac, chew thy bitter thumbs! And here I am, wasting my damn life trying to invent people by means of the written word!" His face became suddenly suffused: he rose towering. "Get to hell out of here," he roared. "You have made me sick!"

Mr. Talliaferro rose obediently. His hopeless dejection invested him again. "But what am I to do?"

"Do? Do? Go to a brothel, if you want a girl. Or if you are afraid some one will come in and take her away from you, get out on the street and pick one up: bring her here, if you like. But in Christ's dear name, don't ever talk to me again. You have already damaged my ego beyond repair. Do you want another drink?"

Mr. Talliaferro sighed again and shook his head. "Thanks

just the same," he answered. "Whisky can't help me any."
The large man took his arm and kicking the blind outward
he helped Mr. Talliaferro kindly but firmly into the alleyway.
Then the blind swung to again and Mr. Talliaferro stood for
a time, listening to the frantic typewriter, watching planes
of shadow, letting the darkness soothe him. A cat, slinking,
regarded him, then flashed a swift, dingy streak across the
alley. He followed it with his eyes in a slow misery, with envy.
Love was so simple for cats—mostly noise, success didn't
seem to make much difference. He sighed and walked slowly
on, leaving the thundering typewriter behind. Presently he
turned a corner and heard it no more. From beyond a cornice there came at last a cold and bloodless rumor of the
dying moon.

His decorous pace spaced away streets interesting with
darkness and as he walked he marveled that he could be
inwardly so despairing, yet outwardly the same as ever. I
wonder if it does show on me? he thought. It is because I am
getting old, that women are not attracted to me. Yet, I know
any number of men of my age and more, who get women
easily . . . or say they do. . . . It is something I do not possess,
something I have never had. . . .

And soon he would be married again. Mr. Talliaferro,
seeing freedom and youth deserting him again, had known
at first a clear, sharp regret, almost a despair, realizing that
marriage this time would be a climacteric, that after this he
would be definitely no longer young; and a final flare of freedom and youth had surged in him like a dying flame. But
now as he walked dark streets beneath the hot heavy sky and
the mad wilting gardenias of stars, feeling empty and a little
tired and hearing his grumbling skeleton—that smug and

dour and unshakable comrade who loves so well to say I told you so—he found himself looking forward to marriage with a thin but definite relief as a solution to his problem. Yes, he told himself, sighing again, chastity is expected of married men. Or, at least they don't lose caste by it. . . .

But it was unbearable to believe that he had never had the power to stir women, that he had been always a firearm unloaded and unaware of it. No, it's something I can do, or say, that I have not yet discovered. As he turned into the quiet street in which he lived he saw two people in a doorway, embracing. He hurried on.

In his rooms at last he slowly removed his coat and hung it neatly in a closet without being aware that he had performed the rite at all, then from his bathroom he got a metal machine with a handpump attached, and he quartered the room methodically with an acrid spraying of pennyroyal. On each downstroke there was a faint comfortable resistance, though the plunger came back quite easily. Like breathing, back and forth and back and forth: a rhythm.

Something I can do. Something I can say, he repeated to the rhythm of his arm. The liquid hissed pungently, dissolving into the atmosphere, permeating it. Something I can do. Something I can say. There must be. There must be. Surely a man would not be endowed with an impulse and yet be denied the ability to slake it. Something I can say.

His arm moved swifter and swifter, spraying the liquid into the air in short, hissing jets. He ceased, and felt for his handkerchief before he recalled that it was in his coat. His fingers discovered something, though, and clasping his reeking machine he removed from his hip pocket a small round metal box and he held it in his hand, gazing at it. Agnes

Mabel Becky he read, and he laughed a short, mirthless laugh. Then he moved slowly to his chest of drawers and hid the small box carefully away in its usual place and returned to the closet where his coat hung and got his handkerchief, and mopped his brow with it. But must I become an old man before I discover what it is? Old, old, an old man before I have lived at all . . .

He went slowly to the bathroom and replaced the pump, and returned with a basin of warm water. He set the basin on the floor and went again to the mirror and examined himself. His hair was getting thin, there was no question about that (can't even keep my hair, he thought bitterly) and his thirty-eight years showed in his face. He was not fleshily inclined, yet the skin under his jaw was becoming loose, flabby. He sighed and completed his disrobing, putting his clothing neatly and automatically away as he removed it. On the table beside his chair was a box of flavored digestive lozenges and presently he sat with his feet in the warm water, chewing one of the tablets.

The water mounted warmly through his thin body, soothing him, the pungent lozenge between his slow jaws gave him a temporary surcease. Let's see, he mused to his rhythmic mastication, calmly reviewing the evening. Where did I go wrong to-night? My plan was good: Fairchild himself admitted that. Let me think. . . . His jaws ceased and his gaze brooded on a photograph of his late wife on the opposite wall. Why is it that they never act as you had calculated? You can allow for every contingency, and yet they will always do something else, something they themselves could not have imagined nor devised beforehand.

. . . I have been too gentle with them, I have allowed

too much leeway for the intervention of their natural perversity and of sheer chance. That has been my mistake every time: giving them dinners and shows right away, allowing them to relegate me to the position of a suitor, of one waiting upon their pleasure. The trick, the only trick, is to bully them, to dominate them from the start—never employ wiles and never allow them the opportunity to employ wiles. The oldest technique in the world: a club. By God, that's it.

He dried his feet swiftly and thrust them into his bedroom slippers, and went to the telephone and gave a number. "That's the trick, exactly," he whispered exultantly, and then in his ear was a sleepy masculine voice.

"Fairchild? So sorry to disturb you, but I have it at last." A muffled inarticulate sound came over the wire, but he rushed on, unheeding. "I learned through a mistake tonight. The trouble is, I haven't been bold enough with them: I have been afraid of frightening them away. Listen: I will bring her here, I will not take No; I will be cruel and hard, brutal, if necessary, until she begs for my love. What do you think of that? . . . Hello! Fairchild? . . ."

An interval filled with a remote buzzing. Then a female voice said:

"You tell 'em, big boy; treat 'em rough."